RENEGADE PROTECTOR

NICO ROSSO

For Ami.

Chapter One

Dark night hunched over Mariana Balducci as she stood outside the back door of her shop and double-checked the locks. The light in the parking lot behind the building was out, and she was the last to close along the row of stores. For months, every time she heard the metal snap into place on the glass door, it sounded final. Customers avoided her place, and sales were terrible. It was only a matter of weeks or days before she locked up one last time and handed the keys to a stranger.

A shape forty feet away sent a startled shock up her spine. Through the glass back door she peered down the length of her store to where a man stood at her front window. She'd already been on edge from the deep shadows surrounding her, and the figure on the other side of the building froze the breath in her lungs. A streetlight carved out his features enough for her to recognize him. He'd been in her shop that day.

When he'd first come in, she'd thought about walking him through all the organic apple products she had, produced directly from her fifth-generation orchard. But there was a quietness about him that demanded a little space as he discovered things for himself. He was a handsome black man, clean shaven over a square jaw and close-cropped hair. Broad shoulders. Somewhere in his early thirties, around her age or a little older. It was probably a good idea that she hadn't tried to hand-sell him any cider, because when their eyes did meet, an unexpected heat bloomed across her chest. Her mouth had managed only a simple greeting. Anything wordier would've tied her tongue in knots.

The surprising blush on her skin had persisted as he'd walked her store. His thoughtful eyes had captured hers as if he'd already known her and her struggles. As if he understood. But the man didn't say much, and instead of buying anything, he spent most of his time looking at the antique black-and-white photographs on the wall. They'd been passed down through her ancestors, Italians who settled in the Monterey Bay of California and the Mexican families they'd married into. For a moment, she'd considered telling him what little history she knew from the pictures, then maybe asking if he wanted to get a cup of coffee. But her tongue still felt too thick for nimble words, and it wouldn't have been fair to flirt with the man while she was buried under two tons of trouble.

Now, standing at the back of her store, seeing him lurking out there on the other side, she wondered if he was part of that trouble. Usually the men who hovered near her shop or prowled just at the edge of her property outside town wore a more stony expression. Their eyes were hard, with zero sympathy. Predators, sent by the Hanley Development Group to intimidate her customers and scare the hell out of her. All so she'd close up shop and sell her land to them. The damned plan was working.

Mariana kept one eye on the man through the windows of her store and backed quickly toward her parked pickup truck. His body straightened, as if he'd spotted her movement. She lost sight of him when she whipped her keys out and tried to get them into the truck door.

Another wave of fear crashed coldly through her. Clothing rustled close by, way too close to her. The presence of a man loomed from the shadows at the bed of her truck. Was it the man from the front of the store? How did he get there so fast? She didn't even hear any footsteps.

"Back off." She forced her voice into a command and jammed her hand in her purse for a canister of pepper spray.

"You back off," a deep voice growled. A hand swung out and slapped the purse from her grip. "Back off your store. Back off your land. Back off this whole county." Shadows erased the details of this man, but she fully understood the threatening step he took toward her.

"I know who sent you." It hadn't been hard to figure out that the Hanley Group was behind this. A few months ago, they'd reached out to buy her orchard and land. She'd refused. Then the goons started showing up.

The man sneered. "I doubt it."

Her muscles tensed. Words hadn't been enough to end this. Balling her fists, she tried to control her breathing. Panic would only make her an easier target. Until this moment, none of these threats had been overtly physical. The rules suddenly changed, though, and she had no idea what it would take to make it through this night. The man moved forward again, shadowy arms upraised. She had to fight.

All her fury at being bullied, being afraid, feeling helpless, was released in a punch toward his throat. The man turned at the last instant and her knuckles glanced off the top of his hard chest, then found the side of his neck. He flinched to the side. The impact jarred up her arm and threw her off balance.

The man recovered quickly and lunged, barking, "You little—"

She ducked her head beneath her arms and braced for the impact. Two bodies slammed together with a loud grunt, but she was untouched. Her attacker and someone else thumped into the side of her truck, rocking its squeaky suspension. The new man was equally obscured in the darkness. Maybe he was local police. Her ex, Pete, was one of them, and still came around sometimes. But the police always identified themselves first.

The only things the new man spoke with were his fists. He drove them with brutal efficiency into the attacker. Rough, pained wheezes answered that the new man knew what he was doing. While she was in the clear, she dived to the ground in search of her purse. Her attacker might be armed, and she needed any advantage she could get. The idea of the new man getting injured while helping her boiled her blood. She found the purse strap and dragged the bag to her. The fight continued next to the truck. The new man was knocked to the side, then sprang back with a knee into the first attacker.

The brutality shook her. The fights she'd seen at the local saloon were drunken and sloppy. This was high stakes, between two people who knew what they were doing. And if it went on too long, one of them would die.

Her hand finally wrapped around the canister of pepper spray. She crouched low, released the safety and pointed it out ahead of her, toward the men. Their shadowed shapes continued to struggle, each trying to get the upper hand as they slammed each other into the side of her truck. If she released the spray now, she'd hit them both.

At least it would end the fight. She tightened her thumb on the trigger.

A car suddenly screeched into the parking lot. Headlights blinded her. Maybe now the police were showing up. But there were no sirens. The engine sped closer and did not slow. Her vision cleared enough to see the two fighting men. One of them was the black man who'd been in her store. The other man she didn't recognize. He was white, with a shaved head and a mean scowl.

Their melee paused in the light of the oncoming car. With a quick shove, the black man separated himself from the other man, then dived toward her. He wore a thick denim jacket, yet she felt how muscular the arms were that surrounded her. She and the man tumbled to the side, his body taking the brunt of the impact on the asphalt. He remained wrapped around her as they rolled out of the way of the speeding car. It screeched to a stop between them and the first attacker. The bald man jumped into the back seat, and the car peeled off again with the smell of burning rubber and engine oil.

The car was quickly out of the parking lot, then turned up a side street, leaving Mariana in the dark again. With a stranger clutching her to his chest.

"Are you hurt?" His voice was deep and smoky.

She assessed her body quickly. Bruised, definitely, but nothing broken or bleeding. "I'm fine."

With athletic grace, he separated from her and stood. She took his outstretched hand for balance, but hesitated before getting to her feet. The touch of their skin reminded her of the quiet connection she'd thought they'd shared in her store when their eyes met. It had brought on a blush before, and now it shot fire through her veins. But that might be the adrenaline from the fight and nearly getting run over.

She rose and released his hand so she could brush the gravel from her palms. The prickles of pain brought the fear and danger crashing back into her.

"I'm fine," she said again and dragged her foot across the ground, searching for the pepper spray she hadn't been aware of dropping. Anger tightened her throat. "I'm not fine." She fired the words in the direction the car had disappeared. "I'm pissed." She toed the pepper spray and picked it up, glad to be armed again. "I'm tired of being leaned on, threatened, attacked…" Both the languages she spoke ran through her head in an attempt to explain why she was shaking. "*Solo estoy cansado.* I'm just tired. I don't know who you are, but saying thanks doesn't even begin to cover it." He took a step forward, as if to speak, but she continued, "You did an amazing thing."

"My name is Tyler Morrison." He maintained a distance and spoke calmly. "Call me Ty."

"I can't thank you enough, Ty." She wished there was some light to examine his face. "I'm just going to disappear now and find a life where I'm not in someone's crosshairs." If she could find her purse, she could get her keys and drive home to dig up all the paperwork to transfer the deed of her orchard to the Hanley Group and they could stop ruining her life. "I'm fine, and you can go back to your vacation or road trip or whatever it is that brought you to Rodrigo, California."

He spoke evenly. "I'm here for you, Mariana Balducci."

Danger immediately clutched her again. She held her pepper spray and got ready to run. "What the hell does that mean?"

A pool of light flicked across the ground. Ty held a small flashlight on a key chain. She was able to make out the shape of his nose and serious mouth, but his dark eyes remained unreadable. The light landed on her purse and remained there. Neither she nor Ty moved.

Adrenaline continued to rack her body, amplified each second he didn't answer her question. She raised the pepper spray higher in her fist. "Explain," she demanded.

He nodded easily. "In exchange for me helping you out just now, you can do something for me."

"So this whole attack was a setup for you to show up, play hero, then get something in return." For months there'd been threatening phone calls, unexpected letters and unwelcome presences in her store. And here was another man thinking he could push her around.

"This was no game. Those guys were dead serious." Ty shook his head, and the light glinted off his eyes, revealing their depth. "Here's what you can do for me—stay."

She squinted at him, trying to piece together his meaning.

"Make a stand," he continued with a passionate fire growing in his voice. "Fight back."

She barked an incredulous laugh. "I don't know what you think is going on here, but I'm down to my last twelve dollars, my last hour of sleep and my last nerve. Looks to me like the best way to stay alive is to sell out."

"You're not alone in this fight." His jaw was set.

She lowered the pepper spray but stayed on guard. "Yes, you were absolutely there for me just now, but this has been going on for months. Are you going to stick around that long?" She jabbed her finger toward him. "And what do you get in return?"

He bared his teeth. "I get the satisfaction that a good person won her fight."

She swept her purse off the ground. Ty talked tough, but confidence alone wasn't going to win this struggle. "You make it sound so easy."

His flashlight pointed at the door of her truck now, bathing him in reflected red light. "I know it isn't."

"You seem to know a hell of a lot." It was crazy to collect any hope from Ty's conviction. "And all I know is the name you gave me." Which could easily be fake. "How did you find me? I haven't gone public with any of this."

He explained slowly, "But you did go to the police when the extortion started. And that puts things on record."

"So you're a cop?" That might clarify parts of this, but

not everything. Ty certainly had authority in his presence, but if he was here on any official capacity, he would've flashed some identification. Not that she had much trust in the police these days. Pete toed the line with the rest of the local cops, explaining that they couldn't do anything without proof. The goons who'd been coming around had been too slick to get caught.

Ty dropped his voice, sounding like he had a secret only for her. "I'm part of an organization—"

Shattering glass interrupted him. He immediately ran in the direction it came from. Her store. She chased after him toward the back of the building. More glass broke. A car tore away down the street in front of the row of stores.

A yellow light flickered in her shop, making the shadows in the back door dance awkwardly. The light deepened to a dangerous red. It silhouetted Ty as he skidded to a stop at the door. He turned to her, face deadly serious. "Call 911."

She pulled her phone and her keys from her purse as she pressed the emergency-dial button on her phone, Ty took her keys, unlocked the back door and rushed in without hesitation. A wave of heat hit her, and she could only stand and stare at the fire that spread across the floor of her shop. Beyond it were the broken windows, gaping, jagged and dripping with flames.

The emergency operator answered and Mariana implored the fire department to show up as soon as they could.

Ty's shape hurried through her field of view. He moved purposefully, opening drawers in a desk behind the register. "Where's the important paperwork?" he barked over the sound of the growing fire.

She burst into action and ran into the shop. Shouldering him aside, she unlocked the file drawer on the desk and pulled out the fire safe containing her business license, her inspection reports and the archival information she'd collected on the historic building all the shops shared.

Ty held his large hand out to her. "Cash?" She found the key for her register and handed it to him as the heat intensified. An automatic alarm system blared. "Get to safety." He pointed to the back door. She sped in that direction, losing sight of him as he moved toward the register.

The fire grew and the ceiling sprinklers finally hissed to life. She swung out the back door, put the safe down and turned to see the steam from the blaze as it crept up her wooden display tables. Water would kill the fire, but nothing could quench the rage that shook her. The intimidation had been wearing her down for months, but tonight was a direct attack. Her body had been threatened. Her work was burning.

A hunched and wet Ty blasted from the back door, carrying her cash drawer. He handed it to her. The undiminished fire revealed his grim face. "Homemade napalm," he explained. "It's like jelly. The water won't put it out."

The fury felt like it would consume her. "This is how badly they want me gone."

"But they don't know who they're fighting against. The answer's still inside." Instead of backing away from the growing blaze, he sped back through the rear door.

Sirens cut through the night in the distance. She hung up her phone, dropped the cash drawer and rushed to the door. Ty moved through the deadly blaze, one arm curled across his face for protection. He was collecting something, but she couldn't tell what.

"Leave it," she shouted to him through the door. "Leave it! It's not important." Her merchandise was a loss by now, and none of it was worth his hurting himself. He disappeared completely in the flames. She threw the door open. Despite the heat, cold panic raced through her muscles.

"Ty!" She crouched low, beneath the choking smoke. "Ty!" Water from the sprinklers splashed on her as she pressed forward toward the flames. He'd helped her, stepped into her fight, and she couldn't just leave him in the fire.

He burst through the flames in front of her. The two of them retreated for the back exit as relief washed over her. Once they were outside, she saw that he held a stack of the old framed photos from her shop walls. The same photos he'd been examining when he was there earlier.

"It *is* important," he said. "This is why you've got to keep standing up." He shuffled the antique pictures until he got to one of a group of nineteenth-century cowboys and frontierswomen of different ethnicities, posing along a ridge next to a sprawling oak tree.

She laughed without any joy. Her shop burned. Exhaustion dragged her down. "I can't stand up anymore."

The sirens grew louder. He glanced in that direction. "You've got to." He held up the picture. "This is us. This is my organization."

Maybe she'd hit her head during the attack. Maybe this was all a dream. "So you're a cowboy from the past who's come to help me?"

The continuing fire etched Ty's serious face as he pointed to a man in the group. "This is my ancestor. These people formed a group to protect anyone without a voice. People like them. Poor. Immigrants. Women. Workers." He looked again to where the sirens were coming from. He'd fought a man, saved her from the speeding car and dived into her burning shop, and still he stood strong before her. "That job isn't finished."

"Look what they did." Tears burned her eyes as the flames mocked her. A fire truck finally pulled up in front of her store, firefighters rushing out before the wheels stopped.

"I know you're under the gun." He put a hand on her

shoulder, and his energy radiated into her. "That's why I'm here."

She winced as more glass shattered. The firefighters raked it out of the frames so they could access the fire. "I don't know what to do anymore."

His gaze held hers. "We're going to turn around and take the fight to who's doing this."

"Why?" There had to be a catch.

"This is what we do." He handed her the picture of the group of people. "This is who I am." Red and blue police lights flickered into the parking lot. Ty's eyes narrowed as he watched the approaching car. "Don't tell them my name."

"You're not leaving." She tried to hold him with her voice. Ty had been the only good in this terrible night. Hell, he'd been the only good she'd seen since this ordeal began.

He looked back from the approaching police car and into her eyes. "I'm with you all the way. Until it's over." His broad shoulders straightened. He radiated power. "You are not alone."

The police car stopped and its searchlight swept over the back of the shop, then onto her. She blinked. Ty was gone. As if he'd never been there. But his impact was clear. He'd protected her and saved what he could from the shop, including the old photo she held. The stern-faced people stared at her with the same strength and determination Ty had. But he'd disappeared somewhere into the deep shadows.

She needed him back, to feed on his strength if this fight was to continue. And to chase that spark of a connection she'd felt when they'd first glanced at each other in her store. Somehow, they were tied together in all this. For the first time in a long time, she didn't feel alone.

Chapter Two

His lungs burned, his knuckles were scraped and bleeding, his damp jacket soaked a chill toward his aching muscles, and Ty still wanted to chase down those two bastards and make them pay for what they just did to Mariana Balducci.

It had been harder to leave her alone in the parking lot just then than it was to run into her burning shop. But he wasn't ready to try to explain himself to any local cops, and it was best if he stayed off everyone's radar until he had a better handle on who exactly was threatening Mariana and her property.

One detail he picked up tonight: the bald man could fight. His moves were from the street, not a cardio class, and intended to do maximum harm. Ty knew that Mariana had to be tough to run an orchard and her shop alone, but if the bald man had got ahold of her... Ty couldn't consider that outcome.

He watched her interact with the two officers, both white men, from the patrol car, reassured by how she stood strong, gesturing more with anger than defeat. He stood in the deep shadows between an old tree and a cinder block wall on the far side of the parking lot, hidden from the cops' view, even when they looked around to follow the story she described.

But the officers' search of the asphalt with their flashlights wasn't as thorough as Ty wanted. If he'd been in his jurisdiction, every resource would've been in that parking lot working inch by inch, then in the shop once the fire was out. As it was, his San Francisco badge probably wouldn't get him more than a polite cup of coffee with the chief and little more info than a press release.

According to any county and city authority, his business in Rodrigo was unofficial. But when it came to the underground organization he was working to establish, he was on a focused assignment. The mission was Mariana, and he wished he'd had a chance to really explain who he was and why he'd shown up to help.

Hell, when he'd first walked into her shop, he'd wished that he was in her town for completely different reasons. The scents of apples and spices had surrounded him, warming the moment he locked eyes with her. All the data he'd collected from the police report and internet searches didn't prepare him for the strength of her presence. He knew the woman had been under the pressure of intimidation for months, and still she wasn't crushed. Her quick assessment of him revealed a sharp mind. Cautious, yes, but also ready to absorb the world around her. And there was the spark in her eyes. Heat, deeper in her glance. He wanted to know what it was that lit her brown eyes up like that. But he was in her shop for the mission, not to chase down a possibility of a connection with a woman he'd just met. Instead of finding out just how deep the light in her eyes went, he spent the evening scraping his knuckles on another man's face and running headlong into a fire.

The police officers in the parking lot with Mariana finished their insufficient search and motioned for her to follow them around the front of the building. The angriest flickering of the fire had diminished and it seemed like the firefighters were close to putting it out. Ty tensed, watching Mariana walk away and out of sight. He unclenched his fist.

That magnetic pull he felt toward her must've just been his professional protective instinct. The bad guys had already made two tries for her tonight. They'd definitely be back.

Now that the parking lot was empty, Ty took out his phone and thanked his diligence in getting a waterproof case. It wasn't until he tried to key in the code for his phone that he noticed how much his fingers shook. Still cold. And the adrenaline continued to urge him into action. He calmed his fingers as much as he could to unlock his phone and dim the screen. But his thirst to fight only increased as he typed a brief text outlining what had happened this night. Those bastards had come after Mariana and if he hadn't been there…

The text went to two people in his nascent organization. Vincent and Stephanie would distribute the information further if necessary. Helping Mariana was the number one priority. His secondary goal would have to wait until he knew just how bad things were. But there would be no quitting. He'd told himself that before showing up in Rodrigo. Seeing his ancestor in that photo on her shop wall had steeled his resolve. Standing along the ridge in the old picture were the men and women who had founded Frontier Justice over 120 years ago. They'd banded together to help the abandoned, forgotten and hated people the system ignored. Frontier Justice had to be revived. Mariana's life depended on it.

THE FIRE WAS OUT, but the trouble was far from over. Mariana stood outside the broken windows of her shop, nose stinging with the smell of damp burnt wood and plastic. Two police officers stood close by, one of them her ex, Pete. He'd been professional and attentive during his questions, but she still felt his reserve, a by-product of her breaking up with him last year. He hadn't even been the one to offer her the blanket she had draped over her wet shoulders. His partner, Jones, had done that with an apologetic look in his eyes. In the store, firefighters wrapped up their gear, boots sloshing in the water pooled on the floor where her customers were supposed to be walking. Hot, angry tears welled in her eyes. Her work, her life and her history were being destroyed. Ty had asked her to stand and fight, but now that he'd disappeared, taking his confidence with him, she wasn't sure how.

"Over here." Miguel, the lieutenant firefighter, waved her and the two police officers into the shop. Small-town living. She'd graduated high school with both Miguel and Jones, Pete being one year older than all of them.

It was ridiculous to open the front door of her shop while the windows were completely broken out, but she had to maintain some normalcy. Flanked by Pete and Jones, she stepped to where Miguel pointed at the floor. The firefighter indicated a long dark object. "They probably threw this first to break the window." It was a crowbar. "Then this came through with the fuel." Melted glass gaped like a screaming mouth. "Most likely a mason jar with some kind of wick. There's another over here." He waved his hand over the floor a few feet away, next to one of her half-burnt display tables.

Jones pulled out his phone and took pictures of what Miguel had indicated. The firefighter nodded to Mariana. "You should get pictures, too, for insurance."

Her damp phone still worked so she framed up the crowbar and melted glass on the floor. A tear rolled down her cheek and she didn't wipe it away. Her shop had been reduced to a crime scene. If Ty hadn't shown up tonight, someone might've been taking a picture of her lying on the concrete in the parking lot. Cold shudders ran up her spine. She forced herself to stay on task, taking more pictures of everything Miguel had pointed out, jumping in once Jones got what he needed. Pete maintained his distance.

The blanket did little to keep her warm. Ty's steady presence would've been welcome, but he'd lit out like he was a criminal. And what was that organization he'd said he was with? It was somehow tied to the old photos he'd rescued from the walls.

"Mariana! Mariana!" A woman's voice called from the front sidewalk. Mariana turned to see her friend Sydney craning her neck to see into the dark, burned-out shop.

"I'm here." Mariana had recorded all the photos she could and walked toward Sydney.

"Are you all right?" Concern etched the black woman's face. She clutched a hastily thrown-on sweater across her chest and didn't hesitate to step into the puddles on the sidewalk in her untied sneakers.

"I'm fine." Mariana hadn't meant it when she'd told Ty after the attack. She tried to put as much truth in it now to reassure her friend.

"I heard the sirens and jumped on the community loop. They had the address from the scanners." Sydney slowed her progress once she reached the broken glass on the ground.

Mariana separated further from the police and fire-fighter activity, opened the door of her shop and stepped into the embrace of her friend. A long breath racked her, releasing some tension. "It was them."

Sydney squeezed harder around her. "The developers?"

"It had to be." Mariana stepped from the hug and looked Sydney in the face. "They attacked me…in the parking lot."

Worry mixed with fury in Sydney's eyes. "I'm going to take a wrench to every one of their heads."

Mariana whispered, "Someone helped me."

"Who?" Sydney shot a suspicious glance at Pete. She'd

had less choice things to say about him and the police department when Mariana's concerns had been dismissed because of lack of actionable evidence.

"I don't know." And what details she did have weren't quite adding up yet. "I mean, I have a name, but not much else."

"Not local?" Sydney looked about, as if they were being watched.

"Definitely not." Mariana would've remembered if she'd ever seen him before he walked into her shop that day.

"He didn't stick around, though." Sydney couldn't hide her skepticism.

"He's kind of…shady." When Sydney shook her head and took a breath to voice her concerns, Mariana took her friend's hand and continued, "But he was there all the way. And he rushed into the fire to save things from my shop."

Sydney squeezed her hand tighter, looking at the broken-out facade of Mariana's store. "I'm so sorry about what they did." Her friend swung her gaze across the street, to her own shop that sold candles and honey and other byproducts of Sydney's beekeeping. Mariana understood. Anyone could've been targeted by these attacks. But it was only her. And it was for her land.

Jones approached respectfully. "We're wrapped up here for now. Can you come down to the station to put all the details down?"

Mariana nodded and let go of Sydney's hand. "I can do that."

Sydney stepped to her side. "I'll go with you."

"You showed up here," Mariana reassured. "And that's exactly what I needed. You can go home now. I'm good."

Miguel was the last out of the shop and closed the door behind him. "Moretti Construction has a twenty-four-hour number for boarding windows. I'll give them a call."

"Gracias, Miguel." Mariana shook his hand. "Thanks for everything."

He held her hand an extra beat. "I'm really sorry about what happened."

"We'll find them." Jones stood straight, but Mariana couldn't draw from his confidence. The crooks had been too slick to leave a solid trail before. What could the police do now?

Miguel dropped her hand and headed to his fire truck. Mariana patted Sydney's shoulder. "Seriously. I'm good."

Sydney's concern didn't diminish. She waved her cell phone. "Call me for anything."

"You know I will." Mariana smiled a goodbye, but wasn't sure how convincing it was. Sydney kept watch as Mariana moved up the sidewalk with Jones and Pete. Rounding the corner at the end of the building brought relief from the flashing lights of the fire trucks. But a new anxiety arose when Mariana stepped into the dark parking lot.

The attack still shook her, cold fear knotting between her shoulder blades. "Maybe now we can convince the city to fix the light back here." Her voice rang tight. If she could just see Ty and know if he was still around, it might unwind the tension. She thought she felt him watching her, standing by to spring into action again, but it might've just been a fantasy. Maybe she'd just imagined him in the first place and this whole thing was a delusion created by her assault.

Pete offered up only "Yeah."

Jones opened the door to the police cruiser. "We'll follow you there." He turned on the headlights, illuminating her truck and half the parking lot. If Ty had been lurking in the shadows, there would've been nowhere to hide now. She tried to search as casually as possible for him. No sign.

She'd already seen his skills in a fight. There was no question he could stay hidden if he wanted. But she didn't know how to sort her disappointment at not seeing him. It could've been just a matter of safety. He'd been the one to save her this night. There was something more, though. A curious yearning to find out more of who this mysterious man was.

The automatic motion of taking her keys from her purse brought her back to the moment. This was where her night had changed. She unlocked the truck, then walked to where the rescued items from her store were still scattered on the ground. Everything stacked easily, with the photos on top. Serious and determined, the people in the old picture watched her walk back to the truck and load them in the passenger seat.

She was back behind the wheel of her truck but couldn't erase what had happened. The engine turned over, and pop music sprang out of the radio, way too cheerful. She killed the radio and pulled away, leaving her burned-out and soaked store. The police car followed her out of the parking lot, but she didn't see any other cars join the caravan, even from a distance. Ty talked a good game about being with her every step of the way, but his absence left her starkly cold.

Seven blocks later, she parked in front of the police station and went inside with Pete and Jones. Her skin had been so chilled from the wet clothes she didn't even feel it anymore under the heavy blanket. Hot coffee didn't help, nor did the hard plastic seat next to Jones's desk in the large room past the front desk of the station. The lights were so bright she couldn't tell if it was night or day. Jones typed on a computer and Pete sat close. Together they sent questions to her as she recounted the night. Now that she was off her feet, exhaustion dragged her bones heavy.

"I don't know who he was. He didn't say." Most of the questions swirled when she mentioned the man who'd helped her. "It was too dark to really see him in the parking lot." She left out the detail that Ty had been in her shop, and that his deep gaze had inspired an unexpected blush on her chest and cheeks.

"And in the fire?" Pete asked pointedly.

She shot back, "I was a little preoccupied."

Jones looked over his screen. "So we have a black man, over six feet tall, and that's it."

"But I know that the guy who attacked me in the parking lot was white, shaved head, in his twenties, no facial hair." Pete tilted his head and smoothed the back of his blond hair, a move she recognized as frustration. Before he asked, she answered, "The headlights of the car that tried to run me over lit that guy up pretty good, but not the man who helped me."

Pete seemed unconvinced. Jones stepped in. "I think we've got everything you remember." He took a business card from the desk and handed it to her. "Anything else comes back to you, call anyone here. We're all working on this, Mariana."

"Thanks, Jones." Her legs felt like rusted steel as she stood. She shook his hand and nodded to Pete. He tipped his head in return.

Jones stepped with her toward the front door. "You want us to escort you home, check out the place?"

She shook her head. "I've got Toro there."

"Dog?" Jones asked.

"Mean dog," Pete answered. Mariana suppressed a laugh. Toro was a better judge of people than her, and had always growled when Pete's car had pulled up the long drive to her farmhouse.

Mariana walked out of the building, Jones still behind her. "Sure you're okay out there?"

A car eased down the street in front of the station. Ty

was driving, heading in the direction of her home. Relief bloomed in her chest, edged with a hot thrill of seeing him again. He passed, not looking up at her. Whoever Ty was, whatever he was really doing in her town, she would find out tonight.

She turned to Jones, with Pete within earshot in the lobby. "I'm fine."

Chapter Three

A mile away from the center of town, country dark took over the landscape around Ty's car. Leaving his headlights on was necessary, but it also made it impossible for him to move stealthily toward the low rolling hills that surrounded Rodrigo. He shifted his weight, reassuring himself that the automatic was still in its holster on his belt. There'd been no time to change into dry clothes while tracking Mariana to the police station, but he'd added the pistol as extra insurance after the assault and firebombing. If anyone was following him, they'd have a clear target on his vehicle.

Not that it would be a secret where he was headed. The Balducci orchard was at the end of Oak Valley Road, a two-lane deal that ran straight to the hills past neighboring vineyards, farms and horse ranches. Some lit windows stared at him in the distance with yellow predator eyes. Mostly, though, he was surrounded by black and gray. Low clouds blocked the stars. A looming oak sped past, made into a monster by his stark headlights and taking him back to the summer visits to his grandparents' spread, east and inland from the Bay Area. As a child, he'd been afraid of that dark and the countless animals that could be lurking just out of reach of the kitchen window light.

Those creatures didn't scare him anymore. As a cop in

San Francisco, he'd seen the worst of people. He'd seen it tonight and still held a tight fist and clenched jaw.

According to the GPS on his phone, he'd passed the last of the side roads. Ty killed the headlights and brought his car to a crawl. Details in the terrain slowly emerged as his eyes adjusted. The road curved up a small rise ahead. More oaks flanked the asphalt, behind them aging wooden fences. Cresting the rise revealed the first edge of Mariana's orchards. They spread up another hill and curled around a broad clearing that held her farmhouse and outbuildings.

He rolled the window down, trying to pick up any sounds of trouble over his engine. Approaching the dark house like this, expecting danger, with only the light from nature to find it, brought him closer to his ancestor than he ever imagined. Jack Hawkins had ridden this land in the dead of night and through stark days, a .45 on his hip and justice on his conscience.

The road turned into a single-lane driveway. Easing closer to the house brought the barking of a dog. Ty had read all the police reports, studied internet maps and social media about Mariana and her orchard, but there was nothing about a dog. He pulled off into a wide swath of dirt and turned off the car. The dog kept barking, but didn't approach farther than twenty yards in front of the main house. Ty got out of the car and immediately regretted it. Summer was on its way out, and the Pacific Ocean a few miles away sent a cool, damp breeze across the hills and directly through his wet jacket.

"Good dog," he called up to the guard, but the barking didn't stop. The dog was as black as the shadows, making its size impossible to determine. It could've been anything from a mastiff to a Pomeranian. This being the country, and from the depth of the warning bark, Ty figured it to be a reliable threat and wouldn't risk getting any closer.

"At least you're on the job." If there was anyone other than Ty skulking around, the dog would've gone at them, too.

A hitch in the barking alerted Ty to a change in the action. He could see from his high vantage point that a pickup truck moved along the road toward the orchard. Mariana's truck. Easy to remember because he'd been slammed into the side of it. Relief washed over him when he saw she wasn't being followed. Either by the bad guys or the police. There was too much that he and Mariana needed to sort out, one-on-one.

It was clear from her confidence on the curves that she'd driven this road her whole life. In just a few moments, she pulled up beside Ty and his car. Dashboard lights revealed the exhaustion in her face. Her black hair was still back in a ponytail, her clothes unchanged. He wanted to replace the blanket she had around her shoulders with a clean, dry one. Her wary eyes kept him at a distance.

The dog continued to bark, voicing the caution Ty saw in her. She tipped her head toward her guard. "You met Toro."

Ty nodded. "I like him. He's looking out for you." A small smile brightened her face, then disappeared. Ty took a half step toward her truck. "You should get into something warm before that chill gets too deep."

She stared at him for a second, expression opaque. "Leave your car there. I'll meet you at the house." She drove off to the house, Toro bounding to follow. He saw in her headlights that the dog was some kind of shepherd mix, medium sized and athletic.

Ty collected a duffel from the trunk of his car and walked up the forty yards to the farmhouse. By the time he got there, several lights were on inside and the front door was open. Toro paced on the other side of the doorway, head low and eyeing Ty. It was best to pause on the broad porch that stretched the entire front of the house.

Mariana's voice came from inside. "Toro, let him in."

The dog edged away, not breaking eye contact. Ty stepped over the threshold and into a comfortable living room with mismatched furniture ranging from dark wood antiques to minimalist new pieces. Mariana stood on the far side of the room, next to an open cedar chest. In her eyes was the same caution Toro had. In her hands was a lever-action rifle.

Ty carefully placed the duffel on the ground and showed her the palms of his hands. The barrel wasn't pointed at him, but it wouldn't take much for her to swivel it in line with his chest. "I'm glad you've got that," he said, noticing that it wasn't cocked. Yet.

Her gaze narrowed on his duffel. "Are you planning on staying?"

"I'd like to change." He brought his hands down. "The sprinklers hit me when I was running through the fire to pull the valuables from your shop."

She lowered the barrel of the rifle toward the ground and let out a shaky breath, some of the tension releasing from her shoulders. Toro sat near her. "Sorry." Her grip on the rifle loosened. "I'm just…"

"I get it. I've seen it." He turned and closed the front door. "And I've been there."

She tipped her head at the door. "The dead bolt."

He threw it, but wouldn't feel the house was completely secure until he'd gone room to room. "Did you tell them my name? Anything about me?"

"No name, just a vague description." She walked to a small desk in one corner of the room with a laptop on it. Toro followed. "I've never seen you before today."

"Good. Thanks." He slowly pulled his badge wallet from his back pocket and held it open. "I'm a San Fran-

cisco City detective, out of my jurisdiction and technically on vacation."

She stepped forward, still gripping the rifle in one hand,
and took the badge and ID from him. "I don't know how
things are done up in the city, but you suck at vacationing."

"I don't want a vacation." His wet jacket tightened
around him. "I want to help you."

"And I still don't know why." She put his ID down on
the desk and opened the laptop.

"Let me get dry first." He nudged his duffel with his
foot.

She hooked her thumb to a wide hallway leading away
from the living room. Half of it was taken up by a stair-
way to the second floor. "First door is the guest bathroom."

He picked up his bag and walked deeper into her house.
Floorboards creaked under his feet. The scent of a woman's soap drifted down from the top floor, where he supposed the master bedroom was. At the end of the hall was
the kitchen, but he turned to the bathroom before he could
investigate it or the photos that lined the wood-paneled
walls of the hallway.

Once inside, with the door closed, he paused and listened. A chair shifted in the living room. Light typing.
Toro's tail thumped on a rug on the floor. At least Mariana wasn't waiting with the Winchester outside the bathroom. He pulled off his jacket, peeled off his shirt and piled
the heavy material in the narrow shower that stood in one
corner. A quick inspection in the mirror revealed no open
wounds from the fight.

A hot shower would've been heavenly, but it would've
definitely pushed Mariana's hospitality. He quickly unlaced
his boots, kicked out of his remaining wet clothes and replaced them with dry ones from the duffel. Once his keys,
wallet, knife and pistol were secured and covered with an

unbuttoned denim shirt over his T-shirt, he stepped back into the hallway.

Mariana met him at the edge of the living room, the wary look in her eyes softened. Behind her, on the laptop, he recognized a San Francisco news story about an abducted girl he'd helped find. Mariana held out his ID. "The article doesn't say what happened to her dad and uncle."

"They were put away." He reached forward and took hold of the ID wallet. For a moment, she didn't release it. The two of them balanced, he felt her strength. The power of her body had been clear when they'd tumbled on the hard parking lot, but that hadn't been as quiet as this intimate moment in her living room. Their gazes locked. He was close enough to see flecks of gold in her brown eyes and wanted to step closer and search the depth of her darkness. She released her hold on the ID, and the two of them moved apart.

"Do you drink, Detective Morrison?" She drifted to a side table next to the hallway. A few bottles of liquor stood at various levels. Two glasses had been poured with a light amber liquid.

"Ty." The drink was so inviting. Heat in a glass. "Please call me Ty."

She picked up one of the drinks and presented it to him. "Do you drink tequila, Ty?"

"I won't refuse you." He took the glass.

She took the other. "Ms. Balducci."

An embarrassed flush heated his cheeks. "Sorry if I used your name, I…" Telling her about all the files and information he'd read on her wouldn't help to undo the awkwardness.

A smile, tilted wicked, crossed her face. "A joke." She laughed incredulously. "You did so much. Of course you can call me Mariana." She raised the glass and he clinked his against it.

"To surviving another night." Their eyes held again. The tequila was forgotten as he was drawing a new heat from a growing connection with Mariana. The first spark had started when he'd seen her in her shop. But his purpose couldn't be chasing down this possibility with a woman he'd just met. It wasn't fair to her and it wasn't fair to his mission. He blinked, then threw back the tequila. The burn wasn't strong enough to shake the fire he felt in his veins standing this close to her.

She drank hers quickly and put the empty glass down, not making any more eye contact. "I have to change." Rifle in hand, she moved into the hallway and up the stairs, followed by Toro. The door at the top closed and a lock was thrown.

Ty set his glass down and stood at the bottom of the stairs, listening to the ceiling creak with her movement. His investigator's mind always drew pictures, scenarios and possibilities based on details he collected. But that mind usually kept a cool distance so it could observe cleanly. The imagination that saw Mariana in her room, pulling the wet clothes from her body, was not at all professional. He shook the images from his head and brought himself back to task.

"One of the police officers was acting sketchy." He pushed his voice up the stairs and hoped she could hear through the door.

"Really?" She wasn't very muffled. The old house had gaps.

"He was unfocused, like he was carrying a distraction." It still made Ty mad to think of how unthorough the initial investigation was. "Could he be in on this harassment?"

"Which cop?" Her footsteps creaked closer to her door.

"The taller one. White. Blond. Built like a baseball player. A pitcher."

The door at the top of the stairs opened, revealing Mariana's silhouette. Her hair was down, making her look mythical as she descended the stairs. The ground-floor light slowly showed that she wore jeans and a button-down flannel shirt. Toro remained at her side and she still held the rifle. "That's Pete," she said with a smirk. "My ex."

That made sense. "There's the distraction."

"He played third base." Dark hair framed the dusky skin of her face. All the lights in the house seemed to have dimmed to a sultry glow. "What position did you play?"

Toro finally ventured close, and Ty put the back of his hand out to sniff. "Wide receiver on the football field, forward on the basketball court."

"Double threat." She observed his interaction with Toro, then poured another two drinks of tequila.

"I didn't mess with baseball." He ventured to pet Toro's head and the dog leaned into it. "You were a point guard, right?" It hadn't been in any file he'd read. She raised her eyebrows as if asking him to explain. "I can see that you like to call the shots. Your orchard, your house, your rifle."

She quirked a smile. "You should ask Pete about that."

"I'd like to ask him why he didn't spend another two hours scouring that parking lot for clues." Even if they were exes, it was no excuse for shoddy police work.

"Small town." She shrugged. "They don't know how to handle this kind of stuff." Her face darkened. "Or they don't want to." She handed his drink over and swirled hers in the glass. "I sell my spread to the developer, they put in a resort hotel, property values go up, property taxes go up, the town does better, the police department does better."

"That price is too high." He waited until she sipped at

her tequila to taste his. The liquid fire couldn't override the anger he felt at her situation.

She stared into the distance, eyes unreadable. "Hungry?" Without waiting for his answer, she walked into the hallway and down to the kitchen. Toro remained at her heels. Ty followed. The kitchen was larger than he expected, with a broad center island covered in a warm wood butcher block. One wall was dominated by a stove and vent hood that stretched to the high ceiling. Mariana slid a wire bowl of apples to the center of the island and picked two out. "We have plenty of apples. Can't sell any of them without harvesters to get them off the trees or customers to show up at the shop."

She pulled a gleaming knife from a block and quickly segmented the apples. Her hands paused as she pushed some of the slices toward him. He saw her eyes fixed on his hip. His gun. She asked, "Why didn't you pull that on the guy in the parking lot?"

"I didn't have it on me." He reached forward and dragged the pieces of apple to him. "I didn't know it would be this bad."

She set the rifle on the corner of the island. "Neither did I." They silently ate pieces of the apple, drank tequila, then chewed on more apple. Toro glanced between the two of them, like he was looking to see who would give him a handout. Mariana used a piece of apple to point at a slice Ty held. "Do you taste it?"

He'd been eating automatically and slowed down to search. Savoring it this way strengthened the connection he'd been feeling with her all night. Her work, part of herself, was in his mouth, intimate and close. An apple had never made his blood rush like this. "It's…salty." A surprising flavor within the balance of sweet and tart.

Her face lit up with a smile, then changed to something

more serious as she examined his face. "We're only a couple miles from the Pacific. The mist comes in from Monterey Bay, bringing the sea salt with it. There are no other apples like this."

"That's why I'm here." She needed to know only part of the reason for now. "There's too much history here to lose. Your history is here. Your family's. And if you want to stay, I will help you."

"With those ghosts from the past?" She nodded out to the living room, where the old photos lay on a table.

"After the Civil War, the West expanded. People tried to carve out lives for themselves. But the law wasn't always on their side." Shame and anger shook him, knowing that even as a police officer now, the same injustice occurred. "Money was power. My ancestor joined with others to form a group to protect people who couldn't protect themselves. Vigilantes. They rode mostly in California. Black, Chinese, Native American, Mexican. Other immigrants. Men and women. They called themselves Frontier Justice."

Mariana held his look. "You can't be a cop and a vigilante."

He stared deeper into her, hoping she saw his vow. "I can if they don't know. I have to be if no one else will help you."

Her eyes narrowed, cutting him open for dissection. "Do you ever lie?"

"Yes." He was no superhero in a cape.

She loosened her posture, resting her hip against the island. "If you'd said no, I wouldn't have believed you."

He propped his elbows on the thick butcher block. "We live in a difficult world."

Despite her casual attitude, her gaze still held steel. "Are you lying now?"

"No." The night was black and silent outside the kitchen windows. For now, it was just the two of them. In her home.

With an unexpected, electric connection stretching between them.

"And you're going to help me." She leaned forward. Heat prickled across his chest. Did she feel it, too? "No strings. No motive other than justice."

"I will." It wasn't a lie. It wasn't all of the truth.

Her gaze fell to her hands and she seemed to wrestle with a thought. She glanced at her rifle, then Toro. A long breath shook through her. She made a fist, released it and looked him in the eye again. "Stay the night."

Even though he knew the invitation was just for the sake of her safety, the words in her low voice, in that quiet kitchen, fired quick heat through him. The circumstances of his visit to her house tried to ice the flames, but only brought them down to a deep red smolder close to his bones. This job of protecting her had started out feeling important because of the ties to his ancestor. Standing here with Mariana, feeling how hard it was to ask for help and knowing how much she needed it, the job was now very personal.

Chapter Four

Mariana had never shared her bedroom with the rifle before. The door was locked and Toro was curled up next to the bed. She sat on the edge of a reading chair, very aware that Ty was in the guest room below her feet. The rifle wasn't for protection against him. As crazy as his story was, he'd proved she could trust him to help her. Whether or not he could fight off the Hanley Development Group was a different question.

She spoke low into her phone, knowing he could still hear her through the old house. "Hi, Brenda, I couldn't find an after-hours number for you, so I'm leaving this message." Her voice was tired and shook as she recounted the minimum details to her insurance agent. "My shop on Pacific was firebombed tonight. Fire department did a good job, but I don't know how much I can salvage. Call me back and let me know what to do next. Thanks." She hung up and let the phone slip to the rug.

Brenda was a professional, and had to know the steps for dealing with the nuts and bolts of a claim. Paperwork, phone calls, emails. Impersonal. But that didn't stop the cold grip that squeezed the back of Mariana's neck.

Ty had eased that. He knew the violence of the world. And he seemed to understand her. That uncanny perception of his had a way of slipping past her guard. He was

probably doing it just then, staring at his ceiling and seeing her rubbing her hands together in an attempt to wring
out the tension.

It had been months since the guest room had been used,
when Sydney had brought a special bottle of wine and the
two had cooked dinner and stayed up way too late. Inviting Ty to stay had taken all her resolve. After all that had
happened that night, an empty house would've only amplified her anxiety. But when she'd shown him to the guest
room, with the made bed against one wall, she was hit with
just how intimate the silences between them had become.

Talking about what Frontier Justice had been and what
Ty wanted it to be again had occupied her mind like an un-
finished puzzle. She'd put the pieces together as he'd spread
them out. There were still gaps, like why the old photos had
come into her family's possession, even though none of the
people in them had ever been identified as her ancestors. It
hadn't been the time for too many questions, though. Any
more information would've been overload.

She picked up her phone and walked to the bed, turning what Ty told her over again to see if she could draw
any conclusions from what she knew about her own family. The Italian side had come from southern Italy and had
started out as farmhands until they could buy their own
spreads and plant the kinds of foods they understood. It
didn't take long for them to make ties with the Mexicans in
California, marrying into old, established families. Their
voices surrounded her, rising up from the earth of the orchard. Her parents had drawn strength and pride from that
past, but had passed on only a handful of stories before
they were taken from her in a car accident during her first
year of college. She'd been so busy growing up, she hadn't
learned what this land had really meant until she'd returned
to work it.

Ty seemed to understand these connections. She saw how he felt his own ancestors and their struggle for justice in himself. He acted on it, leaping into the fight for her and into the fire for his own legacy. Thoughts of the assault and the fire kept jabbing into her, making her weary muscles ache. Her mind wouldn't allow her to go over it again and again. A new thought took over.

Ty's mouth. Eating the apple she'd grown and picked and cut. He'd taken his time, giving her plenty of opportunities to watch him consider and then savor the fruit. It had almost been like kissing him. Almost. Mariana knew that if she had, she'd still be feeling the power of that man on her mouth. Hell, she might still be kissing him hours later.

She plugged her phone into a charger cord. Sitting on the bed made the mattress groan. She knew he could hear it, too. Her breath caught in her throat with the thought of what Ty's remarkable perception would find if he turned his attention to her body. Usually people couldn't identify what made the apples of her orchard so unique. But he'd tasted the salt. He could probably search out pleasures in her body she'd never discovered.

Mariana blew out the hot breath and shook the thoughts out of her head. He might be involved, or married, though she'd noticed no ring. She'd seen his integrity, so it didn't make sense if he had someone that he'd still be staring so deeply at her. Or maybe it was just her wishful thinking. Throwing too many feelings toward the one man who'd helped her.

She got under the covers, wearing sweats and a T-shirt, knowing her shoes and rifle were close by. Ty's perception was dangerous. She tried to take comfort in how it was an asset in her fight to keep her orchard, but couldn't dim the bright flush across her chest and down her legs that he inspired. The man was probably asleep already, thinking only of justice. She turned out the last light in the bedroom. He remained very much awake in her mind. All he'd told her still hadn't settled into order. But it was the silences between her and Ty she had no defense for.

Stars glittered outside her window. Ty was in her house. Sleep seemed impossible. She closed her eyes and felt him wrapped around her, rolling from danger on the hard ground of the parking lot. Remembering him eating in her kitchen slowed her pulse to a more sensual pace. It was only when she imagined the slow process of handpicking apples from her trees that sleep finally took her.

She woke with a clutch of fear in her throat. The sky was still deep charcoal. It could've been hours or minutes since she'd fallen asleep. Toro stood on alert in the middle of the room, staring at a dark window. The unknown danger burned the cobwebs out of her head with icy fire. She slipped from her bed and grabbed her rifle.

One footstep creaked on her floor and Ty's voice came cautiously low from downstairs. "One car, parked on the road to your place."

She crouched low and approached the window. Among the natural landscape that spread out beneath her house and orchard, a car gleamed in the starlight. It was on the side of the road, small puffs of exhaust showing it was idling. Then she heard the distant sound of the engine, like an angry insect stuck deep between the house's walls.

Ty asked in a clipped voice, "Is there a back way to your house?"

She kept her gaze on the landscape while she hurried to her bedroom door and unlocked it. "Fire roads." She returned to the view of the car. Ty bounded up the stairs. Toro was so intent on the window, the dog didn't even glance at him.

Ty moved to a window opposite the one she was looking out, with a view of the back hill of the property. "Are they passable?"

"They're blocked by gates and chains and dry creeks." The car remained motionless, too far away to see how many people were inside or what they were doing. "Only four-wheelers and horses can get through."

He came over to the front window and crouched next to her. It was amazing someone with his size and strength could move so quietly. His intense presence brought her even more awake. He kept his voice a whisper. "The car killed its lights a mile before coming to a stop."

Anger choked her words. "They're parked on my property. That's after my fence line." As if tonight's attack wasn't enough, they had to come back.

Ty focused out the window. "Have they ever come this close before?"

She gritted through a clenched jaw, "Yes." It was then she saw that his pistol was in his hand. "Are you that good a shot?" It was at least half a mile.

He glanced at her, grim. "They might not be the only ones out there."

She shook off a quick shiver. "Toro would be going crazy." The dog remained rigid, staring out the window.

Without taking his eyes from the idling car, Ty lowered his pistol. "Good thing it's so quiet in the country. Never would've heard them until they were closer in the city."

"You heard them coming?" She couldn't identify exactly what had woken her, but knew it wasn't the noise of the engine.

Ty shrugged. "I was barely sleeping."

"Too quiet for a city guy?" Their whispers didn't reach the glass panes in front of them.

"My grandparents had a spread east of the bay and we used to do summers out there." A smile emerged in his voice. "Chopping wood. Swinging off a rope into the swimming hole. Chasing chickens."

"That's what I was trying to get away from when I went to college." She put her fingers on the windowsill, wishing she knew more of the history of the hands that had built this house. "I didn't know how valuable it was until I came back to make a life out of it."

The steel returned to Ty. "That's why I'm not going to let them take it away from you."

"What happened to your grandparents' place?" Was that why he was so determined to help her?

"The younger generations moved to the cities and the land got to be too much for them to maintain. They sold it off and lived out their lives in a nice little house." He warmed again. "I still see people wearing belts my grandpa tooled. Didn't sell them, just gave them away with plenty of free advice. And my grandma tutored any local kid who needed help."

The lineage started to make sense. "They were Frontier Justice."

Ty's gaze dropped to the floor and his brow drew down. After a moment, he shook his head. "As far as I could find, that organization dissolved around World War One. My grandparents were just…"

"Good people." She moved her hand from the windowsill to brush it against his. "Like you."

He brought his attention to the idling car again, eyes taking on an edge. "I'm trying."

His deflection helped her find some perspective. Yes, he was diligent in helping her, but was she reading too much into the silent moments between them? "What does your girlfriend think about you spending the night at my place?"

"No girlfriend." He kept staring straight ahead. "No wife."

"Married to the badge?" She could see how his intensity might not leave space for another person.

"I'll give you my mom's number." A wry smile curved his mouth. "She can fill you in on all the things I'm doing wrong in my love life."

"I don't know, Ty. I think you've got primo moves." She focused ahead as well, but felt as if she was leaning against his shoulder, even though they were over a foot apart. "You jump into a fight, run into a fire, all just to get into my bedroom."

He leaned back on his heels, as if startled, and looked about the room. "I was just tracking that car. If you don't want me in here..." His voice trailed off as he glanced from the bed to her in her T-shirt and sweats.

What had started as a joke turned serious in the new silence. She hadn't even taken in that he was wearing only a tank top and athletic shorts. The dim light from outside revealed the muscles in his arms that made him move with such sure grace. He was lean, defined, built for purpose, not just for show. "I let you in," she answered.

Outside, the sound of the car's engine changed. Condensation from the exhaust billowed and the car moved forward. Ty crouched lower, pistol in hand. Ready. She clutched her rifle and tried to keep her heart from pounding too hard. Her voice shook. "I've never shot at another person."

"You're lucky," he whispered, face so dark she couldn't see into him. "Remember, you didn't ask for this. These bastards are bringing it to you, and you're just defending your home and your life."

Her palms sweated with the thought of it coming down to a life-and-death fight. But that was what they'd done this night, attacking her the way they did.

The car continued up the road. Her breath caught in her

throat. Ty remained poised, eerily calm. After a few yards, the car swung across the blacktop in a hard U-turn. Tires screeched into the night. The headlights turned back on and the car sped away, having sent its message.

Relief blanketed her as the tension shuddered its way out of her limbs. She leaned the rifle against the wall and sat on the floor. Ty remained at the window another few moments, then joined her, letting out a long breath. Toro curled up at her feet.

Even though the threat had passed, there was still hard intent in Ty's voice. "The Hanley Development Group, right?"

"They're the ones who first approached to get me to sell." It had all seemed so impersonal and businesslike. Two representatives had come to her shop, laid out the idea of their resort on her land, then left with polite handshakes when she'd declined.

Ty knocked the knuckles of his fist on the wood floor. "We're going to give them a visit."

"I've got to take care of things locally first. Insurance. Phone calls." She still didn't know just how badly her shop was damaged. And she had to update her website and social media to let people know the store was closed. Maybe permanently.

"Soon, then." He rose. "If they're hitting you, then we have to hit back." His outstretched hand waited for her.

Her pulse warmed seeing his skin so close. She could stand on her own. She reached up and took his hand. The touch fired her blood hotter. Like a bolt of electricity passed between them. The way his chest swelled with a breath, she knew he felt it, too. His fingers curled strong around her. She flexed her muscles and got to her feet. *Closer*, her body demanded. Still clutching his hand, she could press against him, pull him to her. Bring his mouth to hers.

He stared at her from behind heavy lids. This man had burst into her life. In just a few hours he'd reminded her that she'd forgotten how to want something just for herself. But wanting that kiss, that physical contact, and taking it were two completely different things.

She dropped his hand.

He took a respectful step back and the sultry atmosphere lifted from around him. "Good night, Mariana."

"Thanks for—" how many times could she thank him in one day? "—sleeping light."

An unexpected quirked smile lit him up. "My pleasure?"

The temptation to ask him to stay in her room hit her. Like the way she'd asked him to spend the night at her place. But this wasn't motivated by the need for safety. It definitely wasn't safe to have him in her bedroom. "Good night, Ty."

He nodded and turned for the doorway. Toro got up, followed him for a step, then stopped as Ty descended the stairs. Mariana closed the door and didn't lock it. She placed the rifle next to the bed and sat on the mattress. Toro curled near her feet and let out a satisfied sigh, his job done for the night.

Transitioning to sleep wouldn't be that easy for her. Each tick of the floorboards downstairs was amplified in her ears. Ty returned to the guest room. His presence washed across her skin. But as potent as it was, she knew better than to pursue the attraction. It was only a side effect of all the tension of the night.

She slipped under the covers and stared at the ceiling. *Yeah*, she tried to convince herself, adrenaline keyed her body up and it was easy to focus that energy on Ty. He'd stepped in when no one else had. Now that her body sank into the mattress, exhaustion dragged her into a warm darkness. *But*, her mind objected, *you were taken by him when he first walked into the shop. Before the trouble.* Ty was trouble. She knew that. And as she fell asleep, a long-dormant need inside her was waking up.

AFTER STARTLING AWAKE what felt like every ten minutes, Mariana finally gave up trying to sleep near dawn and left her bed. There had been no more threats that night. Toro rose, much sprier than she was feeling. Mariana went through her morning movements, pausing every few moments to listen for Ty on the ground floor. All seemed silent there.

She dressed and walked downstairs. The sun crested the far hills. Yellow light sliced in through the side windows. At least it would be a clear day, even if she couldn't predict what the next few hours would bring.

As soon as she reached the ground floor, Ty stepped from the guest room. He wore jeans and a hoodie, and looked as fresh as if he'd slept twelve hours after a spa day. Her tired body immediately responded with a surge of energy. Their connection had gone untested last night, and parts of her wanted to find out just where it led. Instead she maintained her distance and her equilibrium.

Ty eyed the rifle in her hand. "You going to hunt up some breakfast?"

"Yeah." She nodded and moved toward the kitchen. "California moose chorizo."

"Just like Momma used to make." He followed her, and both of them came to a stop at the large island.

She rested the rifle against the side. "I just feel safer having it in the room." The same feeling she discovered with Ty.

"I get it." He turned to reveal his pistol in its holster on his belt. "Get any sleep?"

"Who needs sleep when there's coffee?" She collected

the necessary elements to brew a pot. "How long have you been up? I didn't hear you."

He checked his watch. "An hour?" She felt him collecting her details as his gaze tracked her movement. "I figured out most of the creaky floorboards and walked around them."

"Stealthy." She cut up a crusty loaf of bread from a local baker into slabs for toast. "You would've made a good burglar."

"What do you think I did before I was a cop?"

"Really?" She started to assess him completely differently.

He smiled easily and shook his head, more relaxed than she'd seen him before. "Nah. I worked in a couple restaurants through college." He took a couple of slices of bread and put them in the toaster.

For months, her morning routine had been the same. Toast. Coffee. Work on the orchard and work in the shop. Nothing was normal this day. Ty's presence shifted everything. The sunlight came through the windows differently, making her see aspects of her house that had gone unnoticed in…forever. "Was the guest room okay?"

Ty found the plates for the toast in a cabinet and stacked them at the ready. "Upper sash on one of the windows is loose and wouldn't close. A little drafty, but no problem."

"Really?" It felt like everything was falling apart around her as she broke her back trying to keep all the pieces together. "I'm sorry. There just hasn't been time to work on the house. Or enough money."

"It's not your fault those bastards have been after you." He pulled out his phone and set it on the island. "I was reading comments and reviews for your shop this morning."

"Oh, God." She rolled her eyes and shuddered. "So many fake accounts trashing me." The coffee was ready and she brought two mugs to the pot. "And they've been leaning on the harvesters. No one's willing to come out here to work the trees."

"And still your local PD didn't do anything." Anger heated his voice.

She poured coffee into the mugs, the aroma helping to bring her more into the present. "They just kept saying there was nothing concrete to move on."

Ty finished with the toast and brought the plates to the island. "Last night will put everything on the books, but I don't think they collected a lot of actionable evidence."

Her frustration with the police department didn't have the same bite it used to. Ty was there, bringing Frontier Justice from outside the system. "Cream and—" Her phone rang. The screen indicated it was her insurance agent and she answered immediately. "Thanks for calling back so early, Brenda." The woman's concerned voice was just waking up, but she was diligent in explaining the next couple of steps and agreed to meet Mariana at the store within an hour. Mariana related all this to Ty after she hung up.

He nodded with understanding, drinking his coffee black and making mental calculations. "I won't be there for that. The fewer official reports I'm on, the better."

She threw back some of her coffee, hoping it would ready her for whatever was coming this day. "You're only here for the action."

"Until you tell me to leave…" He found a pad and pencil on a counter and scrawled a number. "I'm never farther away than a phone call." Bringing her the piece of paper closed the distance between them. Her body drank in the heat of his intensity. "Usually, I'm much closer than that."

She took the paper and stepped away to enter the number in her phone. Now that she knew she had to meet Brenda, the clock ticked on the day. She and Ty gathered their things and headed out. Hearing and believing what he'd said had taken the cold edge away from being alone in this fight. But as she drove to town followed by Ty, an unsettled question burned into her. How much closer did she want him?

Chapter Five

He still felt her near his skin. It had been an hour since they'd left the kitchen. The drive to town hadn't helped cool him down. Pretending to be interested in a revolving rack of comic books at the front of the small local bookstore still couldn't shake the resonance of her in him. She was standing down the block on the far side of the street, outside her boarded-up shop. She and the insurance broker had gone inside, come back out and now discussed several pages of paperwork on the Asian woman's clipboard.

Even from this distance, the warmth on his chest that had started in her bedroom persisted. It had come as a quick shock. He'd been so focused on the danger outside there'd been no time to assess where in her house he was or what that might mean. Once the car had left, though, the intimacy of standing so close to Mariana in her bedroom bolted, hot, through him. He was in her house to protect her. He was there for Frontier Justice, and following through with the attraction he felt was beyond a bad idea. There was no certainty she was feeling it, too. The way her hand had lingered in his when he'd helped her up had definitely encouraged the idea, though.

Sleeping lightly in the drafty guest room had calmed his body down, but not his mind. The boldness of the Hanley Group's attacks and follow-up intimidation only showed just how hard it would be to dislodge them from getting what they wanted. Mariana had to be safe. Ty had to stay sharp. Could he maintain that edge while giving in to a sudden desire for the woman he was there to protect?

The questions continued to stab at him while he watched her from the window of the bookstore. The insurance broker was wrapping up her business with a handshake and a hug with Mariana. Ty pulled a comic from the rack and took it to the front counter, cash already in hand.

The white woman behind the counter smiled genuinely. "I like that one. It's dark." She rang him up and handed over the change.

"Sweet." He pocketed the change and gave her a wave with the comic as he headed out of the shop. So far, from what he'd seen of the small town of Rodrigo, there was nothing to support the sinister business that had come down on Mariana. People were generally open and nice. A couple of locals had given him hard looks, but that was expected everywhere.

He hurried across the street and down the block. Mariana turned from the direction the insurance agent walked away to face him. She was tired—he could see the exhaustion—but still strong as hell. He wanted to put his arm around her shoulders, give her something to lean on, but couldn't risk invading her space. Instead he would support her how he could. He moved close enough to tell her, "You're doing amazing."

Her thin smile barely registered. "It doesn't look good in there."

"Can I check it out?"

She nodded and swung the door open with a bracing breath. "No power, so we have to use flashlights."

The floor was still wet and the room was close with the smell of damp wood and paper. He ditched the comic book to the side and used the flashlight on his key chain to sweep across the space. Everything he could see was either burnt or soaked.

Mariana's voice shook. "The refrigerator went off with the power. All the apple butter and pies have to be scrapped." She coughed, but he heard it as a cover for a sob.

Immediately he was at her side, shoulder to shoulder, giving her as much of himself as she would take. "I saw how many apples are on your trees. This can all be built back."

Her eyes squeezed shut and she leaned into him. "There's no one to harvest."

"There will be." Determination rose in him. "We'll push the Hanley Group back." He hated seeing her bullied, and feeling her pushed this close to defeat drove him to rage. "They'll be so scared of you they'll never set foot in this county again."

She opened her eyes and searched his face. "You'd better be telling the truth."

He promised through a clenched jaw, "This is no lie."

Her hand coiled around his. He held her tight, hoping to tell her everything with the touch. She whispered, "Tell me again."

"I'm with you to the end." No matter if the electricity that passed between them was real or just his imagination, if she bridged the gap to come closer to him or never approached, his resolve was set. And he couldn't wait to punch a hole through the Hanley Group and send them running.

"You'd better mean it." A deep fury heated her voice. "Because if we're going to fight, I'm going to burn them down."

Her energy fueled his. "All the way down." The two of them balanced on an edge. They'd said all they could with words. He needed to taste her strength. Was he drawing her closer, or was she stepping to him? Her gaze flicked to his mouth. Her lips parted. He knew this wasn't a good idea and refused to stop. Their faces grew nearer.

The front door of the shop opened with a blast of sunlight. He and Mariana immediately parted and his hand instinctively hovered near his sidearm. A silhouette took a cautious step into the shop. Once his eyes adjusted to the light, he saw the curious expression on the black woman's face as she glanced from him to Mariana and back.

"Sydney." Mariana immediately walked to the woman in her midthirties. Ty remembered getting a glimpse of her last night, when he was watching the front of the store as the firefighters were wrapping up.

"I hope it's okay I came by. I saw you around…" Sydney scanned the burnt and soaked shop with concern and hurt in her eyes. She stroked a hand down Mariana's arm.

"Of course." Mariana squeezed her friend's shoulder. The front door remained open, illuminating the genuine caring between these two women. "This is Ty." Mariana turned toward him. He approached and shook Sydney's hand.

The woman inspected him carefully. "You helped her last night?"

"I did." It was easy to tell that Sydney's sharp perception would crack through any attempts at evasion.

"Did you know trouble was coming?" Sydney tilted her head, still wary. Mariana stood by, watching.

"I knew there'd been trouble for a while, but I didn't know it would be that bad."

The woman assessed him up and down. He'd thrown a light jacket on over his hoodie and knew his pistol didn't print through. Still she pierced him with "Cop?"

"San Francisco. But," he added quickly, "I'm here on vacation."

Sydney chuckled. "You really know how to relax." She

clicked her tongue and walked deeper into Mariana's ruined shop. "What station in San Francisco?"

She clearly knew the deeper workings of the city. "Ten-
derloin."

That got her to raise her eyebrows. "Tough spot."

"Where I grew up." It had gone through a lot of changes
since then, and continued to transform as the city evolved.

"I did junior high in Oakland." Her shoulders loosened
up and she appeared like she wasn't squaring him up for
attack or defense.

"I've got a cousin out there."

Sydney looked over a half-burnt table covered with
goods Mariana had hoped to sell on it. "Your whole family's out here?"

"California." He nodded.

"And before?" She looked back at him, sharing a history.

"Georgia."

"Alabama," she answered. Now that they'd covered all
the basics, she looked over the table and talked to Mariana.
"Is any of this salvageable?"

Mariana joined her and picked over the wares. "Jars of
jelly, no. Dried rings, no. The apple peelers can be sold at
a discount once they're dried."

Sydney separated two of the devices. "I cleared a table
at my place. We'll fill it with anything you can sell, and
I'm not taking any commission."

Mariana objected. "A table of my stuff means lost sales
for you. I can't—"

Sydney raised her hand to cut off her friend's concern.
"They burned your place. This is the least I can do." She
strode toward the back. "Did the jugs of cider get damaged?"

Mariana followed and Ty trailed after them. Soon they
were all sorting through what could be sold and what had

to be trashed. Mariana's eyes welled with tears as she separated out all the losses, but she pushed through and filled three plastic tubs with good merchandise.

They carried them across the street to Sydney's shop, where Ty was instantly surrounded by the aromatic warmth of wax and honey. The bright store was decorated in natural light woods. Sydney exhibited the same personal connection to the place and the goods that Mariana did with hers.

Sydney saw Ty looking about and explained, "I'm just working for the bees. They do the heavy lifting."

The three of them organized Mariana's wares on an open table. After a brief debate over who had the worst handwriting, Mariana settled down to write up all the signage explaining what was on sale. Sydney stayed at her side. "You need anything else, let me know. If the local cops aren't helping and we have to hire a private detective…"

Mariana looked up from her work with a serious expression. "Ty is staying to help."

Sydney took a step back, staring at him quizzically. "I thought you were on vacation."

"Officially." How much would he have to tell her before she trusted him with her friend?

"Shady business." She shook her head, but luckily left it at that.

Mariana stood, face set with determination. "That's what they brought, so that's what it's going to take to stop them."

Sydney glanced out the front windows of her shop, as if they were being watched. "I'm in it with you." Her conspiratorial lips barely moved.

Ty saw how good her view of Mariana's store was. "Can you keep a log of anyone unusual around Mariana's place? Date and time, clothes, body type, cars, behavior?"

Sydney took out her phone. "I'll create an online document and share it with Mariana. She can share it with you."

He put a fist out for Sydney. "I like the way you think."
She bumped it.

Mariana brought her in for a tight hug. "Thank you for
everything."

"Be safe." Sydney gave her friend a final squeeze, then
released her. She waved pointedly with her phone at Mariana and Ty as they headed out the door.

Ty paused on the sidewalk. The tallest structures on this
side of town were only two stories, but that still provided
plenty of protected vantages to anyone lurking. Mariana's
shop was one of five in a long brick building that took up
the entire block across the street. None of the other stores
had been touched by the fire. She was the only target. He
asked, "Anyone around here get an advantage if you're
forced out?"

She thought a moment, scanning their surroundings.
"I can't think of someone. We all look out for each other.
And there are empty storefronts a block over if someone
wanted to expand."

"Okay." He crossed the street with her, watching who
might be watching them. No one seemed particularly interested. "But something's not clicking. Hanley Group has
developments all over Northern California. Businessmen in
expensive suits." They reached the front of her shop, where
some shattered glass still gathered at the base of the exterior wall. "These tactics are brutal."

"There's been no contact from anywhere else." She
swung the door open and stepped in. He watched her posture hunch under the burden of what had happened.

"Sydney did great to set you up." He was rewarded by
Mariana straightening.

Her warm smile transformed the room. "She's a god-
dess."

He walked toward the back of the store. "I'm going to

crawl that parking lot." But when they got out the rear door, he saw that no one had cordoned off the space and several cars had already parked on the blacktop. He gritted his teeth.

Frustration made him want to just quit the search, but he steadied himself and set about scanning the ground as he paced back and forth. Mariana moved about the space as well, focused down. She concentrated around the area where her truck had been parked. He'd noticed that this morning she'd parked farther from her store and closer to the side street.

"Tire tracks." He called her over. Black streaks marked the ground where the car had peeled off after collecting the bald man. Hope drained out of him. Any definition in the tracks, which could lead to a make and model of the car, was lost underneath a parked car's tire. "Son of a..."

She ran her hands through her hair. "I couldn't find anything."

"Someone better get fired over this." Small-town inexperience with this level of crime was no excuse.

An ironic laugh huffed from Mariana. "Doubt it."

He couldn't tell if she was mistrustful of the police in general or Pete, the one she'd identified as her ex. "As long as they stay out of my way."

She kicked a pebble across the ground, a dark look on her face. "What do we do now?"

"The most important part of an investigation." She steeled herself and he continued, "Lunch." He strode back toward her store. "You pick. I pay."

They locked up the shop and Mariana led Ty up the street to a small restaurant next door to the bookstore. As soon as they walked in, all eyes were on Mariana. A white man and Vietnamese woman, both in their late forties and wearing T-shirts with the restaurant's stylized sun logo, walked to her with concern on their faces.

The woman reached her first. *"¿Estás bien, Mariana? Estábamos tan preocupados."*

"Gracias, Lam." Mariana clutched the woman's hand to reassure her. *"Todavía estoy de pie."*

The man shook his head. "We couldn't believe what we heard."

Mariana nodded gravely. "Can I catch you guys up later? It's still kind of a whirlwind."

"Por supuesto." Lam waved her and Ty to a small table against one wall. Ty took the seat facing the door.

Mariana sat, a grim look on her face. "Thanks." She busied herself with the slim menu.

"You all right?" Ty focused on her, rather than the dining options.

"I'm fine." The same thing she'd told him in the parking lot after the attack, said with equal venom. Her features softened when she looked at him. "I just… I'm just tired of being the victim. Everyone's staring at me."

"They care about you." He did, too, as much as he tried to tell himself this was just a mission for Frontier Justice. Her response was to move her attention back to the menu. He looked over the farm-to-table vegetarian selections, as well. In an attempt to redirect the mood, he asked, "Do you speak any other languages?" Hearing her ease with Spanish revealed a new facet of Mariana.

"Just Spanish. The Italian side of the family was fully Californian by the time I came around." She set her menu down. "I've never even been to Italy."

"Would you ever want to go?" That sounded too much like an invitation. His imagination took him to a sunlit hotel room with billowing white curtains brushing against

Mariana as she stood at a window and sipped white wine. He bore his attention back into the menu.

"I haven't taken a vacation in…forever." Her wistful smile was impossible to ignore. "I'd like to see some old orchards out there."

Suddenly the imaginary window she stood at was in a villa overlooking rows of apple trees. "Sounds nice."

The return of the man to take their orders thankfully broke Ty out of his reverie before he had the urge to check airfare prices to Italy. He and Mariana made their selections, then were left with silence between them. Her darkness continued. She looked at several black-and-white photos of Rodrigo's main street on the wall. "My folks died before I was ready to listen to all the stories."

"I bet we could piece a lot together with the people out here." From what he'd seen of the town, there was a strong sense of history.

Her gaze locked onto him. "Always the detective." Her darkness seemed to lift, replaced by a warm depth in her eyes. But then her brow came together with concern as she looked at his face. "What is it?"

Pete, the police officer and Mariana's ex, had swung into the restaurant and was making a beeline for them. Mariana turned to see him, the thick clouds returning around her. She brought her worried gaze back to Ty. "What do we tell him?"

"Some truth." Ty hoped his quick wink to her was reassuring. "We'll see what shakes down."

Without asking, Pete brought an empty chair over to their table and sat. "You doing okay, Mariana?"

"Fine, thanks," she answered coolly.

Now that Pete had shown the bare minimum of care for her well-being, he shifted his attention to Ty. "We haven't met."

Ty kept his hands on the table. Pete wasn't asking socially. He was puffed up, lats flexed and neck tight. He was in full uniform, belt heavy with sidearm, Taser and collapsible baton. "Ty," he answered.

It obviously wasn't answer enough for Pete, and his mouth turned down with an authoritative frown. "You're the one who helped Mariana last night?"

Ty maintained a neutral expression. "I couldn't just stand by and do nothing."

"But then you left." Pete shifted in the seat, his duty belt creaking. His arms remained tight.

"Everyone else showed up." Ty shrugged it off. "There wasn't anything for me to do then."

Pete tensed his jaw. Clearly he had no patience for interrogations. "You could've stuck around and talked to us."

"About what?" Ty knew it wasn't fair to bait this man, but he was already pissed off about how little Pete had helped Mariana.

The police officer spoke through clenched teeth. "About what you saw. Any details that might've helped our investigation."

"I barely saw anything." Ty leaned back in his chair and moved his attention to Mariana. She sat straight, tense. "It was super dark, right?"

She nodded. "I already told you how little I could see, Pete."

"But I'm trained in this, Mariana." Pete also stabbed at Ty with his instructive tone. "So something that might seem insignificant to you could turn out to be important."

Professional pride made the muscles in Ty's back tense. He struggled to maintain a calm exterior. "Good point."

Pete didn't seem to hear the venom in Ty's voice. The police officer continued trying to collect evidence. "So Ty here disappears, then reappears at lunch?"

Mariana jumped in. "I saw him on the street this morning when I was cleaning up at my shop. The least I can do is treat him to a meal."

Pete zeroed in on Ty. "And you spent the night…?"

"Hotel" was all Ty would give him.

His mouth a tight line, Pete took a long breath through his nose before trying a smile. "This might be a lot easier if I just saw an ID."

Mariana's eyes went wide. "You don't have to show him."

Several other people in the restaurant watched the conversation. They must've sensed the tension peak. The restaurant owners stood at the front counter, wary of what was going down. Pete maintained his smile, all part of his easygoing intimidation. Ty remained stony, giving Pete nothing back. Slowly, so as to not set off any alarms for the officer, Ty reached into his coat. He pulled out his wallet, opened it and laid it on the table. With his badge facing up.

Pete unclenched his jaw. He looked from the badge to Ty's face and back to the ID.

Before Pete could ask, Ty explained sternly, "I'm on vacation." More questions spun in Pete's eyes. Ty collected his badge and replaced it in his coat.

Pete finally collected some words into a sentence. "I'm sure Captain Phelps would like to get your insight into what happened last night… Detective."

Ty fixed him with the kind of stare he used to wither rookies. "Maybe he can explain why no one set up a grid in that parking lot and crawled it centimeter by centimeter." Pete reddened. Ty had hurt the other cop's pride, and cut off any excuses. "I'll come by after lunch." His tone was final.

Nodding like he had anything to do with the decision, Pete stood. "Sounds good. I'll let the captain know." He gave Mariana a small wave before adjusting his duty belt. "See you around, Mariana."

She smiled weakly, but he was already walking out of the restaurant. The people watched him exit, then turned their curious gazes back to Ty and Mariana. Luckily, Lam came to the table with two glasses of water and diffused the attention. "Everything *bueno*?" she asked.

"Yeah." This smile from Mariana was genuine. "Thanks." Lam left them alone and Mariana leaned across the table to Ty. "*Is* everything *bueno*?"

A list of curses uncurled in Ty's mind, but this was a respectable restaurant. "It's fine," he echoed her words back to her. She got it and let out a long breath. He muttered, "So much for flying under the radar."

She remained close to him, whispering, "You killed that chance when you tackled that bastard in the parking lot." A thought troubled her and she tilted her head. "What was your plan if those guys hadn't attacked me?"

If she wasn't being intimidated by criminals. If he wasn't there on Frontier Justice business. If he could've just wandered into her shop while really being on vacation. "I was going to ask you out to coffee."

Her face grew very serious and she leaned away from him. "Not if I asked you first." It could've been flirtatious, and he wanted so desperately for it to be. Instead it was the truth. They'd had a chance. When he'd first walked into her store, it hadn't been about Frontier Justice or the Hanley Group. It could've just been the two of them, following the electric possibility of their connection. But the attack changed that. Now the police knew who he was. The complications wove out into a web. Coffee dates, slow flirtations and the first blossom of a romance were way too fragile for the hostile environment they were in. His appetite left him and his chest felt tight. He and Mariana had lost their chance.

Chapter Six

All eyes were on Mariana. Throughout her lunch with Ty, she felt the glances. Any local who walked into the restaurant would fix her with a curious gaze. Sometimes sympathetic, or even acknowledging her with a wave, other times just staring. This was what the Hanley Group wanted. Mariana set apart from her community. Targeted.

But not alone. Ty hadn't wavered in his commitment to helping her. Even after they'd acknowledged the missed opportunity of their connection. The mood had remained cloudy, her food tasteless. She chalked it up to yet another thing the Hanley Group took away from her. Ty's determination must've been rubbing off on her, because instead of feeling defeated, she was fired up to finally take the fight back to them.

It would have to wait, though. After lunch Ty split off to visit the police station and she walked to Sydney's shop. She could see people on the street checking out the boards on the front of her place. Even if she could rebuild her life, it would never really be the same. There were scars on her body from when she'd been learning to run the orchard on her own. A fall from a ladder onto a pruning saw left a long line across the back of her left arm. Last night's attack scarred her history.

"Does Toro like him?" Sydney organized a display of honey sticks next to her register.

Mariana hovered near the table with her wares, as if she could protect these vestiges of her store. "Seems to tolerate him fine. Can't say that Pete took a liking to Ty." And yet Ty was voluntarily at the police station right then. Her gut clenched. He'd handled himself coolly at lunch with Pete, but the pressure could really be on now. And what if he got in trouble with his own captain? That could abruptly end his ability to help her now.

"Pete's opinion doesn't carry much weight around here." Sydney's voice remained light, despite her dig.

Mariana tore her gaze from her ruined storefront and walked back to her friend. "Your family's been here for a long time. Did they ever talk to you about a group called Frontier Justice? Nineteenth century. After the Civil War."

"Yeah." Sydney stared at the ceiling, collecting memories. "There was always this story about not long after my people got here, someone was trying to run them off. Bloody times." She looked out her window, eyes unfocused. "And there was some group of gunfighters or outlaws or something, called Frontier Justice, who stepped into the fight. They finished it." A small, private smile crossed her lips. "I don't know if it's true, but my grandfather would tell me that as a kid, he'd still find brass shell casings on the property from those old shootouts." She moved her attention to Mariana. "What do you know?"

"Just heard the name thrown around a little bit." It didn't seem right to connect Ty to Frontier Justice without letting him know. "My parents didn't really talk about it." If they had, she hadn't been paying attention then.

"I'll talk to my folks and see what other stories they can think of." Sydney raised her eyebrows with irony. "Thinking of calling them in for this one?"

Mariana dropped her voice. "I think they showed up on their own."

That drained all the jokes out of Sydney. "What?"

Mariana had already said too much and tried to figure out how to explain without betraying any of Ty's trust. "They went away for a while, but they're coming back—" Thank God her phone rang to bail her out from stammering anything else. She imagined it was Ty, but it was listed on the screen as a private caller, even though she'd added him to the contacts. But he was a crafty guy and probably had a couple of phones for different purposes. "Hello?"

"Do you want to die?" It definitely wasn't Ty's voice. "We don't care how much help you've got." Ice chilled her bones and froze her breath in her chest. "You think you get out of one little fight and you've won?"

Sydney must've read Mariana's body language because she hurried to her, whispering, "Who is that?"

"We're going to keep coming," the rough masculine voice continued. "And your best move is to get out of the way."

Blazing fury thawed her. Frontier Justice had helped Sydney's family, and Ty had brought it back with him now. "If you get too close," Mariana hissed into the phone, "you will feel my hands around your throat."

The man chuckled. Her anger hardened and sharpened to a cutting edge. He sneered, "Your boyfriend's back."

Ty appeared on the sidewalk at the front window. Mariana hurried out to him. "They're somewhere here." She scanned the street but no one there caught her eye. "They're on the phone." The man had hung up. Ty put a hand on her shoulder and gently moved her back against the facade of the shop, then shifted his body between her and the street. His gaze swept low and high, and his hand hovered near where she knew he wore his pistol.

He spoke quietly, his attention on the street. "What did he say?"

"More threats." She fought to maintain her balance as hot and cold swirled through her. Ty radiated calm danger. "Then he said you were coming back just before I saw you."

"Rooftops." He searched again, then turned to her. "You all right?"

"I can't wait until I can stop answering that question." She held up the phone. "Private caller, no number."

"Wouldn't expect anything else." He cursed under his breath.

Sydney tentatively cracked open the door next to them. "Trouble?"

"They did what they wanted to and bailed." Ty huffed out a breath. "And the local police are a little too interested in me. Even called my captain." He straightened his jacket, composing himself. "I have to lie low for a minute. We'll have that conversation with the Hanley Group tomorrow." The word *conversation* was punctuated by a clenched fist.

Sydney came outside and looked over the area, just as Mariana and Ty had. "You have to stay safe."

"We will," Mariana reassured her.

"Same to you," Ty told Sydney. "You're our eyes here, but any bad news and you bail." Sydney nodded. He turned to Mariana. "Do you have any more business at the store?"

"We salvaged what we could. Insurance is coordinating the cleaning crew."

"Too many hiding places in town." Ty remained edgy. "I need to walk your land."

The buildings crowded together on the grid of streets created sinister corners. Someone could be watching from behind the brick structure to the right. Or the concrete-edged roof down the block. The open space of her land would allow her to breathe. "Let's get out of here." She and

Ty said their goodbyes with Sydney and went to do a final sweep of Mariana's shop.

He retrieved the comic book he'd been carrying when he'd arrived that morning. "So…" He scratched at the back of his head. "Officer Pete?"

She was through blaming herself and waved it off. "He worked a lot. I worked a lot. It was fine when we barely saw each other. Then it sucked when he wanted me to move closer to town for his kind of life."

Ty considered for a moment. "Understood."

She found nothing else to collect and locked up the shop, and they stood on the sidewalk at the front for a moment. Ty continually scanned the town around them. Whenever his assessment swept over her, a blush rose in her body. Their connection continued, even though they'd seemed to admit that chance had passed. But part of her longed to have that gaze on only her. So she could let him learn her, and discover how hidden she'd become in her isolation.

He agreed to follow her to her place in his car, and they parted. She knew all the trees and paths and contours of the family orchard. It would be safe. And it was unsettling. She would be alone with Ty again.

HE'D BEEN SITTING in the Rodrigo PD office of Captain Phelps, not learning anything new as the clock ticked away, and meanwhile those bastards had struck out at Mariana on the phone. Ty's blood boiled. Now his own captain had been informed that he'd run into local trouble during his "vacation." Helping Mariana was going to be difficult enough if he'd remained completely invisible. He had to take each step knowing he was tracked.

Driving behind her on the way to her place, he tried to take comfort in getting out of town. The approaches were mostly visible at the orchard. The house had the high ground. It should be simpler there, but he knew it wouldn't be. The more time he spent with Mariana, the more complicated everything became. The intimidation on her house and land. His ultimate task with Frontier Justice. All of it twisted together, melted by the heat he felt when he looked into her eyes. Her strength and intelligence were there, and her pain.

When he'd seen the fear on her face as she'd come out of Sydney's store with the phone in her hand, he'd nearly lost his head. If that son of a bitch had still been on the phone, Ty would've gladly called him down to the street to see who was faster on the trigger. But that would've put the man in the morgue and Ty in a whole lot of trouble.

He found himself standing on the accelerator too hard and nearly tailgating Mariana's truck. Easing off, he tried to reset his calm. Maybe he could help resolve everything with the Hanley Group using only some accurately placed language. The chances of that dwindled with each escalation from the goons.

And here they came again. The sedan that had parked threateningly on this road the night before now barreled down toward Ty and Mariana from a side street on their right. Did she see them? They were coming on fast, not letting up. Ty pounded on his horn and sped to get up behind her. She looked at him in her rearview and he pointed toward the oncoming black car.

He saw her shoulders tense as she gripped her steering wheel. Her truck pulled forward faster. But it was still right in line with getting T-boned by however many goons were behind the tinted windows.

The sedan bounced over a rut, kicked up a cloud of dust and blasted toward Mariana. She accelerated as Ty hit his brakes. The goons' car skidded sideways between them. Its tires caught and the car bolted forward, not far behind Mariana.

For a split second Ty considered drawing his pistol and trying to take out the attackers. Shooting left-handed out of a moving car was a terrible idea, though, and Mariana would be in the line of fire. He hit the gas and brought his bumper to the rear of the sedan. They tapped their brakes and bumped back into him. The impact jarred his car and rattled his bones. He struggled with the steering wheel to keep on the road.

On each side of the blacktop was a deep irrigation shoulder, then farm fences of steel and wood. Trees sped past. If he slammed into any of them, it would be over. Mariana continued to race up the road, but her truck seemed to have topped out and the sedan grew closer. She fishtailed slightly. It wouldn't take much for them to knock her off the road.

Ty stood on his accelerator. His jaw clenched, muscles of his arms and chest tight, as if he could will his car faster. The sedan reached Mariana and edged to one corner of her rear. They were going to try to throw her into a spinout. At this speed she'd roll and…

He couldn't consider it. He had to stop them.

While they were lining themselves up on Mariana, he neared their bumper. Any miscalculation could push them harder into her. The only time was now. He pulled the wheel to one side and clipped the rear side of the sedan. Tires screamed and the car jerked with the impact.

They lost speed and Mariana gained ground ahead of them. But the sedan remained on the road. As it straightened itself, the rear fender slammed into the front side of Ty's car. He steered into the impact and the cars ground together with the sound of crumpling metal.

He pulled away from them for a second, gained traction and speed, then slammed into the sedan again. This time he dented the rear passenger door. They nudged hard against him, and his car neared the steep shoulder on the right of the road.

But he was far enough alongside them for him to pull his pistol without endangering Mariana. Awkwardly, with his left hand, he drew the gun while steering for his life with his right hand. Even one shot would change how this whole mission played out, but these bastards would not quit until someone was dead.

Ty extended the gun out the window. The sedan immediately reacted by swerving away. He fired. The glass of the rear passenger door blew out and scattered. He saw no one sat in the back of the car. The sedan hit its brakes and sent a plume of black smoke into the air. It swung hard to one side, clipping the rear corner of Ty's car.

The world spun around Ty. He tossed his pistol on the passenger seat and used both hands to right the car as it careened sideways down the road. The rear end continued to swing out. Soon he was dragged backward into one of the drainage ditches. Gravel sprayed all around.

His car finally came to a stop. He'd managed to keep from flipping, but was still parked facing up a steep angle. When the dust cleared away, he could see only a flash of the black sedan speeding away. Mariana's truck slammed to a stop at the top of the ditch and she leaped out.

"Ty! Ty!" Her face was drawn tight in fear.

He shouldered his door open and stepped out. "I'm good." Though the ground didn't feel very stable. "You good?"

"Fine." She had to walk sideways down the steep bank.

He laughed at her response. "I'm fine, too."

At least she was able to smile. "That sucked."

"Hell, yeah." He retrieved his pistol and holstered it.

"Did you shoot them?" She squinted down the road in the direction they'd disappeared.

"There was no one in the back seat." The sedan was long gone. He eyed the angle of his car. Calling a tow truck would mean more attention from the local cops and his captain. "Sent a definite message, though."

Mariana was also looking over his car's predicament. "I have tow straps in the truck. Should be able to get you out of this."

"Thanks." He tried to shake out the adrenaline that bounced through him. "Bastards will scrap the car, and they didn't have license plates." But it wouldn't be too hard to find them because he knew they'd be back.

Mariana started back up toward her truck. "Once we get you hooked up, I'll need you behind the wheel."

He waved his understanding and kicked a rock out of frustration. It skipped along the drainage ditch, punctuated by puffs of dust. Sweat made his shirt cling to his back. The day was warm, the sun bright, but the real fire was in his chest. Anger choked him. Those bastards had called all the shots. He had yet to take the fight to them.

Mariana secured two broad yellow tow straps to the hitch of her truck, then descended the hill to him. They tied the straps to the front frame of his car. Not the most professional rig, but it should do the job. He hoped.

"This part of the road's all yours, right?" He couldn't remember if they'd passed the fence that marked her land.

"Yeah, we're on the private property, so no one official needs to be looking in." She dusted her hands on her jeans and started up the hill. "I'll probably have to field a couple curious emails from neighbors, though."

He prepared to get back in his car. "Just tell them you're practicing for a demolition derby."

She stood at the top of the rise, hands on her hips, sunlight revealing an iridescent deep blue within her hair. "I'll tell them a rogue cop showed up and won't stop saving my life."

Neither of them moved. For a second, it was only the two of them. No fires or threats or gunshots. The twenty feet that separated them hummed with a connection. Magnetism that could pull him into the air toward her. And if he could meet her, feel her in his arms, without gravity. Or danger. Just him and her, breathing each other in.

But the world around them was far too real. He climbed into his car and she walked to her truck. Both of their engines revved high. She tugged, her truck straining to keep from being pulled down into the ditch. His tires struggled to catch and sprayed dirt out behind him. After six feet of sliding sideways, his car gripped the earth and lurched forward. Mariana's truck added more muscle to his efforts. He drove along the side of the ditch for a few yards, then angled all the way onto the blacktop.

Both vehicles stopped to undo the tow straps, which Mariana just tossed in the bed of her truck. They stayed free from drama on the rest of the drive to her farmhouse. He parked next to her truck and they were quickly greeted by Toro. The dog circled Mariana, tail wagging. She stroked over his head and scratched behind his ears. The dog grinned.

She held out her hand. It trembled. "How do you do it?" Her voice was still shaken.

"Give yourself credit." He extended his palm to her. Tentatively, she reached forward and placed her hand in his. The tremors calmed. His skin hummed where she touched him. "You've been doing it. You're surviving under their pressure."

Her gaze warmed on him. She blinked slow with a thanks and removed her hand. "Tequila?"

"I'll keep it corked." Instead of heading to the house, he started to walk around the back of it. "Gotta stay sharp now that they're coming on hard." Her footsteps followed, along with Toro. Ty waited for her to catch up. "Have they called before?"

"No." She picked up a slim branch and used it to point the way to a path in the orchard behind the house. "And they hadn't tried to run me off the road."

"They're threatened." Shade from the trees cut the afternoon heat. Walking the incline woke up his legs and let him burn off some of the residual tension from the car chase. "We fought back and they're dialing it up to the next level."

"How far will it go?" She tapped the stick against a row of apples on a low branch. One of them caught her eye and she stopped to pick it. The shaking leaves released a dry green aroma. She tossed the apple to Ty and pulled one for herself.

It was the realest apple he'd ever held. Skin smooth in some parts, rough in others. Warm from the sun. Like it was still beating with the life of the tree. "It'll go all the way." Hiding this truth would only make it more dangerous for her.

They resumed walking through the orchard and up the hill behind the house. He scanned for hiding places and where the clearest approaches were. The trees wouldn't completely obscure someone. An attacker would have to use the shed up and to the left. A portion of old broken fence would slow someone's progress if they were avoiding the path on the right.

If they were on a horse, though, they could step right over it. Being that tall would be impossible within the trees. Outstretched branches would brush a rider off. This fight, if it ever came, would be on foot.

Sunlight splashed against his face again. He walked

higher, out of the orchard and onto harder dirt. Low grass struggled in places, while scrub held firm, and oaks farther away seemed like they'd always been rooted into this ground.

Mariana pulled ahead of him on a sharp bend of the path. Her body moved fluidly, shoulders and hips tilting with the climb. He had a moment to investigate more of that deep blue he'd seen in her hair. Dusk right before the dark. How would those thick strands feel through his fingers? Warm on the surface from the sun. Cooler underneath? Or the skin of her neck would bring its own heat.

She stopped on the crest of the ridge and took a bite out of her apple. Toro sat so he leaned against her leg. Ty reached her and saw the continuation of rolling hills she stared out at. A few miles away, higher mountains rose up. The low sun cut them into hard planes of bright and dark. "There's the fire road." She pointed, holding the apple with her teeth marks in it.

He followed the cut in the low hills as it wound through golden grass and stands of oak. A dry creek bisected the road in a couple of places to expose large rocks. "That fence is the edge of your property?" It was simple metal and wire, stretched just after the bottom of the hill they stood on.

"Yeah." She drew over the landscape with her finger. "After that are three huge parcels the Hanley Group bought up. I found it in the public record after the harassment started. None of that is zoned for development, but my land is. They've already invested millions and can't do a thing unless they force me out."

The assault he'd imagined earlier materialized again. There wasn't much cover once the fire road arced up the hill. After they reached the top, though, it wouldn't take long to dive into the confusion of the orchard. The hill was too steep on the left and right. Any approach would come right where he was standing.

Ty bit into the apple. Sweet and tart, with that hint of salt he'd tasted the night before. The fruit was Mariana's work, her life. It was his purpose, too. His ancestor would've stood on this same ridge, assessing the landscape. The silver of the Pacific would've burned white with the falling sun on his left, the same way it did for Ty. They both wore a gun. They both knew loss and knew justice wasn't easy to come by.

There was so much that Ty didn't know about that man's story. As determined as he felt, his own path wasn't completely clear. Each time Mariana's presence warmed him, the complications became unreadable.

She finished her apple and tossed it down the hill. It rolled and bounced on the steep slope. Ty imagined men on horses, bandannas obscuring their faces, thundering up. Guns drawn. He could tell her things about her property that even she didn't know. But he couldn't, not with everything else weighing on her.

"I can't let them take this." She shook her head and straightened her shoulders.

"They won't." Was that the same promise his ancestor had made?

She started walking down toward the orchard again. Toro ran ahead. "We're not the top." Her voice was distant. Her gaze swept over the trees ahead of her. "We're participants."

Growing up in the thick of the city and seeing what he had as a cop had opened his eyes to many things. Good and bad. Her perception of the world around them awed him. He investigated details. She conversed.

They again passed through the orchard, where she collected a leaf and rubbed it between her fingers. Another conversation. The sun continued to sink, drawing the shadows out across the path. For a moment, her farmhouse looked like a black-and-white photo, like the ones she'd had on the walls of her shop. But an addition on the back of the house he hadn't noticed broke up the old lines. It looked like it couldn't be more than fifty years old.

"Is that room only accessible from outside?" Someone could use the roof to climb into a second-story window.

"There's a door to it in the kitchen. The room is just storage, mostly stuff for my store."

"No flammables?" If an attack came over the back ridge, this addition would be easily hit.

"I keep those in a fireproof cabinet in the barn." She pointed with her thumb at the low barn a hundred yards from the house. New concerns darkened in her eyes. He knew she was assessing the dangers he sought to minimize.

Everything was flammable now. It could go up any second, taking her land or her life. The men threatening her were more volatile than ever. "We'll hold the high ground," he reassured her. He'd fired the first shot. He had to be ready to fire the last.

Chapter Seven

The quiet with Ty continued to warm deep into her. Usually when she walked her land with someone, the talk flowed like the constant breezes over the hills. Sydney would vent about small business ownership, or gush about the view from the high vantage. When Pete used to come up there, he'd muse about building a little cabin as a man cave and base of operations for his mountain bike. Ty had watched. Absorbed. She'd felt his gaze on her, sweeping across her orchard and the hills beyond.

Some of it was tactical. The most recent attack meant more were coming. But she also felt in Ty an appreciation for the surroundings. He was listening, the way she did when new weather was coming in. The same way he listened when she was talking. Not just waiting for her to finish, but absorbing and learning.

They walked around the house. He continued his assessment and she had a moment to see all the things that needed fixing. A gutter or two sagged. Parts of the roof could use extra shingles. Yes, the top sill of the guest room window hung at an angle, with a wedge of space above it. It grew overwhelming. Her shop was in ruins and might not ever come back. Her fruit was unpicked. Even if there was time to fix all these things, there was no money.

The high ground. Ty's potent silences made the words

ring out in stronger echoes. She and Ty stood at the front of the house. Her road wound away from them, past the spot of the attack and into the distance. The air chilled. Fog began to sweep in from the coast. Trees diffused into folk-tale creatures and the contours of the hills blurred. "I'm in this fight with you." The mist turned her commitment into a whisper.

He took a step closer to her, and they stood shoulder to shoulder. "They're going to be sorry they ever came at you."

The sky darkened to a deep blue. She wished she had the rifle in her hands again. "No fear, right?"

"Fear's all right." He looked from the land below to back at her house. "Keeps us alert and safe. Panic, though, is a killer."

"So we plan." Each step was unclear, but she was learning that there was no one else with whom she'd rather be working out this deadly puzzle.

"I've looked at the approaches, have some ideas about limiting an attacker's movement out there." He nodded back toward the upper orchard. "We'll keep assessing the main road." Now his voice took on more emotion. "And tomorrow we'll get up close with the Hanley Group."

"Then we have to work on the second most important part of a tactical plan." She patted her leg and Toro sped up to her side.

Ty cocked his head. "What's that?"

"Dinner." She and Toro turned toward the house. "Nearly getting run off the road burned through my lunch."

"Danger is a great workout." Ty flexed his shoulders. She took advantage of the opportunity to look at how he formed a broad V, ending in a well-formed butt and muscular legs. "How do you think I stay in shape?"

She licked her lips and cleared her throat. "Chasing perps up those steep San Francisco hills." It was easy to imagine him charging up a sidewalk, focused fury on his face and all his muscles moving in perfect coordination.

A darker memory flickered in his eyes. "It's happened." He quickly shook it off and glided up the stairs next to her. "How can I help with dinner?"

"Laundry," she answered. Inside the house, she collected her still-damp clothes from last night and pointed Ty toward the washing machine in its alcove in the hallway. She'd felt the impact of Ty's body, and knew he was a man of action. Anyone who could drive as well as he did could take care of a load of clothes.

"You've got it." He set about getting the machine ready. Something so normal seemed almost trivial after the attacks. But normal was exactly what she needed. One small part of last night's trauma would be washed away.

She stole a look at his butt as he bent to load the machine, then continued on her way to the kitchen. Knife out, onions ready on the cutting board, she stood motionless. Ty continued to work in the laundry area. She felt his energy as if he was standing next to her at the kitchen island. As if he was pressed against her.

The burn of the chopped onions would hopefully erase those thoughts. She broke them down, wiping the tears from her eyes with her forearm, and still couldn't shake the need that drew her to him. It came from deeper inside her than she expected. She tried to justify it as a side effect of his helping her through all this trouble. Of course she'd feel bonded with the man who stopped a parking lot assault and kept her from getting run off the road. But the quiet they'd shared on the back hill resonated even more than that.

"Where do you need me now?" He filled the doorway to the kitchen.

The first answer that came to mind had nothing to do

with household chores. She cleared her throat and answered, "Can you make rice?"

He moved into the kitchen, scratching the side of his head. "I'm better with mashed potatoes, but I can work with a recipe."

"I'll talk you through it." She pointed with her knife at a shelf of pots and pans under the island. "It starts with that pot." Dammit, even these ordinary tasks were still charged. Seeing his hands around the pot gave her a chance to really see how large they were.

He stood still long enough that it was clear he saw her staring at his hands. "Rice?" he asked once her gaze moved up to his face.

Remembering the process helped clear her mind. "In that cabinet. We'll rinse it first." She talked him through the recipe as she assembled what she needed for the rest of the meal. Once the rice was steaming, she moved to the stove with her cutting board full of onions, carrots, bell peppers and herbs. Ty continued to help, straining cans of beans and getting them ready for their turn in the pan.

She'd never cooked with a man before. On the rare occasions where she and Pete had time to share a homemade meal, it had been one or the other at the stove. Usually her. Ty moved easily around her and through the space as he followed directions. A simple dinner of beans and rice was transforming into a feast for the senses.

Once the food was done and plates assembled, she opened the cupboard for glasses. "Wine?"

"Water." The reality of his meaning drew a little chill into the room. Danger was always looming.

She poured out two waters and carried them to the small table in the window nook at the side of the kitchen. The sun had set, turning the window into a mirror. The reflection showed Ty approach with the plates. Her pulse quickened seeing him close to her, as if she was peering in at two other people who didn't know they were being watched. And from the heat in his eyes as he looked at her, she felt like she witnessed the prelude to something very erotic.

But it was just dinner. She told herself that again and again as they settled at the table and began their meal. "Nice work on the rice," she told him.

He toasted her with his glass of water. "Just following your directions."

"Add it to your repertoire." The spiced beans brought a deeper calm. "Where'd you get the mashed potatoes?"

"My mom." He smiled warmly. "Trained me until I got them right before going away to college."

"You're getting a family recipe here, too." It seemed like this plate of food was always available in the kitchen. "My mom, from my grandmother and who knows how far back."

"It's good." His eating slowed, and he focused on the food. "It's great."

The genuine appreciation he showed made her pay new attention to the food. Warm spices embraced her with the hands of family. "It's not too simple?"

"It's not simple at all." As his gaze moved to her face, she felt her skin light up. "It's you."

More heat spread around the small of her back and up her chest. The two of them ate in silence for a while, the quiet meaning just as much as the words. Ty looked about this nook of the kitchen and she watched him absorb the details.

"I'm sorry about your folks." He spoke softly. "I read about them when I was looking into this case."

Pain from losing them would never go away, but she'd learned to let it pass through her, rather than tearing her from the inside out. "Thank you. Your parents are…?" She didn't have files on Ty to search through.

"Still around." His smile returned. It was a tricky grin. Elusive, like he had to hide it before he revealed too much. "Daly City. Dad teaches high school history and civics. Mom's got an office job at a nonprofit for at-risk kids."

"More justice." He came into clearer focus for her.

He nodded with a small laugh. "Family recipe." She watched him tilt his head up, eyes focusing on somewhere else. The past or the future. The kitchen light revealed the shapes of his face and she stared too long. The cords of his neck led to a strong jaw. His mouth, always so expressive, now held in a line, musing. Broad nose. And those eyes, sharp with perception. Her gaze slid back to his full lips. A new hunger that had nothing to do with food yearned deep in her.

"Dessert?" Her voice came out like a seduction.

He met her gaze. "What've you got?" Did she see his need, or was that just her projecting what she wanted on him.

"Apple pie." She stood. "Of course."

He collected the empty plates before she could and took them to the sink. "I'll take a slice."

Now she wasn't sure he was talking about dessert at all. But she hadn't been, either. "Sydney makes them with the apples I give her." She cut broad slices from the pie her friend had given her two days ago. Just two days. Before all this had happened. Before Ty had appeared.

He didn't need to be reminded where to find the plates and brought two small ones, with fresh forks. "Her shop smelled amazing." Without stopping, he backed out of the kitchen. "Laundry's got to go in the dryer."

She moved the slices to the plates and gathered them. "We'll take them to the living room." She caught up to him in the hallway. "I'm sure there are emails from the neighbors I've got to field."

"Hit-and-run. Probably a teenage joyride or a stolen car." He trailed behind her. "The gunshot was a tire blowing out, but I patched it and everything's fine."

The story sounded true enough, infused with his police authority and experience. "They should buy that." She ran over it again in her head to figure out how to word the email. She reached the living room and put the pie next to her computer. Ty sat on the couch, plate in hand. When her laptop flicked on, the first thing on the screen was the article she'd found about some of his police work. He was good at his job. She tried to take confidence in that for whatever was coming next. Those bad guys in the article had been put away.

"It doesn't always work out." His pie remained untouched. Shadows crossed his face as he looked away from the computer screen and out the black windows. "I've found all the evidence, built the case, and the bastards still walk. Money's power. There are back rooms I'm not allowed in where the deals are made." Anger crept into his voice. "Innocent people suffer so someone can keep turning a profit."

She was on her feet and walking toward him before the decision had been made. He looked too alone sitting there. Even Toro approached cautiously. She stood behind the couch and laid her hand on Ty's shoulder. The stillness of his body was a shock.

He continued, "I knew a family who owned a little convenience store. Good location. Too good to pass up for a chain to come in. Someone broke the father's leg in a hit-and-run." She winced and tightened her grip on him. His voice remained even. "I found the driver, I even found the links that connected him to someone at the chain's corporate level. But the lawyers cut a deal, the driver got a slap on the wrist and the spotlight never hit the corporation."

A deep breath made his shoulders rise and fall under her touch. "And they got their location."

"No justice."

He put his hand on hers and looked up at her. "It'll come." Conviction was set on his face. "But it won't make the papers." At times, he seemed made of iron, but she saw—and she felt—how much of a man he was. Flesh and blood. And a heart. "Put their mind at ease," he said, looking again at the laptop. "I'm going to savor this pie." His hand slid from hers and he took up the fork.

She moved back to the laptop, and sure enough, there were two emails from neighbors about the trouble on the road. Ty's prepared story looked like truth on the screen. Typing *hit-and-run* slowed her down as the weight of what he'd just told her combined with what was really intended for her in the assault. Once the emails were sent she picked up her slice of pie and carried it to the couch.

Ty remained in his spot, pie uneaten. He shrugged off her quizzing look. "I told you I was going to savor it." She sat next to him and dug into her piece. He picked up a forkful. "You didn't think I'd eat this without you."

She had to look away, just as he slid the food into his mouth, eyes closed. Just seeing that had ignited a flame down her chest and deep into her belly. His perception could turn so…sensual. "Are you always such a gentleman?"

Dios, she was looking right at him when he opened his eyes slowly to reveal a wicked gleam in them. "Not always."

"Good." A gentleman wouldn't be able to take on the bastards who were attacking her. A gentleman wouldn't be able to feed the hunger she was feeling. And she didn't have to fight fair, either. She took her time with her bite of pie, knowing he was watching.

He licked his lips, fire in his eyes. "Tastes so fine."

"You like it?" she asked in a smoky voice. The couch seemed to sink in the middle, drawing them closer together. The side of her knee touched his.

He rumbled, "I don't think I'll get enough."

She placed her plate on the coffee table. "I want more."

He put his plate next to hers, then turned back to face her. Her breath slowed and her heart raced. His gaze moved over her face. Hot fingers interlaced with hers. She reached forward and placed her hand on his chest. The connection flowed with electricity. He stared into her eyes, not moving. She nodded and curled her fingernails into his chest to urge him forward.

Currents of heat concentrated as he drew closer. The world went dark as she closed her eyes. Everything she needed to know she could feel in his nearness. His mouth met hers and she immediately understood his need. Firm lips brushed against hers in strokes, then pressed hard. She met his intensity with her own hunger.

The flavor of spiced apples mixed with the smoky and earthy taste that was him. Her hand on his chest slid higher until she felt his strong neck. She stroked over his jaw and along the tight curls of his hair. He growled into her mouth and surged his body against hers. His fingers smoothed over her temple, wound into her hair and held there.

The two of them were locked together. His tongue darted out and tested across her lips. She opened for him and teased his tongue forward with hers. They slid against each other, communicating their yearning wordlessly. Their hands were still clasped. The grip tightened. Her body had to have more. Nipples tight, heat gathering between her legs. Satisfying these needs might mean burning everything down.

She parted the kiss and gasped for breath. Their bodies remained knotted close. He leaned his forehead against hers. Her pulse throbbed through her, driving heat to the deepest corners. A tremble started between her shoulders and shot down her arms. The intensity with Ty was too much, too hot.

He must've read her and gently unwound his fingers from her hand and her hair. She dropped her hand from the back of his neck. It glanced against his firm chest as she drew it back. This solid man seemed to be the answer to hungers she'd long forgotten about. But after all the needs were sated, what would be left?

A war raged between her body and her mind. Chaos swirled everywhere. Attacks and firebombings and car crashes. Secret justice. Ty fighting for her, and igniting her. She found her voice. "I have to say good-night."

He blinked slowly. The intensity remained in his eyes as an understanding grew. Standing, he steadied himself and took a step back. She stood as well and the two of them collected their plates. They maintained a safe distance during the procession to the kitchen, yet she still felt how he shook the air around him. The lights were turned off behind them, narrowing the house to only where they were.

Ty stood at the bottom of the stairs. Toro ran ahead to her bedroom. She was halfway up when Ty spoke. "Good night."

She draped the words over her shoulders like a shirt still warm from his body. His kiss still shook her. The hunger remained on his face. Their gazes held for a moment, then parted. He turned off the light and disappeared into the shadows. She walked to her bedroom alone.

Fog from the sea covered the landscape outside the guest bedroom window. The mist held the night quiet. Ty didn't feel quiet at all. He lay in bed, smelling the salty air coming in from the gap in the upper window and trying to concentrate on the comic book in his hands. It was the second time he'd looked through it.

But sweet honeyed apples continued to lure his brain into a fever. The taste on her lips. And the heat of her touch, her body, remained close to him. It didn't reach deep enough, though. Past the skin. That would be satisfied only if he held her against him. Tight. Breathing her in as she dug her fingers into his back.

He tossed the comic book on the bedside table and turned off the dim lamp there. The fog from outside seemed to press closer, hazing the details of the room in the darkness. But he could feel Mariana burning bright above him.

She was right to end the kiss. This attraction, this need complicated everything. The threat was ongoing, and he wasn't sure what it would take to stop it yet. Tomorrow might tell that. But tonight...

Mariana was in too vulnerable a spot, and he would not take advantage of that. Pursuing this desire couldn't be part of the mission. He slid his holstered pistol higher on the mattress next to him. He would fight for her until the end. He felt for her and didn't know how to stop.

Chapter Eight

Sunrise startled Mariana awake. She lay still in bed, listening. There was no sign of trouble and Toro snoozed calmly on the rug. Mostly, she was shocked that she was able to sleep at all. When the lights were out, her mind had been a jumble of insurance paperwork, car attacks and that kiss with Ty. She must've been more exhausted than she'd known to find any rest in the midst of that.

Toro unwound himself and stood when she swung out of bed. He was in the same spot, wagging his tail, when she emerged from the bathroom and put on a pair of jeans and a T-shirt. The two of them came down the stairs as sunlight continued to brighten the house.

A faint metallic sound from the kitchen froze her. Her legs flashed with cold heat and she regretted leaving her rifle in the bedroom closet. But Toro remained cool and trotted ahead to where he was normally fed. She crept forward down the hall, past the closed guest room door. Another sound from the kitchen. Movement.

And the smell of fresh coffee.

Relief swept in and her feet felt more firmly grounded on the floor. Before she reached the doorway she saw Ty in her kitchen, pulling two mugs from the drying rack next to the sink and setting them next to the brewing coffee. Jeans, T-shirt and a hoodie, he seemed perfectly comfortable in her space. Maybe the kiss didn't have to be stopped. Waking up to his making breakfast felt like the start to the kind of life she wanted to lead.

The bulge of the gun on his belt frosted that hope. Deadly reality remained.

He saw her in the hallway and smiled. "Mornin'." His hands remained busy collecting the coffee necessities. "I watched you make it yesterday and think I figured out your formula."

"Looks like you cracked the code." She put Toro's food together, then joined Ty at the counter. "Toast?"

"Bring it on." A new hesitancy tempered his energy. The intimacy of the kiss had told her so much. And she'd expressed her needs to him with it. But ending it the way they had left an air of caution between them. "Did you sleep?" he asked.

"Better than I thought I would." It hadn't solved all her problems, but at least she had the energy to face them. "You?"

"Eventually." It was all he needed to say. Many men would be surly after being cut off, but she saw none of that darkness in him. Not that the attraction had gone away. That magnetic pull still drew her close to him, and it took extra effort not to find the stability of his shoulder when she stood next to him at the island. He poured out coffee. "This'll get us ready for the Hanley Group."

The acid of hot coffee in her stomach suddenly felt less appealing. Tension made her hand shake as she cut slabs of bread. "Right."

"But nothing—" he spoke with quiet conviction "—can prepare them for you."

An attempted confident smile quickly failed. She tried to rally, but didn't even know what to prepare herself for.

"Should I build a battering ram from scraps in the barn? We go in guns blazing?"

"They will gladly open the door for us because they'll think you want to sell." He casually leaned against the island and sipped his coffee, as if planning a picnic. "Once we're inside, we play nice and collect any detail we can. Maybe we'll pick up what scares them, and we can use that to fight back. They flinch, and we'll see it." The iron of his intent was still evident within his casual posture.

Having a plan helped ease her nerves. Having Ty helped…everything. "As easy as falling off a ladder."

"I've never tried that," he mused.

"Can't recommend it." She pulled up the sleeve of her T-shirt and showed him the scar along the back of her arm.

"Damn." He tilted his head to get a better view.

"Pruning saw."

Stepping back, he pulled down the collar of his T-shirt. A scar along the top of his pectoral broke up the smooth expanse of his skin. "Wannabe mobster thought I needed a shave with a straight razor."

The urge to reach forward and touch it pushed her toward him, as if she could erase some of that pain with her fingers. She remained where she stood, hating that she had to suppress this need for contact and communication. "I've only seen those razors in antiques stores." They even looked dangerous in the glass cases, like gleaming poisonous insects.

He reorganized his shirt. "Some punks like them because they're easy to conceal. That particular punk had to wait until his broken arm healed before shaving anything." Subtle swagger glowed in Ty.

She drew the confidence into herself. Falling off the ladder hadn't killed her. The rattlesnakes that had slipped through her orchard had never bitten her. The Hanley Group was just men.

Ty moved toward the hallway. "Can you finish the toast? I've got to change." She nodded and he continued out. Instead of stopping in the guest room, though, she heard him leave the house and get something out of his car. Undisturbed by the activity, Toro let himself out the dog door in the kitchen for his morning rounds.

The toast took her attention for a bit, but she was aware of Ty's returning and closing himself in his room. A few minutes later, a different man entered her kitchen. It was Ty—same bold steps and lean, muscular frame—but he was wrapped in a deep blue suit. A tie with gold and umber motifs contrasted against a crisp white shirt.

Mouth dry, she licked her lips. "Slick." He tugged his cuff and spun quick on his heels. The jacket opened to show he still wore his gun, but it disappeared once he faced her again. Strutting closer revealed that rare wicked gleam in his eye. Her own clothes felt way too functional. It would be better if she was completely naked while he was dressed like that. She cleared her throat and tried to clear her mind. "You city detectives are polished."

His long fingers adjusted his tie. "You've seen what I usually wear. This was for my sister's wedding." Dipping his hand into his pocket, he pulled out a white sachet with a little tag attached. Mints with gold lettering commemorating the couple and the date.

"You must've had the bridesmaids lined up." It came out a little salty, but it was obvious that no one would be able to ignore his striding across a dance floor.

"Just to dance." He scratched at the back of his head. "Two of the bridesmaids were already married to each other and best friends with my sister and her wife, so it was that kind of party."

The context of the wedding quickly shuffled in her head and calmed her jealousy. "Got it." And she had no business feeling jealous anyway. Ty had been in her life for less than three days, they'd kissed once and then she'd said good-night. "I'll change into something more businesslike after we eat."

"You have a knife you can bring? Just in case you need some extra confidence." Any playfulness drained out of him. "With a blade under three inches, so they can't ding you on legalities."

"I do." A dead-serious air hung over the rest of breakfast and muted the food's flavor. Upstairs, all her serious clothes felt too flimsy for a confrontation. The best compromise she could find was her nicest dark-wash jeans and a silky top with a simple jacket over it. She retrieved a folding knife from her work pants and slid it in her front pocket. Tall, ruggedly stylish boots pulled over the jeans finished the look.

For a second she thought to pull her hair back in a bun or ponytail, but threw out the idea. These bastards were already trying to control her. Let her Mexican Italian hair stay wild.

Unease in her stomach grew with each step down to the ground floor. Ty emerged from the living room to meet her. He quickly checked out her outfit. The heat of desire flared quickly in his look, reassuring her that she wasn't the only one who still felt it. "Your hair looks nice like that."

"Thank you." The nerves dimmed in the blush that moved up her. She patted the knife in her front pocket. "This is definitely the strangest date I've ever been on."

With extra chivalry, Ty glided to the front door and opened it for her. "I know how to turn it up, right?"

She made sure Toro was set for the day, then stepped

outside with Ty and locked up. "How are you still single?" It was a joke and not a joke.

Dark sunglasses hid his eyes. "If criminals would stop breaking the law, I could slow down."

Or he could find a woman who kept up with him. "Stupid criminals."

Keys jingled in his hand. "I'll drive. You navigate." They went to his dented but functional car and climbed in. Her house and surrounding orchard grew smaller in the side-view mirror as they drove down the main road. After a turn toward the highway, it was gone from sight. The urge to return tugged at her. That was her home. Her family's roots struck deep into that dirt.

She focused ahead on the Hanley Group. "As soon as I felt them leaning on me, I put all the contact info from the developers into my phone." Pulling up the entry, she mapped a route and relayed the first stage to Ty.

A metallic scraping sound from the dented front end of Ty's car grew steadily as he accelerated to highway speed. The car stayed on track when he pulled the steering wheel back and forth as a test. No stray pieces shook loose and he proceeded on.

Rodrigo merited only two exits from the highway. They sped past the last turnoff to town. Golden-brown hills rose and fell on both sides of the road north. She settled deeper into the seat to watch the shifting land, broken up by agricultural buildings. "I never get to really look at this." Ty glanced at her quizzically. "I'm always driving," she answered.

"Enjoy it until we get to San Jose." He made an exaggerated frown before resetting to a neutral expression. They swept over a long bend in the highway and the Pacific came into view on their left. In the cloudless day, it looked like the horizon had been cut with a razor.

After a few miles, they turned away from the ocean onto another road. It wound into hills, dark with pine. Traffic sped up, taking on a more urban urgency. Scrape marks on the concrete median showed the scars of all the wrecks. Some looked very fresh. The twisting highway didn't help the growing nerves prickling under her skin.

Ty navigated smoothly through the curves and let the faster cars pass and risk their own necks. "I know a cop in the city, Benny. His parents were Welsh, he told me, as if that explained why he had an Everest-sized chip on his shoulder. Do you know why?"

"Something to do with England, but that's all I've got."

"The guy has hands like bricks. He always holds the smallest coffee cup he can find in one of his massive fists during an interview or interrogation. As soon as it's finished, he crushes it, just a little bit. So you can hear it. Maybe the last couple drops drip out. And whoever we're talking to gets scared as hell and doesn't even know why." Ty made a fist and used it to gently tap her shoulder. "That's what we're going to do. Squeeze them. Subtle."

When she shifted her focus from the story to the task at hand, she found that the Hanley Group didn't loom quite as large. But she knew it wouldn't be easy. "Maybe Benny could join us."

"You don't need him to intimidate someone." Ty's eyes were hidden behind his sunglasses, but his mouth remained serious.

"A farmer with no college degree." And her size wasn't going to send anyone cowering behind their desk.

"A woman who shapes trees. Who knows how the earth and the weather come together to create food." He looked at her instead of the road for a little too long. "You scare *me*."

"I don't buy that," she scoffed.

He shook his head. "I could tell you a lot of things to get

you hyped for this door kicking. I'm telling you the truth now. These guys, whoever we're going to meet there, have no idea what you are. And that's going to terrify them."

She ran her hand through her hair and gathered her confidence. "And I have my knife." But she didn't want to consider what it would take to use it.

He revealed his own danger in a smile. "And you have me."

Which was both reassuring and more complicated than ever. There was no one other than Ty who she'd trust to walk with her into the teeth of whatever was coming. But that kiss hadn't stopped echoing through her. As soon as she was distracted enough to not think about it, the hot pulses would wash back over her again. Seeing Ty in his suit hadn't helped. The passing trees flicked the sun on and off his profile and the determined set of his jaw.

The highway swept down from the hills and turned into a flat racetrack. Suburbs surrounded her. New and old strip malls, office buildings and stucco houses sped past. Warehouses and industrial parks crowded next to the road for long stretches. Logos for tech firms she'd never heard of were too convoluted and went by too quickly to read.

Ty drove more aggressively to keep up with the traffic around him. People seemed to change lanes or pass without fear of consequence. She kept hitting an invisible brake pedal on the floor. "You can't drive like this in a small town. Everyone'll know who it is."

"Kill or be killed on the highway." Somehow he kept his cool. "It can be better in the neighborhoods."

That was the world she was rushing into. "Far cry from the orchard."

"Do you know how terrified these suits we're going to meet would be to spend the night among your trees?"

"The call of a horned owl will give anybody the chills."

The paths between the trees were so well-known she needed only a flashlight on the darkest of nights.

"Except you." He raised an eyebrow above his sunglasses.

True, knowing the hunter was watching over her land was reassuring. "We have an understanding." Her phone alerted her to the next move in the navigation. Both she and Ty sat up straighter as they exited off the highway into San Jose. At first they were surrounded by warehouses and she wondered if the map was wrong, but after a block they were met by a stand of gleaming new buildings. They stood at different heights, as if still growing and learning how to best adapt to the sun and wind. A manufactured neighborhood of mixed-use housing and shops crept close to the sidewalk, leaving little room for pedestrians to walk.

"There it is." Ty slowed the car. The address was ahead on their left. A twenty-story building, alternating stripes of concrete and glass.

She unclenched her jaw. The Hanley Group didn't own the whole structure. They were just renters in suite 1550. She owned her land.

Ty brought the car into a parking lot attached to the mixed-use buildings, near a high-end supermarket. Maybe she imagined it, but it sure felt like most of the people they passed checked out the dented front end as he looked for a spot. They parked between two very expensive SUVs. Ty got out and inspected his car as it ticked down from the drive. "Nothing's rubbing where it shouldn't. We should be good for the drive back."

"I bet you're rethinking your whole 'justice is my reward' thing." The damage on the fender wasn't a cheap fix.

He shrugged it off and straightened his suit. "I know a guy with a body shop." With a tip of his head, he brought them into motion. They merged into the flow of people near the market, then broke free of them to get to the street.

Concrete, metal and glass amplified the daylight. She squinted against it to pick out the details of the crosswalk and the building ahead. The architect had curved the ground floor into a welcoming arc. A low oval fountain broke the sun into thousands of dazzling pieces. Ty glided past it all and stayed at her shoulder as they walked through the sliding doors into the lobby.

Her first instinct was to check in at the security desk on the far right, but Ty kept moving toward the elevators. There were several other people flowing in the same current, and she walked as if she belonged. Ty removed his sunglasses, stashed them in his jacket and gave her a discreet wink. Her heart pounded faster. Because they were headed up to confront the Hanley Group? Or was it the way his attention never strayed from her, and he always seemed to know what she needed.

"Fifteen, please." Ty's low voice was so much warmer than the stainless steel interior of the elevator. A woman close to the front punched the button and the doors closed. The ride up was too long for Mariana's nerves. She distracted her mind with thoughts of pruning her trees in winter. Following the lines of branches, seeking the strongest flow of energy through the wood… "This is us," Ty brought her back to the world with a gentle whisper. They eased past the remaining people in the elevator and stepped out to the fifteenth floor.

"Dead ahead." The same Hanley Development Group logo from the business card she'd first received was cut into glass and metal next to a set of gray doors.

Ty put his fist out and waited. She bumped hers into his and stepped forward. The door opened with a heavy swish in Ty's hand. He held it for her and proceeded after with a guarding presence. The lobby was decorated in gray tones, with conceptual drawings of building developments on the walls and another set of double doors on the far wall. She walked to the front counter, where a white woman in her twenties smiled politely at a low desk and adjusted her thick-framed glasses.

"Good morning." The woman scooted her chair closer to her desk. "How can I help you?" Strange to think that the same money that paid her also paid the bald man who'd firebombed Mariana's store.

After sitting in the car, getting worked up, Mariana felt ready for a throwdown. She paused so she didn't sound too confrontational. "I'd like to see Mr. Hebert."

The secretary scrunched her lips to one side and clicked over her computer. "Do you have an appointment, Ms…?"

Mariana leaned on the counter. "Mariana Balducci." She expected some kind of tell from the woman to indicate the importance of what that meant.

The woman's innocent eyes lit back onto Mariana. "I don't see an appointment." A glance at Ty raised the woman's caution. He smiled casually, but not warmly. "Let me see if he's available. Please have a seat." She waved her hand toward the chairs in the far corner, then typed efficiently on the computer.

While the stylish leather chairs were appealing, Mariana and Ty only stood near them. He whispered, "She didn't blink. The bad business isn't run through her desk."

Any second the bald man and whoever his partner was could come bursting through the doors. Mariana nearly jumped when the secretary chirped, "He's got a few minutes, so hold on just a sec." Her pulse kicked faster. Ty's calming hand came to rest on the small of her back. He smiled just for her, the iron still in his eyes.

A moment later, the door on the far wall opened to reveal the man who'd first approached her in her store. Mr. Hebert was a fit white guy in his forties, about Ty's height, with hair just starting to whiten at the temples. He wore slacks and a striped button-down shirt. A wedding ring was his only jewelry. "Ms. Balducci. Nice surprise to see you again." It seemed genuine. "Come on back." He waved her forward. When Ty approached with her, Mr. Hebert's smile wavered. "And you are?"

"Mr. Morrison." Ty shook his hand with a neutral expression.

"We'll use the conference room." Mr. Hebert walked briskly to a glass door on a glass wall that showed a long table lined with chairs next to yet another window revealing the sprawl of San Jose below. Mr. Hebert held the door for them. Outside, the land was carved into concrete pieces for miles and miles until it reached the foothills in the distance. "I honestly didn't think I'd hear from you again."

"But you hadn't completely given up hope." She stood instead of taking the offered chair.

Mr. Hebert's smile wavered. "Sure. I mean, your property has a lot of upsides for us and I'm sure we could work out a deal that would benefit everyone."

It was impossible to gauge if this man was behind the intimidation, or if he didn't even know about it like the secretary. But someone in these offices knew, and the word would spread about her arrival. The nerves that had been shaking her all morning concentrated to hot coals of anger. "My orchard has been on that land for over a hundred and fifty years. Will your resort stand that long? Will it hold the hills together, or break them apart?"

"I'm sorry..." Mr. Hebert stood behind one of the rolling chairs, his gaze shifting between Mariana and the silent Ty. "Are you not here to talk about our offer?"

"I *am* here to talk about your offer." She stepped forward, hands hot. "I saw that you bought the parcels north of my property before you contacted me." Mr. Hebert moved backward. "You must've known those hills aren't zoned for development. Did you just assume I was a sure thing?"

Mr. Hebert's words faltered. "Of…of course not." Having him on the defensive brought out her urge to go for the throat, to curl her fist in his shirt and tell him that she would never sell, no matter what they threw at her. But she knew from Ty that this meeting was just a step to finally stopping the intimidation.

She leaned toward Mr. Hebert, her hands spread on the conference table. "Then maybe you should've waited for my answer before you snatched the other land." The next look from Mr. Hebert gave her a taste of what she needed. A glimmer of fear in his eyes. But not nearly the same amount as they'd made her feel. Mr. Hebert glanced out the glass wall at one of his associates. This older white man in an expensive gray suit shrugged as if to ask what the problem was. When he laid eyes on her, though, his question disappeared and his posture straightened. The older man turned to head down the hall one way, changed his mind, then hurried away in a different direction.

Ty's even voice took over the room. "After investing those millions in undeveloped land, your associate might not like it if you give up the pursuit of Ms. Balducci's property." He waved his hand slowly in the direction the other man had sped off to.

"Mr. Innes?" Mr. Hebert seemed to have been infected by the same fluster that took over the older man. "He's not involved…"

Ty stepped up to stand at her side. He spoke slowly and calmly to Mr. Hebert. "You're not to contact her again. *No one* is to contact her again." Good thing he was on her side, because he was ice cold and damn intimidating.

"W-well," Mr. Hebert stammered, "I don't think you have to worry about that." His hand shook slightly as he indicated the door out of the conference room. Ty swung it open for her and they walked back out the way they came. Mr. Innes was nowhere to be seen.

The woman in the lobby smiled. "Do we need to set up another appointment?" Mariana shook her head and left with Ty. Her heart pounded as if she'd just been in a fight.

As they waited for the elevator, Ty knocked his knuckles into the back of her hand. "You kicked ass."

"You're freaking scary when you go cold." She returned the gesture and wondered if there had been a static shock where they'd touched or if she'd imagined it.

"Absolute zero." Then he smiled with the quiet warmth she'd grown to understand in him.

The elevator opened to show a few businesspeople, most of them on their phones. With each floor down she and Ty rode, her body calmed from the confrontation. Every sentence rang again and again in her head, overanalyzed. Maybe she could've said more. Or got more information. Her brain had been revving so high when she'd been in the conference room.

Once the doors opened on the ground floor, Ty walked slowly, allowing the other people to get ahead. He leaned close. "Hebert doesn't know anything. Mr. Innes, though…" He went silent and stared ahead.

Her pulse immediately raced up again. Two security guards, a white man and an Asian man, both in navy uniforms, stood in the building lobby, necks flexing and hands curved ready. Ty reached into his jacket. She and the men tensed. Only she relaxed when Ty pulled out his sunglasses and put them on.

The guards separated slightly as they approached. The closer they came, the more she saw the hard lines of their faces. Ty raised his hand slightly as a warning. "No need for an escort. We're leaving."

While the guards were distracted with him, she slipped the knife out of her pocket and kept it folded. The guards looked like they were made of stone, hard enough to break the blade. They didn't pay attention to Ty's dismissal and kept coming. In another three steps, they'd reach her. She couldn't see a gun on either of them, but that wasn't a guarantee they weren't armed. Ty definitely was, but how bad would things have to get for him to draw it?

Before the guards intercepted them, they stopped walking and formed a wall to her left. Ty kept moving, so she did, as well. After they'd passed the guards, the two men swung behind them to closely follow. The muscles in Ty's jaw jumped. He growled back to them, "What did I just tell you?"

The men continued to ignore him. One of them hooked his thumb in his gear belt next to a collapsible baton in a sheath. Her palm sweated around her knife. Ty remained amazingly cool. He slowed as he approached the glass doors. The guards didn't adjust their pace and came closer. Without missing a step, Ty undid his blazer and spun toward the men. "Don't touch her." His jacket opened just enough to reveal the gun on his belt.

The guards froze.

Ty's menacing scowl alone would make anyone back off. He effortlessly opened the door for her, then followed her out into the bright day. "We've done all the damage we can. Let's get out of town." She felt the eyes of the guards on her back all the way across the street and let out a huge sigh once she climbed into Ty's car.

He spoke kindly from the driver's seat. "You're still holding your knife." Sore fingers uncurled from around it. Ty asked with surprise, "What is that?"

She opened the steeply curved hawkbill blade. "Pruning knife." She closed it and explained, "It's the only knife I have under three inches."

He chuckled, impressed. "If they'd seen it, I wouldn't have had to flash my pistol. No one's going to mess with you with that knife in your hand." The car kicked into gear and he hurried them out of the parking lot. Part of her expected to see the security guards and a full SWAT team waiting for them in front of the building, but everything seemed normal on the street.

The tall buildings seemed like they were ready to come crumbling down on her in hard and sharp shards. It felt like she'd been tensing her muscles for hours. Relaxing them made her far too vulnerable. "Get us out of here."

"You've got it." He moved more aggressively through city traffic and hit the highway without looking back. They blended in with the rush. Anyone following them would've been lost. She, too, was without a compass until they crested the hills and once again faced the Pacific Ocean.

She wanted to go home. She wanted home to be safe again, and had no idea if what Ty had helped her do today would be enough.

Chapter Nine

There'd been enough talk. Ty brought them back to the coast and felt Mariana slowly decompressing next to him. Replays and analysis would burn her out, so he navigated them to a lunch spot he knew of in one of the small towns north of hers. Their silence during the meal wasn't awkward or charged with unresolved emotions. It was necessary. He took a few minutes to text the content of the meeting to his frontline Frontier Justice associates, Vincent and Stephanie, emphasizing the name Mr. Innes. That man practically tap-danced down the hallway once he saw Mariana. Mr. Hebert wasn't in on it. Mr. Innes was.

After lunch, Ty and Mariana walked a boardwalk near the bluffs over a beach. Her eyes focused in the distance, still processing, but she stood on strong legs and her path didn't waver. The strength he'd seen in her, felt in her, showed up in that conference room. He hadn't known how much talking he'd need to do, but it was her force that sent the message. To say he was impressed was an understatement. More like awed. Her controlled storm seemed like it could take the whole building out.

She stopped at an old redwood fence and stared out at the sea. "Did that do anything?"

He stood next to her, felt her energy calming. "We got a name. Innes."

"But they're still going to come back," she said, resolved.

"Yeah. Until we find the right guy at the top to send the right message to." She was too experienced with the situation by now to believe any deflection. "Today we got to the suits." He leaned his shoulder into hers. "You saw Innes jump."

That brought out a smile. "Felt good." She stayed pressed against him.

"We'll rattle all the bolts out of him." He slid his fingers up her wrist and curled his hand around hers. Too intimate. Once the touch started, his hunger for the heat of her connection struck deep.

She held him. "There's no way to thank you." The sea air carried her whisper into him. "There's no one else I'd want helping me other than you."

Turning, she pulled him toward her. Her head tilted up and he fell into the kiss. The words were still on her lips, he tasted her truth. They met tenderly. She opened to him and the kiss deepened. Heat crashed through him. The link between them he'd tried to deny was inescapable. He would do anything to help her. What had started as a mission was now tied to his heart.

The kiss ended and he opened his eyes back to the bright sun. They stayed at the bluff for a few more minutes. The ocean shone and surged at the beach below, calm and eternal. But their work protecting her and her home wasn't done and it was time to return. Without speaking, she understood, walking readily with him back to the car.

The ride to Rodrigo released more of the tension that had built up on the way to the Hanley Group confrontation. Mariana found a local college radio station and they listened to music they'd never heard before. Once back in town, Mariana's attention grew more focused. "I want to swing by my shop and see Sydney."

"Can I drop you? I need to do a hardware store run."

She nodded. "It's just a couple blocks away." Afternoon deepened the shadows and increased places for someone to hide. He pulled up in front of her store. She must've seen the concern on his face. "I'll be quick, then I'm going right over to Sydney's."

"Meet you there." How would they part? A kiss? A handshake, like teammates? He hadn't left her since yesterday morning. She leaned forward and he met her for a quick kiss. A moment later, she was out of the car and on the sidewalk.

He kept an eye on her in the rearview mirror as long as he could before turning toward the hardware store. Though brief, the kiss's impact remained. The fact that it was so casual, so light, was what shook him. He'd shared brief passion with women before, but nothing sustained. His job would always get in the way and the initial fever would dwindle until they both agreed to move on from each other. The passion for Mariana hadn't gone away. It rooted deeper than he'd known.

The parking lot of the hardware store and lumberyard was filled with pickup trucks and men and women with dust on their boots. Ty's rattling, dented car turned a couple of heads, but there were no comments thrown his way as he got out and entered the store.

More than just hardware, the store supplied everything a homestead needed. Lamp oil, canning supplies, toys and pots and pans. His ancestor had probably walked through a very similar general store in this area, though he wouldn't have seen the two-hundred-dollar coolers or propane grills. Ty moved past the ready-made housewares and headed to the raw materials at the back of the store, basket in hand.

Going through a mental list, he collected what he needed as he wove through the aisles. A countdown ticked in his head. Mariana was still under threat. And everything felt more…complete when he was at her side.

A man walking down the aisle toward him told Ty that he wasn't going to have a quick in-and-out visit to the store. Pete, in full uniform, cruised forward. His rangy frame blocked any exits. Ty imagined the small smile on the officer's face was supposed to be friendly, but it was mostly a sneer of authority. And Pete's gaze remained cool.

"Those don't look like vacation souvenirs," he ribbed unsuccessfully, staring into Ty's basket.

"Good eye." Ty put the basket down and faced Pete. "You just might make detective."

The cop straightened taller. "Don't suppose you've remembered any more details from the other night."

"I'll let you know." There must be security cameras on every aisle in the store. Was anyone watching the two of them squaring off? "Has your department found anything?"

Pete stared over Ty's shoulder like he was reading a teleprompter. "We're still sorting evidence and have put out a call for any potential witnesses to come forward."

Ty suppressed an unhappy laugh. "This isn't a press conference."

"This isn't your case." The cop hitched his thumbs in his belt. "You're staying in town?"

"Nearby." Ty was more than ready to move on. Pete the cop hadn't helped. Pete the ex was one of the last people he wanted to be talking to.

A realization finally dawned on Pete, his eyes narrowing. "At Mariana's?"

"Is there a law against it in this jurisdiction?" Ty was pushing it, but wasn't going to shrink away from Pete. Deliberately selecting an item from a peg on the wall, Ty took a package of sash cord and tossed it in the basket.

Pete blinked at the suggestive coil of rope. His jaw

flexed. He stared back at Ty with more emotion in his eyes than before. "Maybe you can convince her to sell that place. It's falling apart around her."

Anger tightened in Ty's chest. "Maybe I'll help her fix it." Picking up the basket, he showed that he was leaving. If Pete tried to stop him, things would get ugly. The cop remained puffed up for show, but stepped aside.

Ty headed straight to the checkout counter, still heated. The cashier was chipper and he couldn't match her enthusiasm. If Pete and the police had been listening to Mariana all along, she wouldn't be in this mess. She could've been hurt or killed, and Pete's answer was for her to sell. She was still in danger and Pete's biggest reaction was when he figured out Ty was staying with her.

After lightening up for a little small talk with the cashier, Ty saw her stare out behind him with some trepidation. Ty collected his bags, thanked her and headed out of the store. One glance back confirmed that it was Pete looming toward the back of the store, trying to bore a hole in Ty with a hard look.

By the time Ty was in his car, Pete must've been talking trash about him to the cashier, building an ally to keep an eye out. Petty and personal. Instead of working to strengthen the community around Mariana, and anyone else who might be threatened.

A minute later, Ty parked in front of Sydney's shop and walked inside to find her and Mariana behind the counter, sharing a worried expression. "You already heard about it?" he asked.

"What?" Mariana furrowed her brow.

"My neighborly conversation with Pete at the hardware store."

Sydney let out a sound of frustration. Mariana came around the counter to him, concerned. "Was it bad?"

"Pete's a lightweight." Still, the anger hadn't completely gone away. "He just said that you should sell your place."

"Son of a… I don't have time for his…" Mariana ran her hands through her hair in frustration. After a shuddering breath, she reset and turned to Sydney. "Tell him what you saw."

The other woman kept her voice low, glancing out the window. "White guy with a shaved head, over six feet tall. Dark jeans, heavy shoes, jacket over a T-shirt. He walked past Mariana's shop a couple times, looked in the glass door in front."

The description sounded like the man whom he fought in the parking lot. "Time?"

Sydney checked a slip of paper on her counter. "Eleven thirty-eight and twelve twenty-two."

It didn't click. Mariana looked like she was troubled with the same thoughts. "That's when we were at the Hanley Group."

Ty tried to sort the information. "It's when we were there and after we left." So how connected was the bald man to the developers? "Thanks for keeping an eye out, Sydney." Even if he couldn't figure out how it all fitted together, just having pieces to work with helped.

"It's all logged on an online document." Sydney hadn't lost her concerned expression since he'd arrived. "I didn't see him come and go, so no car to track."

"This is all good info," Ty reassured her. "Are you feeling safe?" It wasn't fair to leave her exposed while she was helping them. "Is there something you need here?"

She smiled her thanks. "Warren's picking me up after work."

"Excellent." He started toward the door. "I have to do some work in the orchard."

Mariana first went to Sydney, gave her hand a squeeze,

then met Ty at the front of the store. The afternoon would be leading into evening soon, and he needed the daylight.

Back in the car, Mariana explained that nothing had changed at her store. No progress with the police, and the insurance company was still getting some things sorted before the cleanup. The path to her orchard grew more familiar. He drove on instinct and took in the aging sheds that lined one side of a road, rusting tin roofs and doors that had pulled from their hinges on rotting wood.

Mostly, he wanted to stare at how the late sun caught in Mariana's brown eyes. They looked like polished stone, something mysterious from deep in the earth. She gazed out, sharp. Unbroken, even after all she'd been through.

He parked outside her house and she got out to look back down the long road. "No ambushes." Toro hurried out from behind the house. His tail thumped against the car as he received his welcoming pets.

Ty pulled the hardware store bags from the trunk. "I got some insurance against that." He headed toward the house. "But I can't risk this suit." Mariana unlocked the front door and Toro clicked his claws up and down the inside stairs while the two of them changed into work clothes. Ty still wore his sidearm.

Back outside Toro settled into an easy gait between them for the climb up through the orchard. In boots, jeans and a T-shirt, Mariana walked much more confidently on the land than she did in San Jose. Ty pulled out three spools of heavy-gauge wire from the hardware store bags. "Will it hurt the trees to wrap this around them?"

She inspected a strand from the spool. "Not temporarily."

If the problem with the Hanley Group wasn't fixed quickly, there'd be no way to win. That corporation had more money, more resources. A sustained assault on the house with just him and her defending would finish them.

He stood still to take in this side of the orchard. The trees weren't planted on a perfect grid, and the gaps between them created some worn paths. Unwinding a length of wire, he wrapped it around a tree about two feet above the ground.

"I get it." Mariana took the spool from him and walked to another tree. She coiled it around that side, keeping the wire tight. "Did you get a pair of cutters? I have some in the barn."

He found the new ones in a bag and tossed them to her. The muscles of her forearm flexed in defined lines as she worked the cutters, and the wire was severed with a sharp click. She hefted the spool and Ty pointed her to the next pair of trees. Once that wire was strung, they climbed higher on the hill and continued.

At the top of the hill, they walked to the road that split the orchard. He explained, "If anyone comes down here, they'll hit the wires and get funneled onto here. It makes them exposed targets and slows their approach."

"Targets," she repeated back in a whisper. Her unfocused eyes scanned the orchard and her home below.

"*If* anyone comes." He placed a gentle hand on her elbow.

The clarity returned to her gaze. "Have you done this before?" She walked to the next tree and started winding the wire around it.

"Similar principle." He took the spool and unwound it across a gap. "We locked all the doors but one in a hotel hallway, flushed a suspect down from the floor above right into our hands." She tossed him the cutters and he severed the wire once it was secure.

The spool was nearly empty, so he started a new one

on the next pair of trees. Mariana's pace slowed, her expression pensive. "Has Frontier Justice done this before?"

"Not for a while." Eroding her confidence with too much truth wouldn't help this fight.

She stood her ground, not taking the spool to walk it out. "How long?"

There was nothing to be gained from a lie. Her sharp gaze cut into him and would find it out. "Hundred years."

He expected fury, but got a wry smile. She took up the spool and commenced with the work. After a few more pairs of trees, she stilled again with a sudden realization. "Pete knows you're staying here."

"Some of his best police work." Ty couldn't forget the look on the cop's face when he looked at the rope in his basket. "Is that going to be a problem?"

After a long moment, she shrugged it off. "Hell, who cares what he thinks?" The fluid motion returned to her body and the two of them progressed through the rest of the orchard. The wire ran out as the sun descended toward the glowing Pacific.

A cool breeze smelled like the sea and made the leaves shiver around them. Ty and Mariana collected the empty spools and other gear and walked down toward the house. Mariana knocked her shoulder against his and said, wryly, "Don't tell me, all the hotels in the area are booked and you're going to have to stay the night here."

"Don't need to. I'm staying on my yacht in the bay."

She chuckled, then grew serious. "You're staying until things are safe?"

The question rang through him, shook him. He'd promised that he would stay by her side throughout the trouble. After that? His mind couldn't answer. There was no sensible way to project that far ahead. But an ache deep in his chest urged him to tell her he would remain as long as she would have him.

Her phone rang. "Private caller." She held it for him to see. He nodded and she answered with the phone between them. "Hello?"

The man's voice was loud enough for Ty to hear the sneer. "I can't figure out if you're stubborn or stupid." Ty felt Mariana tense next to him. Her mouth tightened and her hand trembled. His own fury blasted up from his legs and through his chest. If this son of a bitch was standing there instead of hiding behind a phone, Ty would take him apart. The man continued, "What's it going to take for you to figure out there's only one way out of this? And it's an easy way that ends with your bank account full of cash."

Mariana spoke with deadly precision. "If you were a human being, you'd know why I'm never going to sell."

"But I'm not." The man laughed. "I'm one of those nightmares you can't kill."

Mariana's lips curled into a snarl. "So why'd you drive away scared yesterday?" Striking back loosened her posture.

The man was silent. She'd hit a good nerve. He came back with, "I know where you were—"

Ty cut him off, knowing the man's confidence had been rattled. "They're not paying you enough to risk your life."

"It's her life at risk." For the first time some emotion shook in the man's voice as he tried to convince them. "And yours if you're standing too close."

"You're going to get hurt." Ty didn't let up. "You thought this was going to be easy. But this lady isn't easy. *I'm* not easy."

Silence on the other end of the line.

Ty told the man, "The next bullet is for you." He punched

the disconnect button on Mariana's phone and was left with ringing in his ears as his rage ebbed.

Mariana pocketed her phone and turned a circle, searching over the darkening landscape. "Is he here?"

Ty shook his head. "Guy like that couldn't pass up an opportunity to drop a scare like that. He would've said if he could see us."

She shuddered. "Bastards."

He took out his own phone. "He won't stay silent long. I'm going to call in the others." Hopefully they could drop their lives and show up in time. "Get them here by tomorrow." He was midway through writing the text when Mariana's stillness drew his attention. Putting the phone away, he focused on her.

Tears glossed her eyes. She looked at her trees. "You knew how bad this was going to get."

"I'm preparing for the worst." He'd give anything to stop the coming storm from her land.

"We have to save this place." She said it like a promise to the land surrounding them. He'd had ulterior motives for wanting to preserve the orchard and house, but they were insignificant as he looked at her strong profile set against the shadowed hills. Whatever he did now, it was for her.

Chapter Ten

Anger numbed the fear. Or it was the hot water pounding her back in the shower. Jolts of tension still ran up her limbs, spurred by the confrontation at the Hanley Group and the threatening phone call, but she was learning to channel them. Watching Ty operate, smooth until just the right moment to release his fury, she started to understand her own power in this fight. Mr. Hebert and Mr. Innes had been so shaken they'd called security on her.

Not that the trouble was over. She knew better than that.

The plumbing pipes rattled around her. Far cry from a fancy resort shower. They'd probably deck it out with marble for miles, a big glass box around her to catch all the steam from the six showerheads. She had a claw-foot tub, but theirs would have water jets and could seat four. A long vanity with two sinks, instead of her single enameled antique. There must be thousands of expensive hotel bathrooms like that around the world. No one else had a room like hers.

As soon as she turned the shower off, she heard the downstairs one turn on. The pipes got only a moment's rest before clanging like a distant train struggling to find a station. Beneath that stream of water was Ty. Her skin was still warm from her shower. It grew hotter as she imagined his lean muscles glossed wet. Her imagination had him drawing a bar of soap over his chest, then down his abs and lower… She dried herself more vigorously, as if it was possible to distract herself from the need that yearned from deep.

She threw on ordinary jeans over everyday panties. The T-shirt and sweatshirt were functional and comfortable. She brushed out her hair and tried to lose herself in the routine. But nothing felt normal. Every stitch of the clothes was felt by her tuned nerves. The brush in her hair brought back memories of Ty's hand there, holding her during the kiss.

That kiss. And the one today. So different, but all part of the silent communication between her and Ty. She'd only just started to know this connection. The thought of losing it made her chest ache. Pursuing that feeling with Ty, though, left her lost. The path was dark, unknown.

But she had to take the next step.

The shower turned off downstairs. She left the bedroom and went to the ground floor while trying to interpret the sounds of Ty getting dressed. Was that his T-shirt being pulled down over his chest? A belt buckle clinked. His jeans must be pulled across his hips.

A sudden concern quickly cooled her thoughts. Something was different in the guest room. Trouble? But Toro had been cruising calmly through the house. She stood in the doorway and inspected from floor to ceiling to pinpoint what change had caught her attention. Night had fallen outside, but the curtains weren't drawn. She would be in plain view.

Then she saw it. The top sash of the window rested securely in place with no gap on the edge. The tension drained from her, replaced by a fresh energy when Ty stepped into the hallway. He wore a tank top under his partially zipped hoodie, giving her a clear view of how the cords of his neck joined the clean lines of his collarbones. "You fixed it?" she asked.

He glided forward. "The least I can do as a guest."

The nearer he came, the more her confidence grew. She'd expected the opposite, but her need for this man cut through all the chaos of her life with striking clarity. Seeking a connection with Ty wasn't a complication. It was an answer.

She met him in the hallway. "I don't want you to sleep in the guest room tonight."

His gaze deepened on her. The air hummed with electricity between them. It seemed to crackle when he stepped nearer. Her skin brightened, awaiting the contact. His first caress was a whispered "I want you."

The heat of his words cascaded down her body. With her nerves already tuned to him, it was like liquid fire. She needed to burn with his touch and closed the gap between them. "Yes," she told him, her hands curling into his sweatshirt. "Yes." She brought her chest to his and tilted her head up. "Now." Her word ended in a kiss. Ty devoured her and she gave all of herself. And she fed herself on his need.

His hands moved up her back. She held him closer, her sensitive breasts raining sparks from where she rubbed against him. One of his hands swept into her hair. Hot skin contrasted against damp cool. She opened her mouth, asking him deeper. He sank into the kiss and wound an arm around her. The two of them gripped each other.

The ordinary space of the hallway transformed into a spot of ferocious need. She'd understood the hunger as it was building, but was surprised by the urgency. As if the danger could return any second and tear Ty away from her.

A flush burned her skin from her neck, down her chest and belly, to between her legs. From the impression of his arousal in his jeans, she knew Ty felt the same. The strength in his kiss told her, as well. His tongue slid against hers, probed into her, inciting a raw hunger.

She dug her nails into his chest through his sweatshirt and stopped the kiss long enough to murmur, "Upstairs." He nodded, stubble lightly rasping her cheek. Even the smallest texture of his body set her off with an aching want to discover more.

They loosened their grip on each other enough to walk up the stairs. She led and he ran his hands down her waist and over her hips. Once she reached the bedroom, he held her and brought his chest against her back. Her fingers found the fronts of his thighs. His hands searched up across her belly and higher. A moan escaped her throat when his mouth found the side of her neck in a gentle kiss.

Her voice grew louder when his palm swept up over her breast. She arched, pressing into the sensation. He circled her erect nipple and built the fires inside her higher. His kisses continued on her neck. She reached up and stroked down the side of his face. He murmured warm words into her flesh.

All the sensations swirled around her and threatened to sap the strength from her legs. She only needed to tilt her shoulders toward the bed and Ty moved with understanding. He turned her and lifted her with easy strength, allowing her to wrap her legs around his waist and drape her arms over his shoulders. She felt the impression of his sidearm, but would not let that reality take away these moments. Only the small lamp on her bedside table burned, casting a diffused pink across the bedroom. The light drew the lines of Ty's intense face. It shone in his eyes, but only the surface. The depths were unseeable.

The glow disappeared when she leaned in to kiss him again. Coiled around him, weightless in his arms, she was more free than she'd ever felt. Their lips met, open and unashamed. Her body gripped him tighter. Her hips ground against his. He growled into her mouth.

She floated on Ty's powerful legs as he walked her to the bed. Gently, he laid her down there, then leaned next to her. His long fingers ran through her hair with a hypnotic rhythm. She unzipped his hoodie and explored his chest with her hands. The muscles were firm, and his abs trembled slightly when she touched them. That same thrill ran through her. Her clothes, which had seemed so comfortable when she'd put them on, now scraped at her sensitive nerves.

She tugged his hoodie off one shoulder. "Take this off." Easing the fabric off, he gave her a full view of his powerful arms. She gathered the hem of her sweatshirt. "Take this off." He smiled hungrily and helped sweep the sweatshirt from her. His eyes seemed like they would burn the rest of her clothes away.

He started to lift his tank top, then paused. "This?" She nodded and it was gone in a flash. He was muscled like a warrior. She'd seen the scar by his collarbone, but there were others, too, silent reminders of the battles he'd fought and won.

His hands rested on her ribs and gathered the fabric of her T-shirt. "This." The depth of his voice relayed his need, but he waited for her consent. She pulled the T-shirt off, leaving her in a simple bra. This was more naked than she'd been with someone since the split with Pete. Even clothed, she felt more exposed with Ty than she ever had with that man. Ty saw her.

And from the slow breaths that moved him, he liked what he saw. He caressed her with his gaze, then with his hands. Hot skin to hot skin. She soaked it all in and still thirsted for more. Unhooking her bra, she gave more of herself to the sensations. His attention drew a needy moan from her, first as his hand circled her breast, then as his mouth found her nipple. Her eyes closed as she concentrated on the rain of sparks he created. She raked her nails across his back, inciting a deep rumble from him.

He kissed the center of her chest, then moved higher to her throat, her chin and finally her mouth again. Embracing him now brought all the skin of their chests together. The sparks gathered to brighter points of heat. She grew wet. His erection surged against his jeans.

Ty was so powerful, so capable, and still she was able to move him. She proved it further by dragging her mouth across his stubbled cheek and capturing his earlobe between her lips. He hummed pleasure. His arm wrapped tighter around her.

Her hand skimmed down his flat stomach to the waistband of his jeans. His breath slowed. Hers raced. For a second she tried to decipher his rugged belt buckle, but he quickly took over. The metal unclasped. She savored the pleasure of undoing the top button of his jeans, then told him, "You don't need these."

He kicked out of his shoes and socks before pulling his pants away. He returned to her in only a pair of boxer briefs that revealed just how aroused he was. "What don't you need?" he asked with a wicked smile. She grinned back and swept off her jeans. He skimmed his hands up her legs, like he was molding her out of fire. His hands stopped on her hips, over her panties. "What *do* you need?" The smile was gone, replaced by his depth of passion.

A tremble reminded her how new this was. It quickly added to the thrill of finally releasing herself to the hunger with Ty. "I need you."

He hooked his fingers in the waistband of her panties and dragged them down. She swiveled free of them. Completely naked. But unafraid. She tugged at his boxer briefs and he removed them. Neither of them had anywhere to hide. The honest hunger in his eyes told her he didn't want to hide. And she wanted his unique perception on all of her.

His hand moved up the inside of her thigh slowly. His gaze was fixed on her face. She knew his attention was tuned, making sure she was comfortable with every progression. That care only made her want him more. His fingers reached the wetness between her legs and sent surges of heat up through her. She reached out and wrapped her fingers around his erection. He pressed forward through her touch and moaned. They shared the sensation, bodies rocking.

Before she completely ran out of breath, she slowed her pace on him and tilted her head toward the bedside table. "Condom," she explained. He was gone only a moment before returning with the wrapper. He sheathed himself and brought her back into his arms.

He shifted the two of them farther onto the bed, then turned so that she straddled him. He gripped her hips. Their gazes locked. She leaned down and kissed him. Their lips brushed against each other as she pressed backward, taking him inside her. Neither moved. She reveled in the hot expanse of pleasure. It grew in intensity when she began to pump up and down along him.

His fingers dug into the flesh of her hips. His mouth curled into a carnal smile. She braced herself on his chest and rode harder as he thrust with her pace. Her thirst grew deeper. The only relief would be release. The first taste of a climax approached. It built higher on her speeding pulse and rushed breath. Close, it was so close.

"Yes, Mariana." Ty was reading her and must've known that all she needed was her smoky name from his mouth to send her over the edge. The orgasm crashed through her.

She called out, voice filling the room while the waves of fire rolled.

Her shaking arms couldn't hold her any longer and she collapsed onto Ty's chest. He wrapped his arms around her, holding her tight as she found her breath again and opened her eyes. She tried to tell him with a kiss all the pleasure she'd just felt. He growled and turned them so she lay on the bed, him above her.

His muscles were taut all around her. His eyes so hungry. And still he waited. She nodded and scratched her nails over his shoulders. He plunged inside her. She hooked her legs over his and urged him on. He sped faster, growing in urgency. The intensity on his face deepened. She rocked with him. Another orgasm grew with a deeper heat.

If she could just tell him, she could set it free. "Ty…" she moaned, breathless. "Ty…" she whispered.

He surged harder into her, deeper. She came, crashing together with him. After another thrust, he froze and spent himself, pulsing in her. His muscles were stone. The features of his face etched. The power of his release sent her own into the farthest corners of her body.

Slowly, he moved again. His head dipped down for a kiss, where she tasted his salt and breathed him in. He pulled from her and leaned to the side, both of them resting on their backs. She sank into the blankets. Their bodies pressed close along one side. She ventured with her fingers until she found his. They wound their hands tight.

The air settled and rested warm on her naked skin. She turned to look at Ty's profile. His brow was calm, but those eyes did not rest, staring at the ceiling. "What do you see?" The cracks and texture of her bedroom ceiling were well-known to her.

"History." He brought his gaze to her. "Determination." Rolling to his side, he stroked her hair while still holding her hand. "I see an amazing woman who deserves to feel good. To thrive any way she wants."

"I want this." Her fingers skimmed his cheek and urged him toward her. They kissed, and while the immediate hunger was sated for now, the need hadn't burned away in their passion. It remained, deep within her chest. She parted the kiss and let her fingers linger on his face. There was so much more she wanted to learn about him. Time might not be on their side. She shoved the dark thoughts away and tried to savor the moment. "And I want dinner."

He smiled. "I like the way you think." They both sat up and she collected her clothes as he shucked the condom and got dressed. His body disappeared beneath the jeans and tank top, but she still felt the resonance of him throughout herself.

She'd thought that intimacy like she felt with Ty could exist only in the bedroom, but it followed them down the stairs and into the kitchen. He brushed against her or took a moment to give her a kiss on the cheek while they moved about the island collecting food. He sliced another artisanal loaf of bread into slabs that she covered in peanut butter and local raspberry jam. They didn't bother with plates and ate off the cutting board, leaning on the island.

"The fanciest peanut butter and jelly sandwich I ever had." He chuckled between bites.

She lifted her pinkie while holding her sandwich. "Only the finest at Rancho Balducci."

The heat returned to his eyes as he looked at her. "Fine is right." He edged nearer, until his leg rested against hers. Warmth blushed on her chest and neck, as if she was still naked in his gaze. She rubbed her knee up and down on his thigh and was rewarded by a little growl from his chest.

They finished the meal this close, then shut down the ground floor for the night. Back in her bedroom, she arranged for company, sorting the pillows on the bed and putting out another towel in the bathroom. Ty took off his jeans and put them with his shoes by the foot of the bed. She'd never danced this quiet, intimate dance before with someone, but somehow knew the steps with Ty.

She emerged from the bathroom to see him placing his pistol on the bedside table closest to the door. The silent music she'd been dancing to stopped. She went into the closet, took out her rifle and leaned it against the wall next to the bed.

The heat from their bodies had soaked into the sheets and mattress. She focused on that warmth instead of the cold burn that the rifle had left in her hand. Ty slid into bed next to her and drew her close to him. His arms surrounded her. She laid her head on his chest. The steady rhythm of his heart helped hers slow. *Right now,* she reminded herself. No matter what the Hanley Group threw at her, they couldn't take away what she felt in that moment with Ty. He ran his fingers through her hair. She willed time to slow so she could absorb all she felt. Sleep started taking her. Panic scrambled up through her, wanting to stay awake and keep hold of Ty. She had no idea what world she'd wake up to.

Chapter Eleven

Ty watched the sky turn from black to purple to lavender and couldn't stop the day from arriving. He lay in Mariana's bed, soaking in her warmth, hoarding it. Each memory from last night was collected and held tight. Her trust and passion shook him. He'd never known that deep a connection was possible for him. Falling asleep with her hair fanned across his chest seemed like a scene from someone else's life. The sound of her calm, soft breathing now was treasured.

And all of this could be shattered in a second. The Hanley Group had been rattled, but not scared off. Firing back at the goon on the phone had felt good, but Ty knew it wasn't the end of the conversation.

Mariana stirred, voice raspy. "The sun up?"

"Not yet," he whispered back. Her warm hand slid against the side of his thigh, moved higher until it rested on his shoulder with their arms wound together.

"Good morning." Her fingernails gently scratched his skin.

"Good morning." He shifted so he could kiss her forehead. Toro stood up next to the bed, and Ty and Mariana both tightened. Ty strained to hear anything unusual in the waking world around them. His pistol was within reach. Then Toro yawned and scratched at his ear with his back foot, relaxed. The air returned to the room, but the complete calm was gone.

Mariana disentangled herself from Ty and eased to the side of the bed. "I think I'm all out of food. You want to do breakfast in town?"

"Sounds good." Staying in one spot made them easier targets. He rose, giving up the blankets for a chill, and pulled his phone from his jeans on the floor. No contact from the other Frontier Justice members yet.

The next few minutes could've looked like an ordinary morning with an ordinary couple taking turns in the bathroom and getting dressed, except for the rifle Mariana replaced in the closet and the pistol Ty reattached to his belt. The weight was heavier than usual.

Toro was fed before Ty and Mariana headed out of the house. Ty took a minute to listen to the growing day. Birds streaked from the trees, chirping. Far below Mariana's property, farm equipment rumbled. A loose board on the roof of her porch creaked in the breeze. Nothing out of the ordinary. He shifted his holster under his jacket, making it ready.

Mariana stared at her trees. "I've got to get these apples off."

"Once we relieve the pressure, the harvesters will come back." But predicting when that would happen, and exactly how, was beyond him. They'd struck at the Hanley Group and were now in the frustrating position of waiting to see what move the bad guys made next. Unless Frontier Justice came up with some actionable info on Innes. Ty yearned to have something to move on.

"I'm driving." Mariana opened the door to her truck. Ty climbed in with her and shifted some hand tools on the floor over so there was room for his feet. The cup holders on the center console were filled with gardening ribbon, a pair of pruners and work gloves.

Every car they passed on the way into town was inspected, but nothing looked like trouble. Instead of Ty's concerns being put to rest the more the day played out normally, he was set more on edge. The next fight was coming, but when?

They found breakfast at a small busy diner, which probably hadn't changed in the last fifty years. Mariana sat in their booth at the end of the row, staring at her coffee more than drinking it. He shifted his foot forward until his lower leg touched hers. Her stare moved up to him. An attempt at a smile didn't take hold. "How do you stay together under the pressure?"

"We're capable of surviving so much." He'd seen people emerge from horrific circumstances. "We just have to convince ourselves that we're going to make it."

"Simple," she said ironically.

"I know it isn't." He slid his hand across the table. She placed hers on top. The heat from the night before and the quiet calm of the morning returned to him. "But those sons of bitches are convinced they're going to win." Some looks swung around from the men at the counter and Ty lowered his voice. "But there's no guarantee they are. That means we can."

"You're convinced we're going to make it?" From the emotion in her voice, he felt she was talking about more than just saving her land.

He knew how to build a case against a criminal. The smallest details piled up to condemn them. He could pick apart their logic, turn it against them and catch them. In a fight, he knew how to use leverage to get the upper hand, even if he wasn't stronger than the other man. But what did he know about making a relationship work? Only that he felt more like himself when he was near her, and the thought of not seeing her again left an ache in his chest. "You have me for as long as you want me."

She turned her hand over to hold his. "Don't quit."

"Never." The table and public setting kept him from kissing her the way he wanted. A glimmer in her stare showed she was feeling the same.

They finished their meal and headed to the market to replenish her kitchen. Every aisle hid a blind corner and potential threat. Ty was struck with how ordinary it felt to scan for trouble, but casually discussing what to make for lunch with Mariana seemed so foreign.

The cashier, a white woman in her fifties, had a friendly smile for Mariana. "Omar in Produce is talking about doing another local table if you have some apples."

"Plenty." Mariana bagged her own groceries. "I'll bring some." When Ty went to assist Mariana with the bags, it caught the attention of the cashier. Had Pete been fueling fires around town? Mariana saw how the cashier was looking at him, and she jumped in. "Ty's helping out around the place."

The woman nodded with understanding. "Handyman?"

"Whatever needs fixing." He hefted the bags as Mariana paid and they walked out together.

The drive back to Mariana's home was just as ominously quiet as the whole morning. Once they were close enough to see the house, Mariana hit the brakes. Parked next to his car were two other vehicles: an SUV and a sleek sedan.

"What do we do?" She looked at him with worried eyes.

He put his hand on her tense arm. "I know them. It's okay."

The truck slowly picked up speed again, now on the private part of the road. "Frontier Justice?"

"It's a start." Having backup arrive immediately boosted

his confidence. "Vincent Solaris and Stephanie Shun. He's FBI. She's...connected."

"Sounds sketchy for one of the good guys."

"She's a good guy because she got out of the family business." Ty had run up against the periphery of her father's organized crime ring a couple of times during investigations in San Francisco.

Mariana parked next to the other cars in front of her house and got out, looking around warily. He joined her, not seeing the others. A conversation came from around the back of the house, but Ty couldn't pick out the words. After a moment, Vincent and Stephanie appeared. The thirtysomething Chumash man smiled broadly, upbeat, while the Chinese American woman around that age shared some of his enthusiasm, but maintained a cautious edge. Toro kept a distance from them, but didn't bark.

"This place is amazing." Vincent approached, hand extended to Mariana. He wore jeans, cowboy boots and a simple jacket. It didn't show, but Ty knew he wore his sidearm. "You must be Ms. Balducci." She shook Vincent's hand, then the introductions were made all around.

Stephanie glanced to the orchard at the side of the house. "I wanted to try one of your apples, but couldn't presume." Her jeans had a dash of fashion in the function, with rugged boots that probably cost a month of Ty's rent. A draped sweater didn't reveal any pistols, but she could easily be packing in her purse.

Mariana started toward the trees and waved the others on. The shade tempered the sun on Ty's shoulders. He gladly took an apple from Mariana as she offered them all around. "Salty," Ty said after the first bite.

Stephanie nodded as she chewed slowly. Vincent's bemused smile showed up when he tasted it. Mariana ate as well, checking out the newcomers on her property. Toro ventured a little closer. For a few seconds, the only sound was of apples being eaten. Ty brought them back to business. "Anything on Innes?"

"I asked around, but the name and description didn't ring any bells with my people." Stephanie adjusted the edges of her bob haircut with a finger.

Vincent squared his broad shoulders, looking more like a G-man than when he was savoring the apple. "No criminal record. He ran a couple of businesses that declared bankruptcy, but that's not unusual for financial players. Some 'charitable donations' to questionable companies. Probably fronts, but I haven't had the computer time to track them all the way down. They go *way* down."

Ty took the new information and tried out some possibilities. "Could be payments for goods or services. Could be a way of covering debts. Gambling, bad investments."

Stephanie frowned with doubt. "If he was in debt like that, I feel like it would've been on my network's radar."

"I'm working without a warrant." Vincent ran his hand over his clean-shaven face. It looked like he hadn't had much sleep. "Any prying I do takes three times as long because I have to cover my tracks. Still haven't been able to get into all of his banking history. It's a web."

Stephanie, on the other hand, appeared as if she was fresh from a Mediterranean vacation. "Any escalation here?" She glanced between Ty and Mariana without expression, and he couldn't tell if she was speculating on what had changed so drastically since last night.

Mariana answered, "Nothing since a nasty phone call yesterday."

Ty added, "We pushed back, but I don't think it was enough to scare them off."

"So until we can dig up anything on Innes, we're just

waiting for them to make a move?" Stephanie's impatience tightened her voice.

Ty felt the same. "That's the situation." He was more than ready to face off with the bald man and anyone else, just to finish it.

Vincent took a deep breath and looked about the area. "But at least we're here."

Mariana put her hand over her heart. "Thanks so much for coming."

"We had to," Stephanie replied.

"Yeah." Vincent turned toward the house and stared at it. "Thank you for what you're doing."

Ty's gut clenched. Before he could get in front of the conversation, Mariana asked, "What am I doing?"

"This house." Vincent was reverent. "I mean, we're really here."

Stephanie, too, gazed at the structure. "Where it started."

"Where what started?" Mariana grew wary and stepped back from Ty and the others.

Ty wanted to bridge the distance between him and Mariana, but knew it would only force her farther away. "I haven't told you."

Mariana's mouth thinned, her eyes went cold. "I'm not going to like this."

Stephanie looked between them, incredulous. "You didn't tell her?"

Vincent only added, "Oh, man."

Ty's heart sank. There was no good excuse, and the tension was already running so high that he knew any explanation now was going to blow up in his face. "There was no right time." His words sounded scripted and hollow. "We were dealing with the immediate issues."

"And other things," Mariana shot back. "So tell me now."

Ty walked out of the shade of the trees, into the bright

sun. He waved toward the house. "This is where Frontier Justice started, Mariana. This house was the first meeting place."

Her gaze remained stony. "My family built this house."

Though they knew the history as well as Ty, Stephanie and Vincent remained silent. Usually recounting this part of the past energized him, but as he spoke, he knew it was only widening the chasm between him and Mariana. "Your family was one of the founders of Frontier Justice. From what I could find, a rancher was trying to force them from here. Some people, including our ancestors—" he indicated Vincent and Stephanie "—came to help. They beat the odds, gathered in the house and came up with the plan for Frontier Justice."

Mariana closed her eyes, her brow drawn down, for a moment. When she looked at him again, it was as if he was a stranger. One she didn't trust. "So what am I doing now?" Toro hurried to her side and stared down Ty and the others. She fired her words at Vincent and Stephanie, too. "You thanked me for doing something, but as far as I knew, I was only trying to not get killed so someone could build a resort on my land."

"The idea was—" a cold ache settled in Ty's chest "—that we'd start over where Frontier Justice began. We'd use this house as a base of operations."

"My house?" she nearly shouted, pain lacing her words.

That pain lanced through Ty. "If you would allow us. Only if."

Mariana became dangerously calm. "You came here with plans for my house." Her fury could scorch the hills, and Ty almost wished to be erased with it. "Just like the developers, but instead of threatening me, you showed up like a superhero. You got close." Tears shone in her eyes.

"Was that your plan?" She twisted the last word like a knife in his heart.

"No." He choked. Vincent and Stephanie watched cautiously, silent. Ty knew they could see the raw emotions, and could guess what had happened. More explanations would just sound like thin excuses, but he had to try. "My plan was to help you. I didn't expect…the rest." Mariana winced. "I was going to tell you…the house, doesn't matter to me anymore. It was always going to be up to you."

She spit ironically, "Thanks for letting me make my own choices."

The world was slipping from Ty's grasp and he had no idea how to hold on. His ancestor had stood on this land and helped create a group to protect people against impossible odds, but would he have known what to do now? Ty could only tell her, "I never wanted to take anything from you."

Mariana stood as rooted as one of her trees. "Get off my property."

It felt like the blood completely drained from Ty, leaving him bone cold.

Vincent spoke up carefully. "The threat is still out there."

Mariana burned him with her eyes. "I have a dog and a rifle. And I have a phone to call the real police if anything happens."

Before Vincent could say anything else, Stephanie put her hand on his arm and urged him toward the cars. They got in, started their engines and waited. Mariana did not move. Ty knew there was nothing else he could do. He'd threatened the very thing she'd been defending all along. He walked to his car. Mariana watched him, expression hard. This woman, whom he'd held so close, was now so far away.

He climbed into his car and drove down the road, leading the way for Stephanie and Vincent. Mariana and her house grew smaller in his rearview mirror. The road twisted, and when the property came back into view, Mariana was gone. Each breath racked Ty with pain, as if his ribs had been crushed and the jagged points tore him apart from the inside. Mariana was gone.

Chapter Twelve

Rage burned Mariana numb. She had to grip the anger tight to her center, because if she let it slip, the pain would be too great. Ty had hidden himself from her. While he was nestling close in her life, making love to her, part of him was betraying her trust. He wanted her house. Everyone wanted it.

She carried the grocery bags down the hallway to the kitchen, floorboards creaking with every step. So what if Frontier Justice had been founded under this roof? That didn't give any of them the right to come back to claim it. And if her family had helped create the group, then she had the authority to tell them all to disappear.

The bags splayed out on the island, spilling some of their contents. Had her parents never told her about Frontier Justice because she hadn't been ready to listen, or had they not known, either? A series of Spanish curse words she'd heard her mother use when frustrated ran through her mind. Mariana voiced them in the kitchen, but they didn't relieve the fury and agony that gripped her. The shouts only served to scare Toro, who slunk to the other side of the island with his tail low.

The groceries were getting warm, but she couldn't put anything away until she'd erased the evidence from last night. She swept the crumbs from the cutting board and stashed it in the sink. She slid the bread knife back into the block and she braced her hands on the counter for support. The house and the orchard outside seemed to be spinning around her. Ty's face was inescapable. The last thing she'd seen before falling asleep and the first vision of the day. And she saw him, racked with pain as he tried to explain himself to her. A part of her had wanted to reach out to him, but that sympathetic urge was overshadowed by her nearly blinding torment.

She barely paid attention to where the groceries went. The confrontation with Ty kept circling again and again as she picked apart every word. Her eyes burned with tears. She'd just found him, and now he was probably lost forever. But she hadn't known all of him in the first place. Was he fighting to save her house for himself, or for her? It didn't matter. Did it? He was gone. She was alone again.

Toro growled and hurried out the dog door at the back of the kitchen. Her chest tightened with the thought of Ty coming back. The unresolved mistrust and hurt outweighed any unfortunate excitement to see him again. She swung out the side door and stalked around the porch to the front of the house.

Her high vantage revealed no car coming up the road. Toro barked. He was behind the house. Ice ran up her spine. She hoped he was just aggravated at a deer in the back orchard, but it was the wrong time of day for them to be moving through.

The rifle was upstairs in her bedroom closet. She walked carefully to where Toro kept barking, and hoped she wouldn't need the gun. The dog poised, hackles raised and stance wide. His focus was up the hill, along the fire road between the sections of trees she and Ty had worked in the day before. She couldn't see anything worth barking at. "Toro." She tried to call him back. The usually obedient dog wouldn't budge.

Between the dog's warning vocalizations, a buzzing sound grew from the back part of the property. The trees weren't flowering, though, and Sydney's bees would have no reason to swarm there. As the sound grew closer, variances emerged, rising and falling in pitch. It wasn't natural. It was mechanical.

Her legs were running before she knew where she was going. Muscles burned as she pushed up the hill. Right toward whatever was coming. Toro sped next to her. She pulled up just short of the crest and crept forward. The buzzing was closer. She peeked just over the ridge. Four men dressed in black on motocross motorcycles sped toward her property. They swung over the fire road as it emerged from a stand of trees and powered into the short valley before the hill she stood on. Their black shining helmets made them seem more like poisonous beetles than human beings.

"Toro, come," she whispered and ran as fast as she could back toward the house. Her phone was in the kitchen. The rifle was upstairs. As she sped down the hill, she saw a car on the road leading to her property. It wasn't Ty or any of the others who'd been there that day.

The sound of engines grew louder over her shoulders. She lost sight of the car ahead when she reached the house and burst in through the side door to the kitchen. Snatching up her phone, she sped through the hallway and up the stairs. Luckily, Toro stuck with her into the bedroom instead of trying to take on any of the men who were coming.

She grabbed the rifle and immediately levered a cartridge into the chamber. Her front window showed the car had passed the fence line of her property and continued toward the house. Rushing across the room to the back window, she saw no sign of the motorcycle men on the hill, but their engines were yelling.

Standing in the middle of the room, she tried to keep an eye on both the front and back windows. Who would get there first? Her heart pounded. Panic tried to freeze her. But she would not go down without a fight. Frontier Justice had been founded in her damn house.

She held the rifle in one hand and dialed 911 with the other. Before the operator answered, the black sedan screeched to a stop near the front of her house. The doors all opened and four men got out. Each one held a pistol at the ready.

"Nine-one-one. What's your emergency?" The woman was measured and calm.

Mariana put the phone on the floor and opened the front window. "This is Mariana Balducci at the end of Oak Valley Road. There are at least four men on my property..." She leaned her rifle out the window and was quickly spotted by the men in the front. They retreated behind the car's open doors. Three of them pointed their pistols at her. One spoke into a walkie-talkie.

The operator's voice was tinny and small. "Ma'am? Ma'am, are you there? Can you speak?"

Motorcycle engines screamed out behind Mariana. Crouching, she sped to the back window in time to see the four riders just start to come down the hill. But the men in the front were already out of their car and could get to her house much faster. She returned to that window to see them stepping out from the safety of their car and moving forward.

Her throat clenched in fear. She lifted the rifle to her shoulder and rested the barrel on the sill of the open window. The men spotted her and again hurried back. Mariana pulled the trigger and sent a bullet at the front of the car. It struck the windshield and pinged off without breaking through.

Bulletproof.

The motorcycles growled closer at her back.

She forced herself to speak, if the 911 operator could hear her choked voice. "Please send help." But there was no way anyone would show up in time. Mariana had only the bullets in the rifle, and the ones from the box in the closet.

One of the men below sneaked above his car window to point his pistol at her. She fired at him, hoping to at least discourage him or throw his aim off. Her bullet struck the car door with a thud. The man ducked, but recovered quickly and readied to shoot.

A strained gasp filled her lungs. She'd been so focused on the men below that a new car on the road toward her house had sped close, unnoticed. It was Ty's car. Maybe he'd pulled off on a side street and hidden in a stand of trees instead of leaving. She'd turned to walk into her house before he'd disappeared. Watching him drive all the way into the distance would've torn her apart.

A shot rang out and the top corner of her window frame splintered. The men at the car were too occupied with her to see Ty coming. He was only a few seconds away. Another bullet smashed a pane of glass. She shot down at the car, hoping they wouldn't turn to see Ty.

Two blasts sounded from behind her. Bullets whizzed through the back window and slammed into the plaster ceiling. The men on the motorcycles were firing at her.

The initial rush of relief at seeing Ty coming was smothered by a wave of fear. If she had to hold off the riders in the back, she couldn't give him any help at the front. She glanced through the broken rear window and saw the motorcycle men had stopped toward the top edge of the or-

chard to fire from there. All the wires that she and Ty had
set would be useless if they didn't venture farther down.

One of the riders must have seen her and fired another
shot through the window. That one had just streaked over
her head when two more smashed through the window at
the front. Certain death crisscrossed her bedroom.

She threw the rug from beside the bed over the broken
glass at the front window and knelt on it to aim down. The
men took cover, one of them speaking again into his walkie-
talkie. Ty's car sped up behind them on the last rise to her
house. He didn't let up and the car sailed off the ground for
a few feet before slamming into the rear of the black sedan.

Metal crushed. Glass and plastic exploded from the impact. The sedan slid forward and Ty's car listed to one
side. His airbag deployed, so she couldn't see him. Terror
clutched her throat. The man closest to the crash lay on the
ground, unconscious. The other three had scattered away
from the car, but slowly gathered themselves.

One of them swung his pistol around toward Ty's car.
She quickly cocked her rifle again and fired at the man.
Her shot missed, kicking up a puff of dirt a few feet from
the man, but it was enough to send him running for cover.
He made it one step when another blast came from below
and spun him to the ground.

Ty emerged from his car, firing his pistol at the men.
She was able to breathe again. He moved with lethal precision. Two shots, then he slid to cover behind his car. The
first man he had hit lay curled on the ground, clutching
at his side. His fallen pistol was too far for him to reach.

She levered another round into the chamber and scanned
for the other men at the side of their car. Between her and
Ty, they might be able to hold them off.

A barrage from the back hill changed her mind and sent
her sprawling to the floor. The riders had adjusted their

aim, and the bullets pierced the window and smacked into the wall opposite. If Mariana had been standing there, she would've been dead.

Toro cowered in the corner, probably the safest part of the room. But she couldn't hide. Coiling up to a crouch, she braced her rifle on the front window again. Ty peeked up from his cover behind his car and pointed toward the back of her house. "Hold them off!" he shouted, then took aim at one of the men who tried to shift positions at the sedan.

The man shot wildly at Ty, who remained cool and returned fire to send the man scrambling again for safety. Ty yelled up to her, "The orchard!" He seemed to have the men at the front pinned, but she nearly locked up at the thought of leaving him alone.

But another fan of bullets came from the back, through the window and into the wall, this time closer to her. If the riders weren't stopped, they'd riddle her bedroom from their vantage. She crawled to the back window, grabbing a pillow off the bed on the way. Sweeping back and forth with the pillow, she cleared enough broken glass to give her a spot to fire from.

The men were close enough that she could see some kind of walkie-talkie attached to the side of their helmets. They were communicating and coordinating their fire. All four of them aimed at once. She gritted her teeth and fired four shots as fast as she could. Her intent was to send a bullet at each rider, but by the time she got to the fourth, her aim was so far off the round didn't even hit the hill behind her house.

The riders, though, took her counterattack very seriously. Their engines revved high and they sped into the deeper cover of the orchard. She tried to track them with the front sight of the rifle, but they wove too quickly through the trees.

Until one of them hit a wire. The front of the motorcy-

cle abruptly stopped and the back end rose up, pitching the
man over the handlebars and into the dirt. He rolled, body
twisted with pain, at the base of a tree. The others turned
to see what happened and throttled back on their bikes.
They picked their way more carefully through the orchard.

One man abandoned his motorcycle completely and took
cover behind a tree. Another rider was flushed onto the
main path down the middle of the orchard, just like Ty had
planned. The bike made a larger target and she let a bullet
fly at it. She was rewarded with a metallic ping, but couldn't
tell if the machine was damaged. The man sped the bike
back into the orchard but hit a wire and lost his balance.

She shot again at the motorcycle, this time producing
a broken whirring sound that rose in pitch, then abruptly
died. The rider scurried back from the useless bike. Mariana chased him with a shot. His yelp of pain was muffled
in his helmet. The man leaped behind a tree, dragging a
wounded leg behind him. Her stomach flipped over. She'd
been pushed to this violence and hated that she had to cause
this harm.

The other rider who'd abandoned his motorcycle fired at
her. Wood splinters rained down from the window frame.
She shifted her aim to him and pulled the trigger. *Click*.
The rifle was empty.

TY FOUGHT TO keep panic from climbing too high in his
throat. The two men were still crouching on the other side
of the bulletproof car. He could hold them off for now, but
if they coordinated an attack from both sides, he'd have to
pick one of them and be exposed to the other.

Worse than that, the sound of Mariana's rifle from the
second floor had gone silent. Pistol fire continued crack-
ling on the back hill. The bullets hit her house and smashed
windows. Had she been hit?

He wouldn't think it possible. He couldn't imagine her hurt and bleeding. Ty hated that his instinct to not leave sight of Mariana's property had been right. The right thing to do would've been to clear out and respect her space. The Hanley Group didn't care about any of his personal problems, though, and he couldn't have just disappeared, abandoning her to fight alone. He'd known the choice to hide on a side street had been correct when he'd spotted the black sedan speeding up toward the orchard.

Two of those four men were out of the fight for now. The others were blocking his way into the house and to Mariana. She could hate Ty. He could live with that. If she wanted him to walk away forever, he would. After he knew she was safe.

He focused his fear and anger on the two men. They were barely visible by the nose of the sedan. Ty was all the way at the back of his car, which leaned on the rear bumper of the black car. The impact had closed the sedan's back two doors, but the front ones were still open. He recoiled, then broke cover and fired at the men to keep their heads down. Releasing the power in his legs, he sprinted to the open driver's-side door of the sedan.

One of the men stood and shot at Ty, who quickly ducked. The bulletproof window took one of the rounds, the other skipped off the roof of the car. Ty righted himself and fired back. The man fell, dead. Before Ty could line up his sights on the other man, he fled up the stairs of the front porch and hid himself at the corner of the house.

The rifle remained silent from the bedroom. There was still one man between Ty and Mariana.

MARIANA'S HEART SEIZED tight and she sprawled on the floor. Pushing the empty rifle ahead of her, she crawled toward the closet, hissing every curse word she knew in Spanish and English. A new volley of bullets from the back hill chased her. Some streaked from the rear window and out the front. As she passed her phone, she heard the operator still trying. "Ma'am. Ma'am, are you hurt? The police are on their way."

Mariana barked back, "And an ambulance."

To get to the box of shells on the shelf, Mariana would have to stand. She waited until another shot smacked into the back of her house, then forced herself up. A pair of shoes and an old throw pillow tumbled down around her as she searched the shelf. Her pulse thundered in her ears. Finally, she found the box and got back down on the ground.

Shaking fingers dumped the shells from the box and tried to load them. The first two spun out of her grip. She managed to get one in, and established a rhythm for the rest. The shooting intensified at the front of her house, then grew quiet.

Dread knifed at her. Ty was down there. She clutched the rifle and peeked out the front window. *"Dios,"* she breathed out. Ty stood behind the driver's-side door of the black sedan, aiming toward the side of her house.

He caught sight of her and tapped his chest with relief. "You good?" he called up.

"Fine," she answered. "You?"

"Perfect." He tensed, as if seeing something ahead. Past him, she spotted another car coming up the road. Vincent's SUV sped closer, before the police were even in sight. Gunfire crackled from the back hill and punched into her house. Ty pointed in that direction. "Get them!"

"But you—" He cut off her concern with a quick move toward one of the fallen men near him. Ty snatched up a gun from the ground and sped toward her house. Before he was lost from her view by the roof of the porch, Ty dived quickly to the side. Someone shot at him but missed. Ty slid on the ground and rose up, firing both pistols.

A man's voice called out in pain before going silent.

Ty sprinted to the side of her house, shouting to her, "The back!"

Mariana steeled herself and scurried to the rear window. One rider remained on his motorcycle near the top of the orchard. He zoomed back and forth, making a nearly impossible target. The first rider to wreck against the wires remained on the ground, out of the fight. Two others were taking cover behind trees and aiming up at her.

She fired at the man with the wounded leg. He ducked behind his tree. On the other side of the orchard, the man who'd abandoned his bike leaned away from cover to shoot. Ty's voice from the base of her house commanded, "Drop it!" The man didn't move. "Drop it!" Ty repeated, stepping into view below and to the left of her. He stalked forward, holding one gun now, braced with his off hand. "Don't—"

The man shifted his gun toward Ty, who fired a rapid succession of shots. The rider was quite a distance away, but one of the bullets hit him. He flew back to the ground. She swung her attention to the other man in the orchard just as he was preparing to fire at Ty. A single bullet streaked from the right side of her house, dropping the man. Vincent, pistol extended, moved into view and approached the hill cautiously.

The rider at the top of the orchard kicked up a tail of dirt as he sped higher and disappeared over the ridge. When the scream of the engine receded, the sound of distant sirens barely reached Mariana's ringing ears. She stood on exhausted legs. Toro still cowered in the corner. "It's okay, amigo." She barely recognized her own rasping, shaken voice.

Her kitchen door opened downstairs, followed by quick

footsteps. They ascended her stairs and her grip tightened on her rifle. "Mariana!" It was Ty. She lowered the gun and wanted to drop the heavy weight to the ground forever.

Ty appeared in her doorway, worry etching his face. Dried blood striped down the side of his forehead and stopped at his eyebrow. She reached forward, then hesitated. "Are you hurt?"

He must've seen where she was looking and dabbed at his head with his fingers. They came back with blood on them. "It's not bad. From the car crash." He stepped toward her. Empty bullet casings rolled away from his feet. "Any injuries?"

Her body still trembled. There hadn't been time to discover if she'd been wounded. She took a moment to assess, and couldn't detect any unusual pain. "I don't think so." Her scan extended past herself and took in the bullet holes in the walls and ceiling of her bedroom. Both the front and rear windows had been broken out, with large pieces of the wood splintered.

Ty looked the space over as well, with emotion-filled eyes. "I'm so sorry, Mariana."

Her ears were so muffled from the gunfire she didn't know if she whispered or shouted, "Thank you for coming back." He was standing so close. Her body wanted him against her, reassuring they were both safe. She didn't move.

A deep pain flashed over his face. "This isn't how I wanted to come back." The angry ache of their parting sank back into her. She was too tired to wrestle with it. The adrenaline had burned off and all the gravity of the world pushed down on her. The pair of them looked out the front window, at two police cars that sped closer to the property, sirens blaring and lights flashing.

Mariana picked up her phone and spoke to the operator. "The police are almost here. We're okay. Thank you." She hung up and tipped her head toward the coming cars, asking Ty, "What do we tell them?"

Ty took out his badge wallet. "Vincent will take the lead, say something about how he was tracking these men and they led him here, but he didn't know what this situation was."

"Stephanie?" Mariana saw her standing with Vincent at his SUV. The woman was putting a sleek pistol away in her purse.

Ty shrugged. "She's his informant or something like that. Vincent will talk circles around them."

She turned from the front and stared out at the back orchard. Three men lay there, two of them dead. A sob caught in her throat. She leaned the rifle against the wall, where it had been when she and Ty had gone to sleep in this bed together the night before. Everything had changed.

Chapter Thirteen

Ty clenched a fist and released it, but the tension would not let out. He'd fired his gun at men before. He'd killed. A cornered money launderer had tried to shoot his way out of being arrested, giving Ty no choice. This was different. Mariana had almost died. It would've taken only one bullet out of the dozens fired.

He ached from the inside out. She was alive, sitting on the front steps to her home, Toro leaning hard into her side. Ty remained apart from her, near his wrecked car. She might never let him back on her property. Once he knew she was safe, he would disappear. And he would never be the same again.

The local police, including Pete, had already talked to her and Ty separately. To his credit, Pete had kept everything professional. The ambulances had come and gone with the injured and dead men. Vincent now stood with Pete and the other officers, pointing to different areas of the property like a conductor leading an orchestra. His authority was obvious, and the men nodded along with his explanation.

Stephanie sat in the open passenger side of Vincent's SUV. Her gaze shifted between the scene around them and her phone. She locked eyes with Ty for a moment and raised her eyebrows with a question toward Mariana. Ty shook his head. He didn't have an answer.

A flatbed tow truck arrived for the black sedan, breaking up the debriefing between Vincent and the police. While the cops dealt with the car, Vincent approached the house. Stephanie joined him, they gathered Ty and all walked to Mariana, who stood.

Vincent spoke only for the group. "I'm sure I can tie whoever these shooters are to an open investigation and pull FBI authority." He turned to Ty. "You'll need to contact your CO and iron things out."

Ty wasn't looking forward to that phone call. "Within the hour."

Mariana's face was unreadable. "Is my land a crime scene?"

"No." Ty hated all that had been imposed on her. Including what he'd done. "It's your home."

Vincent nodded. "Between my badge and Ty's we've got the pull to wrap this up."

Stephanie looked with sympathy at Mariana. "But you don't have to be here alone if you don't want. I can stay."

Mariana's jaw tightened. "They're not done."

"It doesn't look like it." Vincent watched the car being loaded onto the flatbed. "Feels more personal than business now."

A fire lit in Mariana's eyes. "I'm not just going to sit around here and wait for them to come back."

Ty knew exactly how she felt. He addressed Vincent and Stephanie through clenched teeth. "Give me Innes. Give me everything on him and I will let him know he'll never touch this place."

Stephanie held up her cell phone. "I already pointed more people at him."

"As soon as I'm on a computer." Vincent's mouth twisted

to a frown when he looked at Ty's car. The front left wheel was bent nearly flat to the ground. "You're not going anywhere in that."

Stephanie waved a dismissive hand. "I have friends in the car business. We'll get you a new ride."

"I'm a cop, remember?" Ty was already way out on a limb with everything that had happened with Mariana. "It's got to be clean."

"I know how to bleach paperwork." Stephanie put her finger to her lips.

Mariana spoke to Ty as if they were alone. "I have to be there when you get to Innes."

A hundred reasons why that was a bad idea sprang into his head, but before he could voice any of them, his phone rang. He checked the screen. "My captain." The conversation with Mariana would have to wait. He answered the call and stalked off to the side of the house. Ty's captain hadn't reached his position by jumping to conclusions. He was a good listener and started his questions with a level tone. Ty answered as honestly as he could, explaining the events of the day with a detailed timeline. His Frontier Justice tie to Vincent and Stephanie was left out. It was as if they'd just met.

He looked back to see Mariana still on her steps, talking to Vincent and Stephanie. It didn't look particularly warm, but it still wasn't as iced as things had been when Mariana had kicked them all off her land. A pang still stabbed him each time he thought of that. It always would.

His captain seemed satisfied with everything Ty had given him and wrapped up the call with gentle caution to stay out of any more tangles while on vacation. Ty knew that was impossible, but thanked him anyway before hanging up.

Instead of returning to the group, he stayed at the edge

of the house to look up at the orchard along the hill. The bodies had been removed. The harsh snap of gunfire was now replaced by an afternoon breeze bringing fog from the sea. Somehow, Ty's ancestor had managed to live through his own storm of lead and save this land. Lives were lost then and now. Ty would never be able to release the burden of pulling that trigger, but those men had come to kill, and it was the only way to stop them.

He pocketed his phone and returned to Mariana and the others. She was talking to Vincent, gesturing toward the other side of the house. "That was a hell of a shot with a pistol." Ty had still been revving too high with adrenaline at the moment to be impressed, but damn, it must've been seventy yards in a high-pressure situation.

"You're right," Vincent responded with a small smile. "It was." The flatbed finally got the sedan secured and honked its horn twice before pulling away. Pete indicated that he and the other officers were wrapped up and they got into their cars. As soon as the police left, Vincent asked Ty, "Everything squared with your CO?"

"As good as it could be." A missing detail nagged him. "Why didn't the local captain show up here?"

Stephanie huffed an ironic laugh. "Something was more important than a shootout in his jurisdiction."

Ty's unanswered question resonated like he'd hit a deep vein. "I'll look into him."

Mariana faced Ty. "I'll help." Her eyes were clear, shoulders squared, as if what she'd said wasn't one of the last things he expected to hear. She challenged, "You didn't think you were going to start Frontier Justice without me, did you?"

He was staggered. She stared back at him, chin tilted up. His heart leaped at the idea, but caution threw ice water down through him. Unresolved complications remained.

"Only if you want to." He still felt the stab through his ribs from her anger at his breach of trust.

Her voice heated with emotion. "I want to."

"It was always going to be your choice." Having her join in this fight was an incredible asset. But their personal connection may have been gone forever. "I was never here to take that away from you."

Instead of addressing what he'd said, Mariana turned to Vincent and Stephanie. "Thank you for coming back. Thank you for everything you're doing."

"You're welcome." Vincent tipped his head.

"Anytime." Stephanie reached out and briefly touched Mariana's arm.

Vincent added, "I'll stay on top of this and let you know what I find. There are a few leads…" A pointed look from Stephanie slowed him down. She drew his attention to his SUV, then the road off the property. He smiled understandingly. "A phone call and we're here." He shook hands with Ty, who gave Stephanie a wave of goodbye. A moment later, Ty and Mariana were watching the SUV make its way down the hill and toward town.

Mariana didn't take her gaze from the road to speak. "You can stay."

"I have to." His broken car was a couple of dozen yards in front of them.

She chuckled, and then a serious air descended around her. "You wanted my house."

"I had an *idea* about your house," he clarified. "I told it to them." The SUV was a small dot by now. "Before I knew the circumstances here. Before I met you." That had changed everything.

"So that's how you found out about the trouble. You were looking into my house." She still didn't face him.

"I was digging as deep as I could about Frontier Justice.

Old stories passed down, rumors, fragments from the past."
It had been like sifting through sand to find enough rusty
nails to build something. "This property was mentioned a
few times, along with the fight for it. There weren't any stories that came before it, so I knew this is where it started."

"And you wanted to start it again." There was a slight
tremor in her voice, an echo of the hurt he'd given her.

"I did. Looking into this property, I saw the records of
your complaints and knew I had to do something."

"You had to save the house." She didn't move, but he
felt her moving farther away.

"For you." Her look did turn to him then, doubting.
"What I wanted out of this place never got in the way of
that. And I was never going to try to take this away from
you. It was just a possibility I had in my head."

Her gaze softened slightly. "It's still a possibility." And
her steel remained. She walked from the front of the house
around to the side. Together they stepped higher on the hill,
into the orchard strung with wires. Stepping close to a tree,
she muttered a curse and *"Lo siento, amigo."* Her fingers
ran over the bark, stopping at two bullet holes bored into
the wood.

"Will it survive?"

She continued to inspect the tree. "It should." Something on the ground stopped her progress and she moved
away. Blood spattered across several crushed apples and
fallen leaves.

Ty reached toward her, but hesitated to touch her. "It's
not the first time blood was spilled defending this land."

"This man…" She backed toward Ty. "This was the one
you… I can't imagine what you…" Turning, she put her
hand in his. The late sun caught in her shining eyes. "Are
you all right?"

Her warmth rushed into him through this simple touch.

The care and concern from her sent that heat deeper into his chest. "I am, thank you." But where that left the two of them, he still didn't know. "How about you give me a ride to the hardware store for supplies and I help repair your bedroom?"

She started toward the house, still holding his hand, then paused. "Emails first. I'm sure the neighbors are freaking."

"Don't give any details." He resumed their progress out of the orchard. "Tell them you're fine and the appropriate authorities are on the case. You can't say any more until the investigation is over."

Her attention extended down the hill from her property, toward the rest of the world. "I'll use that on everyone in town, too."

"There'll be a lot of looks."

She brushed it off. "I'm used to those by now."

He remembered the attention they'd drawn at lunch. "It'll be different. More fear, like the violence is coming with you."

Her steps slowed. "Will you be with me?"

"As long as you want." Tentative tendrils reached between them. Fragile, like the smallest doubt could break them.

"No more surprises." She held his gaze.

"You know everything now." And he wanted to learn more of her.

She stopped in front of her house. "I meant it when I said you can stay."

The gravity of doubt lifted from his shoulders. He breathed. His body was free to move closer to hers. She met him, and they leaned against each other's shoulders. "You're safe," he told her and reassured himself. And with her, he was safe.

TY HAD BEEN RIGHT. Fear shone in the eyes of the locals in the hardware store. Only one of them had the courage to approach Mariana and ask after her. She reassured that she was unhurt and gave the standard nonanswer regarding the rest of the details. The same as she'd emailed to her concerned neighbors.

Her texts with Sydney had also been vague, but with the added warning to keep vigilant and not go anywhere alone. Returning up the long road to her property, Mariana explained to Ty how her friend had helped inspire her to join up with Frontier Justice. "She said that her family property had also been defended by our people. It's not far from here. Someone must've been tearing through, trying to grab whatever they could. The same could happen now with the Hanley Group." There was activity at her house in the distance, but it was only the flatbed tow truck Stephanie had arranged for Ty's car. "Even if we hold them off at my place, they'll just find another person to intimidate until they sell off."

"That's the goal." Ty scanned the darkening landscape around them. "Stop them here. Let them know their tactics won't fly anywhere anymore." He tested his forehead with his fingertips. The blood had been cleaned off hours ago.

"Is it okay?" She nodded toward his head.

"Just a little tender." He narrowed his eyes like a tough guy. "I've had worse. Busted a couple guys who'd been robbing construction sites. They came at me with every tool they had before I got them cuffed."

She scoffed. "One time, an ostrich from Mrs. Gonzalez's farm got through her fence and into my orchard." It had been like a scene from a dinosaur movie. "But you know I got a riata around its neck after it nearly took a chunk out of my shoulder."

Ty put his hands up. "You win."

They passed her property line and angled up the hill toward her home. With each yard forward, each second of silence she and Ty shared, the trust continued to build back. He'd owned his words from before and she believed what he told her now.

At the house, the flatbed was just finished chaining Ty's car down. Ty collected the paperwork, shook the driver's hand and didn't even watch as the car was taken away. Before unloading the truck, he walked the perimeter of the house with her, both scanning high into the orchard. They paused every few yards, listening. There was the sound of Toro's tail wagging against her leg, and some birds in the evening breeze. No danger for now. She was able to take the time to taste the salt air, but knew she had to stay ready.

Back at the truck, they hauled out the tools and supplies from the hardware store. Ty carried them to the bedroom as she fed Toro his dinner. Her ears still rang in the quiet. Tension rose in her as she climbed the stairs. Seeing Ty in the bedroom instead of streaking bullets helped shape the space anew.

He was already sweeping up glass, shattered wood and bullet casings and dumping them into a plastic bucket. His calm, smooth movements were almost hypnotic. She moved deeper into the room and he bumped his hip against hers. Her body woke up with the simple contact, reminding her of what this place had meant to her and Ty not long ago. He carefully picked out the shards of glass that remained in the frames. "Once we get this cleaned up, we'll replace the panes."

She stripped the bed down to the mattress and balled everything up. Toro came upstairs but didn't cross the threshold. He watched with a curious tilt to his head as Ty cut glass to size and tacked it into place. She remade the bed with fresh linens and edged around Toro to get the pillows off the guest bed downstairs.

When she returned, the front window in the bedroom was finished and she looked at the black panes reflecting her and Ty next to each other. A few hours ago, he was below that window, a bullet away from death. "We're not doing enough." The words were hot in her throat.

Ty seemed confused. "We decided at the hardware store that framing the new wood in could wait."

"We should be going after the Hanley Group." She paced through her room, stopping to inspect the gashes across the ceiling. "Look what they did here." If she'd known what Hebert and Innes had planned for her, the meeting at their offices would've gone very differently.

"Right now, what we're doing is taking away their power." Ty picked up a spent shell from the corner of the room and tossed it in the bucket. "They shoot at you, and we erase it." He placed his phone on a small side table. "When Vincent and Stephanie dig up something we can use, we move."

"How long?" Her muscles ached.

"Too long, believe me." He went to her, placed his hands on her shoulders. "But when we hit them, it'll leave a mark." Spoken like a lethal vow.

She fed on his determination and tried to release the frustrated tension that yearned to lash out at the men who attacked her. "I'm tired of reacting."

He tipped his head from side to side, stretching his neck like a boxer. "I feel you."

She put her hand on his and lifted it to her lips for a kiss. His knuckles tasted like wood. His eyes warmed, and she knew that whatever was next, she wasn't alone. She released her hold and turned back to the work before them. He'd been right. Making the holes in the walls disappear with spackle was surprisingly calming. Each radiating crack she found was filled and smoothed over with meticulous care. The house was healing.

Ty brought a ladder from the storage room off the kitchen and worked on the ceiling. He asked, "Where's the pistol?"

The question was so casual she couldn't tell if he was joking. "Is this some kind of police detective trick, making me feel guilty when I haven't done anything?"

"Your rifle, it's a .44 Magnum, right?" It leaned against the wall next to the bed. Ty still wore his gun. "Was it your dad's?"

"My mom's. Dad got it for her." She still couldn't figure out where this was heading.

"If he bought a rifle in .44, it was probably because he had a pistol in that caliber." He came down from the ladder, moved it and climbed again to spackle another area.

"The rifle was always in the trunk downstairs, so the pistol would be...up here." The bedroom seemed a little less familiar. The drawers of the antique dresser and bedside tables had long transitioned to only her things. She went to the closet and searched along the shelf, especially where the box of shells had been, but knew that her parents' things had been donated or stored in other places ages ago.

Ty continued working on the ceiling. "Any drawers that are heavier than they should be, or stick when they open?" She approached the dark wood dresser as if for the first time, rather than a piece she always remembered being in her life. The top left drawer persistently squeaked on the wood rails. She dragged it open now and peered inside. Of course it was her pantie drawer. Ty stared down into it with a grin on his face. "False bottom."

She mocked affront. "I beg your pardon." And wiggled a little for him. Pulling the drawer farther out, she removed the pile of underwear and placed it on top of the dresser.

Knocking on the bottom of the drawer revealed an unusually hollow sound. "You've got to be…" A small cutout in the side of the bottom allowed the wood to be lifted up. Underneath was a shining black revolver with a short barrel and walnut grips. She lifted it away from the old towel that surrounded it. *"Madre mía."* It was very heavy. And loaded, she discovered when she swung the cylinder open.

Ty let out a low whistle and descended the ladder to look at the weapon as she held it. "Hand cannon."

She closed the cylinder with a solid snap. Her father's hands had been rough from years of work in the orchard. But he'd been a gentle man who took time to care for his family. His care was revealed in the shining finish of the pistol. It had been used, but put away clean. He'd been the last one to place it in the drawer before she'd retrieved it. She whispered to Ty, "You keep revealing the secrets of this house to me."

"I hope they're not burdens." He was quiet as well as they stood with the artifact of her past.

The thought rolled through her mind. An old pistol rested in her hand, found in a time when she might actually need it. Her home was the founding place for a vigilante group, born from protecting people just like her. The surprises didn't weigh on her. "No, they're…what I need to find." She placed the pistol in the drawer of her bedside table.

At the dresser, she replaced the false bottom and started scooping her panties back into the drawer. Ty stood at her shoulder, an indecent smile on his lips. "I can help with this." Seeing his broad hands on her intimate underwear sent a sudden heat down her chest and between her legs. Before she could act on it, his cell phone buzzed and he went to the side table to check it. "What the hell?" he muttered.

The urge to get the pistol out of the bedside table shook her. "Bad news?"

"Not good." He focused on his phone. "Word from Vincent. The wounded men were transferred to another hospital, out of this jurisdiction. They lawyered up without a word. These sons of bitches are going to disappear without a trace." He clenched his jaw. "Someone's overlording this." A potent energy radiated from him. "The local PD didn't put up a fight." His arm flexed so hard she thought he'd crush his phone. "How does Captain Phelps spend his money?"

"Never seen anything too grandiose." Neither he nor his wife shopped at her store, but she saw the woman at the supermarket from time to time with an ordinary basketful.

"His parents still alive?" Ty waited for the answer, as if setting a trap.

She knew what he'd caught. "They just moved to a house in the new development."

"Guilt money," he growled. "Tomorrow." Ty's eyes shone like a predator, and she was more than ready to go on that hunt. "We go after Captain Phelps."

Chapter Fourteen

Mariana woke up to the sound of gunfire. It rang in her ears, but the bedroom was silent. The windows that Ty had fixed were intact and the holes she'd patched disappeared on the dark walls. Ty whispered like smoke, "You're okay, baby."

"Sorry if I woke you." She felt the vestiges of the dream shock its way out of her legs.

"I was already up." He was a shadow, but warm, and with enough mass to shift the sheets and blankets toward him. She tugged to rearrange and he helped get her sorted. When they were finished, he rested his arm across her hips. "Don't know what time it is."

The sky outside was scraped gray, with a few sparkling stars. "Before five."

"Did your parents teach you how to work that rifle?" His words swirled around her, and she wasn't convinced she'd woken from the dream.

"Yeah. No soda can was safe." She turned to look at Ty, just seeing an edge of light in his eyes. "Pete took me to the police range a couple times."

"Can you handle a pistol?" Edges emerged in his voice.

"A little." Fear from the dream spread under her skin again.

"I know you can." His arm tightened and he drew himself closer to her side. "You held your own in a fight that would've frozen a lot of people." She curled her body into his, breathing with his slow pace. He kissed her cheek and whispered in her ear.

She woke with the sunrise, hearing his word instead of gunfire. "Warrior." Of course he was already up, checking over his phone. He gave her a smile and a kiss before leaving the bed to get dressed. The fixes from the night before on the walls were subtle scars in the daylight. Fresh wood in the windows and a new coat of paint in the bedroom, the evidence of the violence would be erased.

Ty adjusted his pistol on his belt and pocketed his phone. "No new word."

Standing and stretching revealed several bruises across her body. "Did you sleep at all?"

"A minute." Yet he still had a sharp edge in his eyes. By the time she dressed and used the bathroom, he was already downstairs. He called up to her. "Want me to put together some breakfast?"

She hesitated before walking downstairs. "Do I need the pistol?"

There was a pause, and then he asked, "For breakfast?"

"For today." For whatever was coming as they finally took the fight off her land.

"Leave the pistol."

She came downstairs with Toro, who gazed at her for breakfast as soon as she reached the kitchen. Ty stood at the island, poised. She fed her dog and assessed what she and Ty could eat. "Let's drive through. I was in a bad mood when I put away the groceries and probably broke every egg."

Ty's face grew serious. "I owe you those groceries and a whole lot more."

"Keep doing what you're doing." She smoothed her hand down his chest. "And we'll call it even."

A sly smile lit up his face. "Then I'll never stop." He tipped his head toward the front of the house. "Come on, let's go stake out the police."

"Sexy." She pulled out her keys and led the way to her truck. The bubble of laughter Ty had evoked dissolved in her as she drove off her property. Instead of just defending herself, she was striking out. It was what she wanted, and she had no idea what kind of risks she was just about to take.

THEY'RE GOING TO give you a badge after this." Ty sipped bitter coffee from a paper cup. Their breakfast had been finished, the sandwich wrappers stuffed into the fast-food bag they'd come in. Mariana had parked her truck a block away from the police station, among a group of other pickups and cars at the edge of an outdoor farmers market. He focused on the front doors of the station. Small town. No activity. "Police work 101. Sitting."

She shifted uneasily behind the steering wheel. "I'd rather be moving." It was how he preferred to picture her—walking among her trees.

"That's the challenge." He flexed his legs to keep the blood active. "Can't get so settled that you're not ready to jump." A woman approached the glass doors at the front of the low cinder block building.

Mariana shook her head. "Sandy from the city permit office."

Ty's phone buzzed and he picked it up from the center console to see a message from Stephanie. He read it for Mariana. "'The charities Innes donated to are fronts. All of their employees are purchased identities. Still no word on who the money trickles down to.'"

"He's paying for those bastards to kill me." A breath shuddered through her.

"They tried." The work of erasing that trauma from her bedroom wasn't done. And he knew it would take much more than spackle and paint to get Mariana back on stable footing. "He can spend as much money as he wants. They'll keep failing."

She perked up when a maroon SUV parked near the front of the police station. "It's too clean. Dust and the marine layer gets on everyone around here." A glance at the other cars proved she was right. Even the compact town-only cars had a coating of dull dust on their paint. The door to the SUV swung open.

Ty readied his phone. "Call me and get set to move." Mariana dialed his number and he picked up, opening the line between them. A white man in a light-colored suit emerged from the SUV. His face was too far away to distinguish, but his shoes shone as clean as his ride.

Mariana squinted toward the man with the dark hair. "I don't recognize him."

"Go." Ty tapped her thigh with the side of his fist. She sprang from the truck, obviously ready to move. Weaving quickly through the other parked cars, she crossed the street and turned toward the police station. The man in the light suit didn't notice her as he stepped into the station. Her pace slowed once on the sidewalk. She slipped her phone into the pocket of her work jacket. Ty put his phone to his ear and listened to the rustle of the fabric and her muttering something to herself in Spanish. Anything to keep herself calm. He understood, keeping his eyes on her while using his elbow to double-check the pistol on his belt.

She disappeared into the police station. His legs coiled, ready to chase after her. Voices came through the open line to her phone. First Mariana greeting someone, then a woman, probably the desk sergeant, replying. No one else spoke. The man in the light suit must've already passed through the front.

Mariana asked, "Can I talk to Captain Phelps for a second? I'd love to get a rundown of what we know after yesterday." The desk sergeant's reply was garbled, but the tone was apologetic. "In a meeting?" Mariana cued Ty perfectly. The man with the too-clean shoes was seeing the captain. "Maybe I could wait."

Ty didn't need to hear the reply. He slipped out of the truck and headed toward the station. Pressure tightened in him and his heart started to hurry. He played the opening hook to an old-school hip-hop song over and over in his head until the rhythm helped loosen him.

He hung up and stowed his phone and pulled out his badge wallet before swinging through the front door of the station. Mariana sat at a bank of institutional chairs off to one side of the main desk. She stood when he entered and casually put her phone away in her jacket.

The desk sergeant was a woman in her forties with curly red hair pulled back in a ponytail. "How can I help you?" Ty led with his ID, which she scrutinized. "Detective." She tipped her head in a small salute. Her gaze bounced between Ty and Mariana as she put all the pieces together. He was sure that the shootout was big news at the station.

Ty pocketed his wallet. "I was informed that our suspects from yesterday were transferred to a different hospital and I need to talk to whoever signed off on that."

The sergeant shuffled some paperwork and clicked on her computer. "I'm sure I don't know the specifics of that. But the captain might be able to point you in the right direction. Let me run this by him after he's cleared a couple of meetings." She looked up as Mariana walked to Ty's side. "Can you leave a contact number, or would you like to wait?"

Ty stared at the heavy doors that led to the rest of the station. "I'm going to wait." He and Mariana returned to the chairs at the side of the room, but he did not sit. The sergeant typed on her computer, stealing glances their way. He'd seen that the news of the suspects' transfer had been a surprise to her, though the widening of her eyes had been subtle. The corruption at this station was localized.

Mariana murmured, "The suit was already gone by the time I got in and the sergeant didn't seem too happy."

He whispered back. "She's usually the most informed person in the building. It's got to be killing her to be out of the loop."

The doors to the back opened and Ty poised ready. Mariana balanced on the balls of her feet next to him. But it was only the woman from the city permit office. She organized paperwork into her shoulder bag and waved to the sergeant as she breezed past her desk and out of the station. Mariana visibly relaxed. Ty couldn't.

A second later, the doors opened again. The man in the light suit strutted out, face stern but smug. Ty's pulse quickened as he recognized him. The man's stride broke when Ty stepped forward, announcing, "I know you." Charlie Dennis. San Francisco "businessman." Racketeer. One of the strong arms of the Seventh Syndicate, a crime organization infecting the West Coast and beyond.

Charlie pulled up and eyed Ty. They'd done this dance before in Ty's precinct and the courthouse halls. "You're a pleasant surprise."

The pieces were falling into place. The Hanley Group didn't have the muscle to lean on Mariana, so they got the Seventh to do it for them. Once that organization was involved, they dug in deep and corrupted everything they touched. "It's never a pleasure, Charlie." Ty wanted to put a fist in the self-satisfied smile on the man's face. "Charlie Dennis," he told the sergeant. "In case he didn't check in."

Charlie rolled his eyes, then fixed his gaze on Mariana. But he still spoke to Ty. "Down here getting dirty in the country, Detective?"

Ty shifted so he stood between Charlie and Mariana. "I like digging in the dirt. You find things. Sometimes treasure." He stepped toward Charlie. "Sometimes rot, in the roots. And then you slice it out."

The crook was in his fifties, still fit. His scarred knuckles and replaced teeth proved he hadn't spent his whole career in crime intimidating people with phone calls. The small twitch in his right eye told Ty that Charlie's cool could splinter. "Detective…" he said like a warning.

Ty bared his teeth. "Let's get dirty." Mariana backed him up.

But the desk sergeant stood, hands out to defuse the situation. "Guys, this is not how we're doing things…"

"Absolutely right, Sergeant." Charlie shrugged casually and stepped backward. His narrow gaze flicked between Ty and Mariana. "We'll play when I want."

Ty stood his ground. "Or when you least expect it."

Charlie chuckled. "Not while you're out of your jurisdiction." During the syndicate man's dismissal, Captain Phelps came through the rear doors, face tight with concern.

Ty eyed the fifty-year-old captain and squared up with Charlie. "Maybe I'm applying for a new job."

Charlie laughed like a shotgun blast. "Good luck with that." He turned on his heel and breezed out of the police station.

The collar of Captain Phelps's shirt seemed too tight for his bulging neck. His small blue eyes bore into Ty. "Detective Morrison, even if this isn't your station, I expect you to treat private citizens with the same respect—"

Ty shut the captain down with two words. "Seventh Syndicate." He'd never discussed them with Mariana, but from the sober look on her face, she understood there was impact in the revelation.

Captain Phelps tried to deflect. "That's an accusation with no foundation—"

"I've seen his work." Ty was completely over hearing the watered-down press releases from Phelps. "I've done my job."

"Not under my command you haven't." The captain's face reddened.

Before Ty escalated things with a volley of insults related to how the captain ran his district, Mariana stepped in with an even voice. "Why were the suspects from yesterday transferred to another hospital?" Ty and the desk sergeant also waited for the answer.

Phelps waved away the question. "I don't know. The feds took over and won't tell me anything." It was a lie. Ty knew that if the FBI had been behind the transfer, Vincent would've been on top of it.

"So you don't know that Charlie Dennis is Seventh Syndicate." Ty tried to keep himself as steady as Mariana remained, when all he wanted to do was tear the badge off the captain's uniform. "And you have no idea where the shooters who tried to kill Mariana yesterday are. What do you know, Captain Phelps?"

Despite his efforts, Ty raised his voice enough to bring another man through the rear doors. Pete emerged, in uniform and on duty. Phelps held up a finger to him, stopping the officer in his tracks. The captain glared at Ty. "I know that the real trouble didn't start until you showed up. So maybe a call to your captain will convince you to get out of our town and back to your work in the city."

A mean-feeling grin broke out on Ty's face. "Please call my CO." Talking this way to a captain was downright insubordination, but his tenuous respect for this man had slipped to absolute zero once he'd seen Charlie Dennis in the building. "Turn up the pressure," Ty taunted. "Let's see who cracks first."

The captain locked his jaw. "Get out of my station."

Ty deliberately turned from Phelps to look at the sergeant. "Thanks for your help today, Sergeant. Be safe." With Mariana at his side, Ty exited the building.

As soon as they were outside, she exhaled. *"Dios."* She kept her eyes ahead and her voice down. "You'll have to explain what the hell the Seventh Syndicate is."

"They're who've been trying to kill you. Looks like they own Phelps and came down here for some damage control after yesterday." He fought from being overwhelmed with the thought of taking on the entire organization that several law enforcement agencies across state lines hadn't been able to shut down.

"Mariana!" Pete hustled out of the police station and to them. "What was going on there?"

Ty and Mariana stopped to face the officer. Ty inspected his face, seeing genuine confusion and concern there. "You don't know?"

Pete dropped some of his police authority to speak with more emotion. "I get that you think we're a bunch of country idiots, but we can handle our business."

"Then step up and handle it," Ty urged him. "Mariana had made a complaint long before someone jumped her in the parking lot or tried to shoot her on her property."

Pete had no answer.

Mariana took a gentler approach. "I know you know

what you're doing, Pete, but this is big. Bigger than what usually runs through town."

"The feds are here." Ty watched the gravity of his words sink in to Pete. "We're going to need everybody. Everybody who's clean." Pete's mouth pursed and he glanced quickly at the police station. With a tell like that, Ty knew Pete had never worked the streets out of uniform. Ty also looked at the station, then back at Pete. "Question authority."

Pete blinked, stunned. Ty and Mariana left him like that. The officer still stood on the sidewalk when they reached her truck. The shocked expression had left his face by the time they drove past him. In its place was a somber frown. The man's eyes were opening. Ty knew it was hard to discover what the officer now started to see.

Mariana turned off the street with the police station. "Where now?"

He took out his phone and texted Stephanie and Vincent about Charlie Dennis of the Seventh Syndicate paying Chief Phelps a visit. He bet the charities Innes paid to were shells for the syndicate. "Your place. Then San Francisco. We have names now." No more waiting. "We have people to go after."

They reached her house and he collected his duffel, in need of fresh clothes. Mariana put out extra food for Toro and called Sydney to tell her where they were headed. Once she was done, she looked at Ty for more direction. The woman was fierce, and he'd seen how hard she'd fought to protect herself. But they were stepping into a different kind of battle as aggressors, on someone else's turf. Tension showed in her face, and tightened her posture.

He reached out and took her hand. "You don't have to come." Her palm was cold.

But her voice was hot. "Frontier Justice started at my

house. The home they attacked." She shook her head. "They've got to find out that they picked the wrong woman."

"This time," he told her, "we're the ones in the shadows."

Her shoulders set with more confidence. A steely edge shone in her eyes. "Together."

"All the way," he pledged. And he would keep her safe at any cost. Because they were definitely headed toward danger. "Take the gun."

Chapter Fifteen

Driving to San Francisco with the revolver and box of shells in her backpack behind her seat was like riding with a live cobra somewhere in the truck. The legality of it was questionable at best, but Ty's badge might help smooth that over. The lethality, though, was unavoidable. The gun was hers, and she might have to use it.

The closer they got to the city, the more traffic clotted around her. Her heart pounded harder, as if her veins were congested with the cars. People tailgated and cut each other off just to gain a few feet. The mass aggression started to infect her and she wondered if she'd be able to think straight at all once they reached San Francisco.

Somehow immune, Ty leaned casually in the passenger seat, eyes not resting on one spot for too long. "What did you go to college for?"

"History. I was going to map out how the Italian and Mexican American experience wove together in California." She laughed. "Ironic, considering how little I knew about the land I was standing on."

"You weren't going to learn any of that at school."

She hit the brakes as someone cut her off to veer across her lane. Cursing in Spanish barely helped vent the stress of the drive.

Ty remained unfazed. "A BA in criminology barely

taught me anything I used once I hit the streets." Traffic slowed to a stop. Her grip tightened on the steering wheel. "They're not hostile." He waved his hand at the cars on the highway. "It's just another way of being."

"Don't know if I could ever get used to it." The flow resumed and she eased the gas.

"You don't have to." He reassured her with a gentle stroke up and down her thigh. "You've got two shovels in the bed of the truck that are crusted with the dirt of your land."

She'd forgotten about the shovels, but thinking of the mud she'd cleared to open a small irrigation channel helped slide her mind away from the anxiety of the drive. Ty had such an easy way of finding her.

"There's a good record store in my neighborhood. They know their stuff if you're looking for anything in particular." He spoke in a steady, calm stream. "I know a great place I think you'll love. We'll hit it up sometime. No liquor license, so we've got to bring our own bottle of wine. Or beer if that's what you go for."

He was almost able to make her forget about the .44 Magnum she brought to a fight somewhere in the city. "Wine."

"It's a date." He straightened his jacket. "Wear something nice. No one will believe you're out with me."

She scoffed. "I doubt that."

"Ask around. If I'm not eating at the station, I'm getting takeout for home."

"You wear that suit and we'll show them all." Though she didn't have anything in her closet that equaled his level of style and a shopping trip would be in order.

He growled approval. "It's definitely a date."

But she knew that there were no guarantees. Not that she doubted Ty's commitment. The man had proved as te-

nacious as the sunrise. What this night would bring, however, was completely unknown.

The city grew closer and more freeways converged on
their route. Night fell, transforming the cars to rows of
white headlights and red taillights. Ty had them exit long
before she was used to when going to San Francisco and
navigated her through city streets that outpaced the traffic
that slowed on the wide concrete ribbons they'd left behind.

Staying in motion helped keep the anxiety down. After
a hard turn, she heard the shovels clanking in the bed of
the truck and gained confidence from that, too. Still, the
pistol rode behind her, a *diablo* constantly reminding her
that deadly trouble lay ahead.

Ty checked over his phone, light from the screen illuminating his stern features. "No word from the others." He
turned it off and was lit only by the passing streetlights.
Whatever thoughts were in his eyes were hidden from her,
but his voice was calm. "First stop is my apartment."

"I knew this whole thing was just a ploy to get me to
your place." She thought back to the first time he entered
her shop and wondered what that cup of coffee would have
been like if she'd mustered the courage to ask him. But
maybe this was the only way the two of them could be
thrown together.

He laughed. "I'm into really elaborate foreplay." They
pushed deeper into the city. He continued to give directions,
and it was a good thing. She was completely lost by now
in the neighborhoods. Sitting up straighter, he scanned the
street. "This is it." He pulled a garage door remote from
his duffel and a large metal gate slid open at the base of
a five-story apartment complex. She drove down into the
fluorescent-lit concrete labyrinth. Exposed pipes snaked
across the ceiling and down the walls. Cars of all variet-
ies parked among thick pillars, scraped with a multitude

of paint colors. Ty pointed out his spot and she brought the truck to rest.

The elevator didn't reach the parking lot, so they had to walk up the ramp to a lobby door next to the gate. Her phone rang just as Ty opened the door for her. "Private caller." She showed him the screen. The door swung shut and he nodded for her to answer.

The familiar rough voice of the bald man came through. "You missed me."

She fought the chill that the man evoked up her spine. "So you were the coward who rode off my back hill before the fight was over?"

A beat of silence. The man growled a threat, "I might still be there."

"You're not," she answered. "Because the motion lights would be on you." A lie, but he didn't need to know that.

"Keep trying." The man forced a casual tone. "It's cute. But your luck's going to run out. Should've sold out when you could. Now it's a guarantee that you're going to fail. You're going to die."

Fury tightened her shoulders and neck. Pure hate shone in Ty's eyes. She spoke through clenched teeth into the phone. "*You* failed to stop me in the parking lot. *You* failed to kill me on my property. *Your* luck's going to run out."

The bald man clipped out a laugh that didn't sound as brave as she thought he wanted it to.

Ty wrapped his hand around hers and she felt the vibrating strength in him. He leaned close to the phone. "When I have my foot on Charlie Dennis's neck, I'll be sure to tell him that you were the one who couldn't get the job done."

The bald man's voice came through a little too high-pitched. "Now, that doesn't sound like a man of the law—" She hung up the phone.

Ty released her hand and paced off for a moment before

returning. He looked like a gladiator entering the ring. Fists flexing, face stony. If she didn't know him, she'd be terrified by the deadly resolve that emanated from this man. But she did understand there was a human beneath the iron facade. Someone who cared for others, who put his life on the line for her. His gaze found her and softened. He stepped to her. "They're not going to stop until we stop them. But we will stop them."

"Yes." She matched his resolve, though still feeling the uncertain weight of the pistol in her backpack. "We will."

The door to the lobby opened and an Asian man in his late twenties bounded out and said casually as he passed, "What's up, Ty?" He smiled sheepishly when he saw he'd interrupted a moment between her and Ty. But he couldn't have had any idea they were just promising the destruction of a criminal syndicate to each other. "Later," the man apologized and hurried down into the parking lot.

"Later, Matt," Ty called after him. The man threw up a wave without turning around. Ty caught the lobby door before it closed and swung it wide for her. The brief encounter with Matt had helped bring her back to the humanity of the normal world. She breathed easier as she stepped through into the somewhat-dated space, tiled in deep brown and gold-veined mirrors.

The elevator door rattled open when Ty pushed the button and the two of them stepped into the narrow space. More smoked-glass mirrors surrounded her. She leaned back into Ty's chest. His hand rested on her hip. "This building," he said like a connoisseur, "is a sterling example of late-disco-era architecture. Only the finest brass." He toed a brass rail that ran around the base of the elevator.

"I can't wait to see your shag carpet."

"It isn't allowed," he whispered conspiratorially, "but I sneaked my waterbed onto the fifth floor."

"Scandalous."

They reached the top floor and got out into a window-less white hallway. The walls were scuffed, carpeting well traveled. Each apartment had a little sconce above its number. The specter of the bald man's phone call still chilled the air she breathed, but she found herself walking without hesitation beside Ty. When the intimidation had first started, each event would send her day into a tailspin. Now, with Ty's help, she was able to process her fear and anger and keep moving.

Ty unlocked his door and stepped in first. One hand hovered over where he wore his gun, the other he held out to slow her steps. Cautiously, he swept through the front room quickly, then waved her forward. She moved amid the comfortable couch and antique furniture. Most of the surfaces were clean, except for a pile of mail on a side table. Ty checked the other rooms, then returned as she was looking at a painting on the wall of a barn on fire in a field of dry grass.

"My sister's." Pride filled his voice. "These, too." There were several more, some abstract in earth tones, others of somewhat twisted pastoral scenes, like the first. "Grandpa made these." He knocked his knuckles on the long table that held the mail and pointed at a sturdy coffee table in front of the couch. "Hungry?"

She should be, not having had anything to eat since breakfast, but couldn't locate any need for food. "Maybe later?"

"I get that." He went into the small kitchen that was separated from the living room by a brief counter/bar. "Just let me know." After rummaging in the refrigerator, he pulled out a cup of yogurt and ate it standing up.

A neatly organized dark wood bookshelf next to the television drew her attention. There were many technical books on law and procedure, then rows and rows of non-fiction history books. Most of them dealt with the Western expansion of the United States, and there were several volumes on California alone. "I might've read these if I'd stayed at college."

"You're welcome to them. Anytime." He finished his yogurt and poured out a handful of trail mix from a bag. A fantasy took over her mind. Her sitting in her chair by the window, reading one of these books, Toro comfortable on the rug next to her. And Ty shifting the floorboards of her house as he moved about his day.

She put her backpack, weighed by the too-heavy cargo, on the couch. The fantasy seemed close enough to be possible, and impossible in the face of what the two of them stood against. "Thanks," she said vaguely.

Typing on his phone, he drifted from the kitchen and down a short hallway, which had a bathroom and, she presumed, the bedroom beyond. She followed, seeing more of his sister's art on the wall, as well as what appeared to be family photos. There were three black-and-white pictures as well, one of them identical to the photo from her shop wall. Several people, men and women of a variety of races, standing on the ridge. Stern, determined faces. For the first time, she recognized the location. "This is the back hill on my property, on the eastern ridge."

Ty stepped back into the hallway to join her. "You see why we had to save that photo. Yours is the original." She paid more attention to the people than she ever had. Eye to eye with the original Frontier Justice. Her ancestor was among them.

No longer alone, Mariana stood with Ty. "Are there more than us and Stephanie and Vincent?"

Ty's warm gaze moved over her face. "You don't know

what it means to hear you say 'us.'" He stood taller. "Makes me feel like we can really do this."

"But I'm not a cop or a fed, or connected like Stephanie." Though she was willing to fight, Mariana couldn't imagine she was an integral part of this team.

"It doesn't matter what your job is." He put his hand out, palm up. She placed hers in it, capturing the heat between them. "You're one of the strongest." He urged her forward with his hand and they met for a kiss. Sudden need surprised her. Opening her mouth to Ty, feeling his lips against hers, was an antidote to the anger, confrontations, fear and danger around them. She hadn't been stripped of her humanity.

A buzzing in Ty's pocket interrupted them. They pulled away from the kiss and he took a moment to compose himself before checking his phone. "Stephanie," he said.

"I'll talk to her about her timing." Mariana tried to hold on to the comfort she'd felt in the connection with Ty.

He read his screen intently, his body flexing and ready. "She was able to connect the dots between Innes's donations and the Seventh Syndicate. It all fits." But how that helped them, Mariana couldn't puzzle out. Ty continued, "Stephanie had a contact put a trace on Innes's cell phone. It pinged a location here in the city. He's at dinner." Ty's eyes shone, fierce. "Let's get him."

Trepidation quickened her pulse. "I know we're operating outside the law, but it still might be a bad idea to go into a restaurant with guns blazing."

"We're not shooting," he reassured her. "We're going to start the same way they did with you. Fear." His energy carried him down the hall into the bedroom. Most of the space was taken up by the simple wood bed and dresser, but there was a small chair and lamp in one corner to keep it from feeling too ascetic. She watched from the doorway as he opened the tidy closet and crouched to unlock a safe tucked into one corner.

Her confusion grew when he unclipped his holster and put his sidearm in the safe. "But isn't that going too far, considering they've already tried really hard to kill me?"

He stood and closed the safe. In his hands were a different holstered pistol and loaded spare magazines. "It's a clean gun. No serial numbers or ballistics on record." He attached it to his belt, and his jacket quickly hid it. The magazines went into his pockets. His expression was grim. "There have been cops who use this kind of gun to make innocent people look guilty."

"A plant."

He frowned and nodded. "I'm using it to stay off the record. It's another shadow we hide in." The somber mood lifted as he snarled, "Now, let's ruin someone's night."

Chapter Sixteen

The sun had long set and the city did not slow down. Ty had navigated again as Mariana drove the unknown streets into an upscale neighborhood. They did one pass of the restaurant, where she only glimpsed the warm glow within, then proceeded to circle farther and farther away in search of parking. Four blocks away, they found a spot she could wedge her truck into.

She killed the engine and found she couldn't move. The act of driving had been automatic, familiar. The next step was completely unknown. She began to clench her jaw, and her breath squeezed short.

Ty placed a hand on her knee. His voice wrapped around her in the closed car. "The only reason we're taking the guns is so no one steals them out of the truck. They are an absolute last resort." He stared into her eyes carefully. She nodded her understanding. Continuing, he said calmly, "We're going to light a fire under Innes, to lean on him so he's scared enough to call in the Seventh Syndicate. Innes is paying for his muscle and can't take a punch. It's the syndicate we ultimately want to deal with."

"Got it." She hoped her legs hadn't stiffened up too much once it was time to get moving.

Ty flashed her his wicked grin. "Are you ready to get mean?"

"So damn ready." Inspired, she swung out of the truck and started walking in the direction of the restaurant. With Ty, they made an immovable force down the sidewalk. Unlike in her town, people were still out after dark. These pedestrians walked around Mariana and Ty. The night city gathered in hard corners above her and around her. She grew edgy, unfamiliar with the shapes. But Ty was at her side, and she remembered what he'd said. These were their shadows.

The closer they got to the restaurant, the more upscale the people on the street became. It was a cool night and the women wore shiny puffer coats. Shearling boots over expensive denim. Mariana's jeans were for work, but she refused to be self-conscious. These women belonged here, and so did she. The men's tailored blazers and bomber jackets drew clean lines around their slim physiques. Ty made his statement with a powerful presence, eyes blazing in the dark.

They crossed to the opposite side of the street from the restaurant and slowed their pace. Ty eased into the shadows at the corner of a high wall and drew her in with him. From the hidden vantage she could see through the large glass wall that made the front of the clean, modern restaurant. Simple lettering stenciled on the glass announced the restaurant's name: Sage. A door led to the warmly lit interior, where a young Asian woman stood as hostess.

Only a couple of tables were occupied beyond the hostess. Exposed Edison bulbs illuminated the guests and their gleaming white plates and bowls. There was Innes. In another gray suit, yellow tie. A white woman around his age sat next to him, facing another couple of a white man and a woman.

Ty's voice was low and even in her ear. "There's only one valet." She scanned down the street to the small station with a kiosk and chair. "We'll contact Innes when the valet goes to get his car. It's secluded enough."

"Their glasses are empty. It shouldn't be long." And the woman from the other couple was already on her cell phone. "I'll bet she's calling for their ride."

Ty's hand stroked down her forearm. "I couldn't have asked for a better partner."

"Partner with benefits," she whispered back, leaning into his body. They stayed close for countless minutes. Waiting, watching.

The other couple stood from Innes's table. He and his wife rose with them, all smiling genially and wobbling slightly with wine. Ty's muscles tensed against Mariana when two more men got up from a table at the back of the restaurant. "Private security," Ty hissed. "They don't look like syndicate men, just regular jobbers."

Her heart started to pound. "Do we call it off?"

Innes and his wife stepped onto the sidewalk and parted ways with the other couple, who walked up the block. As Innes approached the valet with his ticket, the two guards followed a few paces behind. They wore black suits. One of them was a white man with a slick undercut haircut and no facial hair. The other man appeared Hispanic, with close-cropped hair and a full beard. Their muscles strained the seams of their suits.

"It'll take more than that to stop us." He strode out of the shadows just as the valet skipped off to retrieve the car. Mariana was immensely glad Ty was on her side, because the way he rolled his shoulders as he crossed the street revealed all the power of his body had bad intentions.

Innes saw them coming and scraped a step backward. The woman Mariana assumed was his wife looked at him with concern and placed her hand on his arm. They exchanged terse words, then she saw Ty and Mariana coming.

Mariana felt her own strength surge. For once, the people who'd attacked her were afraid.

Innes made a not-so-subtle gesture with his hand. The two guards edged forward to cut off Ty's progress.

Ty maintained focus on Innes. "No more contributions to your charities." Innes stumbled into his wife as he searched for an escape. Ty pressed, "You paid all that money and the Seventh Syndicate still can't protect you." Innes's wife clutched his sleeve as they recoiled. The security guards were almost to Ty at the curb. Ty took one more step toward Innes. "You'll never eat an apple again without choking."

The white security guard didn't even start with a warning. His first move was to shove a forearm toward Ty. The violence produced cries of distress from Innes and his wife. Ty appeared undisturbed. He sidestepped the attack and jammed an elbow into the security guard's ribs.

Wincing, the man stumbled to the side. The Hispanic security man charged toward Ty. Mariana shoved the valet's chair into his path, slowing him. While he was disentangling himself from the chair, she kicked the toe of her boot into his calf. He hissed through bared teeth and dropped to a knee, clutching his leg.

The other guard recovered and swung out hard at Ty with a backhand. Deathly calm, Ty leaned away from the blow, then struck quickly. The side of his hand caught the guard in the throat, making him sputter. When the man's hands went up to hold the injury, Ty lashed out with a punch right to the man's solar plexus. The guard fell, gasping for breath at Innes's feet.

The Hispanic guard rallied, using the chair to stand. He was more intent on Ty than Mariana, but that changed quickly when she pulled out her hawkbill knife and snapped it open. The dim light on the street glinted on the worn steel. The blade was steady in her hand. She'd used it thousands of times on branches, and hoped she wouldn't have to use it on a man. She warned him in Spanish, "Innes isn't worth getting your handsome face ruined." His gaze flicked to the knife and he froze.

The other security guard caught a wheezing breath and hauled himself to his feet. Rather than attacking, he took a fighter's stance, hands raised and ready. Ty moved on him smoothly. His fists flew in a blur, the first missing, the second catching the man in the face.

The guard on the other end of her knife leaned toward joining that fight. She slid to block him, hissing in Spanish, "All of Innes's money won't keep you from bleeding." Instead of looking at her blade, the man looked at Innes, who tried to back through a solid wall to get away.

Ty's fight wasn't over. The white security guard scowled, slick hair mussed. He grunted with anger and threw a combination of punches that didn't reach Ty, but sent him on the retreat. Out of nowhere, the guard swung a blur of a kick toward Ty's head. Ty put up his forearms to block it, keeping the man's shin from slamming into his face. The force, though, knocked Ty to the side and into the valet kiosk. Her heart jumped into her throat. She was barely holding back one guard, but was ready to jump at the other if Ty was hurt.

The white security guard leaped at his advantage. He flashed a swift punch at Ty. Before it could contact him, Ty dropped to the ground. The man's fist crashed into the edge of the kiosk. From the crunching sound, either the wood or his fingers broke. His cry of pain was cut off by Ty rising up to shove his shoulder in the man's gut. Pushing with his legs, Ty took the man off his feet and drove him backward a few steps and crashing into Innes. Innes yelped and the guard groaned as they tangled to the ground.

Though her heart was pounding, she tried to maintain an impervious front before the other security guard. He rocked side to side, hands curled, conflicted. "Be smart, friend," she told him in Spanish.

Innes's wife scuttled sideways on high heels. Ty aimed his hard stare at her. "Ask your husband about the Seventh Syndicate." He leaned over the fallen Innes, who held up a palm as if that could defend him. "You paid the syndicate," Ty growled. "You think they can stop me?" Ragged breaths hurried from Innes. Pure terror shone in his eyes.

Ty stood and stepped backward. Mariana slid to his side, the knife still out and ready. The other security guard didn't move to pursue. And he didn't move to help Innes or the white security guard, who rolled on the ground, groaning.

With a tip of his head, Ty showed her it was time to go. They slipped quickly into the deeper shadows at the end of the block. It had all happened before the valet had arrived with Innes's car. Ty turned and started walking briskly up an alley in the opposite direction from her truck. He whispered, "We'll double back."

She realized the knife was still gripped in her fist. Urging her fingers to release the handle, she closed and pocketed it. The two of them continued hurrying through streets and alleys. She was barely able to figure out where they'd been. It would've been impossible for anyone to follow. After a few blocks, they emerged onto a street a few yards away from her truck.

Ty put his fist out toward her. "Thanks for having my back."

She bumped it. "You were…" *Ferocious. Terrifying. Sexy* "…amazing."

"That knife of yours is an argument ender." He looked at her with admiration. "You did a great job deescalating."

"I really didn't want to get into that fight." Adrenaline still charged her muscles.

"Well, that guard didn't know it." They arrived at the

truck. "Mind if I drive? Easier than giving directions." She tossed him the keys and went through the foreign motions of getting into the passenger side of her own vehicle. A second later Ty pulled onto the street. The night's activity continued around them, forcing Ty to swerve around a ride service car dropping off its fare. He drove as they'd walked, leaving no trail.

Ty slowed as he climbed a street next to a dark park. On the opposite corner, two police cars sped down, lights flashing and sirens chirping. True to his word, the shadows made the truck invisible.

"I would've, though," she said, her body finally calming.

"Would've what?" He tilted his head with the question, but kept his eyes on the road.

"I would've got into that fight if you'd needed me." The memory of his getting knocked down still made her teeth grind.

He drove to the top of the hill and double-parked far from any streetlights. She could barely see his face, but could hear the emotion shaking deep in his words. "I did need you, and you were right there."

She reached out and gently stroked down the side of his cheek, knowing he'd taken a blow there. "Did you get hurt? Are you okay?"

"Fine." A small smile lightened his face. "As long as I'm with you." His shining eyes scanned past her for a second, then he leaned forward and stole a kiss. It was brief, but electric. A hum still moved through his body the way it did hers, aftermath from the conflict. "I'm hungry." He put the car in gear and pulled onto the street. "I'm starving."

At the mention, she found her own blood sugar dropping fast. "I don't think the last restaurant we were at will seat us."

"I know a place."

It was a good thing he was driving. Her head started to spin. The tension and conflict of the day had depleted her. Buildings and cars blurred by. "Is that it? Innes and the Hanley Group will back off?" Fatigue weighed heavy. How long had she been burning, surviving? Weeks, months?

"Not yet. This was just the setup." Ty shot her a glance, looking as energized as ever. "We're not done."

Her plan for a meal and seventeen hours of sleep dissolved. The city came into clearer focus as she rallied. "The Seventh Syndicate."

"Exactly." Passing streetlights flashed against his face. "Innes paid hundreds of thousands of dollars to his 'charities' with no return. He didn't get your land, and now here we are, jacking up a perfectly nice dinner date. We touched him, brushed off his rental security. He'll want real protection. The Seventh Syndicate will be at his house tonight."

"We get to send them a message." The fear on Innes's face was small payback for all the agony he'd given her. Charlie Dennis's condescending smirk as he left the police station was still burned into her memory.

"After tacos."

"Tacos?"

"I told you I know a place."

"You're speaking my love language." It was easy to banter with Ty now, but saying this had strayed into more serious territory than she'd expected.

He was quiet a moment before responding, "I'm learning it."

"Tacos are a good start." She reached across and slid her hand over his shoulder, resting it on the back of his neck. His skin was warm, his muscles firm, but not tense. A quieter calm took him over as he drove. Neighborhoods came and went, some crowded with tall buildings, some low, clutching to steep hills.

Ty slowed the truck. "Keep an eye out for parking." They found a spot and she followed him toward a bright glow on the night sidewalk. A sign above the tall windows read Taqueria de la Amapola #2. Inside, customers sat at the simple orange-and-yellow tables and booths. Ty opened the door for her and she was hit with the aromas of charred meats and frying tortilla chips. Her stomach growled.

"Magnifico," she sighed, stepping into the restaurant. Above the front counter was a huge handwritten menu, complete with photos of some of the combo plates.

"Hey, Esme." Ty approached the Latina woman at the cash register. She was a little older than Mariana, with long black hair in a ponytail, high cheekbones and a stately stance. "This is Mariana."

"Hola, Mariana." Esme extended a hand. Fine gold rings encircled most of her fingers. Mariana shook her hand, greeting her back. Esme's dark eyes shifted back to Ty and she dropped her voice a little. "Javier hasn't been here tonight."

"He's not in trouble," Ty reassured her. "But he'll be here."

Esme pursed her lips with concern. "You're not just here for dinner."

"Dinner, yes." Then Ty shook his head. "And…"

"Justice," Mariana finished.

After a moment of scrutiny from Esme, she asked, "Balducci?"

The question sent a shiver over Mariana's skin. It was said like a mystic password opening an invisible door. She'd only started to learn the history of her family, yet these people knew so much. *"Si,"* she answered. "Mariana Balducci."

Sympathy filled Esme's eyes. "Are you doing all right?"

"Surviving." Mariana found the side of Ty's leg with her knuckles. "Thanks to Ty. And the rest of you." She took a chance, guessing that Esme was part of the growing Frontier Justice.

Esme's face suddenly shuttered to a neutral expression. "Two number four plates." Her fingers flew over the register, then tore off a short receipt and handed it to Ty. He reached for his wallet and she shook her head discreetly. Mariana saw there was a backup of two more groups behind them. Esme shot her a quick wink, then addressed the next people for their order.

Ty and Mariana moved down the counter where they could see the activity of the kitchen through a service window. A server brought trays from the window to the counter and called out numbers. Ty gripped the receipt and whispered to Mariana under the noise at this end of the restaurant. "Esme's family goes back with all of ours. Taqueria de la Amapola numbers one through three are hers, throughout the bay, with ears and eyes that catch everything."

"And Javier?" A few weeks ago, she had only a couple of friends to rely on, and now there was a whole shady network working to protect her.

"Her brother." His wry smile revealed there were stories to be told.

Esme herself hustled a tray of food from the service window to Ty and Mariana. She walked them down the counter a bit, away from the other people, and spoke under her breath. "I hope you have a fight for Javier. He's been howling at the moon since Dahlia and I don't want him hurting himself or anyone who doesn't deserve it."

Ty took the tray from her. "We have a fight for him."

Relief, then concern washed over Esme's face. "Be safe."

"We'll try." Ty gave her a small nod.

"Gracias." Mariana shared a warm look with Esme before joining Ty at a bent-wood booth against one wall. Pork

tacos, rice and beans and plastic forks. "Perfect," she told him, then dug in. She was halfway through her plate before she realized that their foam cups were still stacked and empty. Without asking his preference, she took them to the machine and returned with the cups brimming with orange soda. "The only way." She put the cups down.

Ty toasted her with his. "Agreed." She knocked her cup against his. If it was a date night in the city, it would be going well. The man certainly knew where to take her for dinner. Not fancy, but nourishing to the soul. But the pistols they carried, the fight they'd been in and the one they headed for told her this was no ordinary date. And still, she couldn't imagine being out here with anyone other than Ty.

They were nearly done with their meals when a new presence in the front door drew Ty's attention. He took on that familiar readiness that made her pulse quicken and her awareness sharpen. A thickly muscled Latino man in his twenties approached their table. He wasn't tall, but his broad shoulders and confident stride were imposing enough. His gaze scanned the restaurant, pausing for a brief greeting to Esme. *This must be the brother.*

The man walked right up to their booth and sat next to Ty. He had the knuckles of a fighter, and tattoos across the backs of his hands. Another tattoo crept out of his T-shirt collar and up the side of his neck. The long sleeves of his hoodie must've hid more ink. He stared at her, hard eyes, with a deeper pain somewhere in there. *"Hola."* Tipping his head back made the light shine on his black hair.

"Hola," she replied.

The man turned his attention to Ty. "What's up, Hammer?"

Ty put his fist out and the man bumped it. "Been a minute, Javier." She witnessed yet another facet of Ty, understanding how he could operate on the streets of this city.

Javier leaned back in the booth and jammed his hands in his hoodie pockets. "You going to get us into trouble tonight?"

"That's the plan."

Javier stared soulfully at the ceiling. "Thank God."

Ty pushed his plate aside and spoke quietly. "The Seventh Syndicate."

"Seriously?" Javier sat up straighter.

"They're the muscle behind this," Ty said. "We've got to hit the hitters."

Seeing a brutally powerful man like Javier react to the syndicate made her nerves start to hum louder. Javier took a long breath and rocked his head from side to side, stretching his powerful neck. When he came to rest, his gaze was on Mariana. "You're Balducci?"

The name used to mean just apples. The orchard up on the hill. Something painted on the fence post that marked her property, and over the door of the shop she ran in town. Seeing the name hadn't been enough to discourage the Hanley Group from contacting her, or to scare them off from bringing in the Seventh Syndicate when she'd declined the offer. The history of that name, its power, had been unknown until Ty brought it and Frontier Justice to her. It was more than a name now. A vow. A weapon to defend herself. She looked Javier in the eye and declared, "I'm Mariana Balducci."

Chapter Seventeen

Mariana's simple statement rocked Ty. He heard her pride and her strength as she said her name. He'd been searching so long for Frontier Justice as a concept, he'd lost track of the people. Never again. Mariana—the woman, the fighter—continued to surprise him and he wanted to go on learning her forever.

Even Javier seemed impressed. He took his hands from his pockets and leaned his elbows on the table so he could crack his knuckles. "Ring the bell."

Ty took his phone out of his coat pocket and laid it on the table. "Stephanie's tracking someone's movement. As soon as he's home, we're knocking on the door."

Javier started to shift, impatient. "And you just decided to have a nice little dinner date over number four plates?" He chuckled as if it was absurd. The laugh died out when he swung his look between Ty and Mariana. "Really?" he asked, incredulous.

Ty stared directly into his friend's eyes. "Really."

"Absolutamente," Mariana added, her chin up, unafraid. Seeing her certainty pulsed a hot bloom in his chest.

"Awesome," Javier grumbled as his gaze dropped to the table.

A recent breakup had shaken the man, and Ty didn't want him to spiral down. "I arrested this punk twice," he told Mariana. "Bailed him out once. I've bought him more beers than he'll ever buy me."

Javier's mood brightened enough for him to scowl at Ty. "You get that government paycheck."

Ty shrugged it off. "As long as Esme gives me gratis burritos, we're even."

Javier shifted his focus to Mariana. "But you've got to know my man Hammer here might look all quiet and serious, but he can go beast. Like, pop!" He flashed a jab halfway across the table. "Suddenly someone's knocked all the way out and Hammer here is just chill, polishing his badge."

"I've seen it." Mariana examined Ty, a small smile on her face.

"You've seen it?" Javier sounded doubtful.

Her smile grew wider. "How do you think he closed the deal?"

"I've seen her fight, too." Ty gazed at her and savored the heat she returned in a look.

Javier stood from the table. "I'm going to sit by my lonesome at the window and let you two get on with your getting on." After one step away, Ty's phone buzzed. Javier froze. Mariana lost her smile.

Ty checked the phone. It was a message from Stephanie. "He's home." He and Mariana got up. All three of them headed for the door.

Javier nudged Ty's shoulder. "Text me the address. I'm not riding with you two steaming up the windows."

Mariana pulled the front door open. "There's no room in the truck anyway."

"You drive a truck?" Javier paused in the restaurant to give his sister a nod. Ty and Mariana waved to her, and Esme waved back, quiet concern on her face. As soon as they were all on the sidewalk, Javier jammed his hands into his hoodie pockets and shouldered into Ty a little harder. "You're a lucky son of a bitch, Hammer."

"For once." Ty pasted Innes's address in the Almaden Valley area of San Jose into a text. Javier's phone rang with an alert shortly after. "Go dark," he told his friend.

Javier gave him and Mariana a little salute and headed down the street in the opposite direction of her truck. Once they were clear of any pedestrians, Ty murmured to Mariana, "Stephanie and Vincent are meeting us there, too."

"Five of us." Mariana rolled her shoulders. He saw her trying to stay loose, but knew the nerves would be growing, just like in him. "How many syndicate men?"

"Unknown." He didn't like jumping in without a solid plan, but the time to strike was now. "But they don't know how many we have, either." Remarkable that it was only a few nights ago that he'd heard her angry refusal to the attacker in the dark parking lot. Ty had leaped into that fight with a pounding pulse, knowing he had to help her. His blood still rushed as he walked beside her, ready to finish that battle.

They reached the truck and she held out her hand. "I drive, you point the way." Tension constricted her voice.

Ty handed her the keys and stayed close. "We're going to make it through tonight."

She spoke quietly. "And after tonight?"

"You'll be free."

A tiny smile broke her serious expression. She shook her head and clarified, "I'll be with you."

The cool night air rushed through him in a long breath. "You'd better be." He moved around to the passenger side as she placed her backpack behind her seat. The metal of the revolver inside clunked against some tools. The clean pistol sat foreign on his hip.

Traffic thinned as the hours pushed later. He directed her

to a highway and they made their way south out of the city and toward San Jose. The shovels rattled in the bed of the truck. Mariana gripped the steering wheel with both hands. His gut clenched. They were stirring up trouble, but going in tight was a sure way to make a mistake and get hurt.

"Are there woodworking tools in that barn of yours?" He stared ahead at the taller buildings in the distance.

"Some."

"Enough to finish the window repairs?"

"I'd think so." One of her hands released the steering wheel and ran through her hair. Instead of returning to the wheel, it dropped to her thigh. "You learned all that on your grandparents' farm?"

"And at my folks' place. We're all handy." He watched her fingers loosen on the wheel. "There's some wood rot on the roof over your porch I could knock out."

"That would be great." She scooted forward in her seat a little, leaning back. "Keep it from squeaking when the wind picks up."

"My cousin in Oakland is a welder, if there's any metalwork to be done."

"Can't think of anything offhand, but that's good to know." Her elbow rested on the door, hand propped gently on the steering wheel. A sense of calm diffused through the cab of the truck, as if the sound of the tires on the highway was the drone of bees on a summer day. Ty's shock nearly ruined it for him. Pockets of stillness before the storm were not unusual for him. He'd learned how to live within the rhythm of crisis and recovery. But what surprised him was that making plans for the repairs didn't wind up his sense of dread. In the past, arrangements like that always worried him as they conflicted with the demands of his work. Now, he found himself looking forward to simple time with Mariana and the house.

His phone buzzed. Both he and Mariana stiffened their postures. Vincent reported in a text that Ty read aloud. "'Eight men on the perimeter.'" He put the phone down. "We're going to fix up your house," he reassured her, and himself.

The city of San Jose rose up around them. He navigated her through some highway complications, then had them exit into a sprawling semirural suburb. The trees grew thicker at the flanks of the road as Mariana drove them toward the low hills at the edge of a short valley. Large homes stood behind stone walls and metal gates. The farther into the hills they climbed, the more space surrounded each mansion.

"Kill the lights," Ty directed. She did and slowed, leaning forward. The terrain emerged in the infrequent high streetlamps and landscape lighting that displayed the impressive front greenery of the houses. The neighborhood was quiet and they didn't pass any other cars. Ty texted Vincent that they were close. A quick response indicated their position. Ty pointed. "Turn right at the next street."

The truck swung into a wide street between walled compounds. Higher, past their edges, the nature of the hills took over. A small white light flashed in the deepest darkness, probably Vincent signaling with his phone. Mariana eased the truck in that direction. The asphalt ended. She stopped next to a broad oak tree.

His boots crunched on dry leaves. Mariana grabbed her backpack and stepped around the truck to join him in the thickest shadows. Stephanie's voice in the dark drew them forward. "Vincent is still over the wall."

Somehow Stephanie made simple black pants and a black military jacket over a bulletproof vest look stylish. Javier stood next to her, still wearing his dark hoodie and a sullen expression. He did light up a bit when he gestured with his shoulder toward the eight-foot-high stone wall fifty yards away. "At least we get to mess up a nice neighborhood."

Stephanie stepped closer to Mariana. "Do you have a gun?" Mariana unzipped her backpack and pulled out the Magnum. Its menace glinted in the dim light. Stephanie's eyes widened. "That's a big *yes*."

"Damn, girl." Javier moved backward.

Stephanie glared at him. "You're not carrying?"

He put his palms out to her. "I've got priors, sister."

"Well, what good are you—"

Ty cut Stephanie off. "He doesn't need one to make them hurt." She hissed something between acceptance and frustration.

An approaching footstep in the darkness drew everyone's attention. Ty noted that Mariana had the sense not to raise the revolver and kept the barrel safely pointed at the ground. Vincent silhouetted against a lit portion of the stone wall. He was shaking his head when he arrived with the group. "Could you guys talk any louder?" He caught sight of the pistol in Mariana's hand. "Thanks for bringing the artillery."

Mariana whispered, "Family heirloom."

"We might need it." Vincent walked the group to the back of his SUV and reported, "Eight around the house. Don't know how many inside." He opened the trunk and handed two bulletproof vests out to Ty, who helped Mariana into hers before strapping his own on. Javier thumped his chest, the body armor sounding solid under his hoodie. Vincent continued, "I've already disabled the motion lights on this side of the compound. Two-story house. The only security cameras are on the front. If we stay on the outside of the driveway, we're in the clear. I'm presuming Innes will take the high ground and be on the second floor once the bullets start flying. Bedroom or office."

Mariana spoke up. "Bedroom." All eyes turned to her. "If he thinks he's under attack, like in a bunker, he'll want to have access to a bathroom and running water."

Vincent nodded. "I'll buy that."

Ty peered into the dark past the wall, but couldn't pick out any details of the house. "We can use the plumbing vents to locate bathrooms."

Stephanie looked at the sky and turned a half circle. "Start at the back of the house. Best views and away from sunrise."

Ty breathed easier, knowing a plan was taking shape. He addressed Vincent, Stephanie and Javier. "You guys draw the guards to the front, hold them down." Glancing at Mariana, he saw her taking it all in, unblinking. But she stood strong, jaw set. "We'll hook around back, quiet, then make our noise when we find Innes and whatever Seventh Syndicate sons of bitches are with him."

Vincent and the others nodded. Mariana put the pistol in her backpack and slung it over her shoulder. She turned toward the compound. "Ring the bell."

Javier hissed out a laugh. Ty couldn't. He grabbed a shovel from the bed of the truck and started walking toward the house. Mariana remained at his side. The group approached the wall. With each step closer, he felt the adrenaline shoot through him. The mission from the beginning was to save Mariana's land. The stakes had increased with each new escalation from the syndicate, and with each silent connection with Mariana. His muscles flared with hot electricity and his pulse raced. Tonight he had to protect her at all costs.

The eight-foot wall stood before them.

Mariana spoke low. "Just a few days ago I was worried

about how to get the apples harvested. And now…" Her hands shook as she gathered her hair back into a ponytail and secured it with a band from her pocket.

Ty stood close and whispered, "I haven't seen your music collection yet."

Javier huffed, "You're flirting *now*?"

Stephanie smacked his shoulder. "Shut up."

Ty ignored them and kept talking to Mariana. "Pick a song. Something you can dance to." He already had one running through his head, the same as he used every time he was walking into a tight situation. "That's your theme song."

Her hips swayed slightly and her whole demeanor unlocked. She smiled at him with only her eyes. "It's a cheesy song, but I love it."

Vincent rocked his shoulders up and down. "I've got mine."

Stephanie tilted her head from side to side. "Same."

"You guys are crazy." Javier coiled and leaped to catch the top of the eight-foot wall. He hauled himself up and peered over the top for a moment before straddling it. He put his hand down. Ty gave him the shovel, which was tossed onto the other side. Then Stephanie grabbed Javier's hand and he helped her up. Vincent took himself over the wall a few feet away. Once Stephanie had gone over, Mariana reached up for Javier. He pulled and she toed along the wall until she disappeared over the top. Javier offered Ty his hand with a smirk, but Ty waved it off and scaled the wall himself.

He dropped down into thick mulch between ornamental trees. He found the shovel and moved beside Mariana. In front of them was a lower row of shrubs, then a wide lawn. A stone patio surrounded the house, complete with an outdoor kitchen larger than Ty's apartment. The tall front door was flanked by even taller pillars. Steps swept down from the door to a large curved driveway bordered by a low wall that went all the way to the front gate. An SUV and two sedans were parked there, all dark, all looking as bulletproof as the car that had brought the men to Mariana's house.

Uplights made the mansion look even more imposing. They also revealed the silhouettes of the guards patrolling the front and close corner of the house. The men scanned into the dark around them, postures alert. Going after Innes outside the restaurant had worked. He'd called in the Seventh Syndicate.

Ty caught the attention of his group with a wave, then pointed out a path that arced amid the landscaping toward the front of the house. The others nodded and he led the way. Mariana stuck close behind him, her hand on his hip. His heart thundered with the touch.

The group crouched lower and lower until they huddled behind the four-foot wall that bordered the long driveway. Javier tapped Ty's knee and whispered, "Before you all start making noise, let me do a little work. That dude on the right corner looks lonely and I'll see if I can clear a path around back."

"We'll start when we see him fall." Ty patted his friend's shoulder and Javier was off. From this vantage, the three guards in front of the house were in view, and a fourth man lingered just around the corner. Ty kept watch on him. None of the shrubs next to the driveway wall gave away a hint of Javier's approach. After a few seconds, Javier's shadow appeared behind the guard. He approached stealthily, raising his arms slowly, the nearer he came.

Ty drew his pistol. Mariana quietly unzipped her backpack and pulled out the revolver. Ty told her, "We're going to fix up your house." Her smile was brief and tight.

Javier struck, coiling his arms around the guard's neck in an unbreakable choke hold. The guard made one attempt to slap at him, then went limp. Javier eased the man to the ground and melted into the shadows toward the back of the house.

Ty took aim at one of the front-of-the-house guards and fired the first shot.

Chapter Eighteen

Mariana jumped as the crack of the gun ripped open the still night air. A guard fell to the ground, clutching his leg and yelling for the others. They fired wildly as they took cover behind the pillars and cars. More men came around the far corner of the house, guns drawn.

Vincent and Stephanie rose just above the low wall, pistols out. Vincent sent a single shot streaking out. It clipped the base of a pillar, near a guard's foot. The guard hurried for deeper cover. Stephanie fired in two-shot bursts that chipped into the steps and dinged off the cars. The damn cars were bulletproof again.

The revolver weighed a ton, and with the short barrel, Mariana doubted she'd be able to hit what she aimed at. Return fire from the guards sent her back below the wall, heart pounding. The fight had just begun and it already seemed impossible.

Ty popped up from behind the wall and answered their shots, then leaned back down next to her. Vincent remained cool, reporting, "One of them got into the SUV from the passenger side."

Stephanie fired another two shots before returning to safety behind the wall. "If they create rolling cover, they'll get too close to hold off."

Mariana flinched when Ty patted her leg. He placed his hand gently there. "Shoot the SUV."

"It's bulletproof." Her rifle fired the same bullets as this revolver, and they hadn't stopped the car at her house.

"I know." He squeezed her leg. "But we still need to announce that you're here."

Cracks rang out from Vincent's and Stephanie's guns. Ty added a couple of rounds toward the front of the house, as well. Mariana took a deep breath and rose up from cover, the revolver in both hands. She extended it out and saw the guard positioning himself in the driver's seat of the SUV. The cock of the revolver's hammer tightened her whole body. She took aim and pulled the trigger.

The pistol bucked hard in her hands and boomed louder than any of the others. The bullet tore through the air and smashed into the SUV's driver's-side door. The guard inside flinched, even though the bullet didn't make it through the armoring. For a moment all the guns were silent and the report of hers echoed off the hills.

"Another." Ty was still at her side. "Then we move." He pointed along the same path Javier used to get around the house.

A couple of tentative shots came from the guards, but they flew wild into the night. The man in the SUV had recovered his wits and was going through the motions of starting it up. She lined up her sights again, this time slowing down the process for more accuracy. When she fired, she was ready for the recoil, though it still jarred her. The blast shook the area. This bullet smacked the driver's-side window, creating a web of cracks, though not breaking through. The impact was enough to send the guard scurrying out the passenger side as he abandoned the SUV.

"Nice one," Stephanie whispered, impressed.

Ty picked up the shovel and crouched to move. "Keep

them busy," he told Vincent and Stephanie, then led Mariana along the edge of the shrubs toward the side of the house. The firing back and forth resumed at the front. None of the bullets were aimed at Mariana and Ty, and her confidence grew that they remained hidden.

They passed the unconscious guard whom Javier had taken out. Large windows on this side of the house revealed a huge dark dining room, complete with a heavy table and chairs, and a modern chandelier that looked like an explosion of glass. Lights deeper in the house showed hallways and doorways, but she couldn't see any people.

Ty put out a hand and she froze. He pointed to the far corner of the house, where another guard lay on the ground. This one actually snored, body slumped and head leaning against the wall. More of Javier's work, she presumed. But that man was nowhere to be seen. Ty waved her forward again and they rounded the corner to the back of the house. Stepping wide to examine the roofline, she spotted a plumbing vent to the left of a wide balcony with French doors. Dim lights shone in those windows, but all she could see was the coved ceiling.

Ty leaned close to her ear. "I think we can get up those stones on the side." Chunky rocks ran from the ground floor to up next to the balcony. He held out his palm for her to wait, then ventured closer to the house. The shadows swallowed him.

A footstep crunched in the mulch to her right. Cold shock washed up her back. There was no way Ty could've come around to that side without her seeing him. She raised the pistol just as a guard emerged between two shrubs. He caught sight of her and started to swing his gun up before freezing. He stared at her gun and she hoped he couldn't tell how much it was shaking in her hand. She'd seen what the bullets did to the armored SUV and didn't want to know what that would mean to the human body.

"Don't," she commanded low through clenched teeth.

The guard seemed to be thinking about it, poised between decisions. Just as he started to act, Ty rose up behind him and swung the flat of the shovel hard into the back of the guard's head. The man spun and fell to the dirt, out cold. Relief shuddered through her.

"Sweet." She nearly jerked the pistol in the direction of the whisper, but recognized Javier's voice in time. He stepped out of the shadows. "I was trying to get around behind that guy." He put his hand out for Ty, curling his fingers impatiently. Ty tossed him the shovel and Javier started toward the front of the house. "Stop making out and get on up there." The shadows reabsorbed him.

Gunfire continued at the front of the house. She approached the house and saw that the stones on the wall would make for good handholds. Putting the pistol in the backpack, she started the ascent. Ty followed close behind. Her muscles savored the exertion and she was soon level with the wide balcony. She peeked over the rail to see a bedroom with grand-scaled modern furniture. Someone stepped across a doorway on the far side of the room, but no one was paying attention to the balcony. She crept over the rail and made space for Ty to join her.

Inside the room Innes argued with another man she couldn't identify with his back turned to her. There were two others, who looked like guards. The man with Innes turned and her pulse raced faster. Ty coiled next to her. It was Charlie Dennis.

Ty reached into her backpack and handed her the pistol. He whispered, "Shoot between the door handle and the lock."

She crept to the center of the balcony and readied the

gun. After a glance to Ty, who nodded, his own pistol out, she cocked and fired. The blast shattered wood and slammed the French doors open. Innes and Charlie Dennis tumbled against each other to get out of the way. One guard ducked.

The other guard swung up a submachine gun and fired at Mariana.

THE BARREL OF the submachine gun spit fire. Ty had no other thought than to get Mariana out of the way. He threw himself into her and they crashed to the floor. Bullets tugged at the shoulder and arm of Ty's jacket. If he was hit, he didn't feel it. He didn't care.

Keeping his body in front of hers, he fired wildly back at the guard. The man scrambled to the side. Mariana extended her pistol from behind Ty and let out a single booming round. Drywall dust exploded from a large hole in the wall. The guard reeled backward and shifted his aim toward her again. Ty fired two rounds into the man before the guard could get a shot off.

Ty rose to standing just as the other guard was collecting himself. This man already had his pistol drawn and tried to run for cover in the huge bathroom off to the left of the bedroom. Ty chased him with bullets until one hit him in the side. He landed on the ground hard, dropping the gun and holding the wound.

Innes, eyes crazed and full of fear, dived for the submachine gun on the ground. Mariana scrambled to it first and kicked it under the bed. Innes reared up, but he was too close to her. She slammed the heel of her boot into his collarbone. He shrieked with the crack and curled into a defensive ball.

Charlie Dennis's face was red with fury. He reached into his jacket as Ty turned his gun on him. Charlie's pistol just cleared its holster when Ty shot him in the shoulder. He staggered back into a wall and the gun clattered to the floor. Ty rushed him, kicking the gun aside and driving his forearm just under Charlie's chin.

Ty hissed, "She is never to be touched." He pressed harder into Charlie. "Ever."

Mariana approached, eyes deadly calm. Relief washed over him at seeing her unhurt. Her voice was even, cold steel like a stiletto through the ribs. "Anything the Seventh Syndicate reaches into my county will get cut off. Do you understand?"

"Answer her." Ty balled his fist into Charlie's jacket. The syndicate man grimaced, veins showing on his flushed forehead. "Answer her."

Charlie wheezed. "I understand."

Ty yanked him off the wall and held up the groaning man. "There are more of us. We're watching you. FBI's looking at your 'charities.' Your bosses will know that you put everyone in the spotlight. I'll see any move you make. Your business here is done." He tossed Charlie onto the ground with Innes, who whimpered, but did not move. With the room quiet, the sound of gunfire could be heard again in the front of the house. Ty shared a quick look with Mariana, both agreeing it was time to get the hell out of there.

She cautiously swung open the door to the bedroom suite. He saw the area was clear and hurried onto a broad landing at the top of a large staircase. A huge foyer reached up both floors. On the far end was the front door. Ty could see a guard taking cover behind a pillar outside through a window next to the door.

He and Mariana rushed down the stairs. Once he hit the bottom, he fired through the window. The surprised guard was hit in the arm. He twisted against the pillar until he gathered his feet and ran away. He must've taken anyone else still standing with him, because when Ty got the front door open, the area was completely abandoned.

Venturing out, he kept his senses on alert. A guard popped up to his left. He and Mariana dived for cover at the edge of the stairs. A clang rang out and the guard collapsed. Javier stood behind him with the shovel. He waved Ty and Mariana forward. "We done?"

"They're done," Ty answered. He and Mariana joined up with Javier and they all hurried along the driveway wall until they reached Vincent and Stephanie's position.

Vincent popped up, unruffled. "Injuries?" Stephanie appeared ready to go to a cocktail party. Everyone took a moment to assess themselves and shook their heads at his question. As a group, they moved back to the side wall and climbed their way off Innes's property.

No one spoke on the way back to their cars. Javier placed the shovel back in the bed of Mariana's truck and dusted off his hands. Ty, Vincent and Stephanie holstered their guns. Mariana placed hers in the backpack. Everyone removed their bulletproof vests and piled them in the back of Vincent's SUV. The clock was ticking. They had to scatter. Ty took a moment to stand before his friends. "Thank you."

Vincent extended his hand. "That's what we're here for." Ty shook it.

"All of us." Stephanie gave Ty and Mariana a nod.

"Anytime and every time." Javier held up a peace sign and strode away. Vincent and Stephanie went to their cars.

Ty held out his palm to Mariana. "Let me take you home." She gave him her keys, and her hand rested on his. Slow heat moved between them, an antidote to the fear and violence they'd just lived through. The touch released, the warmth remained in him. Routine movements like getting into the truck and starting it helped bring his pulse down.

Mariana stowed her backpack and sat heavy next to him. Her expression was blank as she stared ahead.

Vincent and the others pulled out and Ty brought up the rear. They all scattered once they hit the neighborhood streets. Ty took the truck onto the highway. In the distance where they'd just been, police lights raced and made the trees dance in red and blue.

Mariana's voice rasped, "Will they identify us?"

"Not with just their word against ours, and it would only shine a light on how they'd been targeting you in the first place."

"We did enough to stop them?"

He remembered the broken look in Charlie Dennis's face. "We showed we can touch them whenever we want. And now the syndicate knows they're being looked at by us, and the FBI. Cockroaches like that hate the light. They'll stay away."

She turned forward and sank deeper into the seat. Slow and deliberate, she took her hair out of the ponytail and ran her fingers through it. It was hard to keep his eyes on the road as she did. All he wanted was that sensation of her silky hair and the sound of her slow, rhythmic breath next to him.

The late hour swept most of the traffic from the highway. Suburbs and dark hills swept past. Semitrucks roamed like prehistoric beasts. Ty navigated through it all, the only constant the road in front of them in the headlights.

Mariana stared ahead. "I can't believe this night."

"You stood up and stopped them." Awe filled him. "Just like your ancestors."

"Your people, too." She looked at him. The weariness cleared from her eyes, where a new light shone. "Frontier Justice needs a home. We'll do it where it all started, at my place."

"We can find another spot." The idea of using the orchard had always appealed to him, but not the way things had gone down between him and Mariana. "The last thing I want to do is impose that on you."

"I'm choosing it," she declared. Her hand rested on his leg. "And I want you there, too. In my house. In my life."

The old fear he'd felt at commitments other than to his work didn't race in to clamp down his throat. This was what he wanted. Mariana. It felt like he breathed for the first time, an unknown weight lifted from his chest. "You have me," he told her. He placed his hand on hers and they drove that way for miles.

They approached her town, the air smelling of the earth and the sea. Ty had grown to know the local routes. More calm came with the familiar landscape. When he turned up the long road toward Mariana's orchard and saw the clean lines of the hills behind it, his heart sped. Yes, he could live here. With her.

Halfway up that road, two cars pulled in behind them with their headlights off. Ty's awareness sharpened and any calm burned away in a new rush of adrenaline. Mariana tensed next to him and twisted to look out the rear window. "One of them is a police car." Her voice was tight.

Ty passed the fence line border of her property and slowed the truck. Mariana pulled out her phone and dialed. "Are you on duty, Pete?" After a moment, she said, "You'd better get up to my property… Thanks… Stay on the line."

The cars behind kept pace. Ty angled the pickup across the road, blocking the path to her house, and stopped. He left the motor running and stepped out. Mariana came around from the passenger side, pulling on her backpack. He saw her put her phone on speaker and place it on the edge of the bed of the truck just behind them, so it could hear everything.

The other cars pulled up a few yards away. Captain Phelps stepped from the police car. The bald man who'd attacked Mariana in the parking lot got out of the sedan. Phelps mostly looked weary and disappointed, while the bald man's face was set with cold fury.

Mariana stood next to Ty, legs braced. "This is my land, Phelps."

The captain frowned, shaking his head. "Everything would've been so much easier if you'd sold. You'd have lived to enjoy your money."

Ty addressed the captain and the bald man. "Didn't you hear? The Seventh Syndicate is done here."

The bald man spit, "I don't care about what they say." He pulled the edge of his jacket back, revealing a pistol on his hip. "I'm going to finish this job."

Ty looked at the men, both armed. The bald man practically vibrated with violence. Phelps's sagging posture was deceptive. Ty knew the man was ready to draw his sidearm. Before Ty had a chance to reach for his, Mariana swept past him, reached into his jacket and pulled his pistol. She stood between him and the men, gun extended toward them.

Ty's heart hammered. She couldn't take on both of them at once. Phelps put his palms out to her. "I know you think this is your only option, but we can work something out. Seventh Syndicate doesn't have to be part of it. We'll get a new offer on the table. Make arrangements so everyone can walk away happy."

He was lying, buying time. Ty felt the menace in the false negotiation. The bald man edged his hand millimeters closer to his own gun. Why had Mariana made this move to take his gun? Then Ty saw that her backpack was completely unzipped. The handle of the .44 was in front of him, within reach.

Searing electricity shot through Ty's limbs. Life and death were a blink away.

The bald man sneered at Mariana. "You ready to put me in the ground?" His shoulder twitched and Ty burst into motion. He grabbed the pistol from Mariana's backpack and sprang in front of her. The bald man reached for his gun. Ty fired a single shot that slammed the bald man back against his car. He slid to the ground, dead.

Phelps's hand hovered over his sidearm, but his jaw trembled and the rest of him was frozen. Mariana held him in place with the steady aim of her pistol. Far behind him, police lights flashed along the road to her property. The patrol car sped closer. Phelps's shoulders slumped when the light flicked over him. The car came to a stop and road dust washed over the scene. Pete stepped from the patrol car and approached cautiously. Mariana maintained her aim at the captain.

Phelps turned his tired eyes toward the officer. "Pete. I don't think you know—"

"I'm taking your gun, Phelps." Pete stepped to the captain and removed the sidearm. Mariana lowered her pistol. Pete cuffed Phelps and sat him in the back of the patrol car before returning to Ty and Mariana. "Thanks for your call, Mariana."

She went to the truck and retrieved her phone, face neutral. When she returned, she handed Ty the pistol, which he holstered. He placed the revolver in her backpack as Pete called in backup and the crime scene team on his car radio.

The people showed up quickly. Ty and Mariana stood together as the activity ebbed and flowed around them. They answered Pete's questions and Ty promised to call his chief and his FBI contacts to tie it all together with the earlier conflict at the house. The body was photographed and removed, then the cars. Pete nodded solemnly to Ty and Mariana before driving off with Phelps in the back of his car.

Mariana got in the driver's side of the truck and took her and Ty to the house. Toro greeted them with tail wags and trotted with them inside. The first thing Mariana did was to go to the bedroom and place the revolver back in the false-bottomed drawer. He took off his jacket. There were bullet holes in the sleeve, but not his flesh.

She sat on the edge of the bed looking exhausted. But warm life in her eyes had not dimmed. "Forget about the violence," she said. "The fight and the fire and the phone calls and the guns." She shook her head, dark hair framing her face. "Without all that, you'd still be here right now, wouldn't you?"

He sat next to her on the bed, heat moving between their bodies. "From the first time I saw you in your shop, I knew. I knew that I would love to find out what your voice sounded like this early in the morning. And whether or not we have an easy life or a hard one, I can't wait to find out every step with you." He leaned close and her arms wrapped around him. Their mouths met in a kiss that spoke more vows than words could.

Epilogue

Mariana couldn't remember this much activity on her land since…ever. The harvesters worked their way through the rows of trees. Boxes and boxes of apples were stacked in the barn, or were trucked off in a couple of runs a day. Just now a truck eased past her and she waved at the driver, standing between the orchard and the house.

Behind her at the house, Vincent and Stephanie ran countless wires from new satellite dishes on the roof, down into the storage room next to the kitchen. Every time she walked into that converted space, it looked more and more like some kind of NASA ground control. Computers and monitors and radios lined a long table that Ty had built into one wall.

The sound of Ty's hammer was much slower than her pulse when she looked up at him on a ladder, replacing old wood on the porch roof with fresh timber. Seeing him in jeans and a T-shirt definitely chased any chill from the light sea mist that blew across the hills. Though she couldn't complain about seeing him in his suits on a daily basis, now that he'd taken over the job as police chief of Rodrigo. After being the one to arrest Phelps, Pete had been fair and professional with Ty, and the whole department was operating smoothly.

But today, Ty was hers. He secured the piece of wood and climbed down the ladder. "They're wrapping up?"

The two of them watched the harvesters packing up the last of the boxes for the day and head for their cars. Mariana exchanged waves with them, then walked up to the porch. Ty stood with her, his elbows on the new railing he'd repaired last week.

She slid her hand down his arm. "Wait here." He turned and leaned back on the railing. A small smile curled his mouth as his gaze followed her into the house. His keen attention hadn't wavered. It felt like every day, they found a new way to communicate, either with words, simple looks or with their bodies.

Crossing the living room, she could hear more movement in the spare room, along with a murmured conversation between Vincent and Stephanie. Javier had even come by to do some work on the place with Ty the other week, but had lit out before dark. Sydney had spent late nights at the house, recounting all the lore she could collect on the Frontier Justice of the past.

Mariana grabbed four glasses off her bar cart, along with a bottle of tequila. The sound of the glass must've reached the spare room, because the conversation ended and footsteps approached. Vincent and Stephanie caught up to Mariana when she arrived back at the porch with Ty. She set the glasses and bottle on the rail.

There'd been no sign of the Seventh Syndicate near her property, her store or anywhere else in the county. But the electronic brain Vincent and Stephanie were installing in the house did pick up hints about the criminal organization. And as soon as there was a hard target, Frontier Justice would be there.

Ty uncorked the bottle and poured into each glass. Everyone raised theirs. Late sunlight glinted through the amber liquid. The depth in Ty's eyes as he looked at her brought more heat than the tequila ever could. She gazed back at him, and watched his breath slow, filling his chest. He smiled, secret and wicked. The two of them spoke with silence.

Ty toasted. "To the Balduccis."

Vincent and Stephanie repeated it back with reverence and clinked glasses. Mariana stood on the porch of her family house, memories of her parents around her. Their orchard remained, and thrived. And the influence of her ancestors was alive again thanks to Ty and the others. She knocked her glass into Ty's. *"Salud."*

* * * * *

WYOMING
CHRISTMAS
RANSOM

NICOLE HELM

To my husband, who also almost always answers my
questions with "That wouldn't happen," but indulges me
when I say "But could it happen?"

Chapter One

Gracie Delaney didn't care for the nickname "Angel of Death," but in Bent, Wyoming, it was something of the truth. If she came to a person's door unannounced, they knew what was coming.

The fact that she was young, maybe a little girl-next-door looking, no longer fooled people. As the coroner for Bent County, Gracie's work was death.

It wasn't as bad as some people made it out to be. Considering her parents had died in a car crash when she'd been six, and she was the lone survivor of said crash, she'd been intimately acquainted with death her whole life.

Funny, life was a lot harder than death. Death was easy, and it was final. The cause might occasionally be a mystery, but it was a mystery she always solved.

Gracie blew out a breath as she parked her car in Will Cooper's yard. Life, meanwhile, had a hundred mysteries she couldn't figure out. Like why two years after she'd informed Will Cooper of his wife's death, she still came to check in on him routinely.

She'd informed a lot of people of their loved ones'

deaths over the course of two years, and while some re-
actions stuck with her, maybe a few even haunted her,
only Will's reaction had ever caused her to act outside
a professional capacity.

She supposed it was the fact he couldn't accept his
wife had simply skidded off the road and crashed into
a tree. He insisted the detectives had missed or over-
looked things. He'd become obsessed with proving foul
play.

Gracie had felt sorry for him and his inability to accept the truth. So, she'd let him have access to records
she shouldn't have let him have access to. She'd shown
him, over and over again, how the only thing that had
killed his wife was an icy road and a tree.

Still he pushed into this theory that whoever his wife
had been having an affair with had been the one to
kill her.

Gracie got out of the truck and stared at the ramshackle cabin Will currently lived in. He still owned
the pretty little two-story he and his wife had shared in
Bent proper, but rented it out to a family with kids. He
claimed it was because up here he could do his metalwork without any neighbor complaint, but Gracie figured it was something more isolating than all that.

He wasn't a Bent native. He'd moved here after marrying Paula Carson and though he'd lived in town and
been building a name for himself with his metalwork,
Paula's death had changed him. He'd isolated himself
and since he had no family in Bent, no natives had been
too worried about a stranger's hermit behavior.

Except Gracie. For all intents and purposes, she was his only link to the outside world.

God, she wished she could help him.

"You're going to," she said to herself. "Right here. Right now." She'd been playing into his obsession for too long, and it had to stop. No more looks at old reports. No more trips to that road to study curves and angles. She'd still be his friend, but that was it. Like a drug dealer refusing to continue to deal an addict their drug of choice.

Will was going to have to go cold turkey or solo. Her chest tightened and for the briefest second she considered retracing her steps. He'd go solo. She knew he would, and she didn't want him to.

She wanted to fix him. To help him. And yes, maybe she was a little inappropriately hung up on the guy, but that only factored into it a little.

She shook that thought away and started for the cabin. No Christmas lights, not a hint that it was December and even rough-and-tumble Bent had brought out its Christmas decor. But not for Will. She wasn't certain he celebrated anything anymore.

She heard the faint strains of music and bypassed the cabin door, instead walking around the cabin to the back. He had the doors open on his shed, and inside he worked on a metal project.

He'd once had a blacksmith shop down in town, something both local ranchers had used and tourists had gotten a kick out of. But he'd closed it after Paula's death. In fact, he hadn't worked for a year after, living off the rent from the house.

Slowly over the past year he'd gotten back into metalwork. Little artistic projects he made custom for ranches, or occasionally sold to the antique store in town.

Gracie had been hopeful it was a sign he'd give up obsessing over the mystery of Paula's affair and death. Like so many times with him, her hopes had been dashed.

And you are done being a silly, too-hopeful girl.

She nodded to herself as she crossed the yard. He worked, mask over his face, black T-shirt clinging to his chest even with the cold air around them. He was working with some tool that shot a flame out of it in one hand, clamps in another as he heated and twisted metal. Faint lines of grime and sweat streaked across his impressive forearms and his biceps strained against the sleeves of his T-shirt.

She allowed herself a dreamy sigh, because he wouldn't hear her over the noise of the tools. Because this was it. She was cutting ties. Well, she was cutting off the supply of information. She just had a sinking suspicion that meant he'd cut ties with her, too.

He turned off the blowtorch thing, nudging the mask up on his head to reveal his face. A few trickles of sweat dripped down his square jaw, and she didn't know why she found that appealing.

"Hey," he offered. "You bring those pictures?"

Gracie shook her head. "No, Will. I didn't."

He frowned, setting down the tools and pulling the mask completely off his face. "Then why are you here?"

Ouch. She forced herself to smile. "I always come hang out on Friday afternoons."

"Usually with the thing I asked you for, though."

"I'm not…" She cleared her throat. "I can't keep bringing you stuff."

He frowned, eyebrows drawing together as he stared at her. Not just anger, but confusion, as if it didn't make any sense to him.

How could it not make sense? "For two years I've helped you try to undermine both my investigation and the police's. I'm…" She swallowed at the nerves flapping around in her chest and throat. "I'm done," she said, wishing it had come out more forcefully and not so wobbly.

"Done," he said flatly.

"I'm still your frie—"

"I don't need a friend. I never did."

Ouch. Ouch. Ouch. "Okay." She wouldn't cry in front of him. She couldn't allow herself to show the hurt. It was so stupid. She'd all but forced her company on him for two years. He might be the obsessive one, but she was pathetic.

She turned, blinking back the tears that burned in her eyes as she forced her lead-like legs to move back toward her car.

"Where are you going?" he called after her.

"Home," she said, hoping he couldn't read that squeak in her voice. Oh, who was she kidding? He didn't care. If it didn't have to do with the case, he did not care. She'd been a means to an end, and she couldn't be anymore.

"Why?"

She laughed, surprised at the way bitterness could grow just as large as sadness. "You don't want a friend, and I can't keep being your supplier. So." What else was there to say?

Apparently nothing, because Will didn't try to stop her after that. She got to her truck, didn't bother to look back and drove away.

It was time she moved on. Not just for Will, but for herself.

WILL WATCHED GRACIE get into her truck. He had no idea what had just happened. And damn if it wasn't at the worst possible time.

After two years of combing through everything, he'd found a secret file on Paula's computer within an old grocery list. It didn't name the man she'd had an affair with, but it gave some clues. Will thought maybe a few pictures of the accident might unearth a clue that was connected.

Of course, he had those pictures memorized at this point. He had everything memorized. Losing Gracie's help didn't really matter one way or another. Though it was nice to have someone to bounce ideas off of.

Nice to have someone who didn't look at him like he was crazy, especially on days when he thought he *was* a little crazy. After all, what man investigated the death of his cheating wife for two years? Especially after every law enforcement agency involved had found no reason to believe foul play was involved.

But he felt it. Knew it. Maybe his marriage had been

a mess, but that didn't mean he could just *let it go*. Someone had murdered her, he was sure of it. They had to be brought to justice.

Justice would bring him peace. He was sure of that, too.

Regardless of whether or not it was crazy, this was the man he was. Had been for two years, so it didn't make sense Gracie was quitting out of the blue.

Will cleaned up his tools, frowning at the custom order he was making. It wasn't turning out how he would have liked. He was going to have to start over, but right now wasn't the time. He had to work through this thing with Gracie first or his concentration would be shot.

Something had to have happened. Maybe a friend or family member had warned her off him? Gracie was part of the Delaneys, all law enforcement and politicians and upstanding citizens.

Paula, who'd grown up in the Carson clan, had always said that—*upstanding citizens*—with such disdain because Carsons and Delaneys didn't seem to have much between them besides disdain and bitterness.

Will hadn't much cared one way or another about the silly feud so many Bent citizens held such stock in. Land disputes and romantic tragedies that happened over a century ago didn't really interest him, but he'd sided with the Carsons if asked out of loyalty to Paula.

But Paula was dead, and he wasn't building any monuments in her honor. Their marriage and relationship had gone sour before her untimely death.

He hated to think that was what drove him—the

tangle of screwed-up emotions that came with losing someone you'd once loved and then had grown to hate.

He shook his head. It wasn't *that*. It was that he knew something was wrong. For starters, Paula had been on the road to *his* cabin, a place she never went to even when their marriage hadn't basically been over. She hadn't had her purse, and she hadn't been wearing shoes. Which was the opposite of the nearly anal woman he'd been married to for five years.

Now she'd been gone two, and whoever her lover had been was a mystery no one seemed to care to solve.

Except him. Occasionally Gracie suggested it was some warped sense of pride, needing to know the man his wife had chosen over him, more than it was his concern over her death being wrongful.

Wouldn't that make this easier?

He just knew Paula too well for her wreck to make sense, and he couldn't live with himself thinking there might be a murderer out there.

It was likely more emotionally complicated than that, but he chose to focus on the case, on the facts, over those messy emotions that plagued him from where he'd shoved them deep down.

He frowned over at where Gracie's truck had been parked, trying to go through the whole interaction. He'd been a little curt with her, but she knew how he could get when a project wasn't going the way he wanted.

The truth was, Gracie was about the only human contact he had on a regular basis these days, and he'd gotten to taking for granted that it would always continue.

She had to be bluffing. She'd be back tomorrow morning with coffee, an apology and those pictures.

He was sure of it. Certain.

Except the next morning came and went, and so did the next, and by the time an entire week had passed without one peep from Gracie, Will was downright pissed. Where did she get off just cutting him off like that? Abandoning him just like…

He grimaced at that thought as he studied the keys hanging from the hook in his kitchen. He needed food and supplies. Usually Gracie brought him everything he needed so he had to go into town only once a month.

Or less.

Truth be told, everything in his life had narrowed, incrementally, over the past two years. Without Gracie to take his mind off it, this past week had been a glaring reminder.

He didn't like to leave his little mountain. He didn't like to drive. He didn't like to face Bent with its people who knew him and his story. Poor widower. The man who couldn't let the past go.

He didn't trust that world out there, but if he didn't get over it, he was going to starve. He grabbed the keys and started for his door.

But about halfway through he turned around and headed for his—well, Paula's—computer. He could stand to go over the secret file one more time.

He pulled up the document he'd found after meticulously going through every file in her computer, no matter how innocuous the title. This particular file was listed as Grocery List 5/16.

The first page was even a list of groceries. He'd bypassed it he didn't know how many times over the years because it was clearly a grocery list even after a few scrolls. Then he'd decided to not just skim through every file, but to read through every word in case some clue was hidden in the midst of some article about tax law or a random to-do list.

He hadn't found it in any of her files from her job as a CPA, but he had found something in this grocery list. He'd noticed just last week that the list repeated itself after ten vegetables. Which was weird. Why would a grocery list need to repeat itself?

So he'd scrolled. For ten pages. Just the same ten vegetables repeated, and then there was what he'd been looking for.

They appeared to be emails with the to/from stripped out of them, but Paula had kept the dates and the subject lines. Love letters. Well, more like sex letters if Will was honest with himself.

It had been hard to read them, knowing his wife had received them while they were still trying to work things out. Sickening really, but he'd needed a clue.

He *still* needed a clue. So he read them again, sick to his stomach and angry all over again. But he did it. Focusing on every detail, every word choice, every mention of meeting.

He jotted down the referenced meetings this time, then cross-referenced with the computer calendar based on the dates of the email.

And that was when he found his pattern.

Chapter Two

Gracie plastered a smile on her face as the party around her was hitting full swing.

Usually a Delaney wouldn't be caught dead in Rightful Claim, a Carson bar, but the whole town had made an exception to the normal way of town feud bitterness with the engagement party of Gracie's cousin Laurel to the bar's proprietor, Grady Carson.

Gracie was happy for Laurel, probably happier than most of the other Delaneys, who thought the Carsons were a vortex of evil, but the happy couldn't smother her self-absorbed worry over Will.

She hated that she was worried about him when he clearly saw her as nothing, but she didn't think he'd come off his little mountain, and he had to be running low on food.

It's none of your business if he starves to death. That's his own problem.

She wanted to believe that, but whether he cared back or not, Gracie did care about Will. Even if it was one-sided. Even if it was stupid or pathetic, she cared about him.

Gracie made a beeline for the bar. She usually didn't drink, didn't like the way it made her feel a little dizzy, a little out of control, but maybe it would shush some of this endless circling her brain was doing.

It's not your brain. It's your heart.

Yeah, she really needed to shut that voice up, but before she made it to the crowded bar, she glanced at the door as it opened.

Will stepped in. Underneath a cheerful swath of Christmas lights that looked out of place in this rough-and-tumble, Wild West–themed bar, but also somehow perfect.

For a second she figured she was seeing things she wanted to see, and berated herself for being an idiot. But Will was striding through the room, ignoring any looks or comments, and heading straight for her.

She could only stare for a moment. Will rarely came into town, and when he did it was only to the general store, the gas station or the post office. And he never went anywhere when there might be a crowd.

"Will, what are you—"

"I found something out," he said resolutely. "I need your help."

Gracie glanced around the bar. More than a few pairs of eyes were on them. She knew what they all thought, too. Will Cooper was crazy, and silly Gracie Delaney placated him because she didn't know any better.

Well, she'd figured out how to know better, but she didn't need to prove it to the group.

"Let's talk outside," she whispered, not wanting to draw more attention. She hesitated a second, then brazened through. She linked her arm with his as if they were friends, or more, and headed for the door.

Will came easily, and if she wasn't totally imagining things, a tremor went through his arm, maybe his whole body.

She didn't want to feel sorry for him, or be drawn into whatever help he needed, but surely it was important if Will was facing Bent and Rightful Claim and a party.

He pulled his arm from hers after they pushed through the swinging front doors of Rightful Claim. He took a few steps down the boardwalk, raking his hands through his hair, which needed a trim. Even in the warm glow of the town's twinkle-light-wrapped streetlights, he somehow looked a little wilder, a little more desperate than the last time she'd seen him.

Or that's what you want, idiot.

"I didn't know Rightful Claim got so busy," he offered, and though the sounds of the party drifted out into the cold night, it was mostly quiet out here.

"It's a party. Laurel and Grady's engagement party."

"Oh. Guess that explains your truck being here." He blew out a breath, looking away from the bar and out at the night sky, which was a sparkling, vast thing. "It's December," he said, as if he hadn't known.

"Yes. Hence the Christmas decorations."

He looked around. Tinsel-lined candy canes Gracie suspected had been around since before she was born hung off the streetlight poles just as they had when she'd been a kid.

"I'm sorry I'm interrupting. It's just I found something."

"Will—" She couldn't do this. For herself as much as for him.

"I found a pattern, to how they met. Wednesdays. Always at six. I don't know where, but there has to be something there. Wednesdays." His gaze fixed on hers in the cheerful Christmas lights.

She'd told him she was done, but here he was, stepping outside his comfort zone and marching into the bar. She was torn between pleasant surprise that he'd braved some of the things he'd been avoiding more and more and being annoyed he thought he could just waltz into her life and demand help.

"Then what?" she asked softly. Because this was what had brought her to that moment last week when she'd cut him off. When she'd cut herself off. She could keep giving him pictures and files and peeks at evidence and what have you, but *then what*? It was an endless circle, and she couldn't be a part of it anymore.

She wanted him to break free of it, too, but she had no say over him. She only had say over herself. But maybe… Maybe if he actually stopped to think about the question like she'd had to…

"What happens if we follow the pattern?" she prodded.

"We follow the clues and—"

"Then what after that? You find the guy your wife was cheating with? You question him and maybe he even had something to do with it despite all evidence to the contrary. The searching is over, you have your answers, your justice. What then?" Because she'd been foolishly hoping to help him to that *what then*, but she had a terrible feeling she'd spent the past two years only aiding him in becoming more screwed up, more of a hermit and less of the easy-going Will Cooper she'd known peripherally before Paula's death.

And because she cared about him, but had zero actual responsibility or hold on him, she had to walk away.

"We'll have the truth," Will said, as if *she* was the one living in a fantasy world. "I've been searching for the truth for two years. I don't know why you're giving up, but I can't. I can't ignore two years' worth of something telling me this is all wrong."

"What will you do with whatever truth you're after?"

He looked at her a bit like she'd struck him. "Hopefully put a murderer in jail." He shook his head. "Why? Why are you doing this? After all this time, you're just abandoning me. I don't get it."

He actually sounded and looked hurt, instead of just irritated he didn't have help anymore, so she gave him the truth. "I care about you, Will, and I can't keep watching you get worse."

WILL COULDN'T PROCESS those words, or the soft look in Gracie's brown eyes. *Care.* Such a weird word. Such a dangerous thing, to care about someone. You couldn't control what they'd do with that. Couldn't predict it. You could feel safe and happy one minute, eviscerated and broken the next.

Care. No. It gave him a full-body chill. "Get worse at what?" he asked, working to pretend the first part of that sentence didn't exist.

She blew out a breath, lights from the tacky Christmas decorations all around creating a sort of warm yellow glow around her. Occasionally, the few nights he managed to sleep well enough to dream, he'd dream of her, much like this. Something like an angel, down to the glowing.

He wasn't fanciful enough to believe in things like angels, but he wasn't so cynical he couldn't believe that Gracie was part of his life for a reason.

So why was she leaving it?

She blew out a breath. "You said you don't need a friend, but I'm always here if you decide you do. But I'm done playing detective. It was an accident, Will. An *accident*."

"She was not cheating on me accidentally."

"No."

"What changed? Something did, because a person doesn't just walk away after..." It all lodged a little too hard, the words he was saying, a very painful realization he'd come here for the very, very stupid reason of feeling abandoned, and that overly sympathetic look on her face.

He tried to say he had to leave, but he wasn't sure any words actually came out of his mouth. He was moving too fast away from her and this town and...

This was why he stayed up there. When he came down to town, when people were around, talking about things not related to Paula's death, all these messy, confusing, complicated and mixed-up emotions boiled up and over. Who wanted to live in the center of all those things? He didn't understand these people walking through life like it wasn't a relentless parade of suck.

He didn't need Gracie to be his friend. He didn't need anyone to be his friend. He most certainly didn't need fake Christmas crap surrounding him to the point of suffocation.

Who cared if Gracie had a reason for backing out? It wasn't the same as learning your wife was cheating on you, or that she was dead. None of this was the *same*.

But somewhere in the past few years he'd lost how to parse it all. Which meant he'd let this all go—Gracie, her help, anything to do with Bent. He'd figure this all out on his own where he was safe from the way people were complicated, from the way people could betray you.

"Will. Wait."

But he couldn't wait. He had to get back to his house, his mountain. Far away from all *this*.

He turned away from her, hunching against the cold. There were cars everywhere, filling the lot, clogging both sides of the street. He'd had to park two blocks down.

Before turning the corner to where his Jeep was parked, he gave a final glimpse at Gracie standing there in the twinkling lights, hugging herself and looking worried and like a Christmas gift.

He damn well didn't need her worry. Or care.

He climbed into his Jeep and started the engine. He drove out of Bent, so distracted with the roiling set of emotions inside him it took miles to realize something wasn't right.

The engine was making a horrible noise, and the steering wheel wasn't responding the way it normally did. Will frowned. It was pitch-black on this mountain road and not a good place to stop. Even though traffic wasn't a big concern, 18-wheelers sometimes rumbled by toward Fairmont.

If he stopped—

The thought, the hope he could fix this situation, died in an instant. When his foot tapped the brake, nothing happened. He swallowed at the trickle of fear, pressing his foot down harder. A grinding noise sounded—a terrible one—and the brake barely responded, slowing his progress only a little bit.

Will swore as he continued to stomp his foot on the brake. Horrible noise, a slight decrease in speed, but not enough. Keeping his eyes on the road and one hand gripped to the steering wheel for dear life, he fished his phone out from the messy console.

He waited for a straightaway on the road, searched for anything that might slow his car down without killing him. All there was in the dark night, he knew, were rocks and trees and death. He couldn't even see the moon, like some kind of terrible omen.

He dialed Gracie's number, impatiently swearing as it rang over and over again. He remembered the emergency brake, stomped on the lever, but nothing happened.

She didn't answer.

Stupid to call her instead of 911, and still he gripped his phone with one hand, while desperately trying to take the curves of the dark road ahead of him. Screeching tires, increasing speed as the road dipped, entire car shuddering.

"Gracie," he shouted into his phone when her voice mail beep sounded. "I need your help."

But he couldn't explain beyond that because he had to drop the phone to grip the steering wheel with both hands. Except that didn't seem to help. His steering had gone the way of the brakes and now he was careening toward another curve, this time with no hope of doing anything but catapulting over the edge and into a grove of trees.

Paula's trees.

Chapter Three

Gracie chewed her lip as she stared at her phone. Maybe Will had been calling to apologize. Maybe she should have answered.

He was dealing with such complicated emotions and—

Well, no, the problem was he *had* complex emotions, grief and betrayal, and for two years he'd run away and hermited away from them rather than face them, deal with them, accept them.

And she'd placated and enabled him at every turn. She chewed harder on her lip, staring at the voice mail icon.

"Here. Turn that frown upside down."

Gracie looked up at Laurel, who had slid a bottle of beer in front of her at her little corner table where she was sitting. By herself.

"Sorry I'm not reveling."

"Don't worry. The Carsons are doing enough reveling for all of us," Laurel said, smiling fondly at the motley crew around them. Delaneys lined the outskirts of the crowd. Most looking a little sour faced, though a few had imbibed enough to mingle with Carsons.

Gracie looked back down at her phone. She should put it away and celebrate her cousin's engagement. Celebrate the fact the town wasn't imploding over a Carson and a Delaney getting married.

Yet.

"What's up, Gracie? It isn't like you to mope."

Gracie shook her head, gesturing at the crowd. "It's so not important. I'll tell you about it later. Enjoy your night."

Laurel took a sip from her bottle of beer then glanced around the room, her smile going soft when it landed on her fiancé, Grady Carson. He was laughing with his cousins Noah and Ty behind the bar. They made a handsome, dangerous trio.

Gracie glanced down at her phone again, that obnoxious voice mail icon staring at her.

"So, who's the guy?"

Gracie's head jerked to Laurel. "What?"

"I know everyone you know, Gracie," Laurel said with a smile. "They're all here. So the only reason you're staring at your phone and not talking to anyone is…well, a guy."

Gracie tried to laugh casually, but it came out sounding forced even to her own ears. "There's no guy."

"Then what's with the phone staring?"

"I'm in a deadly battle of *Candy Crush*."

Laurel laughed. "Liar."

"It's not a guy…per se. I just finally told Will I'd

stop…" Gracie shook her head. "This is not engagement party talk."

Laurel reached across the table and patted Gracie's
arm. Laurel had never been shy about her disapproval
of Gracie's odd relationship with Will. As a sheriff's
deputy, Laurel didn't take kindly to accusations that
the department wasn't doing its best because the victim had been a Carson, or any of Will's other accusations over the case.

So, it made Gracie feel silly and small bringing it
up, especially at Laurel's party.

"He's not my favorite person, but I know you felt a
kind of obligation to him, and cutting that off couldn't
have been easy."

Gracie forced herself to smile. "And something we
can discuss tomorrow."

Laurel nodded. "Fair enough. Just one little piece
of advice. Either cut all of it off for good, or accept
you're going to be a part of it. Don't sit here in a back-
and-forth. Make a choice and stick with it. You'll feel
a lot better."

"Aren't you going to tell me which choice?"

"You two look far too serious for a party," Grady
said, coming up to them and taking Laurel's hand in
his. "On your feet. You're going to dance with me."

"I'm a terrible dancer," Laurel returned with a laugh,
but she let Grady pull her to her feet. She left her beer
bottle, grinning as Grady gave her a little spin toward
the small throng of people dancing to "Rockin' Around
the Christmas Tree."

But Laurel smiled over her shoulder at Gracie. "You

pick the one you can live with," she called over the crowd and the music.

One she could live with. Gracie frowned. That was the worst advice she'd ever been given. She couldn't live with *either* possibility. She had told him she couldn't help him anymore because she was afraid she was making him worse. She meant that choice, but it didn't make it easy.

She cared about Will. Had even said it to his face and watched him blanch outside this very bar. As if care was some kind of horrible disease she'd foisted upon him.

You decided to cut him off, so cut him off.

She nodded, willing herself to hit the voice mail button, which she did. Then willing herself to hit Delete without listening to a second. For that act, she paused.

She'd cut him off. He didn't want a friend. He was allergic to emotion and she was no therapist, so she couldn't possibly fix him. She couldn't go after him and make things right because he was too closed off, too obsessed, too...

She hit Play, then berated herself. She wasn't going to listen. She was *not* going to listen or get dragged into helping him with things that weren't any good for him.

"Gracie."

Oh hell, she had to listen.

"I need your help." Said in a breathless, gritty voice, as if he was straining against something. Some horrible screeching noise went on in the background, so loud she could barely hear his voice over it.

"Laurel," she yelled, already on her feet, already heading for the door. "Who's on duty at county?"

WILL THOUGHT HE heard sirens. Which was weird. He couldn't hear sirens in his cabin. He couldn't hear anything except bird song, and the occasional rumble of an engine on Fridays.

Gracie. Always Gracie.

It registered, vague and faint, somewhere in the recesses of his brain, that he was cold. And uncomfortable.

No, not uncomfortable, on fire. Painful fire, frigid cold. It didn't make any sense and he couldn't seem to open his eyes.

Well, this was bad.

Something like panic fluttered in his chest, but everything in his body was throbbing with pain. He wasn't at home in his cabin. He wasn't on his mountain. He was somewhere… Somewhere.

He couldn't open his eyes, and he couldn't move without a fiery agony spreading through his body. Things were digging into him and one arm was at an uncomfortable angle tangled up in something hard.

He could still hear sirens, but it was all so far off he wondered if it had anything to do with him or if it was just all in his head.

Then they stopped. Just stopped.

He was going to die, wasn't he? Something had gone wrong with his car. He didn't quite remember what, but everything had gone wrong and he'd crashed and he was going to die.

Just like Paula. Exactly like it.

"Will? Will!"

He must be hallucinating. There'd be no reason Gracie would be out this way. Certainly no reason she'd be his saving grace. Gracie. Grace. He might have laughed if he didn't think his head would roll right off.

"Will? Oh my— I found him!" she shouted, and he could almost hear her or someone or something next to his ear.

"Will. Oh God. Will. Please." When she touched him he groaned, because everything hurt, even Gracie's very welcome touch.

"You're alive. You're alive." She whispered it over and over, her hand still on his chest. He felt the gentle brush of her fingertips across his forehead. Finally a part of his body that didn't hurt.

"Say something, Will. If you're awake. If you can hear me. Say something. Please."

He heard footsteps and a murmur of someone else, but Gracie was talking to him and her fingers were on his face. She sounded desperate and afraid, and he didn't want that for her. No.

He tried to open his eyes again, and this time they went a little. Everything was dark though there was some kind of light, but he couldn't see right. He could tell that. Nothing was right.

His Jeep had malfunctioned. He'd crashed. And he couldn't believe that was an accident.

His vision cleared a little, and he could just barely make out Gracie's face hovering above him. The world around them was dark but some light swathed her face, and he could see every feature.

He had the oddest urge to reach out and touch her face. Touch her hair. Anything to assure himself she was real and here, and that all that worry and fear on her face was for him. *Him.*

I care about you, Will.

Turns out even half-dead after a car accident those words could still haunt and chill him.

"Will, an ambulance is on the way. Don't try to move. But, can you talk? Say something?" She leaned closer, the wisps of her hair sliding across his cheek, which felt like it had been ripped off.

"Say something to me, please," she whispered, and he thought he saw a few tears slide down her cheeks.

Say something. He had to say something. Make all this stop. She could cry when he was full dead instead of just half.

"Believe me now?" he rasped.

A pained expression crossed her face and she looked up, her face turning into a flashing red light.

"The ambulance is here," she said quietly. "I'm going to go flag them down. Don't—"

But he gripped her arm with the one hand that was functioning and didn't feel like it was being stabbed by a machete. "Don't go." He had the panicked thought that if she left he *would* die, and he found he wasn't quite interested in that prospect.

"I'll get them."

Will didn't know whose voice that was. He only knew it was male and Will didn't particularly care for it. Had she been on a date?

But he didn't have time to dwell on that uncomfortable thought as footsteps and voices surrounded them. Then he was being touched and prodded and moved, and he tried to bite back groans of pain, but he couldn't manage it.

Then he was on a stretcher, being moved and jerked into an ambulance.

"Gracie."

"I'm here," she said, and though he couldn't see her with the paramedics looming over him, a slim, cool hand slid into his.

More voices, more movement, a door slam. And through it all, Gracie's hand held his. Like she'd been doing for the past two years. The only person he'd come to rely on.

"What happened?" she asked gently as a paramedic shined a light into one eye and then the other.

"The brakes and steering went out."

The paramedic worked on him, but Will couldn't seem to force himself to let go of Gracie's hand.

"It wasn't any accident, Gracie. It wasn't."

She didn't say anything to that so he attempted to squeeze her hand, even though it hurt like hell.

"Gracie?"

"Deputy Mosely is looking at your car. There'll be an investigation."

Will snorted, then swallowed down a gasp of pain. "Yeah, I know how those go." He could feel her sigh of a breath against his temple. She moved so he could look at her while the paramedic did something awful to his arm that wasn't holding on to Gracie.

Her big brown eyes were filled with tears and worry, and he wanted to look away from that kind of emotion, but God, it hurt too bad to even close his eyes.

She touched his forehead again, a gentle glide of her fingertips. "Rest. Let's get you better, and then we'll figure out what's going on."

"You don't believe me," he said flatly.

"I don't know what to believe," she returned on a pained whisper.

But it wasn't him. Never him.

Chapter Four

"There's evidence of tampering."

Gracie looked up at Laurel, who stood in the waiting room at the hospital, dressed in her detective khakis and county sheriff's department polo, looking serious and stern.

Believe me now? Will's words kept looping around in her head whether she was dozing or awake while she waited to hear the extent of Will's injuries. Which they wouldn't tell her because she was no one to Will.

"Can you find out how he's doing?"

Laurel smiled thinly. "You know I can't. They're not going to tell you anything, either. Why don't you go home? Get some rest. Come back later."

Gracie shook her head, linking her hands in an effort to keep her composure. If she dug her fingernails into the tops of her hands she could focus on the pinch instead of the guilt swamping her.

She'd been *this* close to deleting his message unheard, and she just… He would have died. He would have died. He'd be *dead* if she had done that. "What kind of tampering was it?"

"You know I can't tell you that, either." Laurel was firm, but apologetic. If Gracie didn't know Laurel as well as she did she might have tried to beg, wheedle or manipulate, but Laurel wouldn't budge. She took her badge more seriously than she took just about everything.

"He's in danger," Gracie said flatly.

"I think that's a safe assumption."

Gracie met Laurel's gaze. "You know what this means."

Laurel sighed. "Not necessarily. If it has something to do with Paula Cooper's crash… It's been years. There was no tampering done to her car back then. There's no evidence this connects at all."

"Yet."

Laurel sighed again and slid into the seat next to Gracie. "I'm going to look into it. If I find a link, I'll investigate it, but you both need to understand this is for the police to figure out."

Gracie knew Laurel was right, but she also knew Will had come to Rightful Claim, told her he'd figured out a pattern and then his car had been tampered with. Those couldn't be coincidences.

Laurel would be thorough, Gracie had no doubt. Even if Laurel wasn't getting married to a Carson, Gracie knew her cousin too well to ever think she'd not follow a lead just because the deceased was a Carson. If there was some connection, Laurel would find it.

Eventually. But Will was in a hospital room with who knew what kind of injuries and Gracie knew she didn't have time for eventually.

"Gracie." Laurel's voice took on a sterner tone. "Promise me you two will let the police handle this."

Gracie didn't want to lie to her cousin, but she also didn't know how she could possibly agree.

"Ms. Delaney?"

Both her and Laurel turned to the nurse, who smiled kindly. Melina knew both of them because their work often brought them to the hospital and since Melina had been Gracie's babysitter once upon a time. "Not you, Deputy. Gracie, Mr. Cooper is able to see visitors now, and he's asked for you, if you'd like to go back."

Gracie hopped to her feet, but so did Laurel.

"I'll need to speak with Mr. Cooper."

Melina nodded. "That'll be fine, but he specifically asked for Gracie. Room 203."

Laurel started striding that way, but Gracie hurried in front of her. "Laurel, listen, I need you to do me a favor."

"I'm here in a professional capacity."

"Please, let me go alone."

"Gracie."

"Please, just… Just give me a few minutes alone. I'm not asking you not to question him, I'm just asking that you let me… Look…" She swallowed at the emotion clogging her throat. "Maybe you don't understand why, but I feel responsible. At least partially. If I'd handled this even remotely differently—"

"You don't know what would have happened."

"Maybe not, but… As my best friend and my cousin and just the best human being I know, please give me five minutes alone with him. Personal minutes."

Laurel sighed heavily. "Five minutes. And I'm right outside the door."

Gracie gave Laurel an impulsive hug. "Thank you." Five minutes wasn't enough really. She'd probably cry when she saw him again. After all, she'd cried in that ambulance. Hopefully Will didn't remember that.

Still, she'd need those few minutes to try to work through all this…stuff. Guilt. Worry. The desperate need to fix what she'd almost irreparably broken.

She and Laurel walked silently to the room number Melina had given them. Laurel gave a little nod and leaned against the wall next to the door. She glanced at her watch meaningfully.

Five minutes. Gracie blew out a breath and knocked on the door before pushing the door open. It was a small room, but the blinds were open to the bright sunshine outside.

Will sat in his bed and slowly turned to look at her as she closed the door behind her. One arm was in a cast, and his face was a maze of bandages. There was a hospital sheet over the bottom half of his body so she couldn't see what kind of damage had been done down there.

He was beat-up and clearly a mess, and still he loomed too large in that bed. Like it didn't matter he'd been pulverized by metal and concrete, he could take it. She almost believed it when he simply sat there and stared at her.

"Hi," she offered from where she stood rooted by the door.

"Hey," he returned, and his voice didn't sound like

him at all. She couldn't read his expression, either. Maybe it was just pain.

She walked haltingly to his bedside knowing she had to say whatever it was she was going to say before her five minutes were up and Laurel came in to question him.

He frowned at her as she came to stand beside his bed. "You... You've been here the whole time?"

It was then she realized what he was looking so quizzically at. The dried blood on her sleeve she'd gotten from touching him out there on that frigid roadside.

When she looked back at his face, he was staring hard at hers.

"You haven't slept," he said, as though that were some great surprise.

"I was waiting to hear... I didn't know how bad off you were. You passed out in the ambulance."

"I don't... I don't remember that. The ambulance."

"What do you remember?"

"Your voice."

Gracie inhaled and then forgot to exhale. It didn't mean anything that she was the thing he remembered. It didn't mean he cared or this mattered, and as guilty as she felt about almost letting him *die*, she couldn't let herself get wrapped up in thinking there was some change here. He was still Will, and she was just...his supplier.

"Gracie." His non-cast arm moved and before she realized what he was doing, he'd taken her hand in his. There was a bandage on top of his hand, and still he gripped her tight. She stared at it.

"Gracie, look at me."

She forced herself to take her gaze off his much bigger, and far more battered, hand squeezing hers.

His blue gaze was earnest and desperate. A look she recognized, and one that made her heart pinch. Because before last night she would have felt sorry for him, wondered if he needed therapy.

Today, she knew that desperation wasn't out of place, and that maybe, just maybe, Will's obsession with the case wasn't wrong or sad or an attempt not to deal with the complicated feelings about his wife's infidelity or death.

"You have to get me out of here," he said, his gaze never leaving hers. "As soon as possible."

WILL HURT JUST about everywhere and he knew pretty soon a nurse would come in and pump him full of all sorts of crap.

He preferred the pain. The pain kept him centered, and it reminded him of one simple truth.

He'd been right. All along, he'd been right. Whoever Paula had been having an affair with—whether they'd been involved in her death or not—needed to keep it a secret. He didn't know how someone had figured out Will had a clue, but clearly someone had.

Still, Gracie wasn't saying anything. Her hand was limp in his, but she leaned closer. She was a mess. Maybe not physically abused like he currently was, but exhaustion was etched across her sweet face. She had his blood on her shirt and a rip in her jeans. He wondered if it had come from kneeling next to him on the rough asphalt.

He didn't remember much of anything. Not the crash itself, not the ambulance ride, but he remembered those few seconds of in between where he'd been lying there on fire and freezing at the same time and Gracie suddenly being next to him.

"Will," she whispered. "Laurel is right outside."

He blinked. Then nodded. "We'll discuss it later then."

"There isn't anything to discuss. You have to stay in the hospital till a doctor clears you."

But she still whispered, as if she was afraid her cop cousin was listening. It gave him some hope he could convince her, but it'd have to wait. He was just afraid he didn't have much time.

He *was* hurt, which meant he couldn't fight anyone off. He probably shouldn't drive with his arm in a cast, and hell, he didn't have a car anymore anyway. He'd decided his only chance of survival had been to jump out of the car.

Had he jumped out? He couldn't actually remember it. But they hadn't found him in his car, so he had to have done it.

He lifted his nonbroken arm and pressed fingers to his temple, trying to concentrate on the here and now instead of all the fuzziness around the accident.

Here. Now. He needed help, and Gracie was the only one he could trust. He looked up at her. "You do believe me now, don't you?"

She finally wrapped her fingers around his, just a

slight pressure. "Of course I do. How could I not?" She swallowed, and she lifted her free hand as if to touch him.

He found himself intensely wishing she would, but instead she dropped the hand. "I'm sorry."

"About what?"

"You don't know how close I was to not listening to your message," she said, her voice still a whisper though he didn't think it was about not being heard this time. She looked miserable and devastated. "I was going to delete it. I was cutting you off and it haunts me. If I'd deleted it—"

He hated that look of anguish and guilt on her face. He'd never understood why she'd taken so much of *him* on her shoulders, and he'd never spent much time trying to figure it out. But she'd been helping him for two years, the only actual person who'd stayed a part of his life after Paula's death. She shouldn't feel guilty about anything when she'd been the only one who'd stuck. This girl who had no connection to him prior to telling him his wife had died.

"You would have been right to delete it," Will said firmly. He didn't need her guilt. He needed her help. "I get lost in it all and I don't see beyond it, but you do. You have a life and people who care about you and I know I sound crazy half the time. How could you be as invested in it as me? She wasn't your wife or even anyone you knew."

She studied his face as if she was searching for some particular emotion, but he didn't know what she was looking for, what she wanted. So, he needed to bring the conversation back to where it belonged.

"I need to prove that I'm right. If someone killed her they should pay. There should be some justice."

"You're right. Someone tried to kill *you*. You should have justice, too. And I'm going to help you find it." She held his gaze, bent over him like this, hand still in his. "I promise you, no matter what happens, I'm going to help you find the truth." Her dark eyes blazed with that promise. She had such a certainty about her, such an earnestness. He'd never known anyone quite like her. Dedicated and sweet. She cared about people enough to act on it, enough to help.

He didn't understand her at all, and still she stood over him in this obnoxious hospital bed, her light brown hair glowing near to red in the sunlight streaming through his window. Something fluttered low in his gut, a kind of awareness that prickled over his skin.

He'd noticed before, once or twice, a moment drawn out too long. Noticed the shape of her mouth, or…other parts of her. Exactly like this, a kind of faraway thing that was easy to put out of his mind. They'd always been working on the case. Pictures of Paula's accident or reports about it or… It had always been easy to shift away from that awareness.

Maybe it was the drugs they'd pumped him full of that made it harder to shift now.

But a knock sounded on the door and Gracie all but jumped away from him as if they'd been, well, anything other than just *staring* at each other holding hands.

Laurel Delaney stepped into the room looking very official. Will scowled.

"Mr. Cooper, I need to ask you a few questions."

"About whoever tried to kill me because I got too close to finding the truth?"

He'd give Deputy Delaney credit—she didn't flinch nor did she dig her heels in. She kept that calm, equitable expression on her face and nodded. "There was some evidence of someone tampering with your car. Well, what was left of it."

"Am I supposed to be surprised?"

"Do you have any ideas who might have wanted to cause you harm, Mr. Cooper?"

"Oh, just the man who was having an affair with my wife and probably caused *her* car accident in almost the exact same place."

"Your late wife had no evidence of car tampering. It's also been two years. What would cause someone to come after you now?"

"I found a connection. A clue. It's why I found Gracie at your party. I told her that I had found something, right there in Rightful Claim. Then we talked outside. Anyone could have heard me and gotten to my car."

"So, your theory is we're all living amongst a killer and have been for two years?"

"Yeah, it is."

Laurel pressed her lips together, clearly irritated with his steadfast determination. Still, when she spoke, her voice was even and controlled. "Do you have any evidence? Anything that might be able to help us solve this?"

"There was a piece of paper. In my clothes. I'd written it down." He glanced from Deputy Delaney to Gracie. "Did they find it?"

The women exchanged a glance and Laurel pulled a small notebook from her breast pocket. She scribbled a few things on it. "I'm going to see if we can find a piece of paper. What kind of information does it have on it?"

"Dates. A few phrases I thought might hint at where they were meeting. I have the information on her computer, though." He glanced at Gracie and, without him even having to ask, she nodded.

"I'll run over and get you some of your things," she said.

"You need some sleep," Laurel interrupted.

Gracie opened her mouth, likely to argue, but as much as Will didn't want to agree with Laurel Delaney, she was right. "You've been here all night. You need to sleep."

"I haven't had parents for twenty years. I know how to take care of myself, thank you very much."

"Gracie—"

She held up her hand at Laurel and Laurel stopped. "Neither of you are in charge of me. Now, I will run over to Will's to grab his computer. Is there anything else you'd like while I'm there?"

Since he'd never once heard Gracie use that firm, don't-you-dare-argue tone, he decided it was best to heed its icy warning. "No, ma'am."

"That's settled then. I'll be back." She turned on a heel and headed for the door, and even though he wanted to say more, he didn't. Because Deputy Delaney was still there, staring at him with that inscrutable cop face.

He knew she didn't believe him. He'd never expected her to, but there being evidence of tampering in his car meant she was going to have to investigate this. She was probably going to get in his way or get him killed in all reality. Because she didn't believe enough of his story to not be a speed bump rather than offer any actual help.

"She has nothing to do with this," Laurel said, nodding to where Gracie had disappeared.

"Excuse me?"

"She has nothing to do with this. If you're in danger, by allowing her to help you, you're putting her in danger. Is that what you want?" He glanced at the door, then back at Laurel.

The thought of Gracie in danger made his stomach turn, because he'd certainly never considered that. But the thought of trying to solve this without her had a flutter of panic settling into his gut. He tried not to let either emotion show on his face. Deputy Delaney didn't need any extra ammunition. "You really think I could stop her?"

Laurel's mouth curved briefly. "You could at least try."

Chapter Five

Gracie drove, white-knuckle against the slick, icy roads, and tried to ignore the way exhaustion was creeping into her. She didn't have time to be hungry, or tired. There was so much to do.

Her mind was so busy going through all the things she needed to accomplish—first and foremost convincing Will he needed to stay put in the hospital until his doctors cleared him—she didn't notice tire tracks in the snowy road until she was almost halfway up the mountain to Will's cabin.

It had snowed last night. There shouldn't be any tracks leading up here because any tracks Will had made coming down last night would have been mostly filled—not deep and fresh.

Someone had tampered with Will's car, enough so he'd had to jump out of the vehicle to save himself. It could only be a very bad sign that there were tracks leading up to his cabin now so soon after.

The problem was there wasn't really anywhere to stop or turn around, not with how icy and narrow the winding mountain road was. But if someone was up there, someone who'd purposefully hurt Will, Gracie didn't think it would be best for her to head up there, either.

She studied the road, the snow, the way her truck was beginning to lose traction as she eased off the accelerator. She needed to find a place to stop, to gather her thoughts.

There was a slight flat spot on the curve, though it would mean parking perilously close to a very steep drop off, and she wasn't 100 percent sure her truck would fit the small space. But it was the only choice. *The only choice.*

She repeated those three words to herself as she navigated her truck toward the flat patch. She had to fight the urge to squeeze her eyes shut when the tires skidded on the ice. She gripped the steering wheel harder no matter how badly her hands were beginning to ache, and she carefully tapped the brake as she moved closer and closer to that awful edge.

It took a full minute to realize the truck had stopped and she was no longer moving forward or sideways. She was safe and still, right on the edge of the road.

She swallowed, breathed and then slowly peeled her hands off the steering wheel, wincing at the pain in her joints. But she was okay. Parked and okay.

She turned off the engine, studying the tire tracks that led up and around the last curve before Will's cabin came into view. She kept her gaze on the curve as she reached over and blindly pawed through her purse for her phone.

She pulled up Laurel's entry and hit Call and only when Laurel answered did Gracie remember to breathe.

But at the same time Laurel spoke her greeting, the front of a car appeared on that curve, coming down. Gracie dove across the seats, losing her phone in the process. She lay there hoping they'd mistake her truck as abandoned. There was no way they'd miss it parked here, but they'd have a hard time stopping their own car, especially going *down* the slick road. Of course, they'd gone up it at some point and—

A loud bang almost simultaneous with the sound of breaking glass had Gracie shrieking as shards of driver's-side window shattered over her. She wanted to scream again, but she had enough presence of mind to know she had to be quiet. She had to focus.

The car hadn't moved, so she could only assume the bang and breaking of glass hadn't been them crashing into her, but them shooting at her.

The motor of the other car was still running and Gracie tried to focus on that. She didn't know how many people there were in the vehicle, but surely they'd have to stop for any of them to get out. Were they stopped?

But she listened, eyes squeezed shut, body frozen in its prone position across the front seats. The engine got quieter and quieter until she could barely hear it at all.

Oh God, had they left? Just shot and left?

Please God.

She decided it was safe to move, though she didn't get out of the truck yet. They could have left men behind. That could have been a warning and they were going to turn around at the bottom and come back up.

She had no idea who it was or what they were after, so she could only try to protect herself as best she could.

Find her phone, then try to get to Will's cabin. Maybe on foot. She wasn't too far away and she could get into Will's place and find his rifle. It wasn't foolproof, but it was the best she could do.

She peered down at the floor of the truck and grabbed her phone. The previous call had ended, but Gracie redialed Laurel's number as she carefully maneuvered back into a sitting position. She glanced at where the car had to have gone, and didn't see or hear anyone returning, so she pushed out of her truck and onto the snowy road.

"I have two county deputies headed toward Will's cabin," Laurel said by way of greeting. "What the hell is going on? Did you crash, too?"

"No. I… Someone drove down from Will's cabin and shot my car."

"Shot? Jesus, Gracie, did you call 911?"

"No, it just broke my window. I'm fine." She stumbled a little bit in a drift of snow as she tried to jog the distance to Will's cabin.

"Someone is shooting at you. You're not fine. This is not fine."

"I parked on the road and I'm walking up to the cabin. Hang up with me and tell your deputies to stop anyone going down this road. I'm going to hole up in Will's cabin, with his rifle, and wait for someone to give me a ride home. I'll deal with my broken window later." But Laurel wasn't listening. Gracie could hear her talking to someone else.

"I've radioed them to stop anyone coming down from that road, but did you get a look at the car? Color? Make? Anything?"

Gracie tried to think back to the brief glimpse of car she'd seen before she'd dived across the seats. "I can't... I don't know. I didn't get a good look. I tried to hide."

"That's fine. That road shouldn't have any traffic on it, and as long as we're not too late someone will stop him. Now, you—"

Gracie smelled the smoke before she saw it. At first she didn't think much of it. It was winter. Fireplaces or bonfires or— But then she saw the smoke and broke out into a dead run, ignoring Laurel's words in her ears.

The cabin came into view and Gracie gasped. "Call the fire department."

"Gracie, what—"

"I have to see what I can save."

"Gracie!"

But she couldn't listen to Laurel tell her it was dangerous. She clicked the phone off and stared at Will's pretty little cabin up in flames. Whatever evidence he'd collected over the years likely going up with it.

She couldn't let that happen.

WILL KNEW HE was being an ass to the nurses. He felt a modicum of guilt, but no one would let him out of here and he didn't think that was legal. The only thing keeping him in this obnoxious bed was the fact he wasn't quite desperate enough to rip the IV out of his arm.

He eyed the needle attached to his broken arm. Surely it couldn't be that difficult to take it off. He peeled one side of the tape off, but before he could start experimenting with medical equipment removal, his door flew open.

Not gently or with a knock like the nurses did either, and visiting hours were over. Gracie had never returned with his computer, but he figured she'd taken a much-needed nap and he'd get his hands on it tomorrow.

Instead, Gracie stumbled into his room as if she'd been pushed, and he frowned because there were black smudges over the same clothes she'd been wearing this morning. It looked like she'd had the same black on her face and tried to wash it off but instead left a streaky kind of gray complexion.

Laurel was behind her looking furious.

"What's going on?" he demanded.

Laurel jerked her chin at him. "Tell him," she ordered.

Gracie heaved a sigh, looking at her feet, then the window, anywhere but at him or Laurel.

"There was a bit of an incident," Gracie said cryptically.

"What the hell does that mean?"

"Well, when I got to your cabin…" She cleared her throat. "It was on fire."

He struggled to sit up straighter. "Fire. What? I don't…"

"She's leaving out quite a few pieces of the story," Laurel said, anger and frustration written on every line of her face. Which was weird, because mostly he'd only ever seen Laurel cool and calm and detached. Cop-like. This was not any of those things.

"I drove up to your cabin, and when I got there—"

"Before she got there a strange vehicle came down the mountain from your cabin, shot at *her*—"

"At my car. I don't think they saw me."

Laurel flung her arms up in the air, as agitated as he'd ever seen the woman. "I can't believe you're being so ridiculous. You are too smart for this, Gracie Delaney."

"You are overreacting, *Laurel Delaney*. My God, I am a grown woman and—"

"Someone needs to tell me what the hell is going on," Will demanded.

"—you can't boss me around anymore. I'm not your ward and I never was."

"I am not trying to boss you around. I'm your cousin. I love you. You—"

"Ladies," he said fiercely.

"—were reckless and foolish and you need some damn sleep."

"I will—"

Finally he used his fingers to whistle as long and as loud as he could. Both women glared at him, but at least they'd stopped yelling over each other.

"I want an explanation and I want it now since apparently my house was *on fire* and Gracie is covered in…" His brain clicked to the most horrible thought possible. "You weren't in the cabin, were you?"

"Well, not…not exactly."

"Stop talking in riddles," he said between clenched teeth, grasping the IV tower to fight the impulse to cross the room and give her a little shake.

"When I saw the cabin was on fire, I... Well, I carefully poked around to see if I could get to your comp—"

"You did what?" Will demanded, jumping out of bed.

"Sit down," Gracie and Laurel ordered in unison.

He didn't sit down, but he didn't move toward them since he was in a ridiculous hospital gown. He stood next to his bed, furious, and holding on to the damn IV tower with everything he had.

"What possessed you to risk your life for *anything* in that place?" he said, doing his best to speak normally instead of a growl. It didn't go so well.

Gracie turned to Laurel. "Would you give us a few minutes alone?" When Laurel only scowled, Gracie reached out and squeezed her cousin's arm. "Please."

Laurel huffed out a breath. "Fine. But I'm right outside, and in ten minutes you are done here. Ten minutes and we are getting you some dinner and a bed to sleep in."

Gracie nodded, then just stood there as Laurel marched out of the hospital room. Finally she turned to face him, a paltry smile curving her lips. "So, how are you?"

She was standing there covered in black soot. She'd been... He could picture it all too well and it made him sick to his stomach. "What were you thinking?"

"It was your evidence. Two years of your life. I was careful. I'm not stupid. But I had to try."

"This isn't your fight. You shouldn't have... You shouldn't have done that, Gracie. It was just things. You could've..." So many could'ves and they all horrified him down to his soul.

"What does it matter?" she asked, and it finally clicked why her voice sounded all wrong. She'd inhaled smoke.

What did it matter? She'd risked herself and… "It matters. Of course it matters."

"Why? You don't care about me."

She could've shot him for the force of that blow. "Gracie," he exhaled.

"I'm not saying you actively wish me harm, but I'm kind of nothing to you. A means to an end. So I was being your means, and in the end I didn't do anything. I couldn't get to the computer." She shrugged, and he couldn't read her at all. "So, I don't know why you're scolding me or why it matters."

He could only stand there and stare at her. She wasn't making any sense, and he just wanted… He just… There was something all twisted up in his chest or his gut and he couldn't unwind it. He couldn't make sense of how much he didn't like her saying *you don't care about me*.

"I did what I had to do," she continued in that same maddeningly even voice, like this wasn't messed up. "I was careful. I don't need scolding or disapproval. I'm a grown woman. You should be more concerned about the fact someone burned your cabin down."

"I'm more concerned about the fact someone shot at you and then you decided to run into a burning building."

She folded her arms across her chest, her nose going up in the air. "Those are gross exaggerations."

Screw the hospital gown. He crossed the room because maybe erasing the space between them would help him make sense of her.

But she was standing there, soot covered and exhaustedly pale. "You will not risk your safety for this. Do you understand me?"

"What I understand is you're not the boss of me, Will. You're not the anything of me."

That horrible knot in his chest only tied tighter and sharper. It didn't make sense. *She* didn't make sense. His hand itched to…do something, touch her or…something. Which also didn't make sense and so he just stood there frozen and confused. Something like anger starting to work through him.

"You know what? I don't care. I don't care if I'm not your boss or in charge of you or what, you won't dare risk your life for this again. Period. This is my thing and whoever this person is, he's after *me*. You won't be hurt in this. I won't allow it. Go home. Get some sleep and… You'll stay away from me until this is solved."

"Like hell."

Something inside of him snapped, that tight knot maybe. Because he stepped closer. So close their noses were almost touching and he could see the darker flecks of brown in her eyes. "Get it through your head that I cannot bear the thought of you being hurt by this."

She stared up at him, though something in her posture softened. Then she reached out. If he wasn't so churned up or whatever he might have sidestepped her cool, small hand pressing against his cheek.

It was nearly impossible to breathe through that. All those tight knots inside him loosened, but the spaces filled with something else. Something familiar and dangerous and he shoved it all away and used his good hand to pull hers off his face.

But he didn't let her hand go. It seemed odd her hands were so small when she was such a force. So strong and determined, but her hand in his felt fragile somehow. So he met her gaze, and that didn't help him understand anything that was happening, but at least it gave him her to focus on.

"Go home. Get some sleep. Be safe, my God. But you need rest. You know you do."

She swallowed. "Okay, on one condition. You promise you'll stay put. Do what the doctors say. Don't try to get out of here. Not without me. Please."

He glanced at the IV stand, then her hand in his again. He had to get out of here. He knew he did, but... "Okay." He squeezed her hand. As much as he needed to get out of here, he needed her, too. "I promise."

Chapter Six

Gracie would admit to precisely no one she felt like she was going to pass out and throw up at the same time.

She stepped out of Will's hospital room, and maybe she could blame the dazed double vision on the fact Will had voluntarily touched her. He'd taken her hand and squeezed it and made a promise to her and…

She was probably hallucinating, really.

"I don't want you going back to your house," Laurel said, popping up out of seemingly nowhere. "It's not safe."

"They or he or whoever it was didn't see me."

"They saw your truck. Which Vanessa has taken care of by the way."

"A Carson is taking care of my truck? Vanessa Carson at that?"

Laurel wrinkled her nose. "I know, but she promised to be on her best behavior. I would have had Cam do it, but I gave him a different job."

"Laurel, please tell me you didn't."

But Laurel didn't tell her anything. She led her to the

entrance of the hospital and there was Cam, Laurel's brother, freshly home from a stint as a marine.

"I don't need a bodyguard. Cousin or otherwise," Gracie grumbled.

"And here I was hoping to get some practice in," Cam replied. For as military as he appeared on the outside, Gracie had grown up with him. Cam was strong and somewhat detached, but he was kind. All the Delaney cousins had made her feel welcome and part of the family even when their parents hadn't.

"Cam's going to start a security business now that he's home for good."

"That's great," Gracie replied, trying not to seem ungrateful. She smiled at Cam. "I don't need security."

"The shot-out window on your vehicle says otherwise," Cam replied gently. "It isn't safe for you to be alone until Laurel determines what's going on. I'm going to take you to your place to gather your things, then we'll head to the Delaney Ranch."

"If I'm not safe, why would you bring me home? I'm not sure your father would care for that."

"Dad can deal," Laurel said firmly. "I've already told him as such. I've also told Cam to bar the door to your bedroom until you've slept eight hours."

"I don't like this," Gracie said firmly. But exhaustion had stolen her will to fight or do much of anything.

"Feed her before she sleeps," Laurel instructed Cam.

Gracie figured she must be really be exhausted because she couldn't even work up a comment about how she didn't need someone forcing her to eat. She could only follow Cam out to his truck.

Cam said something, but Gracie yawned and couldn't make it out. The next thing she knew, she startled awake in a dark room. The bed was comfortable and something about it all was familiar.

But she didn't remember getting here. She didn't remember anything from the hospital parking lot on.

Her phone chimed and she realized that's what had woken her up. She glanced at the time on her phone screen. Five in the morning. Which meant she'd actually slept something like twelve hours if not more. The light of the phone also gave her a clue as to where she was.

The Delaney Ranch. When her parents had died, she'd bounced around from family member to family member until fifth grade. Then she'd landed at the Delaney Ranch with her four cousins and had stayed through high school.

Though her cousins had been great, Gracie'd had no illusions Uncle Geoff considered her one of his own. Even if she was his late brother's only child.

Gracie scrubbed her hands over her face and tried to focus her brain on the present. Text message. Someone had texted her. At five in the morning?

She opened the message. From Will.

Meet me at my cabin.

She frowned at her phone. Will had promised to stay put. He had promised. Why would he be at the cabin before the sun even rose and when it had been on fire not all that long ago? Besides, he didn't have a car. His had been totaled. How would he have gotten there?

Something didn't add up and she needed to figure it out.

Coffee. Good lord, she needed coffee. And food. She got out of bed and stumbled to the door. It was weird, as many years as she'd spent living at the Delaney Ranch, it had never felt like home. She'd been a permanent guest at best.

On a sigh, she headed for the kitchen. The smell of food and coffee about made her whimper.

When Gracie stepped into the kitchen, her cousin Jen was standing in front of the big stove, humming all too happily for 5:00 a.m. She turned and smiled at Gracie. "I'd hoped you'd sleep longer."

Gracie only grunted. Jen moved to the coffee maker and poured a generous mug before sliding it in front of Gracie. "You just let me know when you're functioning. Cam's doing some kind of recon nonsense. Dylan and Dad are doing the ranch chores." She frowned. "Dad's been acting so weird this week," she muttered.

"He doesn't want me here."

Jen waved it away. A few minutes later she put a plate full of eggs, bacon and toast slathered in butter in front of Gracie.

"Have I ever told you I love you with all my heart?"

Jen grinned. "Not since you lived here and I made you breakfast back then."

Gracie dove into the breakfast and coffee and felt almost human once she was finished. But feeling human meant figuring out what was going on with that cryptic text message.

"Do you know where Laurel is?"

"Sleeping, hopefully. But she has to be back at it tonight, and she did say you could wake her up if it's important."

"No. That's fine. I don't suppose you have a car I could borrow?"

"Sorry. I've got to be at the store at seven, but I can drop you off somewhere. Cam could probably pick you up whenever you need another ride."

"Cam and Laurel didn't insist you keep me here till I have some kind of shadow?"

Jen laughed. "Of course they did. I'm just not listening."

Gracie chuckled, but it died as she stared at the text message on her phone again.

Surely Will wasn't up at that burned-down cabin freezing his butt off waiting for her. He wouldn't have broken his promise to her. She really hoped.

"Can you drop me off at the hospital?"

"Sure, but they're not going to let you in to see Will at this hour."

"I know, but I'd rather wait there than here. I don't want to run into your dad. Sorry."

"*I'm* sorry," Jen replied.

"Don't be. You're perfect and my favorite person right about now."

"How about some more food?"

Gracie frowned at her phone. Something wasn't right. But if Will had broken his promise… "Sure, I'll take a little more."

WILL STARED AT the needle in his arm. He'd promised Gracie he'd stay put, but it was almost seven in the morning and how long could he be expected to reasonably keep a promise?

Someone had tried to kill him. Someone had burned down his cabin, and all the evidence he'd compiled over two years trying to figure out who his wife had been sleeping with was certainly gone.

Which meant he *had* to be so close. Or at least they thought he was. But what had he done differently in the days leading up to his car being tampered with that might lead someone to think he knew?

The only thing he could think of was going into Rightful Claim. Had someone in that bar heard him talk to Gracie and assumed he'd come up with the killer's identity? Panicked and messed with his car? What exactly had he said that night? All he remembered was telling her he had new information.

And her telling him she cared about him.

But that wasn't important right now. What was important was someone must have overheard that conversation and thought he had more information than he did.

No matter how often he tried to tell himself to be methodical and rational when working this all out, the only reason to tamper with his car, burn his cabin, shoot at Gracie—*Christ*—was they had killed Paula in the first place. An affair wasn't a big enough thing to cover up with murder, but murder certainly was.

Which meant he couldn't be stuck here. Both a sitting duck and ineffective when someone was out there trying to get rid of him and all his stuff. When someone had shot at Gracie, who had nothing to do with this. Not really.

Keeping his promise to her was only putting her in

more danger. Yeah. Exactly. He ignored the pit of guilt and began to pick the edge of the tape on his arm.

Again, just as he was getting somewhere, the door opened.

Gracie stepped in, but stopped short at the sight of him. "You're here," she said, frowning.

"Of course I'm here. Where else would I be?" He surreptitiously smoothed the tape back into place.

She looked down at the phone she was holding in one hand. "Did you text me a few hours ago?"

"Text you? What? I don't even have my phone. Laurel said they didn't uncover any of my belongings from the accident. Burned or lost in the snow."

Gracie's eyes widened and she let out a whoosh of breath.

"What's going on?" he demanded.

She took a few careful steps toward his bed. "Or maybe your stuff was taken," she said gravely. "Someone texted me from your number at five this morning asking me to meet them at the cabin." She held out the screen to him and he squinted at the text.

Meet me at my cabin.

"Someone has my phone and is trying to lure you to them." He flung the blankets off his body. Luckily they'd let him change into regular clothes last night so he didn't feel completely ridiculous, even if they were too-big sweats someone had left him at Gracie's behest. Because his clothes were burned up. "We have to get out of here."

"You haven't been cleared."

"They said they might release me today. We're just speeding it up a bit. Gracie, someone is after me. Actually, no, worse. Someone is after *you*."

"I think I've survived a little better than you have," she said, gesturing at his cast and IV and probably him in general.

"I won't give them a chance to do to you what they've done to me."

Dark brown eyes studied him with a kind of emotion he could only guess at. Something like hope, a warmth he hadn't seen from anyone else in years. For *years*, Gracie had been his only source of good.

If she'd felt pity for him, she'd hidden it well. Or maybe her pity didn't suffocate like the town's pity had when he'd still lived down there.

"Laurel has my cousin basically bodyguarding me. Sort of. I may have slipped away this morning."

"Don't slip away again," he said firmly. "Let someone watch out for you." He pointed to the phone still in her hand. "Someone is trying to lure you to an isolated spot, and using me to do it. You need to be protected." He didn't like the idea of this random cousin protecting her, but she was a Delaney. She had a million people on her side, and he had to trust that.

Her eyebrows drew together. "Who will protect you?"

Protect him? He'd never had anyone protecting him. Not really. He'd never known his dad, and for as long as he could remember his mom had been the one in need of protection from a string of men who'd always taken advantage of her. Then she'd married Phil and basically washed her hands of her useless son. He'd had Paula by then, and even though he couldn't believe his wife had *never* loved him, it hadn't lasted. Not the way it was supposed to.

"Will."

He shook his head. This was all ancient history. He needed to focus on a little more current history. Who was after him? What kind of man had been sleeping with his wife? "It doesn't matter. I don't need protecting," he muttered, trying to turn away.

But Gracie grabbed his good arm. "It matters to me. We're in this together, Will. You're in danger." She frowned down at her phone before shoving it into her coat pocket. "And I guess it's possible I'm in danger, too." She let her hand drop from his arm.

"Which is why—"

"We protect each other." She stood there, fierce warrior that she always was. It amazed him, the weight this tiny woman carried on her shoulders, how that sweet, soft demeanor could fool a person into thinking there was no steel underneath.

But he remembered, quite clearly, the day she'd come to his door to tell him Paula was dead. A quiet determination. A sense of purpose. A strength he'd envied when it felt like his world had been pulled out from under him.

"Then you have to get me out of here. I can't sit here and wait around. I have to get out there and figure out what's going on. I don't care if the police *are* looking into it this time. I'm the one who's been looking into it for two years. Paula's lover might have destroyed my evidence, but he can't destroy the things I know. I just have to work out the puzzle."

"*We*, Will," she said resolutely. *"We."*

"So, you'll get me out?"

"First, you have to understand and accept you can't shut me out of this. If I help you get out of here, then you are stuck with me until this is over. Cam and Laurel won't be happy with me, but they can't… Laurel can't bend the rules and Cam won't."

"But you will?"

"If you promise me we're in this together? Yes. I know Laurel did everything she could with Paula's case, but sometimes even our best isn't enough. You're right. You have the most evidence, the most stake. They're bound by rules. I don't have to be. But that doesn't mean we should work against them. I'm going to text Laurel about your number texting me. We want them investigating, too. We're just going to investigate…our way. Together."

He didn't want to risk her, but he couldn't do this alone, either. Not with a broken arm. She was the only one he trusted. She was the only one he had, and that wasn't just because of the circumstances he'd been living in the past year. It was her. Her strength and steadfastness and support.

He'd just have to be strong enough and smart enough to protect her, for as long as he needed her. He held out his arm with the IV needle in it. "All right. We're in this together."

She smiled and nodded, pulling her phone out. She typed in a text to Laurel about the phantom text message, then shoved the phone back in her pocket. "Okay, so how do we get out of here?"

"First, you're going to have to pull this out of me," he instructed.

She looked at the needle grimly, but she nodded. "Don't look."

Chapter Seven

"Crap," Gracie muttered.

"What?" Will demanded. His eyes were still squeezed shut even though she'd removed the IV needle a full minute ago. She'd even bandaged it up with a Band-Aid she'd found in one of the cabinets.

"I don't have a car." She released his hand reluctantly. "The IV is out. You can open your eyes."

He opened his eyes and looked down at where the IV had once been attached to his arm. "Not bad, coroner."

She smiled a little at that. "I may be used to working on dead bodies, but I do know something about basic bandaging. My car is at Carson Auto. I can't get it without Laurel or Cam finding me. It might not even be fixed yet."

"We have to try."

Gracie glanced at her watch. Surely Cam had found out Jen had given her a ride over to the hospital by now. He'd be mad and he'd be here any second. But Will was right: they had to try.

Gracie believed in doing things the right way, but she'd been willing to make exceptions for Will. Laurel would never approve of this. She'd want them to sit tight and wait and let the police do their jobs.

But sometimes the right way didn't get the truth. Clearly, since Paula's death had been ruled an accident. Gracie would have to leave Laurel and Cam and their rules behind if she wanted to help Will right now.

"We won't go out the front exit." She frowned at him. "You need a jacket."

"I'll live."

"It's December. You're injured. You need a jacket."

"Where are you going to find me one?"

That was a good question. There weren't any places in town that sold winter coats. Fairmont would be the closest place they could go for one. She could go prowling the hospital for unattended coats, but they didn't have time and she didn't want to draw attention to herself.

Her phone buzzed and she glanced at it, bracing for another text from Will's number. But this number was worse.

Cam.

If you're not in my truck, which is parked outside the main entrance, in three minutes, you will be sorry.

She had no doubt. But Cam waiting for her outside did give her an idea.

"We're going to have to be sneaky. And I'm going to feel super guilty about it, but it's the only way."

"Fine with me. Just save the guilt for once it's done."

Gracie nodded, but she couldn't help wincing as she typed up the lie.

Can you come up to Will's room instead? With an extra coat if you've got one. He lost his in the fire and they're going to let him out this afternoon.

Will read over her shoulder with a frown. "He's not going to help us. I can guarantee you that."

"No, but he might bring you a coat. I'm going to meet him in the lobby and ask him for the keys. I'm going to tell him to bring you the coat. While he does that, I'm going to move his truck to the back entrance, and you meet me there as soon as he leaves."

"Wow, that *is* sneaky. I'm impressed."

"What can I say? I'm an evil genius. Now it's your turn. We have to figure out where the heck we're going to go."

Will swore under his breath.

"Precisely. Get to thinking. I bet you have less than ten minutes all told." She shoved her phone into her pocket then forced herself to smile at Will. "Let's just hope this works."

He rubbed his good hand over his chin as he studied her, and something about the study was…different. Not his usual baffled *what is with you* or his calculating attempts to try to get her to do something. This was almost like he wanted to understand some piece of her.

She was clearly hallucinating.

"Good luck," he muttered.

Gracie nodded and headed for the door. "Back exit. Soon as he leaves. Or we're toast."

"Aye aye, Captain."

She didn't look back. Couldn't allow herself the precious seconds. She had to be in the lobby before Cam got to Will's room. She jogged down the hallway, then paused to make herself look calm and ambling before she pushed out the doors into the lobby.

Cam was already halfway across the room. He looked furious, but he had an old work coat swung over his arm.

"You're lucky I'm more pissed at Jen than I am at you."

"I only came to the hospital. I don't see what the big deal is."

"Do you recall someone shooting at you yesterday?"

"Not *at* me, per se."

His scowl deepened and Gracie hadn't thought that possible. "How can you be this resolutely obtuse?"

"Years of practice," she muttered. "Anyway, why don't you take the coat up to Will, huh?"

Cam's scowl morphed into something softer. "Why can't you take it up to him?"

Gracie tried to hide her wide-eyed surprise at his very reasonable question. "I can't… I can't…" Cam's eyes narrowed suspiciously, but Gracie knew at least one of Cam's weaknesses. Distressed female emotion.

She sniffled and looked away, working up looking emotional and hurt. If she pretended that she was upset over Will she had no doubt Cam would rush to do what she asked without demanding answers about what was going on. "Trust me, you don't want to know," she said in a wavering voice.

Cam grimaced. "Do I need to break his other arm?"

"No. Just…" She took a deep shaky breath, hoping she wasn't overselling it. "Give him his coat and let's go, please. I'd like to wait in your truck, though. They might let him out and I just… I can't…" She made a little noise, hoping it sounded like a sob.

"All right." He handed over the keys, looking supremely uncomfortable. "At least pay attention to your surroundings. Someone could be out there, Gracie. Someone *is* after you."

Gracie nodded, keeping her gaze averted in the hopes he thought she was crying.

He muttered something but he headed for the hallway to Will's room. She tried to walk at a normal pace toward the front entrance, but once she got out the doors she broke into a dead run toward Cam's truck parked in the very front.

She wasn't totally foolish. She looked around to make sure no one was following her. But she didn't think whoever had tried to kill Will knew much about *her*. Especially if she wasn't in her shot-out car.

Adjusting the seat so she could reach the pedals, she started the ignition at the same time. She peeled out of the parking spot and drove as quickly and safely as she could to the back of the hospital.

For every second that ticked by, she worried about what could happen. Cam could stop Will. A doctor could stop Will. Whoever was after him could intercept him in the hospital and really, truly harm him.

When the panic breathing came, she started counting through it. She would have made a terrible cop on a stakeout because she was ready to run screaming into the hospital, and when she glanced at the time on her phone she realized she'd been sitting here for no more than two minutes.

But those minutes crept by until her nerves were strung so tight she was one second away from turning off the truck and marching inside.

But that was when Will appeared out the back exit. Well, a lump in a coat that looked like the one Cam had been holding stepped out the door, but he walked right to Cam's truck and opened the passenger-side door.

He struggled a little bit while getting in, his injuries clearly hampering his mobility. Gracie tried not to let that worry her even more than she was already.

"So, where are we going?" she asked once he was seated and was struggling to fasten his seat belt.

"Let's head toward Fairmont for now," he said through gritted teeth, clearly in pain. So much so he was pale with it.

But she couldn't be distracted by pain or worry. Couldn't be distracted by the fact Cam would be furious, and might even stop her if she didn't get out of here now.

"Hold on to your hat," she offered before gunning the accelerator.

WILL TRIED TO think through the throbbing pain in every part of his body as Gracie drove far too fast down the highway to Fairmont. Past the scene of his accident, and then Paula's. It was strange to watch those places fly by knowing nothing was left of either wreck.

"Your cousin is going to come looking for his truck." Will felt the need to point it out.

"I know."

"Laurel probably already has county on our tails."

"She's not on duty until tonight," Gracie replied in that breezy way she had when she was lying about something.

"Okay, so say we make it to Fairmont undetected. Then what?" He winced as a bump had him hitting his elbow against the car door and jarring his broken arm.

"Then we… Well, I don't know. I got us out of the hospital. You come up with the rest." She heaved out a breath. "I'm having second thoughts, Will. What are we going to solve by running away?"

"We're not running away," he said firmly. "I mean *I* am running away from being stuck in that hospital, but we're not running away from the problem. We need somewhere to hunker down and think and…"

There were almost no businesses along the highway from Bent to Fairmont. Not even a gas station. But they'd just passed a sign for a motel two miles off the highway.

"Turn around."

"What?" Gracie demanded.

"Turn around and turn left at that sign."

"Why?" But she was slowing down. She reached a center divider and got onto the opposite side of the highway.

"There's a motel there. Off the highway. It might buy –

us some time since Cam and Laurel probably assume we've either gone to your place or Fairmont. They won't guess a motel." He had to hope.

"But why a motel?"

"I want to see if Paula ever stopped here."

Gracie was quiet after that, following the signs for the motel. The road toward it was windy and hidden, and there was a good chance no one would find them back here. It would buy them some time.

"I'm going to park the truck in this back lot just in case," Gracie said, pulling onto a patch of gravel behind the motel that was probably there for employees.

It was a squat sprawling building. Ramshackle at best. It may have been white once, but now it was just grayish brown—a mix of peeling paint and snow and mud. A few windows that had apparently been broken had been repaired with duct tape.

Will couldn't imagine his put-together late wife ever coming to a place like this. She would have run screaming in the opposite direction before ever parking. At least, that's what he'd thought, but he'd never imagined her an adulterer. But the mysterious "night" meetings, the coming home smelling like someone else, the giggling text messages she refused to show him.

He'd let a lot of it continue without confrontation for too long because he hadn't wanted to believe it. Not just the affair, but that everything he'd thought was true about her was a lie.

Gracie turned off the ignition and turned to face him. He couldn't exactly read her thoughts, but clearly she thought he was crazy. What else was new?

"What are we going to accomplish here?" she asked gently. The kind of gentle he didn't like from anyone, let alone her.

"I don't know who's after us or why, but I'm sure it has to do with the affair. If we can piece together the affair, then we can piece together what happened that night she died. And there's no way everything that happened in the past two days doesn't connect to that."

"I don't think you're wrong exactly, but… We're in danger. You especially. The further we dig into this, the more in danger we are."

"I know. And I hate that you're in danger because of me, but we can't go back now. We're already here in danger. Now, the only choice we have is to figure it out before they hurt you."

"Us. Hurt *us*."

"Look, Gracie…" He didn't know how to articulate what he wanted to say. "You shouldn't worry about me. Keeping you safe is our number one priority."

"Why would you be less of a priority than me?"

"We don't have time to argue," he muttered, moving to push open the car door.

"Then don't argue. Our safety is the number one priority. And for what it's worth, I can't find an argument for the theory it connects to the cheating, but I also know it isn't easy to… Well, you didn't want to know who the guy was."

"No, I didn't." Sometimes Will forgot Gracie had been there in those first dark days. So much so he wasn't even sure of all the things he might have laid at a stranger's feet when he'd been so blasted off his feet by her unexpected death.

He'd built himself up to a confrontation. To demand to know why she'd betrayed him. Instead, he'd gotten Gracie on his doorstep informing him Paula was dead.

He didn't have time to go back there. He had to move forward. "I didn't want to know much of anything about what an idiot I was when I was still in the midst of it, but I do want to know who killed her. I want there to be some justice for that. There's no reason to take these drastic measures against us if someone didn't kill her."

"Yeah, I think you're right, but..." Gracie looked at the building in front of them. "What are we looking for here?"

"We'll go in and ask if anyone knew Paula or remembers anything about her." Something he'd avoided for too long. He'd spent two years poring over records and emails and *things*. He'd never wanted to deal with people who might question why he needed answers for the death of a woman who'd been cheating on him.

There was no answer with that question, or, if there was, he didn't want to find it. He'd never wanted to find it.

But he couldn't hide anymore. He couldn't keep shying away from hard questions people might ask when Gracie's life was in danger.

"I'm sorry this is happening to you, Will. It isn't fair," she offered, apparently mistaking his hesitation for trepidation over the unfairness of it all. When in fact he was afraid he'd forgotten how to be a person who dealt with other people.

"Life isn't fair," he returned resolutely. Because it was true. Life had never been fair, so whether he knew how to be with people or not anymore, he had to do it. He reached for the door handle, wincing as he remembered that he wasn't sturdy or healthy. He had a broken arm and a million bruises.

"Let me open the door for you," Gracie said, already hopping out of the truck.

"No. You're not going to treat me like an invalid, broken arm or not." He got the door open himself before Gracie could hurry over and do it for him. He got out of the truck, trying to hide the shudder of pain that went through him when his boots landed on gravel.

He stood there in the parking lot for a second just breathing in the frigid Wyoming air. Everything hurt, body and soul, but he wasn't dead, even though someone had tried to kill him. And more important, Gracie was here, and he had to do everything in his power to protect her.

"I could do the asking. I can handle this and you can stay here," Gracie offered hopefully.

"You're the one who told me we were in this together, Gracie. That means no one stays behind. Besides, maybe she never stayed here. It's not her kind of place, that's for sure. And if she did, it'll be good for me to know. It's been a long time."

"Why is it good for you to know how awful she was? She's dead and it shouldn't matter. You're alive and good, and everything she did to you was wrong."

"But not wrong enough to die over."

"No, I know, but—"

"Paula might be dead, and drudging up the affair stuff might suck, but as much as I need to find out who killed her, I need to learn from my mistakes. You asked me what I thought would happen after I found out the truth, what would be next, and to be honest I don't have a clue. But something will have to change." He strode toward the motel, the strangest sense of purpose washing over him. Not that obsessive, driving need to find out what was right, as if answers would magically fix the broken things inside him.

An end. So he could have a new beginning.

Gracie fell into step next to him. "Her cheating on you wasn't your fault, so I don't think you need to learn anything."

Will smiled ruefully. "Maybe it wasn't my fault per se, but I wasn't a very good husband."

"How could anyone be a good husband to someone who could do what she did?"

Even though Gracie looked fairly young, he didn't often think of her that way. She had such a confidence and strength about her that often had him thinking she was older than she was. But the truth was that as much death as Gracie had seen in her job, she was still quite a few years younger than him and clearly had lived the kind of life that led you to believe in the goodness of other people.

All he had in him anymore was distrust. And something like, well, he didn't like the word *fear* because it seemed cowardly, but there was a certain amount of discomfort at the thought of letting anyone into his life. Clearly he didn't have the right instinct when it came to people.

He looked at the woman pulling the front door open. Maybe Gracie was the one exception to that. He might always be wrong about people, he might be a distant, warped human being these days, but he couldn't deny Gracie's goodness. Who could?

That was not why he was here though. He was here to solve a problem. Keep Gracie safe and figure out who'd killed Paula.

The order in which he thought of those two things was weird, but he didn't have time to consider it. He stepped inside. It smelled like cigarette smoke and maybe mildew or mold. Gracie wrinkled her nose and again Will was struck by how wrong this all was.

Paula was all about upscale and nice things. Any time they'd gone on vacation she'd insisted on the nicest amenities.

But she'd wanted to live in the run-down town of Bent, even when they'd had opportunity to move elsewhere. She'd always explained that away as wanting home, but maybe that had been an excuse.

"Maybe I'm going about this all wrong," Will muttered, staring at the water-stained walls of the motel lobby.

"You want to leave?"

"No, not this. I mean maybe I'm going about Paula all wrong. I assumed whoever she was cheating with was someone from our present, but I never thought about her past. She wanted to stay in Bent. When we decided to move here, she said she just loved home. This whole time I've been thinking the affair happened later in our marriage, but…"

It made his stomach roil, but if he could be betrayed later, why not always? "Maybe it was going on all along. Maybe the connection to this guy isn't one I ever knew or even considered, because maybe it's from her life in Bent *before* I came along."

"An ex-boyfriend?" Gracie mused.

"It's possible. I met her in Colorado when she was in college. She was the one who came up with the black-smith shop idea for me, and suggested I move here. That's when we got married. I didn't know much about her life before that. We didn't dwell on the past, but she wanted to live here. I liked it, too. It was fine with me."

Surely she'd married him because she'd loved him. Surely the affair didn't go back all the way to the beginning of their lives here.

One way or another, he had to find out. Paula was gone. Someone had killed her. Someone was after Gracie and him. He couldn't shy away from the emotional wounds the way he had been doing.

He nodded his chin toward the front desk, where a middle-aged woman in a bright red wig sat, a cigarette dangling from her lips. As the door closed behind them, she made a half-hearted attempt at hiding the cigarette.

"How long you want?" she asked brusquely.

"How long?" Gracie muttered confusedly, further proving to Will just how naive she was.

"How much for a whole night?"

"Big spender, eh?" the woman said with a raspy laugh. "Thirty."

Will went for his pocket before he remembered he had nothing, including no wallet or ID since they hadn't been recovered from his accident.

"Here," Gracie said, sliding two twenties onto the sticky counter. "For tonight and a few hours tomorrow."

"My, my," the woman said with a wink. "Can't say as I blame you." She took the cash, then without getting out of her chair or even looking, reached back and pulled a key off a row of hooks. She put it on the grimy counter and slid it toward them. "Here you go. Get out by noon tomorrow or I'll charge extra."

Gracie looked at the key like it would bite, so Will pocketed it. "Before we go to our room, can I ask you a question?"

The woman eyed him suspiciously. "You know, someone warned me this morning about anybody asking questions."

Will exchanged a surprised look with Gracie. It had to be connected. Had to be. "What exactly did he say?"

She held up a hand, her nails painted the same red as her wig. She rubbed her thumb against her fingers. "He said a few Benjamin Franklins."

"How many would it take for you to tell us about this warning?"

"I'll be generous since you're easy on the eyes, sweetheart. A thousand."

He didn't particularly want to part with that kind of money, but the bigger issue was accessing it. No ID, no cards.

"I don't suppose I could appeal to your moral compass and have you answer some question about a murdered woman?"

She narrowed her eyes. "What murdered woman?"

"Paula Cooper. She died in a car accident two years ago on the curve of Highway 61 near Bent."

The woman studied Will for quite a few minutes. She even took a drag of her cigarette before she answered. "Car accident. That ain't murder."

"It is if it was caused by someone purposely."

The woman's sharp gaze dropped to his casted arm. "That what happened to you?"

"Someone tampered with my car after I found evidence my wife was killed. I don't consider it a coincidence. If you know something and you're keeping it from me, you can be charged with being an accessory to a murder once they figure this all out." He wasn't sure that was true, but it was a decent enough threat. "Because I will find out who did this. I will make sure the full extent of the law crushes every person who had anything to do with her murder no matter how peripherally."

"Pretty big talk for a man whose dead wife was stepping out on him."

Which he hadn't mentioned. At all. Will's heartbeat picked up. "She came in here, didn't she? With another man?"

The woman shrugged then sighed heavily, dropping her cigarette butt into an overflowing ashtray. "I shouldn't say anything, but I didn't care for those threats I got this morning. I don't know much about much. But I saw the girl who got killed in that car accident quite a few times here with a man and they'd go into a room. But he wasn't the man who came to see me this morning, the man who used to hang around while they did it. I never trusted *that* man."

"Why?"

"Sometimes my daughters work here. Didn't like the way he looked at them. Didn't like the insinuations he made about them in my hearing. Got so bad I stopped scheduling them on Wednesdays because that's when he'd always be here waiting for them. Watching them."

Wednesdays. The computer and the days and Wednesdays. Will leaned across the counter, which had the woman edging back.

"Who is he?" Will demanded.

"Don't know. Just came and skulked around. Guy she came with, don't know him, either. Always paid in cash. Pretty nondescript looking guy. Middle-aged. Hair wasn't brown or blond, somewhere in between. No facial hair, no scars, no tattoos. The watcher, though… Usually all bundled up. Couldn't tell what he looked like, but scary guy."

"What else? Surely if you paid that much attention you know more than that."

She crossed her arms over her chest. "Maybe I do. But any more costs you."

"Look—"

"You come back with a grand and I'll tell you what I know. It might get you what you want."

Will shared a look with Gracie. She shrugged. He fingered the key in his pocket. He hated to walk away, but threatening her wouldn't do any good, clearly.

"Thank you. I'll be back with the money." He'd figure out something. He had to.

He strode to the door and once outside, he started for the room number on the key he'd been given.

"What are you doing?" Gracie asked, standing next to the front office door still. "We need to go get that money."

"How? We can't go back to Bent and I don't have any of my cards anyway. We need to plan first. We'll head to the room and figure something out."

She clearly didn't care for that idea, but she followed him nonetheless.

Chapter Eight

Gracie didn't know how to explain this nervous roil in her gut. Something about being in a room that was clearly not meant for sleeping made her very, very, very uncomfortable.

By the hour.

She knew what that meant, what people did in these kinds of motels. Maybe she was sheltered enough to be a little shocked by such a thing, but she wasn't stupid. At least that's what she was trying to convince herself of.

She was not stupid, and it mattered not at all that Will and her were alone in this room meant for…

She should be thinking about how awful this must be for Will. To stand here and know your wife had come to this seedy, disgusting place only to sleep with another man. And be watched by yet another man. It was too much and too gross.

Gracie wished she had the words to comfort Will, but he seemed more like a man on a mission again. The old Will, whose entire mind was consumed with Paula's crash.

It was stupid to be disappointed, considering he'd apparently been right this whole time. It was clear he had every reason to be somewhat obsessed with the matter again. They were in danger, and she was a foolish little girl for expecting anything to ever be any different.

"My cousin runs the bank," she said into the quiet of the smelly room. "I could call him, but I have a feeling Cam and Laurel told the whole family not to do anything for me after I stole Cam's truck. Maybe we should have Laurel question that woman. She might be more forthcoming to a police officer."

"I don't know her, Gracie, but I'm gonna guess money is more of a motivator than a county deputy."

He had a point, but she couldn't shake the terrible feeling in her gut. They shouldn't be here. Something was off and wrong.

"So, where can we come up with a thousand dollars? My checkbook is back home, and I only have a twenty left. If we go to the bank or an ATM in Fairmont someone is going to see us and stop us. There's no way Laurel doesn't have the county on the lookout for Cam's truck since I technically stole it."

"A cab. I can take a cab. A twenty could get me to Fairmont, don't you think?"

"Maybe." She sighed, digging her wallet out of her purse. "I've got my credit card if it takes more. I've got enough in my checking account. We should be able to withdraw a grand. We'll just have to use whatever ATM is closest to the highway. Still, it's a safer bet than heading back to Bent."

"You're right. But I think it's safer if I go and you stay here."

"I don't think we should split up." That bad feeling dug in deeper and she hugged herself trying to ward it off. "I don't want to split up."

"I don't want to, either," Will said gently. "But I think it's the safest way. If I get caught, they can't do anything to me. All I did was leave a hospital. You technically stole a truck, and I think they'd use that against you if it meant they could keep an eye on you."

He was right. It sucked, but he was right. Laurel would no doubt throw her in a cell to keep her safe.

"Will—"

But he railroaded right on. "I'll call a cab. Take it to Fairmont. I'll be gone an hour tops and I'll be back with the money and we'll get our answers. We could have this solved by tonight. I'll pay you back as soon as—"

"I don't care about the money. I care about… What if something goes wrong?"

Will turned to her and gently placed his good hand on her shoulder and squeezed. He looked right into her eyes, certainty and confidence stamped into his expression. "You stay put. The worst thing that happens is your cousins find you and if they do, well, at least you'll be safe."

"When are you going to understand I want you safe, too?" she asked, not sure why her voice came out a whisper or why she thought it would be a good idea to step closer to him.

But he didn't step away, and his hand was still on her shoulder, and for a second she saw a glimpse of what she'd seen in that hospital room. Something different than that laser-beam focus.

But then he shook his head and stepped away, his hand sliding off her shoulder. "We'll both be safe and careful. We have to do this. There isn't another option. This is the first lead we've had. Until Laurel finds something from that text message to you, we have to keep working on our own. I can't wait around. *We* can't wait. We all have to be working toward figuring this out, and like you said in the hospital, we can bend the rules. Maybe with the police department going by the book, and us not, we'll meet in the middle. But we can't stop or wait."

He was right, of course, horrible gut feeling aside. But what was a gut feeling? Wasn't it just worry—and of course she was worried. There was nothing to *not* worry about in this whole situation.

There were no other options. They needed money and they needed to know what that woman knew. Much as Gracie wanted to be skeptical, Gracie had believed the woman's story. She'd known some, and she still knew more. They needed that information.

"Just don't get hurt. Or caught. Or... Just be careful." She swallowed, refusing to give in to the urge to reach out and touch him. She was being overdramatic and so was her gut.

Will called the Fairmont cab company, outlining his plan multiple times while they waited for it to show up. Will stood at the grimy window. "There he is."

He strode for the door, but before he disappeared out of it he stopped and looked back at her. He gave her another one of those weird new looks she wanted to read into, but kept telling herself not to because she was too old to be a mooning idiot.

"Lock the door. Don't open it for anyone. If I'm not back by nightfall, you call Cam or Laurel to pick you up. I don't want you here alone at night. Got it?"

She nodded, but she didn't promise. Because she wasn't about to promise anything if he didn't come back.

WILL SAT LOW in the back of the cab. He had his hood up, trying to obscure as much of his face as possible from the cab driver. He spent the whole drive focusing on Paula and what little he remembered her telling him about her adolescence in Bent.

If he didn't focus on that, he'd focus on Gracie saying *I don't want to split up*, and the way she'd looked at him pleadingly. He'd wanted to give in to that. He'd wanted to give in to too much, and none of it made sense.

Finding Paula's killer was the only sense he could focus on.

Everything in Fairmont went smoothly. The cab took him to the closest bank, waited for him while he walked up to the ATM. He typed in the PIN Gracie had given him and the cash came out without a hitch. Driving back to the hotel, there wasn't so much as a slowdown for wildlife.

Dread pooled in his stomach. He couldn't label this feeling or make sense of it, but it was persistent. Like working on his last ironwork project and knowing it had been all wrong even as he'd gone through all the right steps.

The cab pulled into the lot of the motel and Will scanned the area before he got out. It looked as empty as it had when he'd left. Fat snowflakes were falling from the gray sky and Will struggled to get out of the cab after paying the driver.

He huddled in the oversize coat and trudged toward the room he'd left Gracie in. He had the fleeting thought he should just go talk to the motel lady himself, but with this awful feeling in his gut, he had to make sure Gracie was okay.

She'd been right when she'd said they should stick together. Being apart gave too much room to worry when he had to be thinking and focusing on this whole thing. He wanted to believe Laurel would find something this time, but how could he trust the woman when she and her department had ruled Paula's death an accident?

He knocked on the door, then moved so Gracie would be able to see him out of the peephole, assuming it worked.

She pulled the door open, eyes immediately darting around the lot, as well. "That was quick."

"Everything went just as it should have." He patted his coat pocket. "Let's go talk to her."

She nodded, but he could tell she had that same gut feeling he did. This heavy certainty of impending doom. But there was no way to get rid of that aside from continuing to move forward.

Gracie locked the door and they walked side by side to the front office. It didn't escape his notice they both spent a lot of time looking around the parking lot as if someone would jump out of the trees or mountains and take them both out.

Gracie stopped short and held her hand out to stop him, too. "Will." She nodded toward the door to the front office.

The window was broken out, when it certainly hadn't been an hour or so ago.

Will swallowed. "Stay here. Call the police."

"No. I call the police and you stay here with me. We can't split up. Everything is all wrong." She pulled her phone out of her pocket and kept her grip on his good arm.

"Don't give them your name. As soon as we make sure she's okay, we're out of here," he murmured as she dialed 911.

She nodded and spoke in low tones to the 911 operator claiming of a break-in at the motel and possible threats and refusing to give her name before she ended the call.

"We have to check to make sure she's okay," Will said. "We can't wait for the cops."

Gracie nodded and they edged forward together. They didn't speak as they moved against the wall of the office. Gracie tried to push forward, but even with the broken arm Will blocked her out, keeping her behind him.

She huffed out an irritated breath, but he ignored it. He glanced back at her when they reached the door, a nonverbal *stay put*.

He wasn't great on reading other people's nonverbal

communications, but he was pretty sure the look Gracie gave him was *in your dreams*.

Will used his good arm to reach forward and give the door a push to see if it would give. When it did, both he and Gracie flinched and froze.

But the door merely squeaked one way, and then clicked back closed. They waited, painfully, to see if someone would come out. If something would happen.

"We have to go in," Will whispered. "She could be hurt."

Gracie nodded soundlessly. So, this time, Will reached out for the knob. He twisted and threw the door completely open. When nothing happened again, he moved into the space of the open door.

Gracie was at his heels, but the room was empty. Completely empty.

"Something's wrong," Gracie whispered.

That's when Will heard a movement and something that could be classified only as a groan. They both hurried toward the front desk, and behind it, sprawled on the floor, was the poor woman from earlier.

They both hopped the desk, kneeling next to the woman. She had a horrible bruise blooming across her cheek and temple, but her eyes fluttered open.

"Ma'am. What happened? What hurts?" Will asked, grabbing her hand. He didn't know how to check for a pulse or what to do in a medical emergency, but it seemed right to give her some kind of human connection.

She groaned again, trying to move, but Gracie urged her to remain still.

"Didn't tell 'em anything," she said, proving she was at least a little with it.

"Here." Gracie grabbed some towels that had maybe once been stacked somewhere but were now scattered across the ground. Will helped her sit up a little and Gracie placed the towels under her head as a make-shift pillow.

"What did they do to you?" he asked.

The woman smiled ruefully then winced. "Tried to beat it out of me. That ain't the way to go about it. You don't lay a hand on me and get what you want. I'll live. Just a little bruised."

She tried to sit up but Gracie wouldn't allow it. "You just lie still till the paramedics get here. You could have a concussion, or something could be broken."

"Don't think so. Well, maybe the concussion. I'm not sure how long they've been gone. Guess I passed out. I'm all right. Let me sit up."

Will helped her into a sitting position and even though she groaned again, she did seem in decent enough shape. It was a relief, and yet someone else had gotten hurt in this whole mess and that wasn't a relief at all.

"Don't know why they left." She furrowed her brow. "One of them got a call, I think. Or you would've been toast." She smiled ruefully.

"Will," Gracie whispered. "Sirens."

He heard them, too. "Help is almost here. Stay put. Don't move."

"You go on. I'll be just fine. And I won't tell 'em any-thing. Except about the bastards who tried to hurt me."

"Thank you. Really. Thank you." Will pulled the cash out of his pocket and pulled open the drawer to her desk. "Thank you."

"But I didn't tell you—"

"You were hurt. That's enough. We'll come back if we can." He stood and Gracie stood with him. "We have to get out of here," he said, grabbing her arm and jerking her toward what he hoped to God was a back entrance to the parking lot where the truck was parked.

"He drives a black Ford F250," the woman yelled after them. "The man who was with your wife. Never saw what the watcher drove, but he knew the guy in the truck and your wife, pretty sure. It's not much to go on, but it's something."

"Thank you," Will replied, already pulling Gracie toward the back.

"Where are we going to go?" Gracie demanded, but she followed.

"I don't know." They needed somewhere safe and off the beaten path. If only whoever was doing this hadn't burned down his cabin. Wait. "You said they burned down my cabin, but what about the shop?" He found the exit to the back lot and pushed through it.

Gracie already had the keys out and jogged toward the truck. "No, no, I think it was fine."

"We'll go there," he said firmly, running to the passenger side.

They both got in and Gracie started the ignition.

"I hope she's okay," she said, pulling forward in the lot.

"She has help now. Real help. Now, we need to figure this out before anyone else gets hurt."

Gracie nodded and pulled out of the parking lot. Through the trees, he could see the flashing lights of a police car pulling off the highway.

"Hurry," he muttered, more to himself than to Gracie. But she hurried just the same.

Chapter Nine

It was hard to look at the wreckage of the burned-out cabin and not feel both sadness and fury.

"I just don't understand people. How can they hurt all these innocent lives? What do they think they're going to accomplish?"

"Well, getting away with murder would be my guess. Park the truck behind that cluster of trees. It might give us enough of a camouflage that if someone happens up here they won't see it."

Gracie nodded, but she felt beat down. A black Ford F250 was nothing to go on in Wyoming, and what were they going to figure out hiding up here? She should call Laurel. They should let the police handle this. Everything was too dangerous.

Still, she parked the truck in a little grove of trees and about a foot of snow and didn't voice any of her concerns to Will. She was afraid of what his reaction might be.

He was immediately out of the truck, striding through the snow toward his shed of a shop. He didn't even look twice at the wreckage of his cabin, all burned-out boards and collapsed roof.

Gracie couldn't help but look at it. The black jagged remains seemed so grotesque against a fresh inch or so of snow that had fallen only at these higher elevations.

She watched Will stop short at the door of the shed. He, too, was broken and bruised, no matter how fine he walked. That poor woman had been hurt for only the bad luck of working somewhere where people did bad things and would do even worse things to cover it up.

Panic clawed at her chest, but she couldn't give time to it. She followed Will over to the shed, where he stood frowning at the door.

"Someone broke the lock," he said, gesturing toward the hook on the door where a padlock usually kept the door closed if Will wasn't working in it.

"Maybe we should—"

Before she could offer a caution warning, he lifted his leg and kicked the door open. The sight before them made Gracie gasp. His tools were strewn everywhere, many completely broken. Everything had been torn off the walls, ripped or bashed to bits. Even his worktable had been cracked in half.

"Will, I..." But she didn't have the words.

He started forward, picking through the debris. "Well, it should be safe to spend the night here. I doubt anyone will be looking for us in the wreckage." He kicked one of his metal pieces that Gracie couldn't tell if it was a ruined finished piece or just a piece Will himself hadn't finished.

All of this was too much. Even knowing what his

reaction would be, she couldn't keep silent. "I should call Laurel."

He turned to face her, that *all about the case* expression on his face. The past two years were coming to a culmination and honestly Gracie didn't know how to deal with that any more than she knew how to deal with the fact these horrible people were out there wanting to hurt them and anyone else who might come into their path.

"If you want to go, Gracie, then I want you to go."

Shocked, she stepped forward. "I'm not *going*. We—"

He shook his head, went back to kicking debris out of the way as if all of this was nothing to him. Just unimportant casualties. "I can't sit back and trust the police. Maybe if anyone had believed me for one second in the past two years I could. I know their weaknesses and I can't wait around hoping that changes."

"I believed you," she said, unaccountably hurt. How many hours had she poured into him? When would she get it through her head? When would she accept this? The only reason he was tolerating her was that she was a means to an end. No matter how many times in the past few days he'd looked at her like she was *Gracie* not the *Angel of Death*. It was an illusion.

"Did you believe me? Or did you just support me?"

"So all that support, all that help, all that *being there*," she said, fisting her hand against her heart so it wouldn't hurt so dang much. "All that only mattered if I believed your story one hundred percent all the time?"

"I was right, wasn't I?"

In all the frustrating times she hadn't been able to get through to him for two long years, she'd never wanted to punch him so much as she did right now. But he was standing there with a broken arm, that horrible blank expression behind his eyes, and even now when he was being such a jerk she wanted to soothe him.

"Like I said, Gracie, if you don't want to be here, then that's what I want for you."

She looked around at the trashed workroom, the broken man in the center of it all. Nothing she felt made any sense. He *had* been right all these years, and didn't he have a right to be a little bent out of shape that no one had believed him?

Except she was helping him and she still felt alone. Separate from whatever was going on in his head. An accessory at best. When she'd risked so much for him, and he couldn't even acknowledge it.

She didn't feel sad anymore. She felt *angry*. Livid. That she was risking life and limb for him, for the truth, and he couldn't even *see* it.

"I helped you when no one else would. I broke you out of the hospital and stole my cousin's truck and gave you a grand to pay off that poor woman. I have cared for you and helped you and all you've done is act like I'm the enemy or a burden or should just leave." Her voice cracked but she couldn't let that stop her. "All you've done is act like this one thing—solving this case—is the only thing in the world that matters." She flung her arms out wide. "It matters, but a million things exist around it. Don't you even care they burned down your cabin?

They trashed your shed? You don't even look surprised or hurt or anything. You just want me to leave?"

"I didn't say I wanted you to leave," he replied in that flat, emotionless voice she hated. "I said if you wanted to go, if you want to trust the police, then you should."

"How is that different?" she demanded, something like panic and hysteria winning over every rational voice in her head that told her to calm down and deal with this some other time.

"There is someone after me—"

"Us!" she screeched, and this time she moved toward him, stalked toward him really. He stood his ground, but he looked at her warily and it was *something*. Wary instead of blank. "Someone is after *us*. I am a part of this. That woman back at the motel is a part of this. We're not ghosts you can walk through. We're real-life people putting stuff on the line for the truth. For *you*."

"Can't we have this conversation once we figure out who the hell killed Paula and why? Why would we think about anything else in *this* moment?" He made a gesture around the shed with his good arm. "It's just stuff. But finding out who did this—"

"Won't change the fact that your cabin is gone and your things are broken. It won't change the fact Paula cheated on you, and it doesn't ever change the fact that she's dead. Yeah, you were right, Will. We should absolutely find out who did this. Congratulations. When that's all over, you will have nothing left." She poked him in the chest. "Nothing."

They stood there, facing off, Gracie's breathing too

fast and heavy, while he stood there rubbing his chest where she'd poked him.

"What do you want me to do, Gracie?"

"Acknowledge *anything* that is happening. The wreckage, that poor woman, *anything*."

"By doing what? Stopping trying to find the guy? Cry about my lost stuff or someone getting hurt? Plan my new, empty life when someone's still after me? What am I supposed to do? Do some yoga and *breathe*? While a killer is out there?"

"You're supposed to look around! Acknowledge that I have sacrificed for you. That the motel woman, who doesn't know you from Adam, protected you. Open your eyes, Will. Just because we're focused on finding out who did this doesn't mean you can't acknowledge that life exists around you. That *I* exist around you."

But he didn't. He stood there with the hint of a frown turning down his lips. Her words clearly hadn't penetrated at all, and why was she here? She could be wrapped up in the Delaney Ranch, safe and sound with people who loved her taking care of her.

Her best bet was to leave. To work with Laurel and Cam and try to find the man from the outside.

Because the inside with Will wasn't ever going to solve anything. It would just be half steps of trying to stay safe, of Will keeping everything to himself.

If she truly cared about Will, she had to do the thing that would give him the best chance for being safe, and she didn't think her being with him was it anymore.

She stepped away from him, backing away. "If I'm not your partner in this, if you can't even react when something like this happens—" she pointed to the debris "—then there's no reason for me to be here."

With that, she forced herself to turn, to walk toward the door, to not look back. True care wasn't giving someone what they wanted all the time. Sometimes it was doing what needed to be done to protect them.

She was no good to him here, next to him, because all she could focus on was the ways he didn't see her, the ways he didn't see anything and that wouldn't solve the case.

Will had finally gotten his way. The case was all that could matter.

WILL STOOD FROZEN, watching Gracie step out of the shed. He couldn't catch a breath somehow, but this was right. She'd be safer far away from him, and he'd be free to focus on the important things.

The important things were not the wreckage of the cabin that had become his haven. It was not years of work having been destroyed, the debris of it all around him. And it wasn't Gracie's brown eyes wanting something from him.

What could she want from him?

This was the right move. Letting her go. He'd be safe here and he could work through the things he knew. Connect the dots. That motel. A black Ford F250. Paula's past.

Without Gracie.

He was moving forward before he fully realized it. She couldn't go. It wasn't safe for her to go. It was safer if they were together, fighting it their own way without the police. It had to be safer.

He pushed out the door. "Gracie, wait," he called before he realized she hadn't gone very far.

She was standing in the middle of the snowy yard, just staring at the horrible blackened skeleton of his cabin.

He stared at the snow. She wanted him to feel the horrible loss of that, but then how would he ever move again? If he looked around and accepted what he saw, how did any of it matter? How did he not give up?

He forced himself to look up—not at the cabin, but at Gracie. She'd turned to face him and she had tears on her cheeks.

It just about killed him, and again he was moving forward without thinking it through.

"Don't do that. Please don't do that."

She used a hand to wipe one cheek, but before she lifted it to the other, he beat her to the punch, using his fingertips to brush the tears off her cheeks.

Her breath audibly caught, and he didn't know what he was doing, what he was trying to make happen. He didn't understand any of the things happening inside his chest, the jittery feeling of coming to life all over again. The sun was bright and the snow was cold and his cabin and workshop were in ruins and...

And Gracie was here. She'd been through all of it. Holding him up. But it was his turn. His turn.

Awkwardly using his good arm, he managed to pull her to him. Not a hug so much as a lean into each other, because he only had the one movable arm and she didn't reciprocate. He should probably move or something, but she sniffled against his chest and it felt as if the world shifted. Back to being right after being crooked for so long.

Maybe he was delirious.

"I don't want you to go," he murmured against her ear. His nose was somehow buried in her hair and she smelled like flowers and smoke and he was suddenly hit by the fact she'd run into those charred matchsticks of ruin and tried to save his stuff.

"I appreciate that, Will," she said softly, one of her arms tentatively coming around him.

Will couldn't remember the last time he hadn't wanted to be anywhere but where he was, thinking what he was thinking, but everything about Gracie's arm around him was where he wanted to be.

"But maybe it's for the best if I help the police. You don't need me here and—"

He pulled away, trying not to wince as he moved his broken arm all wrong. But he grabbed her upper arm with his good hand and looked her right in the eye. "I do need you here. I absolutely need you."

Her eyes widened, but she didn't say anything to that. She merely stared at him. Eventually she shook her head, that sad determination creeping back into her expression.

He couldn't let her voice those doubts, voice that look in her eye. He couldn't let her keep thinking everything that was all wrong.

"If I open my eyes, if I look around like you want me to, then I have to accept all this is real." The tide of emotions he'd been warding off for two long years threatened to spill right out of him, but Gracie's eyes were his focal point. His reality. He could beat anything off if he could stare at her.

"I would have been lost without you these past two years," he said, something he'd known all this time but had refused to admit to himself let alone out loud. But once he started admitting things, once in this moment of things hurtling out of his control as he almost watched her walk away, it all came spilling out. "Utterly, horribly lost, but if I stared that in its face, then I'd have to accept what a mess I was. That I'd never really dealt with any of the fallout of being cheated on, because instead of divorce or closure, she died. She was *killed*. It's so much easier to want to find the answer to that than deal with the complicated emotions of losing someone you'd loved but didn't anymore. Someone you were so angry with, but didn't deserve to die."

She reached out, her cold fingers brushing against his cheek. In this moment he could admit what he hadn't allowed himself to admit for a very long time. He wanted Gracie to touch him, see him. He wanted *her*, but it was too complicated, too hard and it would mean moving on.

He hadn't been ready to move on. He'd shied away from anything that meant accepting the things he'd felt, dealing with them, and then even scarier, facing new feelings.

"Will, if you accept all these bad things, then you can move forward. Ignoring them means never building a new life." She rested her palm against his jaw and he wanted, more than anything, to stay here. Right here. Answers and murderers be damned.

"Gracie." A new life. For two years that had seemed like the worst possible thing to want or go after. Paula's life was over, and whether he'd loved her still or not, everything about that night felt like it was somehow his fault. His inability to prove someone else had ended her life was his failure.

He didn't deserve a new life, except when Gracie was touching his face, he couldn't help but see it. Want it. Need it.

Chapter Ten

Gracie didn't understand anything that was happening. Most especially the naked emotion on Will's face, which was something she'd surely never seen.

He lifted his good arm and placed his hand over hers on his face. She thought he'd pull it away like he had in the hospital the other day. She'd thought he'd do anything but rest it there, somehow warm against her cold one.

Everything in her chest pulled too tight, and it was hard to breathe. All of this was different, and different was scary. Almost as scary as the situation they were in the middle of.

She should step away from his hand. Step away from him and this. Stick to her guns. But she cared too much, even if it made her stupid.

"We don't need to have this settled to move on," she said gently. "You don't have to have all the answers to plan your life. All the things that happen in a day *are* your life."

"So, crazy murderers after us is my life?"

It wasn't funny, but she found herself smiling. "For today. Yes."

His mouth quirked into that almost smile she used to desperately try to wheedle out of him.

Will's hand moved off her hand, but not to do anything remotely expected. Instead, it slid into her hair, behind her head, and it pulled her closer. She could see a myriad of emotions in his expression. A confusion. A hurt. A warmth she'd occasionally caught sight of before and then convinced herself she was only seeing what she wanted to see.

"Why?" he murmured, and his mouth was so close to hers she could feel his breath. She could see the diamond pattern to that pretty blue of his eyes. She could count the whiskers on his cheek if she wanted to.

There weren't many things she *didn't* want to do when it came to Will. But his question made no sense. "Why what?"

"Two years, I've kept myself shut down. Separate. I haven't been good to you. But even when you gave up on me, you didn't really."

"That isn't true. Well, not fully. You let me help you, and you let me be a part of something that hurt. It might not make any sense to you, but I… Ever since my parents died, even though I bounced around a lot and nobody really wanted me, they all made sure to shelter me. Hadn't I seen enough horrible things? No one ever let me help. No one ever let me be there when something bad was going on."

"Because you were there. In the car with your parents when they died."

She blinked. "How do you know that?"

"You told me. I might not have always admitted to listening, but I was. I was listening." He almost sounded surprised, as though he hadn't realized it himself.

"Well, yes. So, it's not like you were awful to me. You gave me something I'd been searching for. Even if it's a little messed up. It was nice to feel like I was needed, like I could help. You're a good man, Will Cooper. Amidst all this, you were always so *good*."

His fingertips against her scalp pressed harder, bringing her even closer to him. Their bodies brushed and Gracie forgot all about the cold and the people after them. She could only think about his mouth, right there, so close, and somehow he was doing this. Pushing this.

And he wasn't running away.

"I've needed you this whole time," he said, and his lips were so close to hers she could practically feel the words against her mouth. "I don't know anything about being a good man. I know less about moving forward or new lives or living period. Not anymore."

"I could teach you," she whispered, moving onto her toes so she could be that much closer to what she wanted. A new life. Moving forward. It might be the completely wrong time, but how could she not take what she wanted when it was right here? She knew how precarious it all was.

"I think you could," he murmured, and then he closed that last distance, his mouth finally, *finally* meeting hers.

A dream come true that was nothing like her dreams. This was fire and heat and a kind of need that had her shaking at her core. It wasn't sweet or even pretty. It was deeper than all that. Elemental. It had an edge, and if she had any sense to be scared by it, his kiss had obliterated that sense.

"Finally," she murmured against his mouth, making up for the fact he had a broken arm by holding on to him with both of hers.

Not that it mattered. Even with only one good arm, Will held her exactly where he wanted to, his mouth moving against hers as expertly as if they'd done this forever.

She wouldn't mind, but as she shifted against him, he made a little noise, something like an *ouch* he tried to hide in a cough.

She pulled away. "I hurt you."

He shook his head, but it was no use denying it. He was a mess, and she'd forgotten all about it in the haze of that kiss.

Kiss. Amazing, perfect, life-changing kiss. It didn't matter she'd only been kissed a handful of times before. She *knew* this one would change her life.

"I'll live. That's the point, right? Living."

She grinned up at him, feeling some hope in the midst of all this danger. "I like to think so."

He heaved out a sigh and looked around as if he wasn't sure of where they were or how they'd gotten here. She felt the same. Her heart racing, her mouth still tingling.

Will had kissed her. Will. In the middle of all this hell and worry and confusion and danger, and he'd kissed her like she was the center of the universe.

"We're still not safe."

Because they couldn't ignore reality forever, Gracie agreed. "No."

He looked around, and this time when his gaze met the cabin she saw the hurt, the loss. "We should go."

"Go where?"

His eyebrows drew together, but when his gaze returned to hers, there was a determination there that she didn't recognize. It wasn't the blind certainty he'd been following for the past two years. It was different, not that she understood how.

"We're going to your cousin."

She took a step away from him, afraid this was some kind of trick. He was going to make them split up now or— "What? Why would we go to Laurel?"

"We need to find the truth, and I don't know that the police can find it, but maybe you taught me something after all. Doing it alone while they do it alone doesn't solve anything. Maybe we have to work together. We should be safe while we do. So, we go to Cam. We talk to Laurel. They can't bend the rules, no, but four heads are better than one. If there's a new life to be built, we don't risk this one."

We. She might have argued with him, except it was impossible to argue with *we.*

WHILE GRACIE DROVE from the remains of his cabin back down to Bent, Will kept an eye on the road. He couldn't explain what had changed in him up on that mountain, or what had changed in him when he'd pressed his mouth to Gracie's.

But something had changed. Big. Monumental. Or maybe some piece of his old self had finally broken through years of grief.

Was that what that cloud had been? Not just grief that Paula had died, but grief over the dissolution of their marriage. Because this fog, this turning in on himself and shutting people out had started before Paula had died.

Then she had died and he'd had something to blame it all on. Something to drown himself in.

But since that day Gracie had come to his door with the news Paula had died, she'd been there. This one lifeline, and in that small connection he'd maintained some piece of his old self, no matter how buried.

Now that he realized it, recognized it, had to face fully the fact that life went on and there *were* new lives to have, he couldn't possibly risk anyone else in his single-minded attempt to find Paula's murderer.

There had to be some trust. He might not trust the Bent County Sheriff's Department, but Gracie trusted Laurel and Will trusted Gracie. He didn't know much about Cam Delaney, but Will was somewhat aware he'd been in the military, and that kind of experience would be helpful in keeping Gracie safe.

In keeping them both safe, from whatever lay ahead.

In the falling afternoon light, there weren't very many cars on the road, and Gracie drove them to the Delaney Ranch. It was a vast, sprawling piece of land dotted with perfectly kept buildings, except for one rather ramshackle cabin in the midst of spindly leafless trees in the back. The mountains in the distance looked like they'd been placed there for a slow-moving movie landscape shot and everything glittered with ice and snow. Wreaths lined the fences, and bright red bows dotted each north-facing window. Every tree in the sprawling front yard was covered in sparkling white lights shining through early dusk.

"You really grew up here?" Will asked, trying to imagine having this kind of space. This kind of vast freedom.

"Part of the time."

"I don't think I would have left."

She smiled ruefully. "You would have."

He turned to look at her and the little thread of hurt that went along with that statement. She didn't talk about herself much, but when she did, he listened. He knew her parents had died in that car crash with her when she was six. He'd known she'd spent some years in Colorado before moving in with her uncle and cousins here, but he'd never gotten the sense she'd been unhappy. "Why do you say that?"

"My uncle never wanted me here. He was never cruel or mean, but it's tough to be a teenager where you know you're not wanted."

"I think that's tough for any age group."

She stopped in front of the main house, which looked like a sparkling ad for a ranch vacation Christmas. She turned to him, something soft and a little scary on her face.

Because he might have found some old piece of himself in that kiss, but he still knew he'd grown clumsy with people, with emotions, especially the soft sort.

"I imagine you're right. But I had my cousins, and I have this job that I love. I did all right. I'm doing all right." She pulled a face. "As long as we figure out who's trying to hurt us."

He laughed in spite of himself. "Priorities and all that." But there was something close to vulnerability lurking in Gracie's eyes. He'd never allowed himself to name it before, but that's exactly what it was and he couldn't imagine it stemmed from anything other than a childhood of feeling not particularly wanted.

He could relate to that. He'd forced himself to believe he was different from just about everyone else, but the real reason Gracie had stuck, that he'd allowed her to stick when no one else in his life had these past two years, was a certain kind of understanding.

"You know, it's not like I just *suddenly* noticed I'm attracted to you," he said, because he had a sinking suspicion that was what she'd been telling herself on the drive over.

She raised an eyebrow. "Oh, really?"

He shrugged. "There have been moments."

"What kind of moments?"

He laughed at her straightforwardness. One of the many things he liked about her. Another was that it almost didn't feel odd he was laughing, truly laughing, for the first time in years when they were in the midst of this nightmare.

But something good had been loosed inside him, and he wanted that to last even if someone wanted him dead.

"I think we'll have plenty of time to discuss that later.

For right now, let's go inside and face the wrath of your do-gooder cousins."

"There's nothing wrong with being a do-gooder."

"As long as sometimes you acknowledge you have to break the rules."

"Hey, I was the one who stole a truck to break you out of the hospital."

"Yes, Gracie. You are the queen of bad girls."

She rolled her eyes at his sarcasm, but she pulled the keys out of the ignition and pushed her door open. "Time to face the bad girl music."

Will got out of the truck as well and walked with her up the shoveled walk to the front door. It was one of those giant double doors, and the wreaths that adorned both were bigger than Will's head.

Having lived in Bent for not quite a decade he'd understood that the Delaneys ran the show. Gracie's uncle was the mayor and owned the bank, while her cousin ran it. Laurel was a sheriff's deputy, and another Delaney sibling ran the general store. The Delaney name was splashed over everything. He'd understood they were a big part of the town, but he hadn't fully taken that on board until he'd stood right here in the front of this sprawling house in the midst of this picture-perfect ranch.

Gracie knocked on the door. He didn't know why that struck him as odd. He'd certainly never bust into his mother's house without knocking, but Gracie was, well... She was far different. He was surprised she didn't belong just everywhere.

When the door opened, it was neither Laurel nor

Cam, but Geoff Delaney. Gracie's uncle. Mayor of Bent. A man who looked quite unhappy to see his niece.

"Well, well, well," Mr. Delaney said, crossing his arms over his chest. He was a neat, well-put-together older man. But there was absolutely no warmth in him as he gave Gracie a disapproving look. "You've been causing quite the commotion, Grace."

"Hi. I'm sorry. If Cam is still looking for me—"

"You stole his truck. Of course he's looking for you. Half the town is looking for you. What you've done is very inconsiderate and childish. Instead of coming inside, I suggest you head down to the police station and turn yourself in."

"Surely that's not necessary," Will said, the words out of his mouth before he had the sense to keep his mouth shut and his nose out of her family business.

"No. He's right. We'll go. I'm sure we can get a hold of Laurel there."

Will couldn't believe what he was witnessing. As much as he didn't get along with his mother and even less with his stepfather, they wouldn't have treated him like a criminal. They'd be ambivalent, sure, but not cold and dismissive. Besides, he'd deserved their censure. He'd been a surly ass of a teenager.

He couldn't imagine Gracie being anything but sweet and kind. Giving. Someone treating her casually cruelly didn't add up. At all. "You'd think family would want to help their own," Will said, glaring at Mr. Delaney.

Gracie pulled on Will's good arm, trying to get him off the porch. "It's not important. Let's go find Laurel and—"

"*I* would think a stranger would mind his own business," Mr. Delaney said, his voice harsh and even darker than it had been when talking to Gracie.

There was something about that voice that Will couldn't quite place or put together, but it gave him a strange chill. So he let himself be pulled back to Cam's truck by Gracie.

They got back into the truck and no matter that Gracie tried to put on a brave face, Will could tell she'd been upset by that whole interaction.

He was bothered by it, too, and not just the way her uncle had treated her with such coldness. Something about Mr. Delaney's voice was weirdly familiar. The kind of familiar that made him edgy, suspicious.

His eyes caught the giant four-car garage as Gracie turned the truck around and headed back out to the highway.

"Gracie, this is going to sound very, very strange, but what kind of car does your uncle drive?"

"Oh, one of those giant Ford…" Her head whipped toward him before she looked back at the road. She began shaking her head. "No. That's… No."

"He drives a black Ford F250."

"I could name ten people from Bent who have black Ford F250s. We don't even have a year on it. My uncle is… Will, no."

"It's an awfully strange coincidence."

"But it is a coincidence. It's impossible my uncle had anything to do with this. He prides himself on being moral and good and the mayor of the town. He would never kill someone."

"He wasn't very nice to you."

"There's a big difference between not nice and cold-blooded killer. Honestly, if he wanted to murder people, I think the Carsons would have been wiped out years ago. It's a weird coincidence, sure, but I'm not sure why you would make that jump. It's a big jump."

"Something about his voice was familiar." Will wished he could place it, understand it. "Something about this is all messed up. I think we need to look into your uncle."

Chapter Eleven

It was impossible. It was insane. But as she drove Cam's truck toward the police station, Gracie couldn't help but try to connect the very confusing dots.

"My uncle would have been like twenty years older than your wife at least."

"Gracie, don't be naive."

Gracie scowled. "What? That's gross."

"Plenty of women have relationships with older men. Much older men. We're not exactly close in age, and you did kiss me."

She gave him a doleful look. "You are eight years older. Not an entire lifetime." She shook her head, turning onto the road that would take them around Bent toward the Bent County Police Station. The route down Main Street would be quicker, but this way they might be able to avoid detection till they got to Laurel themselves. "I just can't imagine my uncle being wrapped up in any of this. I can't."

"Maybe you're right. Maybe this is all coincidence. But I can't ignore a coincidence just because you're related to it."

He was right. Objectively she understood he was right. But she knew Uncle Geoff. He wasn't the nicest guy, but a murderer? It didn't add up.

"If we tell Laurel about what happened at the motel—"

"We cannot tell Laurel about this coincidence. This is her *father*. I wouldn't say she idolizes him, but she certainly respects him and loves him. You can't ask his kids to look into him being a killer."

Will nodded, and Gracie tried to concentrate on her driving, but her gaze kept moving back to Will.

"We need to talk to a Carson," he finally said.

Gracie wrinkled her nose. "Why would we talk to a Carson?"

"Paula was a Carson. She wanted to live in her hometown. I didn't really have one of those, so I didn't question it. It sounded nice, to have a hometown."

"It is."

"But she wasn't close with her parents. I wasn't either, so I didn't question that, either. But if we put those things together—hometown but not being close with your family."

"I hate to break it to you, but I love Bent and my uncle isn't my favorite person."

"Yeah. Yeah, but I spent two years looking into Paula's present. Her job, the people she worked with. Her friends. I never went back to before we met because that didn't make sense. But she wanted Bent even though she could have had a better job elsewhere. She wanted Bent even though she wasn't particularly close with her parents. Maybe it's nothing, but a Carson might be able to tell me that."

"Okay. Which Carson? I have to warn you though, I'm not sure how far we're going to get in a basically stolen truck, or with a Carson for that matter."

"She'd go drinking with a group of second cousins sometimes. One was in the army or something and they'd get together when he was on leave. I'm not sure I ever met him since he wasn't around much. Ty, I think. Ty Carson. You know where he lives?"

"Yes, but Ty Carson is Grady Carson's cousin. Grady Carson is engaged to Laurel. And they all live together either on their ranch or in Rightful Claim."

"Jeez. Small-town life is no joke. Okay. Well, we'll try to find Ty. Ask him about Paula. Her parents never believed me regarding the affair, and they'd lost their daughter so I never pushed there. But the second cousins were more friends. Maybe she said *something*." He frowned, but kept barreling forward. "We'll talk to Ty about people in Bent Paula might have had a history with. Maybe he doesn't know about an affair, but maybe he says something that clicks. We won't mention your uncle or anything else. We'll focus on the past. If it doesn't lead us anywhere, and Cam and Laurel don't find us first, we'll make our next choice from there."

"Okay, we can try the Carson Ranch first. If Ty's not there, Noah might know where he is. But I have to warn you, Grady and Laurel might be engaged but that doesn't mean Carsons love Delaneys. Particularly Delaneys who deal in death."

"I'll admit, I never paid much attention to Paula

when she was ranting about the feud. Because I think a century-old feud is ridiculous, but I never got the sense one side was evil."

"You must not have been listening hard enough."

Will smiled a little at that. "What I mean is it sounded like a bunch of misunderstandings and blame. Sure some of the ancestors along the way were jerks, but it always sounded like a bunch of people trying to do the right thing—and just not agreeing on what the right thing is."

"And by 'not agreeing' you mean 'feuding bitterly over it.'"

Will shook his head, but Gracie supposed he wasn't wrong. Except for the people who were after them who definitely didn't want the right thing, all the Carsons and Delaneys she knew were mostly good, mostly trying to do the right thing. Maybe not so much in the past, but now.

All her interactions with Ty and Noah and Grady over the past few months since Grady had gotten involved with Laurel hadn't just been civil—there was a kindness there, too. She had to admit that they weren't the odious, evil caricatures the Delaney side often made them out to be. Most especially her uncle.

"You don't think it could all connect to the feud, do you?" Will mused.

Gracie wanted to immediately deny it, but the fact of the matter was the people she knew who took the feud the most seriously were her uncle and Jesse Carson, who'd been in jail for the past two years. "How was Paula related to Jesse Carson?"

"Max and Jane Carson are her parents."

"If I have my family trees correct, I think Max is Jesse's brother. That would make him Paula's uncle. Sound right?"

"I think so. What does Jesse have to do with any of this? I'm not sure I've ever even met him."

"He's in and out of jail, so it doesn't surprise me you might not have had any family gatherings with him. But I was just thinking about the people who take the feud the most seriously, as in would possibly cause physical harm to someone from the other side."

"And you came up with Jesse Carson? She definitely wasn't having an affair with her uncle."

"No, but I was thinking about Jesse Carson and *my* uncle. They take the feud very seriously." Gracie didn't have to look at Will to know he was giving her a lifted eyebrow, *but you don't think your uncle is a murderer* look.

And she didn't, but that didn't mean there wasn't some more complicated connection here. She couldn't rule anything out. Just like when she was examining a body, she couldn't let her assumptions or presumptions rule her findings. She had to let the evidence speak for itself.

Somehow they made it all the way around Bent to the other side where the Carson Ranch spread out as if it was in an Old West standoff with the Delaney Ranch on the exact opposite side of town. Facing each other. Always ready to fight.

But where the Delaney Ranch was all polish and sparkle, the fence in front of the Carson Ranch was rundown and old. Gracie took the turn onto the gravel road that led them up the hill to the main house.

"I guess it's possible that Cam and Laurel gave up and went back to their own lives instead of trying to find us," she offered.

"Judging from the red and blue lights flashing behind us and a very angry man marching at us from the tree line, I don't think so."

Gracie flicked a glance in her rearview mirror, and sure enough a Bent County Sheriff's Department cruiser was behind them. When she looked to the tree line, Cam was marching toward them on foot.

Gracie offered Will a somewhat sheepish shrug. "I guess we won't be talking to any Carsons."

"We could always make a run for it."

Gracie laughed as Cam stormed toward them. "I know for sure that I cannot outrun a marine, and maybe you could if you weren't broken and bruised. But you are."

He made a scoffing noise. "I'm not *that* broken."

"Then why are you still sitting here? Make your run for it," she challenged.

He reached out, surprising her by gently touching a stray strand of hair and tucking it behind her ear. He looked at her, his expression not exactly grave, but certainly not cheerful. "We're in this together. No matter what. Deal?"

She inhaled and smiled at him, because Will had kissed her. Will had wanted to come back and be safe. They were in this together. "Deal," she returned, more hopeful than she'd been in days.

WILL STEPPED OUT of the truck at the same time Gracie did. Both Delaneys barreled toward them, even as Will and Gracie stood still.

When they approached, there was nonstop yelling and demands, though Will couldn't make out any of it since Cam and Laurel were yelling and demanding over each other.

Gracie held up her hands, giving them both quieting looks. "I know you're both angry."

The two started shouting again, but Gracie waited them out. Patient. Strong. She had such a presence about her, and for the first time in two years Will wanted to get beyond this case, beyond the truth, and really figure out that *what then* on the other side.

"I'm sorry," Gracie said, sincerity all over her face. "I know you think I was in the wrong, but I did what I had to do."

"You could have been killed," Cam and Laurel said in unison. Then they both gave Will almost identical murderous looks.

"We thought we'd be better off trying to figure this out alone, but we both realized we were wrong. We actually went by the Delaney Ranch to talk to you, but you weren't there, so we started talking. Will has some theories."

Laurel started. "Will can shove his theories up his—"

Cam cut off Laurel. "Easy," he muttered, calming his sister down. "What kind of ideas?"

"I never really looked into Paula's life before we met. I assumed whoever she was having an affair with, whoever would have killed her, it would have been someone in her life since us moving to Bent."

"We still don't have evidence Paula was killed, Will." Laurel shook her head. "I'm sorry, but—"

"*I'm* sorry," Will interrupted. "But I do believe that's what happened, and as long as Gracie's in danger, that's the lead I'm going to follow. Paula was a Carson. I know she used to go drinking sometimes with Ty Carson. I wanted to talk to him."

"Ty has spent most of the past ten years in the army," Laurel replied.

"But not all. He'd come home for leave and spend some time with Paula. Him and some other second cousin I can't remember. But I know they did, and Paula would always tell me not to bother to come with. It was 'family time.' So, maybe she talked to Ty or something, or maybe they just know something about an ex or relationship before I came along that might give us a lead."

"Is it smart to focus on the murder and cheating as one thing?" Laurel asked, and Gracie appreciated that there was an amount of gentleness in her voice that hadn't been there before.

"I don't have any other angles, and…" He flicked a glance at Gracie and she stepped forward.

"We found a motel Paula used to go to. We talked to the woman who ran the motel and she told us—"

Laurel swore. "You better not mean the Tick Tock Motel between here and Fairmont." When Gracie only smiled sheepishly, Laurel swore again. "You are *killing* me, Gracie."

"Listen. She told us Paula used to go in there with

a man. And another man used to watch them. She told us the kind of car the man who was with Paula drove."

"And got her skull bashed in the process," Laurel added, glaring at Will.

"I'm sorry she got hurt," Will said. "I take responsibility for it, I do. I wasn't thinking beyond finding the truth, and I'm trying to take more care, but until this man is caught, anyone could be hurt."

That seemed to cut through at least a little bit of Laurel's irritation, if possibly none of Cam's military blankness.

"Did you find anything about Will's phone?"

Laurel shook her head. "No. Whoever used it to text you has it turned off, so it's not traceable." Laurel eyed Gracie then Will. "I'll take you up to the house. If Ty isn't there, someone will know where he is. But if we're working together it means I need to know everything, and it means we need to be able to trust each other. You can't run off again."

"Of course not," Gracie said gently. But Laurel wasn't looking at Gracie, she was scowling at Will.

He was tempted to stare her down, or maybe promise Gracie wouldn't run off again. Laurel didn't have any say over him. But Gracie was looking at him expectantly, with just enough concern in the set of her eyebrows to have him giving in.

"We won't run off," he promised.

"You know what will help with that?" Cam asked, his voice alarmingly casual. "Giving me my truck back."

Gracie winced, but she dug out Cam's keys and handed them to him. "I am sorry. It was the only option."

Cam raised one eyebrow, very slowly. Quite the trick.

"Okay, maybe it wasn't the only option, but it was… Well, I'm sorry."

Cam nodded, pocketing the keys. "And you two are under my protection until further notice, which means I'll follow you."

Will chafed at the idea of someone "protecting" him, but surely what Cam meant was Gracie. Will could pretend he needed protection for Gracie's sake.

Unfortunately there was one thing he couldn't do for Gracie's sake. "There is something we found out that you should both know about."

Gracie squeezed her eyes shut in dismay, but she had to know this was information they needed to share. "The woman at the motel told us the man my late wife was having an affair with drove a black Ford F250."

"I guess that's *something*," Laurel said. "But it was a few years ago. It doesn't mean whoever it is still drives that, or that this necessarily connects."

"But it's something to go on." He almost opened his mouth to remind Laurel her father drove that kind of truck, but Gracie's gaze was pleading.

Well, clearly he wasn't going to get anywhere with convincing a man's family members he was a liar, cheater and possibly murderer.

But that didn't mean it wasn't the theory he'd be working to prove.

Chapter Twelve

Gracie couldn't blame Noah Carson's greeting scowl when three Delaneys showed up on his porch. One even in uniform.

"No one's dead, are they?" he asked, glaring in Gracie's direction.

"Not today." She managed a wan smile. "Things have been very quiet. Unusual for this time of year."

He rolled his eyes before the sound of a young boy shouting *no* started emanating from the house. A pudgy little toddler appeared on his hands and knees before sitting back on his diaper and lifting his arms. "No!"

Noah scowled at them, but when he bent down to pick up the boy everything about him softened. "Well, I guess you want to come in," he grumbled, moving out of the doorway.

Laurel and Cam went first, which irritated Gracie a little. She wanted to be running this show because she knew more. She knew Laurel had worked hard on the case of Paula's accident, but Gracie had an intimate acquaintance with it. Two years' worth of going over it with Will.

But they were all working together now, and Gracie had to let some things go. Laurel was the cop. The one who'd have to actually build a legal case against whoever they found guilty.

Please, God, let us find the guilty party.

"Is Ty here?" Laurel asked.

Noah narrowed his eyes as he settled the baby in a high chair. "What do you want with Ty?"

The front door swung open and Addie Foster, arms heavy with bags, stepped inside already talking.

"Sorry I'm late. I was talking to Jen and… This is a lot of Delaneys in our kitchen. Did someone die?"

Addie might be newer to Bent than the rest of them, and her Delaney relation was far down the line, but she'd certainly picked up on the history quickly since moving here to become Noah's maid earlier in the year. Of course, based on the kiss they shared as Addie transferred the bags to Noah, and Noah's carefulness with Addie's baby, Gracie had to assume things had gotten rather personal.

"No one's dead," Gracie said almost simultaneously with Laurel.

"Ty's in trouble," Noah said.

"No," Laurel corrected. "We need to talk to him. There isn't any trouble. It's about someone he used to know."

"This seems very ominous," Addie said, eyebrows drawing together in concern.

"The case I'm working on is serious, but Ty hasn't got anything to do with it. He just had contact with someone and we want to talk to him about anything he might have heard."

"So, what's with the posse?" Noah demanded.

Laurel crossed her arms over her chest and stared Noah down. "Are you going to tell me where Ty is or do I have to text Grady?"

Noah grunted. "Stables."

"Thank you," Laurel said. She patted the baby on the head as she moved back for the door.

"Couldn't you give us a clue as to what's going on?" Addie asked as the group followed Laurel back to the front door.

"Sorry, Addie. It's fairly unconnected though, and hoping Ty might remember a conversation from a few years ago is a pretty big leap."

"What confidence," Will muttered, and Gracie nudged him disapprovingly.

They filed out the door and since Laurel knew her way around the Carson Ranch, they all followed her, trudging through the snow to a large building that was clearly the stables.

When they reached the building, Laurel walked right in. In the tradition of all the Carsons, Ty was a large, intimidating-looking man and the glare he sent Laurel had Gracie taking a few steps backward.

Of course, that only knocked her into Will, who let out an *oof* when she jarred his broken arm.

Ty studied them all with a kind of calm that reminded Gracie of Cam. Ty had been in the military, too. There was a stillness to it, but there was a sense that he was ready to strike at any moment that put Gracie a little bit on edge.

"This feels like an ambush, Delaney. Or should I say Delaneys." He tilted his head. "Plus that guy." He squinted. "I know you."

Will rocked back on his heels. "Will Cooper. I was married to Paula."

"Paula." He sighed. "A shame about Paula."

"Something has recently happened that leads us to believe—"

Ty held up a hand, and Gracie was shocked to watch Laurel snap her mouth shut. She was clearly irritated, but she quieted nonetheless.

"Are you here on official business, Deputy?"

Laurel pulled a face. "Sort of."

"Sort of?"

"Ty—"

"No. You talk," he said, pointing at Will.

"You're such a caveman," Laurel muttered, but she turned to Will and gave him a little nod as if to give him the go-ahead.

Will cleared his throat. "Ah, well, I haven't ever thought Paula's death was an accident."

"Pretty common knowledge."

"Right, well, it looks like I might have been right."

Ty looked to Laurel. "Officially, right?"

"Possibly."

"Hell. But what's it all got to do with me?"

"You knew Paula," Will said firmly. "You were friendly with her. Maybe you knew, if not who she was having an affair with, someone who might have known something. A mention of someone that seemed off. Something."

"That was years ago, man. And only when I was on leave. I don't know…"

"It's a long shot, but if you think of anything, I'd appreciate—"

"Bent County Sheriff's Department would appreciate the information," Laurel finished for Will.

Ty rubbed a hand over his beard. "I don't know. But Kayleigh might. Kayleigh Gentry. I don't know how close they were at the end there, but they were really good friends as kids. The three of us would always get a drink when I was in town."

The twisted web of feud nonsense just got more complicated. "Kayleigh is Jesse Carson's daughter," Gracie murmured gravely.

Ty nodded at Gracie. "Yeah."

She shared a look with Will. She'd thought any connection to the feud had to be a reach when Will had first suggested it, but now she wasn't so sure.

"If I think of anything else I'll let you know," Ty said, nodding toward Will.

"You'll let *me* know," Laurel said firmly.

Ty flashed a grin and gave her a little shrug. "Guess we'll see."

Laurel grunted and whirled on a heel to leave the stables, Cam, Will and Gracie following. Once they were outside the stables, heading toward their vehicles, Laurel whirled on Will.

"If he says *anything* to you, I want your word you'll immediately share it with the police."

"We came here to work with you guys. That's what we're going to do."

Laurel didn't exactly seem thrilled with that answer, and Gracie had to admit it filled her with a certain kind of trepidation considering Will hadn't given his word at all. But Laurel marched for her cruiser, and Gracie followed at the same slow speed Will did.

"You're not lying, are you?" Gracie said in a low voice she hoped Laurel couldn't hear.

Will gave her an enigmatic look, then simply shrugged.

WILL HAD NO desire to be cooped up at the Delaney Ranch, no matter how comfortable it was, but both Cam and Laurel had insisted they spend the night there. Gracie hadn't put up a fight, either.

He wanted to hunt down Kayleigh Gentry, not wait around for Laurel to decide when it was appropriate. Not spend the night in the same house as Gracie's uncle.

"I thought we'd be working *with* them, not be their prisoners," he grumbled as Gracie showed him to his room.

Gracie laughed, a pretty, bright sound as she pushed open a door. It seemed every room in this monstrosity of a house was magazine perfect and decorated for Christmas.

"I probably should have warned you neither Laurel nor Cam are very good at compromise. But you're in luck."

"I am?" He tried to focus on what she was about to say, but there was a very big bed in the middle of the room, and as much as they'd traveled here, there and everywhere all day, he hadn't been able to put that kiss out of his mind. Every time he looked at her, he could only think to that one perfect moment where he'd felt her mouth under his, where he'd suddenly, glaringly remembered that there were things in the real world that were worth engaging in.

"I may have a few get-around-Laurel tricks up my sleeve," she continued, clearly clueless to what he was thinking about.

She looked so pleased with herself and they were finally really alone for the first time since their drive to Bent and—

And on the chase for a potential murderer, that she might not believe was the man who owned this house, but Will had some suspicions.

But she looked so happy, and he'd forgotten that happy could be a thing. For years he'd existed in something else and the more he'd isolated himself, both before and after Paula's death, the less there'd been any of this. He hadn't realized he'd missed it till it was here, gorgeous and irresistible right in front of him.

"Why are you looking at me like that?" she asked, smoothing an almost shaky hand over her hair.

"Like what?"

"I don't know." She wrinkled her nose. "Usually it's more like looking through me, but that's... I..."

"I never looked through you." No, she'd always been twin sides of a coin existing in one person. A lightness he'd wanted but had been afraid to look too hard at. "I purposefully ignored you."

"Why?"

"I've been in a bad place for a lot of years."

"You were getting better, you know," she interrupted, stepping toward him, always ready to go to bat for him. "Maybe not with the whole going-to-town thing, but your art pieces, getting back into that, was a big step and—"

"You don't need to defend me to me, Gracie. You're right. Something was changing and I tried to shy away from that, too, but you were always there. You've been the…" He was crap at words. Always had been. Even knowing she deserved them, he really couldn't come up with anything.

So he closed the small distance between them and reached out to touch her cheek. Unlike that kiss from this afternoon that had exploded out of nowhere, he took his time. To feel the soft texture of her cheek, to move closer inch by inch and actually watch the pinkish color rise to her cheeks.

He let himself forget everything and just exist in this moment. There was something so completely life changing in breathing this in, letting things go, and giving in to everything that Gracie had ever been to him these past few years.

But before he actually got the chance to sink into all that, someone knocked on the door.

Gracie squeezed her eyes shut, a soft groan escaping her mouth. "Oh, right." She stepped away and gave her head a little shake. "Jen. Jen knows Kayleigh and was going to get me her number. So, that's…"

"Jen," he finished for her, finding some amusement

in how flustered she seemed. He'd been such a mess for years, flustering anyone felt like a kind of power.

"Yes. My cousin Jen."

"Jeez, how many cousins do you have?"

"Oh, lots. Lots. Delaneys never leave for long. I should answer the door. I should answer it," she stuttered.

"You might want to stop blushing."

She opened her mouth, something like outrage threading through her features. "You know you have absolutely no room to poke fun at me, Mr. Hermit."

He grinned. "That so?"

She made a little huffing noise then moved to her tiptoes and in a smooth move she pressed her mouth to his, quick and not nearly enough, before giving him a sassy little look. "That's so," she muttered, walking to the door.

She opened it for yet another Delaney. Will tried not to sigh. It was a strange change in his life to finally want to be done with this. He didn't want the puzzle anymore. He wanted after the puzzle.

"So, I got you that phone number," Jen said, handing Gracie a sheet of paper. Then she turned and smiled at him. "Hi, Will."

"Jen." He vaguely knew her as the woman who ran the Delaney General Store, though he wasn't sure why he'd never put together she was also Gracie's cousin. There were just too many people in that damn family to keep track of.

"How much is Laurel going to hate me for letting you have this?" she asked, smiling at Gracie.

"Depends on what we get out of it."

Jen grinned at that. "Noted. Well, I'll let you two get to it. I know it's late, but if you want some dinner, I left some chili in the Crock-Pot for Dad."

"Is it just going to be us and him tonight?"

Jen pulled a face. "Cam will be around, but he's out front working on some kind of video monitor to put at the entrance." Jen rolled her eyes. "You want me to stay and play buffer?"

"No, no. Don't go through any trouble on my account."

"It's not any trouble. I can talk spreadsheets and profit margins with Dad and give him the thrill of his Saturday night. I'll keep him in his office so you don't have to deal if you want to go eat." Jen patted her pocket. "I've got my phone on me, so text if you need something you don't want to risk running into Dad for." She squeezed Gracie's arm, then gave Will a wink and disappeared out the door.

Gracie looked down at the paper in her hand. "So, do you want to call her, or should I?"

Will stared at the paper, too. Thought about Laurel wanting to work together. Thought about all Gracie had done for him these past two years. The fact she was staying here in this place that made her uncomfortable and avoiding her uncle, all for him, when he hadn't done a thing in two years to deserve it.

But she'd seen beneath the bitterness and the shell. She'd been the support he'd needed to pull himself out of something dark, and in this moment he didn't care about the case, about murderers or his broken arm or Paula's death.

"I think we should wait."

Chapter Thirteen

"Wait? Wait for what?" Gracie asked. He was staring at her so intently and she didn't get it. They had a lead and he wanted to wait? This was not the Will Cooper she knew. Oh. His injuries. "Is your arm bothering you? Did you want some ibuprofen? Maybe some sleep would—"

"No."

He touched her cheek again, just as he had before Jen had knocked. As though he was touching something beautiful and precious and Gracie hadn't a clue what to do with *that*. Yes, she'd had an unfortunate crush on Will for most of the past two years so there'd been a certain level of fantasy about him touching her, kissing her.

But somehow all those silly fantasies didn't match *this*. She didn't have people in her life who looked at her like she was a marvel, who touched her like she was precious. She had protectors in Laurel and Jen and Cam, but no one had ever focused on her exactly like this.

"Gracie, I want to start living my life." He said it so earnestly, and still those blue eyes were focused on her. Not through her, not on anything else but her. Will

Cooper was staring at her like she was the center of his world.

It wasn't about the case, or his dead wife or anything else. That might be why they were here, but that wasn't why he was talking about his life. *She* was why he was talking about living. *She'd* gotten that out of him.

"I want that, too. For you. You have a lot of life left to live, and I think you'd be good at it if you gave it a shot."

He laughed, a low rumble of a chuckle that drifted across her temple. "What on earth from the past two years makes you think I'd be any good at it?"

She looked up at him, trying to speak past the way his fingers drifting down her neck backed up the breath in her lungs. "You're good at going after the truth, and you make beautiful things out of metal. You could make beautiful things out of life, you just have to want to."

He kissed her then, and she couldn't understand how it could be softer, sweeter, while still filling her with all the same things she'd felt up on the mountain earlier. Fire and heat and need. There was a sharpness to it all, no matter how gentle he was. The jagged, painful rightness of finding a new beginning in the midst of something bleak and ugly.

His good arm held her tight against the hard length of his body, and his mouth explored hers with a kind of studied leisure that had warmth pooling through her. Her knees felt weak—her heart felt too big for her chest.

Though it was gentle to begin with, everything softened second by second. Well, except him. His body seemed harder and harder and more this pillar of stone and strength and she wanted all of that more than she'd ever wanted anything.

She raked her fingers through his hair. She arched against him, chasing this edgy, desperate need she'd never felt with anyone else. Not like this. It had always been Will. The one man she'd ever wanted to give herself to.

There was a bed. There was time. She could finally have this thing she wanted and nothing else had to matter. Nothing else. Just for a little while.

"Gracie?"

She didn't know what he was asking, but it didn't matter. "Yes."

Then heat didn't begin to describe what exploded between them. It was so much more, so much bigger than anything. He kissed her everywhere and she slid her hands under his shirt, taking care to be gentle against his broken arm—the hard cast the only reminder he was even hurt at all.

His hand slid over her breast, and even through the fabric of her shirt and bra, he found her nipple with his thumb, brushing against it even as he kissed her mouth, with something like *hunger*.

"I'd take off your shirt but I'm sadly one-armed these days, so you're going to have to help me with the whole clothing removal."

She had her shirt off in seconds, no matter how her heart jittered. "Now let me help you."

He sat on the edge of the bed and she moved to stand in between his legs as she carefully peeled the shirt off him without jarring his broken arm.

She let the shirt fall, standing in between his legs as he looked the short distance up at her small frame. He looked at her like she was a gift or a prize or something wonderful and for one horrible second she was so afraid. Because it didn't make any sense that anyone could look at her that way.

"Are you sure… Are you sure I'm not just convenient?" she whispered.

He laughed, a full-on grin she'd never seen on him as he curled his hand around her hip and drew her even closer. "Oh, sweetheart, I'm not sure anything about you is *convenient.* Convenient would be spending the rest of my life holed up in a cabin ignoring the world. *Convenient* would be letting whoever is after me finish the job."

"Don't say that!"

"I'm just saying there isn't anything about wanting to get back out there that's easy or convenient, but it's what I want. *You're* what I want. A life with you in it. A real one, too, not one centered on a mystery or the past."

"I used to think I should say something, or let you know that I… I mean, I've…"

"You're attracted to me."

She had no idea why that cocky glint to his blue eyes made her feel that much more like Jell-O but it did.

"God knows why," he muttered.

It was that hint of bafflement that soothed some of those nerves, some of that insecurity. "I'm attracted to you and I *like* you, Will. Because even at your worst, you're a good man. But you weren't ready to hear any of those things."

"No, I wasn't."

She cleared her throat, trying to focus on what she wanted to say more than the nerves fluttering around in her stomach. "Are you ready now?"

"To know you think I'm a good man, no. To try to be that man, yes. To act on this attraction, hell yes. Part of me thinks we should figure everything out first. Who might have tried to hurt us both. It's such a big, all-encompassing thing. But my life for the past two years has been trying to figure it out. Shutting everyone and everything down until my life was only finding out who did this. We're so close to something, when I haven't been close to anything in years."

Her hope and giddiness sank a little. "Right."

"But you were right back there at the wreckage of my cabin. It's all life. Finding it out. Exploring this thing with you. You don't know what kind of time you have. You don't know what's going to happen or not, and if you're not moving forward toward the things you want, you're likely to never get it."

She threaded her fingers through her hair, holding his head at an angle that kept his gaze on hers. "What do you want? I mean specifically out of life?"

"I'm not sure quite yet. I like what I do metalworking wise, so more of that. And I like you. I want more of *you*." He drew her as close as he could stand to him. "What do you want?"

She blinked at him, trying to reconcile a million things, most of all that he was asking what she wanted and waiting for an answer.

"Don't you know?" he asked, cocking his head.

"Yes, *I* know, but you've never stopped to wonder what I want before. I'm still getting used to this new you."

His mouth quirked—more and more, she was getting that reaction out of him. "Just because I didn't ask didn't mean I didn't wonder. This me isn't new. It's just been hidden under a lot of ugly things. You're the only thing I've wanted to crawl out of it for."

She sucked in a breath.

"I'm probably a bad bet," he murmured.

She leaned down, smiling. "I'll take it anyway," she offered before pressing her mouth to his.

WILL CURSED HIS broken arm. He could deal with not having both hands to peel off her pants. Watching her shimmy out of them, or help him with his, well, no one could complain about that. Naked except for her underwear, she was gorgeous. And even though the pale hue of her skin gave an aura of delicateness to her, the strength of all Gracie was emanated from those dark eyes, all certainty and heat.

He wanted to be on top of her—he wanted to be able to move. He wanted this moment in time to be the best, most explosive thing she'd ever experienced.

And he had one functional arm and a million bruises to ignore. He only had one hand to touch her. One hand to use to explore the gorgeous curve of her breast, the soft, sumptuous skin of every part of her. The way her skin was as soft as velvet, but the muscles under all that skin were the truth of her.

Of course, he also had a mouth. He used both as best

he could, until she was panting, saying his name like a prayer. Until he was so hard it hurt and all he could think about was losing himself in everything Gracie had always been to him.

He managed to sprawl out and maneuver her on top of him, though he had to hide a wince at the tinge of pain that went through his broken arm. "You're going have to help me out here," he managed to grind out. But it wasn't the pain of his arm that had his voice scraping against the sweet, heavy *need* of the room. It was clawing frustration thinking he couldn't give her everything she needed.

"Oh. *Oh.*" She blinked, looking down at her hands splayed over his chest as if she hadn't quite realized how she'd gotten here. "Um." She swallowed, looking uncertain for the first time. "I haven't…er…" She pulled a face. "It's just…" She trailed off, looking adorably embarrassed.

Until he figured out what she was trying to say. "Wait." She didn't mean… "What?"

She blew out a breath. "Well, I haven't exactly done this before."

He felt something like frozen. Well, his brain was. Other parts of him were fine and not at all affected by the information, especially when the warmth of her was pressed to the hardness of him, even with the underwear barrier. Will swallowed, but Gracie just kept babbling.

"I was just so focused on becoming a coroner, and it's a small town so the dating pool is small and then I was hung up on someone there for a while."

Someone. He scowled, surprised at the sharp bolt of jealousy. He didn't consider himself the jealous type.

Wouldn't he have figured out Paula was cheating a lot sooner if he had been? "Who were you hung up on?"

She laughed, looking down at him with one of those adorably baffled smiles. "Um, *you*. Have you really not been paying attention?"

"I didn't realize it had been a while." He studied her, the round face, the wavy brown hair, the expressive brown eyes he'd been dreaming about long before he'd admitted to himself she haunted him everywhere. "How long's 'a while'?"

"None of your business," she said primly. Primly while she was straddling him in nothing but her underwear. Then she smiled, as if finding all of her normal poise and strength in the blink of a moment. "But I want it to be you, Will. I want it to be now."

Some little voice in his head told him it was too much, some of that panic he usually felt going to town thrumming through his veins.

But she pressed a kiss to his mouth and it was gone, because she was everything he wanted, and he'd give his life to give her what she wanted. "Gracie. I don't have any sort of protection."

A flush washed up her neck into her cheeks. "I mean, I'm on the pill. So, it'd be… I mean…"

"I haven't been with anyone since Paula."

She smiled at that, some of the flush receding. "Yes, Will, I'm pretty well-aware of that."

"I just meant after the whole cheating thing I got… checked out and, you know, we'd be fine. Everything's fine."

She laughed against his mouth. "We really need to stop talking."

He laughed, too, a real deep laugh and it was such a strange thing to suddenly remember a time when he'd had reason to. A relief and comfort to find it again. To find it with her, and have the promise of a future to keep doing so.

They awkwardly struggled out of their underwear, laughing all the while, and it was in that laughter they came together, each other's names on their lips, a long, slow glide to that connection he hadn't realized he didn't just want, but needed. He needed Gracie in his life—wanted her there, too.

The laughter was gone and there was only her sweetness and warmth. She was pouring hope inside him, filling him with something he'd never truly had before.

She was a sunrise on a new beginning. It didn't erase what had come before, but it made hope spread out like light. When she shuddered against him, he lost himself inside her, determined for this new beginning to be everything they both wanted.

Chapter Fourteen

Gracie couldn't remember ever feeling both so perfectly relaxed and so giddy she just wanted to giggle.

She'd *finally* had sex, and it had been perfect. Amazing. And it had been Will, who dozed next to her, his good arm holding her close.

She should sleep, too. They'd been through so much these past few days, but she was too full of adrenaline and excitement. Too happy.

But happy could end in a moment. She knew that better than most, and she supposed Will did, too.

Nothing had been solved, per se, and she found herself not caring in the slightest bit. Oh, she still wanted to figure it all out, but she wanted this, too. She wanted both: the good and the bad. She wanted a hope for the future, even when things weren't great in the present.

She pressed her cheek to Will's shoulder. She could see the pattern of bruises across his torso, the sharp pop of the white cast against the warmer tones of his skin. His dark blond hair was a tangle, and he needed to shave. He was so handsome, even disheveled and beat up, and somehow this had happened.

A future had happened.

Which meant they had to absolutely figure out the very problematic present, because come Christmas she wanted to celebrate it with the man she loved.

Love. She wanted to laugh out loud again. She wanted to laugh and laugh. She'd fallen in love with Will a while ago, during those glimpses into the man he was. She hadn't let herself really dwell in that, think about that, but it had been there.

Watching him choose to be that man she knew he could be sealed the deal.

She couldn't sleep. Not with love and mysteries battling it out for prominence in her head. As carefully as she could, Gracie slipped out of bed. She needed to move to think, and she needed... A list. She needed to write out the next steps. Just like with work.

Work. Jeez. She pulled on her underwear and her shirt, and then went in search of her pants. Once found, she dug the cell phone out of her pocket. No phone calls or messages. Usually she spent a few days in the office a week, even when things were slow, but she was up to date on all her cases, so unless she got called in there was nothing going on at the moment, and with the holidays a lot of people took time off. Her absence wouldn't be missed as long as she didn't get any calls.

She opened the notes section on her phone and began to pace trying to come up with a to-do list. They needed to contact Kayleigh. Maybe they should look into Jesse. Then there was her uncle who had the same kind of truck and...

She closed her eyes and took a deep breath. There

was a lot to look into, but they could only do one thing at a time. She had to prioritize and organize.

"Back to work, huh?" Will murmured sleepily from bed.

She winced and turned to face him sheepishly. "Sorry I woke you."

He shook his head, motioning her back to the bed. "We have to figure this out." He struggled into a sitting position, the blanket falling to his waist, and for a second she just stared at him.

This gorgeous mess of a man was something like hers, and she would do just about anything to protect him. And herself, so that they really got to experience this.

"I made a list," she said, moving to her side of the bed. She scooted next to him and handed it over.

He rubbed a hand over his face before he took the phone and squinted at it. "Okay."

"I start thinking about what to focus on and I get overwhelmed. I don't know where to start. There are so many threads."

"Well, I'd say we pick one. One at a time. We just have to be methodical. And if you and I are methodical, and Cam is protecting yo— Us," he quickly corrected since she'd been opening her mouth to do so. "And Laurel is pulling her own threads, so we pick one."

"Okay. But which one?"

"I think we follow the Kayleigh Gentry connection. It's a weird long shot but I haven't attempted any weird long shots in two years. Maybe it's time."

"Okay, but I don't think we should call Kayleigh. If

she knows something, she might cover it up if we call first. But if we can catch her off guard—"

"And without a cop—"

"Yes. But we can't go back on our word. I know you didn't promise Laurel exactly, but I don't want to wiggle out of that on a technicality. We said we'd work together. We should."

"We can't take a cop with us."

"We need Cam. If Cam came with us as our security, then we'd be staying safe, and we could report it all to Laurel after. She might be irritated, but it isn't going off on our own."

"Okay, but we need Ty, too. To put this Kayleigh woman at ease or have her meet us somewhere."

"One will be easy to use without Laurel's approval. The other?"

A knock sounded on the door and they both froze.

"Gracie? Will? I need to talk to you guys." Laurel's voice was all no-nonsense policewoman.

"Oh my God," Gracie hissed. "I'm pantsless!"

"I'm a lot more than pantsless," Will replied, sounding far too amused.

Gracie scrambled out of bed. "Well, fix it!" she whispered as forcefully as she could.

"I have one arm," Will replied, holding up his cast.

"J-just a second," Gracie called toward the door, her voice too high-pitched. "She's going to know," she muttered, scurrying for her pants.

"Is that a problem?"

Gracie stopped with one leg in her jeans and one leg out. When she'd been thinking about futures she'd been thinking about her and Will and relationship stuff and *love*, not dealing with her overprotective cousins.

He got out of bed, all too perfectly naked, which was quite the momentary distraction. He grabbed his boxers and pulled them on, though she could tell it hurt his arm a little bit.

"You should have a sling."

He raised an eyebrow. "Should I?"

She was an idiot. "And Laurel knowing isn't a problem exactly. Or it won't be. The timing... Laurel is going to lecture me about the timing."

"So?" he asked with a shrug as he picked up his pants.

"What do you mean 'so'?"

"I mean so what if she lectures you? She's not your boss. You're an adult. She's not in charge of you in any way."

"They look out for me. They took care of me when no one else did. They mean a lot to me. Laurel can be overbearing, but she means well, and she's always been there. It doesn't mean I have to do what she says, but I care. I do have to listen."

"You aren't beholden to the people who love you, Gracie. Not like that."

Laurel knocked again. "What the hell is going on in there? Are you hiding something or... Oh God, Gracie Delaney, you're not... Do I need to come back?"

Gracie had to answer even though Will's seemingly offhanded comment had struck her like a blow. She finished fastening her pants and then she helped Will get his shirt on.

They stood there for a second, Will studying her with one of those unreadable glances she thought sex would magically stop. But there were parts of Will she still didn't understand, and parts of everything she didn't understand. She felt young and stupid and out of her depth.

But Will kissed her temple, light and sweet. "She should respect what you want, because you're smart and determined and have always made good choices. You don't have to prove yourself to her, and if she loves you, she won't want you to, either."

Which was more than a blow. Something like an explosion, and Gracie didn't know how to sort through all the debris so she moved to the door and opened it to Laurel.

Laurel's narrowed gaze went from Gracie to Will. "Can I talk to you in private?" Laurel asked, and even though she was still glaring in Will's direction, everyone knew she was speaking to Gracie.

"I don't really think that's necessary."

Laurel sighed heavily. "I came by to tell you that I'm going to stay here tonight and go over some things with Cam and I thought you might want to join us."

"Of course," Gracie replied overbrightly.

Laurel raised an eyebrow at Will.

"Sure," he said, getting to his feet. "We were just discussing some ideas ourselves."

Laurel rolled her eyes before sailing off into the hallway. Gracie knew she should follow, but she only stood there for a few moments before she felt Will's hand on the small of her back.

"You ready?"

She glanced up at him and there was something about his expression—he was calm and in control, sure, but there was something more. Like he was sincerely asking if she was ready, as if he was really paying attention. It dawned on her that him saying he'd paid attention in spite of himself, or while pretending not to, was true. All this time while she'd thought he'd been clueless he'd just been trying to keep himself separate.

But he hadn't been able to.

She rose to her toes and pressed her mouth to his. "Let's solve this, huh?"

"Sounds like a plan."

Will sat on a couch next to Gracie. Laurel was pacing the floor and Cam was sitting unnaturally still in an armchair.

"You need a presence. This is a police investigation," Laurel said through gritted teeth.

"But you're off duty right now," Will pointed out.

Laurel scowled at him, and he knew he wasn't doing himself any favors in terms of winning over Gracie's family, but someone had to speak the obvious truth. Not to mention the fact they had to play this carefully.

"Whoever messed with my car heard me say something to Gracie in Rightful Claim. Or saw me or something. For two years I've been poking into this. Something had to be the catalyst two years later. We can't be too careful. If Kayleigh has some knowledge we have to be careful it isn't the kind of knowledge that could get her hurt."

Laurel frowned at that, but Will could tell he'd scored a point.

"I think I should go alone. They know what I know. They know I'm a threat. I've already been targeted. Why not keep it focused on one person?"

"Because that puts you in danger again," Gracie said, clearly irritated with his suggestion. "And if they did overhear us at the bar, they've connected me to this, too. If they saw me at your cabin when they set the fire, I'm a target, too."

"Neither of you is going alone or together," Laurel said firmly.

"I have an idea," Gracie said. "One where we all get our way."

Will almost scoffed, but then he looked at Gracie and knew if someone could find a compromise amid all this, it would be her.

"We have Ty meet Kayleigh at Rightful Claim. Laurel and Cam can be there. If you're talking to Grady or pretending to do wedding stuff or something, no one will question it. Will and I can come in and I can go up to Ty to say something, and we can start a very casual conversation. Will can play the obsessed, cuckolded husband and not let anything go. She might give us information, she might not, but it's worth a shot."

"Is that acting?" Laurel asked, her gaze slowly turning to Will.

Maybe because Gracie had just talked about these people protecting her and taking care of her, he could finally understand that Laurel wasn't just a hard-ass cop with no give in her. She cared about Gracie and didn't want her hurt. Which reminded him that he had to care about that, too. If he didn't get along with her cousin, that would hurt Gracie.

So he held Laurel's glare and offered a truth he wasn't 100 percent comfortable voicing, even if it was the truth. "People change, Laurel. Sometimes they get out of the crap that held them down because someone helped them out."

It softened her, clearly and completely.

"It's a good plan," Will said to Gracie. "A good compromise."

"It is," Laurel agreed. "But which one of us is going to get Ty to go along with it?"

All Delaney eyes turned toward Will.

Which was how he found himself outside Rightful Claim at midnight, Gracie at his side. Laurel and Cam had already gone inside when Ty roared up on his motorcycle.

"Hey," he offered as he strode up to the two of them. "Kayleigh's already inside. Maybe give us a few minutes to get a drink. Relax into it."

"Sure," Gracie said with a nod.

"And just a heads-up, Delaney, Kayleigh's Dad, Jesse Carson, is out of jail. I know you know he takes this feud even more seriously than your uncle, so I'd be careful in there. Maybe just let Will come over and make sure Laurel and Cam stay on their side of the tracks so to speak. You don't want to add any more volatility to this mix."

Will slid a glance to Gracie to find her already looking his way. They both waited to speak until Ty was inside while Christmas lights glittered above and Christmas music quietly soared from inside.

"Why does this one name keep coming up?" Will murmured quietly, watching the streets for anyone who might be paying too much attention or listening too carefully.

"I don't know. There was the man having an affair with Paula, but also the man watching them. Maybe Jesse knows something. Maybe he's the watcher."

"He's been in jail for two years," Will said thoughtfully. "It might explain the timing. It's not that someone overheard us that escalated this. It's that he got out of jail."

"When we go in, you go to Ty and Kayleigh. I'll go to Laurel and see if she can find out what kind of car Jesse drives."

Will nodded. He didn't mention that her uncle could still also be a person of interest, but he supposed he didn't have to. They were all looking for the truth. If Jesse knew something her uncle had done, that would be a truth that came out. That was the important thing.

"Let's go."

She squeezed his hand. "Be careful."

"You, too. No leaving without each other, got it?"

She nodded and tried to pull her hand away, but he wasn't quite ready to let it go. So he pulled her to him instead. She gently placed her hand above his cast. "You need a sling. And probably a checkup."

"When this is all done, we'll figure out both."

She smiled up at him, sweet and hopeful, and he had to believe for the first time in a very long time things would work out okay. One way or another, he would find a way to get this future they were laying the groundwork for.

"I like the sound of *we*," she murmured.

"Me, too." Then he kissed her in the middle of Bent proper, with twinkling lights and quiet music and the odd hush of evening snowfall drifting around them.

....

Chapter Fifteen

Gracie's heart was beating in overdrive as she and Will dropped each other's hands before stepping into Rightful Claim. There was so much riding on this interaction and she was trying really hard not to get her hopes up, but how could she not?

All they needed was one clear-cut clue and this could be figured out in a matter of hours. But she also knew, through two years of living this mystery, it could stretch on forever.

Laurel and Cam sat at bar stools toward the back, Grady behind the bar. As Gracie walked toward them, Laurel leaned over from her side, Grady leaned in from his and they both grinned at each other.

Gracie wanted that. Laurel and Grady were as different as night and day, as Carsons and Delaneys, but they loved each other. They clicked. Despite the differences. It was special.

Cam watched Gracie as she approached, and she had no doubt that even though it felt like his eyes were on her, his attention was really focused on the table in the corner where Ty and who she presumed was Kayleigh were sitting.

Will hadn't gone over there yet. He'd gone to the far side of the bar from where Laurel was and ordered a drink from Vanessa Carson, who eyed all the Delaneys on the other end suspiciously while she filled a mug with beer.

"Hey there, AOD," Grady greeted, that razor-sharp Carson grin angled her way.

"Oh, we're shortening it these days." She took a seat next to Laurel. "Cute."

"Well, I like to have nicknames for all the Delaney girls. Laurel here, for instance, is—"

Laurel leaned over the bar and slapped a hand to her fiancé's mouth. "You rethink that line of conversation, Carson, or you will be very, very sorry."

Grady laughed against Laurel's hand and when she finally took it away, he winked in Gracie's direction. "She's crazy about me."

Cam cleared his throat, and both Gracie and Laurel glanced toward the corner. Will was approaching the table where Kayleigh and Ty sat. Ty looked relaxed and polite if uninterested. The blonde who was certainly Kayleigh looked… Well, Gracie didn't know if she was reading into things or what but she suddenly seemed uncomfortable as Will approached.

"I knew Ty wasn't in here for a good time," Grady said, disgustedly glaring at his cousin. "You owe me an explanation later, princess," he muttered before heading down to the other side of the bar and Vanessa.

Gracie looked at Laurel wide-eyed when she didn't

pitch a fit at someone calling her princess. "*You* let him call you princess?" she demanded.

Laurel's cheeks flushed pink, but she lifted her chin loftily. "We should focus on the task at hand."

"Uh-huh."

When Laurel and Gracie both looked again at the table in the corner, Cam shook his head. "You two focus on the bar and pretend to be gossiping," Cam said. "They're going to notice if we're all three staring at them."

Gracie turned back around and looked at the drink Grady had placed in front of her. She wasn't going to drink it, so she stole a glance at Laurel, who was doing the same in her direction. "Princess? Really?"

Laurel glared at Gracie this time. "I love the man. Annoying nickname or no. You make certain allowances when you're in love."

Gracie tried not to flush under Laurel's watchful eye.

"You know, love can be confusing. Sometimes incidents can cause people to confuse a certain shared experience or sympathy for—"

"Did I imagine you and Grady falling in love in the midst of you solving a dangerous crime that actually involved you being kidnapped for a bit?"

"That was different."

"How?"

"We didn't have a bunch of dead-wife baggage."

"But you had plenty of Delaney and Carson baggage." Which reminded Gracie of Ty's little tidbit from outside, and the reason they were here, and a much more comfortable subject. "Did you know Jesse Carson is out of jail?"

"Yes, I'd heard. A week ago. I try to keep tabs on that psychopath. I do not trust him."

"His name has come up a few times over the past few days and Will and I were wondering if he's connected to all this somehow. He was Paula's uncle, so not in any affair, but… I don't know. There's all these little clues and none add up, but we should see what kind of car he was driving two years ago. Just to be thorough."

Laurel nodded. "I'll have to go through the proper channels officially for the record, but I might be able to bend a few rules to get that information a little sooner on the down-low." She frowned down at the drink she hadn't touched. "I don't understand any of this."

"I don't, either." Gracie didn't want to add to Laurel's frustration, but it seemed necessary. The more they all knew, the more eyes were on the lookout. This needed to come to an end. "You know who drives that kind of truck."

Laurel's expression shuttered into something blank, and because Gracie at times had to use that expression in her line of work, she knew what it was. It was the mask you put yourself behind when something personal hit. But Gracie wasn't a victim Laurel was trying to solve a case for.

Gracie reached out and put a hand on Laurel's arm. "I don't think it's possible, but I think we have to look at every impossible angle. Especially with the history between him and Jesse."

"We will look at every angle."

"Laurel—"

Laurel quieted her with a steely-eyed glaze. "He's my father, and I love him. But if he did something wrong, that won't change what I have sworn to do or the laws I've promised to uphold. Quite frankly, he was one of the people who instilled that responsibility in me, so if he has *anything* to do with this, I absolutely will make sure he's brought in."

For some reason it made Gracie think about what Will had said earlier. *You aren't beholden to the people who love you.* She had no doubt Laurel would do what was right, but she wondered if she was taking too much of that on herself. "I know you love your job, and you take it very seriously, but there are times when it's okay to step back and let someone else handle something. You don't have to take on every hard thing, especially if it involves people you love."

Laurel stared hard at her hands, which she'd linked together on top of the bar. "If this all connects back to Paula's death, I failed the first time around."

"Hey. You know that isn't true. You know you can't blame yourself when you didn't have the tools or evidence or means necessary to find an answer. We're human."

"Knowing something and feeling something are two different things. You can't tell me that part of why you stuck in Will's life so long was that Paula's death weighed on you even if it wasn't supposed to."

Gracie considered that, but it didn't sit right. Especially with Will's words from earlier about not being beholden to people. Usually she'd accept Laurel's view as truth even if it didn't feel right, but she shouldn't. She shouldn't. "No. It was him. Not her, not the accident. Something about him."

"Uh-oh," Cam muttered, interrupting that moment with Laurel. He swiveled in his seat, ducking his head toward them. "Jesse Carson just walked in."

Laurel swore, hunching herself around her untouched drink. "If he's connected, I don't want him seeing us here. Especially together. One at a time, we split up. Gracie, you go to the bathroom. Text Will to meet you back there once he can extricate himself. I'll go up to Grady's apartment. Cam, you follow me and go out the back. Watch the front for when Jesse leaves the bar, what he's driving and what direction he's going. Got it?"

Cam and Gracie nodded wordlessly.

"You first, Gracie. Keep your back to the front of the bar, but otherwise keep a leisurely pace. No attention drawing. No panic."

"Yup." She got off her seat and it was hard not to look back, to try to catch a glimpse of Jesse, or to see how Will was faring. But Laurel was right—even without a connection, Jesse was dangerous. They had to take every possible precaution.

She walked into the bathroom, stepped into a stall, then pulled out her phone and texted Will, hoping he wasn't so focused on everything that he ignored his phone.

"Who's this?" a large, balding man who looked like a stereotypical biker approached. His question was aimed at Kayleigh, and he jammed a thumb in Will's direction as he asked it.

Kayleigh slid her hand over Will's forearm and Will tried not to grimace. He was very much not used to women flirting with him anymore, and the fact she was Paula's cousin and he was almost positive married, based on the ring on her finger, made it extra weird and a little gross.

"This is Will," Kayleigh replied. "What are you doing here, Dad?"

"Got some business to take care of." The man who, if he was Kayleigh's dad, had to be Jesse Carson, eyed Will. "I know you?"

"Maybe," Will returned with a casual shrug as he carefully pulled his arm away from Kayleigh. He hadn't gotten much out of the woman. She kept going on about how talking about Paula made her too sad, or how the past was best left in the past. Even with Ty's casual attempts at moving the conversation toward Paula, she didn't bite.

Something about it was off, that Will knew, and the appearance of Kayleigh's father confirmed all his suspicions. If only he could figure out what any of his suspicions actually meant.

Maybe Jesse was the answer.

"I was married to Paula," Will offered when Jesse still said nothing else. "We didn't attend a lot of Carson family functions, so I'm not sure we would have ever run into each other. But you were her uncle, right?"

Jesse grunted, narrowing his eyes at Kayleigh, and then at Ty. "So, who's gonna go get me a celebratory get-out-of-jail drink? Ty? I'll take something hard. Have Grady put it on my tab."

Ty rolled his eyes, but he got up to do Jesse's bidding nonetheless.

"And you," he said, giving Kayleigh an intimidating glare. "You have to go to the bathroom."

"Excuse me?" she all but screeched.

"Do as you're told, girl. Or I'll tell Cyrus a few things I don't think you want your husband to hear about."

Kayleigh huffed, muttering things about being an adult and not being bullied by her jerk of a dad, but she got up off her stool. "Whatever," she muttered.

Will nearly jumped when her hand drifted across his butt as she walked behind him to go to the bathroom.

Jeez. He pretended to watch her go, but he was really scanning the bar for Delaneys, who had scattered and disappeared. He frowned and turned back to Jesse.

"Looking for something?" Jesse demanded gruffly. "Maybe a few someones."

"Huh?" Something was off and weird. Why was this man maneuvering people so they were alone?

"I hear you've been looking into Paula's death, that you think it's shady. That true?"

Will's throat felt dry but he took a sip of his beer and did his best to keep the building panic under wraps. "Never settled right with me. The way she died."

"Me neither. I've been in jail, of course, but I had methods of investigation from the inside."

Will didn't trust this man, but all of this could lead him somewhere. "What exactly are you saying?"

Jesse leaned close. "I have information. Evidence. And it all ties back to your girlfriend's uncle."

Will's body went to ice. Not just because Jesse was implicating Gracie's uncle, but that he knew or assumed a relationship had developed there. He didn't like Gracie being on this man's radar, especially when tied to this. It hadn't occurred to him it might be used to hurt her, and for the first time he regretted grabbing life by the horns before solving this mystery.

"You want the information," Jesse continued in that low, conspiring tone. "Then you and the girlfriend meet me outside in ten."

"I don't know what you're—"

"And if you don't, I guess you're just out of luck." With that, Jesse gave him a hard pat on his broken arm that had Will hissing in pain.

Jesse laughed as he sauntered out of Rightful Claim.

As much as Will didn't trust Jesse, he couldn't think of any reason Jesse would have to lie. To say he had evidence when he didn't. He searched the room again, but all the Delaneys were missing. What the hell?

He fished his phone out of his pocket to find a message from Gracie.

Meet me in the back by the bathrooms.

He immediately moved for the back, trying to ignore the searing pain in his arm. Kayleigh bounded out of the bathroom and though Will tried to do a sidestep that would keep her from seeing him, she pounced.

"Hey, sweetheart. Dad gone?" She grabbed on to his good arm.

Will tried to extricate himself, but she only scooted closer, cornering him against the wall as she trailed a fingertip up the zipper of his coat.

"Look, I have to—"

The women's bathroom door swung open again and Gracie stepped out. *Thank God.* "I have to talk to my girlfriend." He slid away from Kayleigh's body.

She scowled after him, and then at Gracie. "A Delaney? You can't be serious."

"It was nice seeing you, Kayleigh. See you around and all that." Will waved awkwardly and walked over to where Gracie was standing by the door frowning. "Save me," he whispered.

That frown didn't leave her face, and she studied him, then slowly turned her gaze to Kayleigh.

"Aren't you married to Cyrus Gentry?" Gracie asked, as if she was totally confused by the whole situation.

Will didn't think she was.

Kayleigh huffed and turned on a heel, stalking back out to the main portion of the bar. Before Will could tell Gracie what Jesse had said, she peered up at him.

"*Am* I your girlfriend?"

Will rocked back on his heels, taken completely off guard by the question. "Er. Well, I mean, we slept together. Which was a first for you. I should hope I'm something to you."

Her mouth curved, a small self-satisfied smile. He wished he had the time or place to enjoy it. "We have to go."

"What?"

"Jesse told me he has evidence, but he'll only give it to me if we meet him outside." He took her arm and started propelling her toward the front. "Where did the other two go?"

"We didn't want Jesse to see us." She pulled her arm away, stopping them before they got into the thick of the bar. "We need to get Laurel before we go out there."

"There's no time. I don't know how long he's going to wait, and he said it was this or nothing. Text her as we walk out there."

"Cam's waiting outside to watch Jesse," Gracie said, pulling her phone out of her pocket. "So we won't be out there alone. Let's go out the back."

Will nodded and followed her to the back exit.

Chapter Sixteen

They stepped out into the back. It was weirdly dark, no Christmas or parking lights shining. It didn't make sense, but Gracie was never out this late. Maybe there was some reasonable explanation.

The door to the bar snapped shut and they were plunged into almost complete darkness. Will stopped walking, holding Gracie to get her to stop, as well. "Something isn't—"

Someone in the dark snatched her phone out of her hand before she could hit Send on the text to Laurel. She reached out for whoever it was but found nothing but air. "Hey!"

"You won't be needing that," a low voice said, far too close to her ear. She moved closer to Will, but she could tell she accidentally jarred his broken arm by the way he hissed in a breath and she jumped back.

"Jesse, if you have evidence—"

"I'm in charge here, son. You'd do good to remember that."

It was all wrong. Even though it was dark when it shouldn't have been, Cam should be here. He was supposed to watch Jesse. Even if Cam was staying out of sight, he would have noticed the light situation and done something. Warned her or gotten Laurel or done something.

Now Jesse had her phone, and she might have written it off as threatening bullying but too much was wrong and off.

"I want my phone back," Gracie said, determined to be strong and pretend like nothing was wrong.

"Little Delaney bitch wants her phone back. We all want something, sweetheart. Delaneys are finally going to be out of luck."

"That's enough," Will said, a dangerous growl to his voice.

But Gracie knew they weren't in control here. This was all wrong and they were in the weaker position. She tried to reach back for the door behind her, but a meaty hand curled around her arm.

"Let go of me," she warned.

"Sorry, sweetheart. You're coming with me."

She tried to wrench her arm free, and she could feel Will moving forward. But there was a sickening crack of something, and then a thud.

"Will?" she whispered, suddenly boneless with fear, thoughts of fighting back disappearing as she tried to reach out for Will.

But Jesse's grip only tightened.

"Might live through that. Might not." Jesse's voice was low and pleased. Gracie's stomach turned as he started dragging her away.

She fought. Kicked and jerked and pulled, but he was

so much stronger than her. When he got to a truck, the engine roared to life and as he jerked open the passenger-side door, the dome light came on to reveal Kayleigh Gentry in the driver's seat.

What the hell was happening?

But Jesse hefted Gracie easily and tossed her into the truck. She tried to scramble back out immediately, but he blocked her with his body as he slid into the passenger seat.

With the light, she could fight back more effectively, but Kayleigh slammed on the accelerator and the unexpected movement of the truck caused Gracie to fall forward into the dash. Which allowed Jesse the chance to grab her arms again and pull them behind her back. He pulled her onto his lap and Gracie struggled to free herself, but he only laughed.

Then his voice was in her ear. "You don't want to excite me, sweetheart."

She nearly retched right there. But she stilled. She could kick across at the steering wheel or Kayleigh's leg on the accelerator to make Kayleigh crash, but there was too much risk she'd die since she was sitting this close to the windshield. She could keep fighting Jesse, but he could outmuscle her so easily it was a waste of energy.

She'd have to wait it out. She knew Bent and the surrounding areas as well as anyone. They couldn't take her anywhere she wouldn't know how to escape from. As long as she could escape Jesse's too-tight grip, she might have a chance.

Then there was the fact Jesse had her phone. If it

was still on, it was possible Laurel could trace it even if Gracie couldn't get a message to her.

She had to calm herself. She had to focus. Except she kept going back to that sickening crack and the thud afterward. What about Will? Would someone find him there in the dark?

"What did you do to Will?"

"Nothing your family hasn't done to mine," Jesse replied as if they were discussing the weather.

She wanted to ask about Cam, but she was afraid that might tip them off. She had to hope Cam was unharmed and had seen them take her and was following. Or something. The less these two knew about which Delaneys knew what, the better.

"I don't know what I have to do with this," Gracie said, trying to do her best to sound calm and unafraid. "Or how you're involved in Paula's death, or—"

Jesse laughed, squeezing her wrists so tight she whimpered.

"I did what I had to do to protect my family. To stand up for them. And somehow *I* ended up in jail when your uncle is the one who deserves so much worse than that." Jesse's evil smile glinted in the headlights of an oncoming car. "Now I finally have the means to make him pay and pay."

She wanted to cry, or scream, but neither would help her any. Or Will. God, Will. The only way she could help him was to survive and get out of here. So instead she paid attention to where they were going. Down Main, like it was the most normal thing in the world.

But it could be good. Maybe people would see them.

Laurel would have to come searching for them soon, and she would have people who had witnessed where they went.

Of course it was late and Bent was pretty much closed down for the night and—

Positive thoughts. There was no room for negativity. She had to get through this, so she had to believe she could.

Kayleigh drove out of town, but not far. It only took a few more minutes for Gracie to realize she wasn't being taken to some off-the-beaten-path, hidden-away place at all. They were driving right up to the Delaney Ranch.

"What is this?" she demanded as Kayleigh drove onto Delaney property, as if this had been their planned destination all along.

"Would have preferred your cop cousin, honestly," Jesse said, something like black, evil excitement twisting his features. "I knew it'd be a lot easier to get you though, and I don't have the time to be picky anymore. Your uncle will think twice before messing with my family again."

Gracie swallowed. "If you think I mean anything to him, I hate to break it to you—"

"Damn Delaneys are always so naive. He doesn't need to love you, little girl. You're a Delaney. Blood is all that matters. It's all that ever will."

THERE WAS A BLACKNESS. A terrible pain. Was he back on the side of that road? His arm sure hurt badly enough, but there was something hard on it. And the person calling his name, over and over, the fingertips touching him, it wasn't Gracie.

If it wasn't Gracie, the blackness seemed like a better place to stay.

But something wasn't right about that. Because Gracie wasn't here. She should be here. Where was she?

He struggled to open his eyes, to move. Someone was saying his name. It just wasn't Gracie.

"He's coming to," the woman said. "You both need an ambulance."

"No one is getting in an ambulance until we figure out where Gracie is. He'll need stitches, but there's no major damage," a man's voice said.

They didn't know where Gracie was, and that made him fight the darkness even harder.

"You're not a doctor, Cam," the woman said—Laurel. It had to be Laurel talking. And she was talking to Cam, who was the man's voice.

"I dealt with plenty of medical emergencies as a marine. He'll live. How long will the trace take?"

"They have to contact the phone company. Once they get through, it should be soon."

Will tried to speak, but his tongue felt five times its normal size and he couldn't make any part of his body move. God, his arm hurt almost as badly as when it had been originally broken. He had a sudden flash of Jesse hitting it inside the bar.

Jesse. He tried to speak again. "Jesse. Jesse took her."

Laurel peered down at him. They were outside in the parking lot, but there were lights now. Laurel had a flashlight, too. "We're pinging her phone. Presuming she has it. Will, are you okay?"

"Jesse has it. The phone. He has it."

"Good. Even better to ping him. Did he say anything? Anything at all that could give us some idea of what's happening or where they were going?"

It was fuzzy. Flashes here and there. He glanced at Cam and frowned. The man had a dried streak of blood from his temple down his cheek. "You're bleeding."

"Lead pipe to the temple. Just like you. Yours is worse."

"I want to sit up."

"You need a hospital," Laurel said. "This is probably your second concussion in a few days. You both need a hospital."

"I'll live," he said, struggling to get up. Cam ended up helping him. He was woozy, nauseous, but Gracie was missing. *Missing.* With that giant man who'd hit both him and Cam with a lead pipe.

"Why didn't he just kill us?" Will muttered, feeling like he'd been bruised and battered. Well, he supposed he had been.

"Murder is a little more jail time than battery," Cam replied. "But he's certainly racking the charges up. Can you remember anything?"

"He came in. He made Ty and Kayleigh leave, and you were all gone."

"We didn't want him to see us," Laurel replied. "The three of us in a Carson bar, even with me engaged to Grady, is just a little too weird."

"I think he knew." Will took a deep breath and let

it out. It seemed to help with the nausea and the pain, but not with the roiling fear that Gracie was with that lunatic. "Or something."

"Yeah, he knew something enough to take me out using Kayleigh as a damn diversion," Cam muttered, clearly disgusted with himself.

"He was talking about Delaneys, something about Delaneys getting what they deserve, but I can't figure out what he meant exactly, or why he'd want to take Gracie. We have to find her."

"The department is going to call me as soon as they have the trace information."

Laurel sounded so calm, seemed so absolutely fine with her cousin being kidnapped by a psychopath, and he might have yelled at her for that but he saw the way her hand trembled before she curled it into a fist and stood.

"We need to get inside. You're both freezing and hurt."

But just as she said it, the door opened and Grady stepped out. "Carson grapevine worked. Someone saw Jesse's truck on the road up to the Delaney Ranch."

"Why would he go there?"

"Wish I knew. You sure they don't need an ambulance?" Grady asked, nodding toward him and Cam.

He probably did. He felt worse than he had after the car accident, and he hadn't thought that was possible.

But Gracie was out there. And Jesse was taking her to Delaney property.

"We all have to go," Will said, trying to get to his feet. It took the wall and Cam's help to get him there, but after a few woozy seconds things smoothed out. "We have to go."

"I don't want to take my cruiser, or your truck for that matter, Cam. Both are way too conspicuous."

"What about Gracie's truck? Isn't it at Carson Auto? Doubt Jesse would know it. Unless he's the one who shot the window out. Even then, it's fairly nondescript."

"I'll go ask Van," Grady said, immediately disappearing back inside.

"I guess he didn't smash your brain completely to bits," Laurel offered, sounding a little surprised.

"Laurel, Cam, I know you aren't going to want to hear this, but this somehow connects to your father. I don't know how. I really don't. But after all these little threads, and now Jesse Carson is headed for your father. He connects."

"If he connects, then we will deal with that. I promise you."

Vanessa Carson came out the door, and made a quick hand motion. "Follow me to the shop. Faster to walk probably. Gracie's truck is fixed."

"Thanks, Vanessa," Laurel said, but Vanessa just grunted.

Laurel and Vanessa moved at rapid speed down the boardwalk to Carson Auto. Will's head and arm ached and burned with every step, but he thought of Gracie. Alone. In the middle of something that had nothing to do with her.

By the time Will and Cam caught up with Laurel, she was already sliding into the driver's seat. Cam went for the front seat, so Will used his good arm to awkwardly open the back door. Damn, everything hurt.

Vanessa pulled a face at the awkward, overly gentle way he and Cam moved. "You two look like crap."

"Yeah, thanks," Will muttered, sliding into the back seat. Laurel was pulling out of the garage before Will even had the door closed and all he could do was lean back in the seat and hope like hell they could solve this once and for all.

All that really mattered was that Gracie was safe and unhurt. He couldn't even consider the possibility of anything else because it hurt worse than his many injuries.

Laurel's phone went off. She pulled the phone to her ear. "Delaney."

Will strained to hear whatever the person on the other end was saying, but it was no use. The few seconds that passed were agony, even as Laurel drove them toward the Delaney Ranch.

She dropped the phone. "Pinged at the ranch house." She swore, a rare sign of emotion. "What the hell is Jesse Carson doing?"

"Feuding," Cam returned darkly.

"That's not an answer."

"It's not a reasonable answer. But it's an answer."

"It connects to Paula," Will said firmly.

"Paula is a Carson," Cam pointed out. "Maybe Jesse believes what you do. That someone killed her. This is revenge. He thinks it was a Delaney."

Will didn't want to say it, but it was important. "Look, it could have been a Delaney. The woman at the motel said the man having an affair with my wife drove a black—"

"Gracie told me," Laurel said quietly. If there was emotion in her over her father being implicated, she didn't show it. "At the bar. She told me Dad might be involved."

"He could have been having an affair with Paula. It's possible."

"He's just as big of a hater of the Carsons as Jesse is of him. I can't imagine him messing around with one. Let alone a married one."

"Okay, well, maybe he wasn't. Maybe Jesse only thinks he was. The truth isn't as important as whatever Jesse thinks is the truth. It has to connect, or he wouldn't have used me as part of it." A memory slapped him, hard and painful, and Will couldn't believe it had slipped away. "Wait. He told me. He told me when he talked to me he had evidence your father was involved. That's how he lured us outside."

Laurel pulled through the archway to the Delaney Ranch, a determined set to her jaw. "Well, we're about to find out the truth, one way or another."

"Nothing is more important than Gracie not being hurt. Not even the truth," Will insisted.

Laurel turned off the lights and pulled Gracie's car off the drive up to the house. Though the night was dark, the Christmas lights of the main house and a cabin off in the distance lit their drive. Instead of heading for the main house, Laurel drove toward a cabin on the far side of the property.

She stopped the car behind the cabin, hiding them from the view from the main house. She turned to Will.

"Gracie is the most important thing, which is why we need to have a plan before we head in there. A plan we all agree to follow no matter what. A plan that minimizes surprise and damage. Once she's out, we'll find the truth. Period. But no one risks themselves."

Will couldn't make that promise. He'd risk himself a thousand times over to keep Gracie safe.

Chapter Seventeen

Gracie was shaking. She didn't know if it was fear or cold, or possibly both, but she couldn't stop it no matter how many times Jesse warned her to knock it off. They had been crouched in the snow next to the porch of the Delaney house for she didn't know how long. Jesse had tied her hands together, with just enough extra rope so that he could hold on to the end of it and jerk her this way and that or pull her like a dog.

Gracie couldn't take it anymore. "He's asleep. Are we going to wait here all night? You'll freeze to death just as much as I will."

"Shut your mouth, girl." He jerked her rope so hard she fell over without her arms to break the fall. The ground was hard and the snow was cold and piercing.

Jesse and Kayleigh laughed like it was a good-natured prank.

It made her want to give up, but she knew she couldn't do that. She and her uncle might not be close, but she couldn't let Jesse hurt him. And what if no one had found Will? What if Cam was hurt, too? There was too much riding on her surviving. She couldn't let the Carsons' cruelty get to her.

Gracie struggled onto her knees. In the distance she thought she heard a car engine. It could be her imagination, a desperate hallucination. It could also be a truck on the highway in the distance—they usually didn't hear traffic up here but it was a cold night. Engine noise could travel. But she didn't want to take the chance it might be help, and the Carsons might see or hear it and hurt whoever could possibly be coming for her. So she started coughing. Coughing and coughing, even when Jesse told her to shut up and jerked the rope again.

She simply fell into the snow and coughed some more.

Jesse swore up and down, threatening her with all sorts of things, but she didn't stop coughing. She had to try to mask the sound just in case.

When Jesse kicked her in the ribs, hard, she squeaked at the sharp, unexpected blast of pain. She had to stop coughing because it hurt too much and it was taking everything she had to try to breathe through the crushing pain in her ribs.

"Are you sure you sent it to the right number?" Jesse demanded of Kayleigh, though Gracie had no idea what Kayleigh was supposed to have sent. There was some kind of plan they'd clearly devised before they'd taken her, and Gracie couldn't figure any of it out. Most especially why they were here.

Before Kayleigh could answer her father, a light inside flipped on. It illuminated the satisfied grin on Jesse's face and if Gracie wasn't in so much pain she might have had the wherewithal to get more afraid.

Jesse pulled her by the rope and didn't give her a chance to get to her feet. He dragged her through the snow as she wriggled and struggled to find a way to get up. It was only once they got to the porch that he stopped dragging her through the snow.

She tried not to sob, even though that was what she wanted to do. This was painful and demoralizing and she didn't understand how she was in the thick of it. Jesse jerked her to her feet just as the front door opened.

Her uncle stood there looking as polished as he ever did. His short hair didn't have one sleep-flattened section, and he wore a robe like most men wore a suit. He looked at the trio of them with regal superiority.

When his gaze met hers, some of that faltered for one second before it smoothed back out. "Grace," he said in that disappointed tone she'd known all of her life with him. He frowned at her. "I should have known it would come down to you."

Gracie didn't have a response. She didn't have anything. She could only stumble forward as Jesse pushed her inside.

"Carson, I don't know what you think you're doing, but surely you know it's only going to end in jail time. Again." He looked at Kayleigh with that sneer of disgust Gracie didn't think he was trying to hide at all. "And bringing your daughter into it. You've made a misstep here."

"Have I?" Jesse asked, studying the vast living room bathed in a warm glow from the chandelier above. The

Christmas tree lights were off, but the prettily decorated tree stood big and full in the corner, cheerful and
mocking.

Jesse jerked the rope again and this time it propelled
Gracie forward into an end table, sending a shooting
pain up her leg and knocking over a lamp in the process. It crashed to the ground.

Jesse sat on the couch, still grinning, as he jerked
the rope again. Gracie was ready for it this time so she
didn't fall, but she did have to take the steps toward the
couch as he pulled on the rope.

"What is this about, Carson? It's the middle of the
night. Some of us are gainfully employed and have
meetings in the morning."

Gracie wished she could be shocked he was so calm,
so completely unconcerned with the fact Jesse had her
tied up like a rabid animal, but all in all it was about as
much as she could expect from her uncle.

"This is about revenge, Delaney. It's about your people stealing everything my people were ever owed. It's
about the crap hand we've been dealt by Delaneys since
the beginning of Bent."

Uncle Geoff sighed heavily. "I'll never understand
why the lazy, shiftless Carson clan has convinced themselves they're owed anything when they won't do a hard
day's work to save their lives."

Jesse only smiled, and that was when Gracie knew
this was very, very bad. Because she expected him to
rage. To pounce. To fight. Every Carson she'd ever come
into contact with who was obsessed with the feud was
always ready to brawl. Usually because a Delaney had

done exactly what her uncle had done—been a condescending jerk.

But Jesse was calm. Happy. It was all so very scary and even as she worked to get her hands out of their bonds, she knew they were too tight.

"I have proof you were involved in the crash that killed Paula Cooper."

Uncle Geoff scoffed. "I didn't kill anyone."

Jesse laughed, an edge of bitterness and something else Gracie had a bad feeling was insanity.

"No. Of course not. Wouldn't want to get your hands dirty. But it just so happens I know who killed Paula, and with that knowledge, I can make sure the police think you did it."

Geoff's face was expressionless, but Gracie knew enough to understand that only meant he had some deep, violent emotion he was hiding.

It occurred to her that by witnessing this, hearing this, Jesse's intent was not to use her as a pawn. He was going to kill her. Because if she knew he was framing Geoff, she couldn't possibly be trusted to live.

The panic beat so hard she could barely hear what they were saying over it, and it seemed the more she struggled against the rope holding her hands together, the tighter and more unbearable it got.

"Don't think for a second your precious daughter can stop that from happening," Jesse was saying. "No one is going to let her weasel you out of this. I'm going to put you in jail just like you put me in jail."

"You put yourself in jail when you robbed one of my tellers. As for Laurel, unlike Carsons, Delaneys have morals and standards. Which means Laurel will seek the truth. I don't need her to get me out of a lie, because your lie will be discovered. Honestly you think you'd learn at some point you can't hurt me, Carson. I'm untouchable, and smarter than you."

Gracie winced, not at the bonds this time, but at the way her uncle was poking at this angry, vicious man while he had her in his mercy.

"Morals and standards," Jesse repeated, rubbing a hand over his chin. Gracie watched the other hand hoping against hope his grip on the rope loosened. "Is that why you were sneaking away to hotel rooms with my married niece?"

Gracie waited for her uncle to deny it. To use that same calm, assured voice to say it wasn't true. Jesse was mistaken or lying again.

But he merely looked grim.

"Oh my God," Gracie whispered, staring at her uncle's face. He didn't look at her, nothing in his gaze changed, but she knew it had to be true. *He'd* slept with Paula. Jesse had been the man watching them.

"No matter," Jesse said happily. "What's incredibly immoral is killing, and you're about to kill your niece. A shame for both of you."

"What on earth? You have lost your mind, Carson. I'm not going to kill Grace. You can't make me."

"A niece for a niece. It's only fair. I had to end Paula's life, you have to end this one."

Gracie tried not to react, but she shook harder nonetheless. Jesse had killed Paula.

The blood had drained out of Geoff's face. "You killed Paula. Why would you…"

"I warned her. I warned her that if she let a Delaney touch her again she'd face the consequences. They were a little more dire than I'd planned, but she brought it upon herself. So, still your fault. Now, let's get on with it. Kayleigh?"

Kayleigh produced two guns from her purse and handed them to Jesse. He laughed, low and oh so pleased with himself.

"See, the beauty of my plan is that I don't have to make you kill your niece. I only have to kill her, and make it look like you did. Two murders? Oh, you're going to rot for a very long time."

"I SHOULD HAVE made you two go to the hospital," Laurel whispered irritably as they finally made it to the house. Both he and Cam had encountered mild dizzy spells on the trek through the snow, causing them both to fall, but they'd gotten back up. They were both upright.

As for Will, he was upright with a pounding headache and a roiling nausea settled in his gut, but he wasn't about to stop. Gracie was in that house somewhere, in danger. He'd deal with his injuries once she was safe.

"We're fine," Cam said shortly, and Will knew if he said it himself it would sound hollow and weak compared to Cam's forceful military surety. So he kept his mouth shut.

"The lights are on. Dad's the only one home and it's two in the morning. What on earth is this if they've got the lights on?"

Cam moved toward the window, but unless marines had X-ray vision he wasn't going to see anything. All the curtains were drawn.

"We have to go in there," Will said. It felt like stating the obvious, but both Cam and Laurel were clearly more predisposed to caution.

"We have to be careful," Laurel countered.

Screw caution. Will knew she was a cop and used to tense, dangerous situations, but he didn't know how she could stay calm or *out here* when Gracie was inside.

"I'm going in there." He didn't have to listen to these people or take orders from anyone, and he wasn't letting Gracie be at the mercy of any of those people.

"You're hurt and one man. If you bash in there you're likely to get both of you killed. And possibly our father."

"Or he's involved."

Neither Laurel nor Cam said anything to that, and he'd give them a little credit for not immediately jumping to their father's defense.

"We need to do this tactically. One person stays outside to assess the situation while two people move in from two different entry points," Cam said.

"Laurel should stay outside," Will said firmly. When she started to protest, Will just kept talking. "You've called backup, and you need to apprise them of the situation. Besides, you're bound by certain regulations. Cam and I aren't."

"He has a point," Cam said, pulling a set of keys out of his pocket. "I'll take the garage side entry, and Will can go in the back. Laurel stays here in the front. We'll assess the situation inside and then report immediately back. No heroics, just information gathering. As long as things aren't dire, we'll come back out and wait for more police."

"Will doesn't have a weapon."

"He doesn't need one if we're just information gathering."

Of course, Will wasn't planning on just information gathering, but they didn't need to know that. Maybe they had the patience to wait around and *assess* situations, but Will couldn't damn well breathe knowing Gracie was in danger.

Cam handed him a key. "This will get you in the back door. You'll be in a mud room, the door will likely be closed. On the other side of that door is the kitchen, which opens up into the living room. It appears the living room lights are the only ones on, so I wouldn't venture past the kitchen. Just try to see who's in the living room and listen if you can hear any conversation. All we're doing is figuring out what's going on. Remember, Gracie can hold her own."

Of course she could. But she shouldn't have to. So Will didn't say anything—he just started walking around the giant house, fighting against the dizziness and nausea plaguing him. He could give in to that later. Once Gracie was safe.

He made it to the door, cold and somehow exhausted. Everything felt about three times harder since Jesse had knocked him out, but he had to keep pushing. As carefully as he could with shaking hands and double vision, Will managed to get the key into its hole.

Another deep breath and then he pushed inside with as much finesse as he could manage. The room was mostly dark, except a slight sliver of light that snuck in through the door. Cam had said it led to the kitchen.

Will crept toward it and then reached out to slowly pull it open enough so he could slip through the crack. It creaked as he moved it, and in the thundering silence of his own mind it sounded supersonic. He froze.

He froze and he waited and nothing happened. He heard no footsteps, no voices. Just his own ragged breath and his heartbeat drumming in his ears. Once he got that mildly under control, he moved through the small opening he'd managed. The door squeaked again, but he had to believe he wouldn't be heard this time any more than he'd been heard the first.

He crept through the kitchen toward the opening on the far side. The one that supposedly led to the living room, where the lights were on.

The light from the living room was bright enough if anyone came into the kitchen they would definitely see him. Which had him looking around the perfectly clean, ridiculously expensive-looking kitchen for some kind of weapon. He'd prefer a gun, but a knife would have to do.

He slid a butcher's knife out of the knife block on the counter, then crept toward the opening again. The closer he got to the opening, the more he could hear voices.

Low and very nearly calm. At least they sounded calm, but then Jesse laughed, low and dangerous, and Will knew there was nothing calm about what was going on.

He edged as close as he could without risking being seen.

"See, the beauty of my plan," Jesse was saying, in

that same casual voice that Will could only regard as wildly out of place and maybe a little psychotic, "is that I don't have to make you kill your niece. I only have to kill her, and make it look like you did."

It took a moment for those words to make any sense. They still didn't even as Will stepped forward into the opening to the living room. It didn't need to make full sense to know that Gracie was in trouble.

And barging in, knowing Jesse was likely armed, would only get them all killed. He had to do something without drawing attention. Something to give him some kind of advantage or just even footing. He had to get Gracie out of there.

Holding his breath, he looked out the opening of the kitchen. Will took in the scene. Jesse lounging on a couch as Kayleigh handed him not one but two guns. Gracie's uncle standing next to a chair looking calm and collected if a little pale.

It took Will a few more seconds to find Gracie, sitting on the floor, hands tied behind her back while the end of the rope was held tightly in Jesse's fist.

There was only one light on. A giant chandelier hanging from above. He'd only need to get the light off to find some kind of advantage, or maybe spur Cam and Laurel into action. Jesse would still have a grip on Gracie, but it would be harder for him to hurt her, and Will had a straight shot to her if he didn't get disoriented.

He looked to the left wall, searching for a light switch. Nothing. As he turned his head to look to the other side of the wall, he had the misfortune of catching Kayleigh's gaze.

Her eyes widened. "Daddy," Kayleigh said, a kind of whispery tone as if she didn't believe what she was seeing.

Will looked away, diving toward the right wall and a row of light switches. He slapped his hand against them, flicking them all off, hoping against hope he'd found the right switch.

When they were plunged into darkness, he didn't have time to sigh in relief. A gunshot went off.

Chapter Eighteen

Gracie screamed when the gun went off. But there was no sound after it. No moan of pain or thud of someone falling over.

Oh God. She prayed with everything she had that the bullet missed everyone in the room.

She didn't have time to pray for long. Not tied up in a room with two people who wanted her dead. She jerked her hands and body as hard as she could and nearly sobbed in triumph when she'd clearly caught Jesse off guard enough for him to let the rope go.

She rolled, trying to keep a clear picture of the room in her head. When she stopped, hoping she was at least somewhat near the front door, she realized the entire room was silent. She could occasionally hear a shuffle, an intake or outtake of breath, but no one was talking.

Which only made her heart pound harder. The curtains were drawn, letting none of the lights outside shine in, so she couldn't see anything. Getting to the door was possible, but if she opened the front door it would draw attention to where she was. She doubted Jesse would be afraid to shoot indiscriminately. Really her only hope was that he had some concern for his daughter, and she had to wonder about that since he'd involved her in this whole thing.

Who had turned off the lights though? Had it been an accident? There were too many questions. Too many what-ifs.

But Jesse hadn't had a chance to kill her, so there was that. She reached out, feeling the floor around her and trying to get a better gauge of where she was in the room.

"All right, who turned off the lights?" Jesse's voice growled, and Gracie was somewhat relieved at how far away his voice sounded. She'd gotten some distance from him.

"It was Will Cooper," Kayleigh said, her voice shrill and maybe a little frightened. "That bastard came in through the kitchen."

Gracie nearly gasped with relief. Will was alive. Will was *here*.

"Thought I killed him," Jesse said, and Gracie would never get used to the conversational way he discussed killing and hurting people.

Will. Will was here. Suddenly relief and happiness at him being alive morphed into fear. Now that was two people she cared about in danger, and she had absolutely no clue how to save any of them.

A phone. She had to get to a phone. If it was in its base, there should be one in the far corner by the kitchen entry, and maybe if she headed that way she could find Will. Either way, if she could get a phone and dial 911…

Maybe it would lead Jesse to her, the movement or the sound, but she had to try.

She started crawling in what she hoped was the right direction and as she moved she realized she could hear shuffling getting closer and closer.

Something brushed her hand, followed by a sharp intake of breath. "Gracie?" someone whispered. Will. It *had* to be Will. It definitely wasn't her uncle, and Kayleigh and Jesse wouldn't whisper.

When a warm hand touched her shoulder, she was 100 percent certain it was Will. She didn't want to answer since the room had fallen silent again, so she reached out with her other hand and put it on top of his on her shoulder. She felt his whoosh of relieved breath, but it was also too loud in the quiet room.

"Kayleigh, get over to me and then I'm going to start shooting and hope I hit something."

Kayleigh said something in return, but Gracie couldn't hear it because Will was whispering in her ear.

"Can you get us to the front door?"

She carefully turned her mouth to his ear, doing her best to whisper as softly as possible while Jesse and Kayleigh bickered as they tried to find each other.

"We can't leave my uncle."

"Laurel's outside. Police on their way. Cam's somewhere. We need to get you out and let the others handle the rest."

Gracie swallowed. Help was here. A lot of it. She squeezed his hand and then maneuvered herself, hopefully back toward the door. She put Will's bad hand on her back, hoping he got the hint she was going to guide him to as close to the front door as she could manage.

They moved along, and as she moved she listened to Jesse and Kayleigh practically yelling at each other at this point.

"How can you not find me, girl? We weren't that far apart? Don't make me start shooting without you."

"I can't see anything!" Kayleigh cried in return. "I cannot believe you'd threaten to shoot me. What kind of father are you?"

"What kind of useless are you that you still sound far away?" Jesse demanded, a cruel, awful growl to his voice.

Gracie picked up her pace. She didn't doubt Jesse might snap and start shooting indiscriminately if Kayleigh didn't reach his side soon. She reached out to crawl forward, but found wall. Not door. Wall.

She didn't let herself panic, though she wanted to cry in frustration. Instead, she started feeling along the wall, trying to find a hint of anything that might give her a clue as to where she was.

Her hands brushed a hard corner. She felt around it, determining it was the windowsill. There were the curtains. But which side of the window was she on?

She tried to count her breathing and focus on that over fear that silence had descended again. *Inhale, one two three. Exhale, one two three.*

She nearly cried out when her fingertips ran from wall to another hard edge. The door frame. Oh, thank God. She felt along until her hand found the doorknob.

She reached back and took Will's hand, leading it to the doorknob, as well.

His hand closed over hers and his mouth was at her ear again. "I'm going to open it. You're going to go out and find Laurel."

"What about you?"

"I'll be behind you."

She swallowed, then squeezed his hand again, a nonverbal yes. She pulled away, on her hands and knees to the side of the door so Will could pull it open.

She heard something click, and the door squeaked as it opened, a little shaft of Christmas light glow edging through. It would draw attention, but Gracie didn't hesitate. She crawled out the opening onto the cold cement of the porch. She turned to help Will out, but the door closed instead.

Then it exploded as a bullet smashed through it.

And into her.

WILL COULD ONLY SIT, frozen and in shock that the bullet hadn't hit him. He'd felt it whizz by him, and then heard the exploding crash of it smashing through the door.

The door Gracie had just gone out of.

He'd promised to follow her, but he'd known her best chance of survival—since Jesse had been specifically targeting her when he'd walked in—was to get her the hell out and let him and hopefully Cam stop Jesse.

But a bullet had gone through the door Gracie was on the other side of.

Please God, let Gracie be okay.

Another gunshot went off, and if this one passed near

him, he didn't feel it. Instead, something on the other side of the room crashed.

The lights suddenly flipped on, causing Will to wince and close his eyes on reflex. But he immediately forced himself to open them.

Cam was standing there, his own weapon drawn and pointed at Jesse. Will turned his attention to the large man in the middle of the room, his daughter cowering behind him.

Jesse smiled and Will didn't think, didn't hesitate. He got to his feet and ran full force at Jesse. He was more than shocked that a gunshot didn't go off before he crashed into Jesse's large, hard body.

He swore viciously as they both fell down, trying to reach out for the gun or land a blow with his nonbroken arm. But it was all flailing limbs and painful landing on the hardwood floor.

Jesse swore and threatened, but he must have lost the gun because he was using both hands to try to toss Will off him. Will managed to land a blow to Jesse's gut with his knee, but the victory lasted only seconds before Jesse was twisting his broken arm.

Will fought to escape that painful grasp, fought to land any blow. He got a few in, but still Jesse twisted his broken arm until Will was shaking and sweating.

Will felt himself being nudged out of the way by a boot, but it got Jesse to let go of his arm so he could only feel relief flood him. Everything hurt and ached and Gracie…

Will stumbled to his feet and looked at Cam, who had

his boot shoved into Jesse's neck and had his weapon pointed straight at him.

"You can't shoot me," Jesse growled, attempting to spit on Cam. He missed his mark and his eyes searched the room, but Kayleigh had taken off through the back, as if she could escape.

"Watch me." Cam flicked a glance at Will. "Go see if the cops are here yet."

Will was already scrambling for the door, aching arm forgotten. Screw the cops. Was Gracie okay?

He stumbled out the door, and there were two police cruisers. One had its lights on, the other was completely dark. Laurel stood talking to another deputy, while two other deputies stood on the porch, guns drawn on him.

"That's Cooper," Laurel shouted, striding forward. "What's the status?"

"Cam's got Jesse. Kayleigh went out the back."

"Mosely, Jackson, get Kayleigh Granger. Hart, go in and arrest Jesse Carson. Get statements from Cam and my father. I'll handle Will's."

The men moved at Laurel's orders.

"Where the hell is Gracie?"

Laurel dropped her crossed arms, running a hand through her hair that was falling out of its rubber band. It was the way her arm shook that had Will's stomach pitching.

Laurel cleared her throat. "She…"

"What?" Will demanded, and the only reason he didn't reach out and shake Laurel was that every inch of his body felt like lead. Painful, cracked lead.

"It was all his idea!" came a scream from the other

side of the house. "He threatened me! You have to let me go." The two deputies who'd gone after Kayleigh had her handcuffed and were bringing her toward one of the cruisers.

"Where is Gracie?" Will demanded when Laurel turned all her attention to Kayleigh.

"Will."

"Just tell me," he said, and he didn't have it in him to care that his voice broke.

"The bullet that went through the door hit her. I had the first deputy on the scene rush her to the hospital."

"She was…"

"Breathing? Yes. But it was not good."

"Why are we here? I have to go." He started walking. God knew where. He didn't have a car. Couldn't drive. But how could Laurel just let her be taken away to the hospital alone?

"Will, we have to handle this here." She caught up with him and gripped his good arm. "We cannot go running off to the hospital. I know you're scared. *I'm* scared, but we have to handle *this*."

"Like hell we do," he returned, pulling his arm out of her grip.

"Do you want Jesse Carson to go to jail?" she demanded.

Will stepped forward, furious she'd even question it—that she'd still be standing here when Gracie was being rushed to the hospital. After being shot. "He will rot there if I have anything to do with it."

"Then we have to do this right. We need statements and proof and they need to be arrested on the complete up-and-up. We wouldn't be with her in the hospital anyway. This is what we can do for her. This is what we *have* to do for her. Will. Us being in that hospital doesn't change anything. Us making sure this scum gets everything he has coming to him? That's something."

Will swallowed at the horrible tide of emotion rising in his throat. Somewhere in his brain he knew Laurel was right. Being with Gracie wouldn't change anything.

"How bad was it?"

"I don't know, Will. They're going to call me the second they have any information and we'll go to the hospital immediately once we get everything taken care of here."

Will nodded, looking back at the house where Jesse was being lead out the door. He struggled the whole way, trying to knock the deputies over, trying to land an elbow. But the deputies just kept pulling him toward one of the cruisers, Cam behind them, his gun still drawn.

Jesse looked around the yard, then at Will and Laurel standing. He struggled more in the handcuffs and the deputies' grips, but they didn't let him go.

"Where's the little bitch?" Jesse called. "Did I get her?"

Sucker shot or not, Will calmly walked over and punched Jesse right in the nose, satisfied by both the sickening crack and the howl of pain.

"Oops," Will said to both deputies who'd stopped pulling Jesse forward and were staring at him in shock.

"He assaulted me! I want to press charges!" Jesse screamed.

That got the deputies back into action and they struggled to get Jesse into the back of the car, Jesse fighting and yelling about Will and a broken nose the whole way.

"It doesn't solve anything," Laurel said softly. "But that was satisfying to watch."

"Laurel."

"Come on. We need your statement."

So he went with her, back toward the gigantic Delaney house now glittering with light. Enough light he could see the pool of blood on the porch. Gracie's blood.

He wished he'd done a lot more than break Jesse's nose.

Chapter Nineteen

You're too strong to give up.

  We're only getting started.

  All you have to do is open your eyes.

  I am sorry.

Gracie couldn't make sense of any of the voices that came or went. They all existed in a gray fog. She couldn't isolate one from another, but they kept coming. Someone would take her hand, or whisper something to her, but she couldn't open her eyes. She couldn't even seem to breathe, though it wasn't a struggle exactly. She just didn't seem to have any control over anything.

Grace. She hadn't heard that voice in so long and it sent a weird, twisted pain through her side. Her mother's voice. No one called her Grace nicely, lovingly. She hadn't been able to stand it after losing both parents, and only Uncle Geoff had refused to abide her wishes to go by Gracie. But he never said Grace kindly, not like this. It had been almost twenty years since she'd heard that voice.

  Grace. You'll be all right.

She remembered those words. Her mother's last.

You'll be all right. She'd believed it. She'd always believed it because that had been Mom's parting gift to her.

When Gracie's eyes opened, it was as if someone had pulled her straight out of the fog. She hadn't made the choice to open anything, but suddenly her eyes were open and everything was a cloudy white.

Nothing made sense about any of this. Where was she? Why did she hurt? She didn't remember anything.

"Gracie."

Except she did remember that voice, and even though it took a supreme effort she didn't know she had in her, she turned her head toward it. Will's face was a little blurry, but it was Will. Right there. Oh, thank God. "I remember you," she whispered.

He made a noise she couldn't explain, but he leaned forward and pressed his forehead to the back of her hand. Because he'd been holding her hand.

"Well, that's something," he croaked. "Are there things you don't remember?"

His voice sounded so scratchy. So…something. But her head was pounding too much to really figure it all out. Her throat was dry and she felt so incredibly heavy.

"Hurts," she muttered even though that wasn't the right word for it. No throbbing pain or sharp discomfort. Just everything was too heavy, too hard.

"What does?"

"Everything."

"Oh, Gracie. Hell. I think you scared thirty years off all our lives. I'm supposed to go get everyone the second you wake up."

"No, don't go." She tried to hold on to him, but after the failed attempt she realized he hadn't made any move to go. Will. Here. Hers. But she didn't understand how she was in the hospital, and he wasn't. Wasn't he hurt? Jesse had hurt him. But after that? "It's all a jumble. What happened?"

"You were shot. Narrowly missed your spine. They say you were lucky."

"Shot." She squeezed her eyes shut trying to make sense of that. Of anything. Shot. Lucky. "Who shot me?"

"They've got you on a lot of medications. They said it'll take some time to come out of it. Make sense of things. It's okay if you're confused. It's all going to clear up."

"Will."

He kissed the palm of her hand, just a light brush of his lips. "That's me."

She managed to move her arm, reach up and touch the bandage on his head. "He knocked you out. Jesse. Jesse Carson. He hit you with something and knocked you out. You're okay. I didn't think you were okay."

Will gave her hand a light squeeze. "Lead pipe. Managed to get both me and Cam. But we're fine. A few stitches and a concussion for the both of us. I was given the extra-special warning that if I sustain another concussion my brain's probably mush, but I'm mostly okay. Sitting here instead of lying there, huh?"

"You pushed me out the door." It was fuzzy, but starting to come together. Jesse had taken her to her uncle's house and… Something she should remember. Something she should tell Will.

"I should have followed you out that door," Will said gravely, still holding on to her hand. "I should have done so many things differently. Like not listen to the psychopath in the first place. You'd be okay."

"No. I mean, first of all, I am okay, but he wanted me all along. It didn't really have anything to do with you. He wanted to punish my uncle." She tried to read through the fog. "I can't remember."

"You don't have to. Jesse is going to jail, and everyone else might be a little banged up here and there, but we're all going to live and that's what's important."

"But you blame yourself."

"I should have—"

"You can't tell me being alive is what's important and then tell me you should have done things differently. You can't sit there and blame yourself. The only blame for today goes on Jesse's shoulders."

"You're going to have this same guilt fight with Cam and Laurel, just to warn you."

She closed her eyes, unaccountably exhausted. "I don't want to fight. I want to go home."

"You're not quite ready for that, but waking up was a start."

"Mmm." She tried to open her eyes, but sleep seemed like a much cozier idea. Maybe in sleep she could find the answers.

"Gracie?"

"Hmm." But she was floating away, and whatever he said after that never quite reached her.

I LOVE YOU.

Will looked down at Gracie's pale face, gut twisted into knots over how much strength had leaked out of her in just thirty-six hours. She hadn't heard him say those three words, and maybe it was for the best. Probably shouldn't utter them in a hospital room to a gunshot victim.

The door opened and Laurel walked in, dressed in her uniform.

"She woke up for a second," he offered.

Laurel rushed over to the other side of the bed, peered down at Gracie. "Why didn't you come get us?" she hissed in a whisper.

"She didn't want me to leave."

"You could have used the nurse button."

"I didn't think of that at the time."

Laurel scowled at him. "What did she say?"

"She didn't remember everything. Still a little mixed-up, but she knew who everyone was and had a little idea of what happened. What's the update on Jesse?"

Laurel moved back to his side of the bed, then pulled him out of the chair and back toward the door. In a low voice, she spoke. "Charges include attempted murder, aggravated assault, coercion. I could go on, but even if he pleas down, he's going to be spending quite a bit of time in jail."

"What about Kayleigh?"

"She'll likely get off as she's given us almost all the information to prosecute Jesse to the fullest extent."

Will frowned. He didn't particularly like that Kayleigh wouldn't suffer any consequences, but maybe she really just was a pawn in her father's scheme.

"Now, visitor hours are over, and if you make the same scene you made yesterday about leaving, I will have to arrest you."

Will scowled. "Someone should be with her."

"Jen's in the waiting room. Since she's family, they're letting her spend the night." Laurel frowned, something like concern in her eyes. "They kept you overnight last night. Where are you going to stay tonight and how are you going to get there?"

Will glanced at Gracie, asleep in bed, an idea forming. He watched her as he lied to Laurel so the fib wouldn't show on his face. "Gracie said I could stay at her place. I just need a ride."

"I can do that. Should you be alone with that concussion?"

"It's been over twenty-four hours. They said I was fine to be alone after that." He turned to Laurel and smiled.

"Okay. Follow me."

"Just one second." He felt a little weird with Laurel watching him, but he couldn't just walk out. He went over to Gracie's bed and dropped a kiss to her temple, whispering a goodbye and those three idiotic words one more time.

He walked back to where Laurel was waiting by the door. She had a speculative look on her face and Will hunched his shoulders against it.

"What?"

"I didn't like you, Will. For two years, you've been

nothing but a pain in my side and a constant worry because I knew Gracie had a thing for you and I thought you weren't interested. But you were right, and you've been... Well, I'm glad you're as head over heels for her as she is for you. Or I'd have to break some laws to cause you physical harm and probably lose my job."

"You could always have Grady do it and avoid the job loss."

"Smart. I'll keep that in mind."

"I wasn't not interested. I was clueless, and still healing I guess. So. It wasn't like that. Just so you know."

Laurel smiled, slinging her arm around his shoulders. "Now that I know, I can mock you mercilessly. I am marrying a Carson after all, and mocking is their way of life."

"I think I prefer the Delaneys."

"I think you're about to be dealing with a whole lot of both." She took a deep breath. "I've talked to my father."

"Ah."

"The affair didn't start before you guys moved here. There was no past connection. Do you remember Paula applying for finance officer?"

"Vaguely. She didn't get the job. That was only three or four years ago, right?"

"Right. She didn't get the job, but my father was the one who interviewed her." Laurel pulled a face. "He said they hit it off. They started meeting for drinks in Fairmont. Then, well, it escalated from there."

Will didn't know what to say. He supposed it was some kind of relief she hadn't been cheating on him the whole time. A relief he'd been wrong about *some* things.

"In addition to that, based on what Kayleigh told us, Jesse tampered with your car and burned down your house in the hopes you'd back off so he could arrange his revenge for my father."

"Why didn't he just kill Cam and I back at the bar?"

"He was trying to get my father in jail, not wind himself back there. Your saving grace, I guess."

Saving Grace. No, that was the woman in the hospital bed. The woman he was ready to build a future with. Because Paula, affairs and even this horrible incident was in the past.

It was time to plan his future.

GRACIE WASN'T SURE she'd ever been so happy to see her little house in her entire life. It seemed like months or years since this had all started even though it had been only two weeks now.

There was a dusting of snow over her Christmas lights lining the eaves, and thick clumps in the sparkling trees. The lights were on inside, adding another warm glow of welcome to the lights. No more white, sterile hospital. *Home.*

"Is someone inside?"

"Will," Laurel said, eyebrows drawing together. "He said you offered to let him stay at your house. I gave him your key."

"Oh. I don't remember. Maybe when I was out of it I did, but I'm glad I did. He doesn't have anywhere to go." She yawned and tried not to wince as Laurel helped her up the walk. The wound still hurt, and she imagined it would for quite a while, but she'd been lucky the bullet had passed through her side and not hit any important organs.

Her recovery had been stellar and now she was home just in time for Christmas tomorrow. And Will was inside. She smiled at that.

Laurel turned the knob and pushed the door open, helping Gracie with that last step. She was too exhausted to fight all the help she was getting, though she imagined she'd be done with it in a few days.

For today, she was glad to be home. Her Christmas tree twinkled from the corner and Will stepped out of the kitchen with a big grin on his face.

This was exactly what she wanted for Christmas. Maybe without the gunshot wound and his broken arm, but they'd get through those things all the same. Heal. Move on and forward.

"Welcome home," he offered with a smile.

Home. Will in her home. It felt infinitely, perfectly right. She stepped toward him and when she reached him she simply leaned right into him, gingerly to protect her side and his arm, but he wrapped his good arm around her and this was right where she wanted to be for a very long time.

"I guess I'll leave you two alone, huh?" Laurel smiled warmly. "Take care of each other, and for the love of God stay out of trouble."

"Merry Christmas, Laurel," Will offered.

"Merry Christmas, guys." She left, pulling the door closed behind her.

"Christmas," Gracie murmured, looking up at Will. "How did it get to be Christmas Eve?"

"I wish I knew." He used his good hand to brush some hair out of her face. "Oh, I'm glad you're here."

"Me, too," she replied emphatically.

"And I have a Christmas gift."

"But it isn't Christmas."

"It's our Christmas. You're home, which is my gift, and what I'd made for you survived my shop's destruction, so Christmas miracle or something."

"You made something for me before?"

"I did. I'd convinced myself I was going to sell it to the antique store while I made it, but it was always for you." He released her then bent under the tree and pulled a terribly wrapped lump that might contain a box somewhere under crumpled edges and too much paper. He cleared his throat. "It was hard to wrap with only one workable arm."

She swallowed, feeling teary as she carefully pulled the wrapping paper away from the box inside. She pulled the lid open to find an iron door knocker in the shape of a flowering rose.

"You were always talking about how much you liked my door knocker. I'll install it for you, too, once I've got two good arms."

"Will. It looks just like the rose bushes I planted in front of your cabin."

"That was kind of the point." He smiled, and she realized a tear had escaped only when he reached out to brush it away.

She waved a hand in front of her face. "I'm blaming this emotional response on the meds."

"I don't mind an emotional response," he said, still touching her face.

The gift was thoughtful and gorgeous and proved Will had been paying attention even when he hadn't wanted to. It was too perfect, really. She didn't deserve it or him or this seemingly happy beginning.

Which reminded her of something she'd completely let fall into that fog that still clouded some of what had happened that night.

"Gracie, I lo—"

Oh God. No. "Wait."

"Huh?"

"Oh God. I haven't told you, all the things I pieced together. I didn't tell you." She turned away from him, panic bubbling through her. She hadn't told Will and it changed everything. *Everything.*

"Tell me what?" he insisted, moving so that he was in front of her again.

It was going to end things. How could it not? "I…" She didn't want to lose him, but how could she keep that secret? It was too big, too awful and likely to come out in Jesse's trial anyway. "Will, I know who Paula was having an affair with," she whispered.

He didn't say anything, just gave her a quizzical look.

"It was my uncle," she forced herself to say. "That's why Jesse was going to hurt me. That's what prompted Jesse to try to punish Paula—a relationship with a Delaney. I…" She shook her head, feeling tears well in her eyes as she looked down at his perfect gift.

She thrust it back at him. He wouldn't want her now.

Not when she was connected to the man his wife had slept with.

"What are you doing?"

"You can't possibly want…" She forced herself to look at him and he only looked confused. Not shocked or angry or anything other than slightly concerned. "You don't want me now," she said firmly. "I'm related to the man who—"

"Gracie, I knew all that. Kayleigh told the police everything, and Laurel explained it all to me. Why Jesse was there, how he was involved with killing Paula. I knew it was your uncle days ago." He took her by the shoulders, ignoring the gift she still held out to him. "I don't care who you're related to. I love you."

She could only stare at him for a few awful seconds. But he was still touching her. He knew and he'd given her this and said that. "But…"

"No buts. I love you no matter what. I'm not saying I want to have Christmas dinner with the guy, but that's also because he treats you like crap from what I can tell. But I love you, and I'll make sacrifices for you, Gracie. You've been there no matter how little I deserved it, and you infinitely deserve the same from me. Why would any of that stuff you had nothing to do with change my mind?"

No one had ever said that to her before. Not so certainly. Not without equivocations. But Will just *loved* her. No matter what.

"I love you, too," she whispered.

He grinned. "I kind of knew that."

Which earned him a laugh, but then she winced and

placed a hand over her side. "Oh, don't make me do that for another few weeks."

"We should get you to bed," Will said, taking the present from her finally and putting it on the table next to the couch. "I'd carry you if I had two arms."

"Man, we really are a pair."

"A pair of survivors."

She smiled at that, walking with him down her hallway toward her bedroom. Survivors. Yes, they'd both survived a lot, and now they had each other to lean on to survive the rest.

And what could be a better Christmas gift than that?

* * * * *

COMING SOON!

We really hope you enjoyed reading this book. If you're looking for more romance, be sure to head to the shops when new books are available on

Thursday 13th December

To see which titles are coming soon, please visit
millsandboon.co.uk

LET'S TALK
Romance

For exclusive extracts, competitions
and special offers, find us online:

For all the latest titles coming soon, visit
millsandboon.co.uk/nextmonth